F[illegible]
PROFITS

A gripping, action-packed thriller

PAUL BENNETT

Nick Shannon Thriller Book 3

JOFFE BOOKS

Revised edition 2021
Joffe Books, London
www.joffebooks.com

First published by Warner Books in Great Britain in 1998

This book is a work of fiction. Names, characters, businesses, organizations, places and events are either the product of the author's imagination or are used fictitiously. Any resemblance to actual persons, living or dead, events or locales is entirely coincidental.
The spelling used is British English except where fidelity to the author's rendering of accent or dialect supersedes this.

ISBN: 978-1-78931-968-2

Beware of false prophets, which come to you in sheep's clothing, but inwardly they are ravening wolves.

Matthew 7:15

You are covered against all eventualities — except those that actually happen.

Unofficial motto of Future Assurance PLC

CHAPTER ONE

Have you ever lost the will to live? Me, neither — although I've come very close on a couple of occasions. Could claim I'd read the book, got the T-shirt, seen the video and played the virtual reality game without the need for a headset: that's how I can recognise the signs in other people. Detective Superintendent Collins was looking more like a candidate for psychotherapy with each passing moment.

The three of us — Collins, DI Walker and myself — were sitting in broody silence in the tenth-floor conference room of one of those featureless modern office blocks you encounter in every major city across the whole globe. This particular product of a life-sized concrete-and-glass construction kit was situated in Richbell Place. The lowest levels, including the basement cells, housed Holborn police station; the upper two-thirds was the home of the likes of us in the Fraud Squad.

The conference room had been recently decorated in an ingenious choice of matt emulsion that was not quite blue and not quite grey. At times of extreme boredom, I found myself wondering what this shade was called. So far I'd not been able to reach any conclusion, colour charts being an esoteric area full of cryptically phrased names like Thanks Vermilion and

Freudian Gilt. I'd crack the code eventually, though — maybe even a little later, judging by the programme for today.

The room could sit eight in comfort; the acrimonious meeting that had just finished had involved nineteen people. The cramped conditions hadn't helped; but, even if we'd been stretched out on sun loungers sipping rum punches around a swimming pool in Barbados, the general mood would still have been one of depression and despondency.

The attendees at this ill-tempered gathering of the 'Liaison Group' were ourselves and representatives from the drug squads. (Contrary to public perceptions, there is no longer a single specialist 'Drug Squad', the equivalent of the Fraud Squad: each of the eight Metropolitan Areas has its own team of officers dedicated to drug-related crimes.) The topic, as ever, had been Prospekt.

For the last three months, Collins, Walker and I had concentrated on this one case. Prospekt Holdings Ltd, to use its full trading name, was a venture-capital company, existing solely to invest in other companies: its income was derived from interest charges, dividends and selling its shareholdings at a profit. Its public face was a titled chairman (sole function to lend respectability) and a financial director (dubbed Corkscrew by us) with a reputation as a shrewd operator who could spot a good deal with vision only surpassed by the Hubble telescope. So much for the official line.

We knew, but could not prove, that Prospekt was a front for the laundering of drugs money — an operation so big that Prospekt didn't count money, it weighed it. Corkscrew employed all his skills to collect, scrub clean and put back into circulation the dirty money of the barons for whom he worked. And he did it too damned well.

With equal certainty — and equal lack of evidence — we believed that whoever was the ultimate decision-maker at Prospekt had authorised at least five murders — including the only person Collins had ever loved: Louise, his ex-wife. When my boss had heard of her death and been in his darkest hour, I had sworn an oath to help him bring Prospekt to justice. OK, so it was a rash promise to make. But — and call me old-fashioned if you like — when I give my word I like to keep it.

The attack on the problem had been two-pronged. From our side, we had started with Prospekt Holdings and worked down through the eighteen individual operating companies it owned, searching for some line in their accounts that would substantiate our hypothesis. The second front was the responsibility of our colleagues in the drug squads. They had begun at the bottom, targeting dealers and attempting to locate a path that would lead upwards.

Eighteen officers — and one humble civilian, yours truly — all working with a common purpose.

Stake-outs. A succession of suspects questioned.

Countless hours scouring columns of figures.

Innumerable meetings.

And what was the sum total of our achievements?

Bloody zilch. The biggest, fattest, most absolute zero imaginable.

The dealers had been as tight-lipped as quality controllers in a lime-juice factory. The columns of figures had produced nothing but eyestrain and headaches. The meetings had degenerated into fruitless buck-passing and blame-casting.

If anything, we had actually made matters worse. Prospekt, either alerted by this flurry of unrewarding activity or just simply playing safe, was progressively liquidating its assets in this country and switching its operations to God knows where. The trail — such that it was — hadn't just gone cold; it was positively arctic.

When you're going nowhere, all you can do is change direction. That was why we were still sitting here, waiting expectantly for our guest to arrive. The bright spot on the horizon was that we were due to receive information on a possible fraud in an insurance company, a case that could provide a welcome distraction from insoluble problems. The dark cloud — and the reason, in addition to Prospekt, for Collins's gloom — was that the messenger would be Metcalfe.

* * *

Metcalfe could bore for England. The man was a natural. And what Nature had so richly given him, Nurture, in the form of years of guarding the pennies of other people's money, had honed to the peak of perfection. It didn't matter what the subject was. Or how much — how little, even — he knew about it. In no time at all, with that effortless grace of a true expert, he could produce screams for mercy from any audience. Anoraked, bobble-hatted, pebble-glassed train-spotters had been known to crack when Metcalfe was in full flow. So Collins stood no chance. When God had handed out patience and tolerance, Collins hadn't seen the point of joining the queue.

Listening to Metcalfe was the mental equivalent of being stretched on the rack, each sentence a further pain-inflicting crank of the handle by the torturer. He'd been going on now for twenty minutes, never once varying his delivery in pitch or volume. He had yet to reach the point of the story.

In a show of understanding and solidarity, I penned Collins a short note. Slid it surreptitiously across the table to him. 'Got a razor blade?' it read.

Collins scowled at the interruption. Reluctantly dragged his mind away from wistful daydreams of life at the sharp end of police work and back to the bluntness of mundane reality. He gave me a puzzled look. But, then again, that wasn't unusual.

I nodded my head fractionally in the general direction of Metcalfe, rolled my eyes skyward, and drew the imaginary blade across my wrists.

Walker registered the interchange. She shook her head pitifully at me; dipped into her wide repertoire of withering looks and, having selected one of the more contemptuous variety, sent it searing through the air with an accompanying silent mouthing of 'Grow up, Shannon'.

In typical fashion, my mind wandered off to search the archives for a fitting quotation. Came up with the story of some saint (name not in the file) who had reputedly said: 'Lord, give me chastity — but not yet.' All I had to do was change chastity to maturity. Then, with a clear conscience, I blew Walker a kiss.

The mime act went unnoticed by Metcalfe, all possible sources of disturbance rendered harmless by the impenetrable shield of his focused mind.

Metcalfe is the kind of person who doesn't stand out in a crowd — even if you stretch the definition to include only two people. He was that bane of police eyewitness reports, Mr Average: average height, average build, averagely brown hair (neither light nor dark), similar colouring for the eyes. Normally Metcalfe was human wallpaper: no part of him registered on the conscious mind. But today there was a twinkle in the eye.

I made an effort to concentrate. Tried to remember what he had been talking about.

It was hopeless.

Within seconds, the constant drone of his voice had me hypnotically drifting back to my inner thoughts. Thankfully Walker, newly promoted and eyes already gazing longingly on the next rung of the ladder, was taking copious notes. But that's Walker for you — dedicated to a fault. The way her pen was filling pages of her notepad she was probably taking down a verbatim account of the entire monologue. I found myself wishing Metcalfe would cough, just to see if she would prove my theory by writing down 'cough' in brackets. Or maybe she would use hyphens. Walker can be unpredictable at times.

To give Collins his due, he was trying hard to keep awake, methodically working his way through the limited range of distractions available. He had begun by drawing back the vertical blinds and forcing the rusty window wide open: smoke was sucked out and replaced by the cool breeze of what is known in this country as 'flaming June' — 'flaming' being an expletive rather than an adjective. Moved on to making minute adjustments to the amount of grubby white-shirted cuff showing beneath the sleeve of the ash-flecked dark blue suit. Pulled at the knees of his trousers to prevent them bagging

— further. Combed his long lank ginger hair with the tips of nicotined fingers. Forensically inspected the table-top with its tell-tale collection of stains from cheap ballpoints and thick tannic police-canteen tea. Now he lit another cigarette and blew an intentionally impolite smoke ring.

Metcalfe ignored the gesture with the contempt of a professional who had seen it all before, and many times.

I tuned into a subordinate clause of a complex sentence from Metcalfe's mouth, stifled a yawn, and went back to arranging my favourite jazz pianists into an All-Time Top Ten. Fats Waller at number one (because he never took himself or his music too seriously), Art Tatum at two (since he was technically the best, although prone to pomposity), Oscar Peterson . . .

I shook my head in self-rebuke. Nick Shannon, what are you doing? Thirty years old and here you are debating with yourself about a bunch of people most of whom were dead before you'd even been born.

'Finally,' Metcalfe said, smiling proudly at each of us in turn — it took more time than smiling proudly at all of us simultaneously — 'I thought it best to bring the matter to your attention.'

'Let me recap,' Walker said — not for my benefit, but for Collins's. 'You are in the process of auditing an insurance company,' she said.

It was a bad move. The phrasing was ambiguous, could be interpreted as a question rather than clarification. Metcalfe was provoked to reply.

'Not me personally, you understand,' he said.

The long-winded garden-path explanation that followed was purely for his own self-gratification. Audit work, as I knew from first-hand experience, was the punishment meted out to the young and enthusiastic. A kind of accounting equivalent to attending a public school. A make-or-break exercise. If you survived, you could cope with anything that life threw in your path; if you didn't, you turned into a walking psychiatric casebook fit only for a cardboard box under the arches of Charing Cross station — or a career in the Church, the armed services or politics.

'But the crux of the matter,' she persisted, her dark eyes flashing a warning against further interruptions, 'is that there is an unexplained difference on the sales ledger. A difference you felt should be brought to the attention of the Fraud Squad.'

'It may be nothing, of course,' said Metcalfe, covering himself for the charges Collins was preparing — wasting police time, assault and battery on the eardrums, grievous bodily harm to the sensitive areas of the brain. 'There is still a lot of detailed checking to be done. But, in the light of current developments—'

'How much?' said Collins.

'Well,' Metcalfe said, consulting the pile of notes. 'The precise figure seems to be . . . Ah, here we are. Fifty-four pounds.'

'*Fifty-four pounds*,' Collins echoed loudly. He slumped back in his seat. Reached in desperation for his cigarettes. Checked his watch. 'Do you mean to say that we've sat here for the last thirty-seven minutes' — his tone implied that it had seemed more like thirty-seven years — 'and all for fifty-four pounds?'

'I admit that it is a small sum,' Metcalfe said, a small smile flitting across his lips.

Collins opened his mouth, bit back a tide of invective, and let his head drop into his hands. He peered out through outspread fingers.

'But,' our torturer continued, 'I did say in the light of current developments.'

'I think it might help us,' I said, seeing again the uncharacteristic twinkle in his eye, 'if you told us about these "developments".'

'Of course,' Metcalfe said. 'Should have brought it up at the beginning, I suppose.'

Collins closed his eyes and winced, probably mentally pinching himself to check whether this wasn't all a very bad dream.

Metcalfe dug around in his briefcase and produced, with a magician's flourish, a copy of *The Guardian*. Passed it at a snail's pace across the table.

Walker moved her chair closer so that the two of us could read at the same time. She finished before I did — it was her unidentifiable sweet-smelling perfume that put me off. Not the delightful contrast of the light-tan linen suit against the Aphrodisiac coffee-and-a-dash Nubian-princess skin. Or the dark blackberry colouring of her full lips. Or the . . .

There was a black rectangle around a short piece on the 'Home News' page. Its significance wasn't apparent, but instinct told me this wasn't a *non sequitur*.

I tapped Collins on the shoulder. Placed the paper under his opening eyes.

'The man in this report,' I said to Metcalfe, as Collins caught up with proceedings. 'Where does he fit in?'

'Oh, didn't I say? Finance director. Of the insurance company, that is.'

'Well, Mr Metcalfe,' Collins said, politeness personified now that he had finished reading. 'You best tell us all you know about him. And the company.'

It didn't matter that the sum involved was fifty-four pounds. Could have been fifty-four pence and still had the same effect on Collins.

When it comes to journalism, there's nothing that cheers up a bored policeman more than a sentence that starts: 'The dead body of . . .'

CHAPTER TWO

Collins is my boss. So is Metcalfe. Confused? Me too, much of the time.

Well, the theory of the arrangement went like this. Jameson Browns, the firm of accountants where Metcalfe was a partner, paid my salary. *Salary*. Monkeys formed picket lines rather than accept the peanuts I was getting. But, then again, monkeys could afford to; they weren't encumbered by all the disadvantages that came from being a convicted murderer.

There were mitigating circumstances, I hasten to add: my 'victim' was my sixteen-year-old sister, reduced by a hit-and-run accident to a paraplegic, able to move only her pretty head — and incapable of brushing away the tears. But society, represented by a judge who thought Adolf Hitler would have been a better man if he hadn't been so damned liberal, demanded a minimum of seven years of my life in settlement of the debt. During my time inside, I had channelled my anger and energies into study and passed the exams to become an accountant. Jameson Browns — God bless their ulterior motive of tokenism, the ex-con joining the representatives of the ethnic, homosexual and disabled communities to complete their set of minorities — had given me the opportunity to acquire the two years' on-the-job experience that was mandatory in order to become certified. Pun intended.

In my first year there I had uncovered a complex fraud. Were Jameson Browns proud of me? Did I get a lip-smacking bonus and the keys to the partners' washroom? Un-huh, as our American cousins would drawl. The fraud happened to have been perpetrated by someone inside their firm. After that, I was an embarrassing reminder to my employers of the principle of 'Physician, heal thyself'. Metcalfe, my superior in Acquisitions and Mergers, had promptly volunteered my services to the Fraud Squad.

That's how I came to be working for Collins. I was part of the Fraud Investigation Group, a loose-knit panel of supposed experts — in the country of the blind the one-eyed man is king — who act as consultants.

So much for theory.

The practice was that each owned me when it suited them.

And, as a natural corollary, disowned me when it didn't.

It made me feel a little like Candide, except that in my case Pangloss believed we lived in the worst of all possible worlds. Still, it didn't lack for interest or excitement.

Especially working for Collins.

There were three sides to the job. My official job specification was to bring years of training to bear on the more complex cases. My unofficial role, as spelled out by Collins, was to teach him street-cred (spreadsheet-cred?). My self-appointed task was to keep him out of trouble. To prevent terminal boredom from leading him to commit professional hara-kiri. Six months Collins had spent with the Fraud Squad, and each moment as enjoyable as a typical day in hell. You know how it goes — headstands in the ordure, Barry Manilow CD on repeat play in the background, own-label pot noodle for lunch. Collins was a front-line cop who had plunged into a world of desktops and committee tables. Metcalfe would have loved it.

‘Well?’ I asked Collins. I was sitting, the knees of my long legs jammed uncomfortably against the badly planed edges of his desk, in the bare-walled monastic cell of the tiny makeshift office. Metcalfe had at last departed, Walker was deep in concentration outside Collins’s room diligently transcribing the notes of the meeting. ‘How did you get on?’

It was a rhetorical question. Which is a fancy way of saying just plain stupid.

‘Bloody Commander,’ Collins said, reaching into his drawer for the comfort of the whisky bottle. ‘Too little imagination.’

‘Or too much,’ I replied.

‘And what is that supposed to mean?’ Collins said, tipping the cold remains of a mug of coffee into the plastic pot of an ill-treated spider plant. It perched precariously on the short length of narrow window-ledge left after the creation of the room from a small square of the main open-plan office. The plant’s sole purpose was as a receptacle for coffee dregs. Impossibly, it thrived. Caffeine addiction perhaps? Feeding off the intense emotional aura of its owner? Or just too scared to die? Whichever it was, I’d been there myself.

Collins poured a large measure of whisky within the concealing pottery of the mug. Waved the bottle in my direction.

I shook my head.

It was still only eleven thirty. I didn’t have Collins’s total disregard for timing — or his suicidal tendencies. OK, you can take nutrition too far, but his idea of a balanced diet was a large Scotch in each hand.

‘Unless,’ I said, ‘you’re practising for the grand finale of Temper Tantrum of the Year, I would hazard a guess that the Commander saw through your little subterfuge and caught sight of your hidden agenda.’

‘Subterfuge? Hidden agenda? Come on, Shannon.’ He spread his hands in an unconvincing gesture of complete openness. Glanced conspicuously at the piles of routine paperwork littering his desk. ‘What do you take me for? I know nothing of such things. I’m just a simple detective.’

'And a bored one,' I said. I lit a cigarette. Exhaled the smoke in what I hoped was a suitably derisive stream. 'The only reason you're interested in this insurance company is so you can poke your nose into the murder inquiry.'

Collins feigned a look of maligned innocence. 'Our job is to stamp out fraud, Shannon. Big or small. Makes no difference. It's the principle that counts. A man should live or die by his principles.'

'I think I'll change my mind about that drink,' I said.

Collins is such a terrific influence. In his presence I smoked more and drank more than was good for me. Christ, I didn't even like whisky that much. A glass of Bushmills from time to time, maybe. When my quarter-Irish blood needed a liquid reminder of its roots. But certainly not this cheap mass-produced hooch that the Scots exported to England as revenge for Flodden Field.

'So the thought never crossed your mind?' I said, sipping warily and waiting for the harshness to mug the back of my throat.

'Maybe a little,' he said, shrugging his shoulders.

'Maybe a little, eh?'

'What *are* you, Shannon? Counsel for the bloody prosecution? So what if I do want to give a little behind-the-scenes assistance? The local CID might benefit from my experience.' He composed his face into a butter-wouldn't-melt expression. 'I only want to help,' he said.

His sincerity was very touching — no, make that entirely lacking.

'Shame on me,' I said. 'There was I thinking you just wanted to beat them. You know, be the first to catch the killer? And use that success as evidence that you're wasted in the Fraud Squad.'

He glared at me. Then became thoughtful. Shook his head. Sagged back in the chair. Evidently decided that confession might be good for his soul.

'I should never have taken this job,' he said.

'You weren't given much option,' I said. Collins had a disciplinary record that made Dennis the Menace look like Goody Two-Shoes: it was a bit of a hindrance when sitting opposite his superiors at the bargaining table.

'I wasn't given *any* option,' he corrected. 'Except bloody resign, that is.'

Collins had been stitched up with the dexterity of the finest Savile Row tailor. Used by the power-brokers as a pawn in a high-stakes game where winning meant maintaining the status quo. One that patently didn't work.

The Fraud Squad, and its sister organisation the Serious Fraud Office, had come under increasing criticism (well deserved) from media and government alike for its dismal record in terms of the numbers of cases brought to trial (too few) and the proportion of prosecutions resulting (too low). Collins, a self-confessed no-nonsense, results-driven copper, had been transferred to head the specially created 'C' Squad in order to demonstrate the open-mindedness of those under fire and their willingness to consider any remedy. It was an experiment designed to fail. A preparatory manoeuvre to clear the air for the shout of 'We told you so. The old ways are still the best.'

'Christ, Shannon,' he said, 'I'm going nuts here. Square peg in a round hole. I'm a street copper. I understand villains — proper villains, that is: murderers, bank robbers, drug dealers. Granted they're not "nice" middle-class criminals like fraudsters — that's why it's so much more rewarding putting them behind bars — but I talk their language, know what's going on inside their heads. Fraud isn't my game — too bloody subtle for one thing, too bloody devious for another.' He took a long, reflective draught of the whisky and turned sad eyes in my direction. 'It's killing me here, Nick. Like some bloody cancer. Slowly. Painfully. A little more each day. I've got to do something.'

'Whatever you're thinking, sir,' I said seriously, 'forget it. You can't afford to disobey the Commander.'

'Now, would I do that, Shannon?' he said.

For some strange reason, reassurance didn't exactly flood over me.

'Don't get involved,' I pleaded. 'Just leave it well alone. If you put your head on the block, they'll have to hold a sweepstake to decide who has the privilege of wielding the axe.'

'Thanks for your concern, Shannon,' he said, 'but, as I told you, I have no intention of going against the Commander's orders.'

'In that case,' I said with relief, 'let's drink to your new-found wisdom. Cheers.'

I raised the glass.

It never reached my lips.

One word from Collins acted like the shutter of a camera, transforming me into a static snapshot, arm frozen in mid-air.

'However,' he said.

I groaned. Shook my head sadly. And waited for the inevitable underhand plan.

'I've been thinking,' Collins said.

Here comes trouble, my sinking heart warned me prophetically. Collins doesn't think, he plots.

'You need a break, Shannon.'

'Oh, no.'

'You've been working too hard on the Prospekt case. A change would do you good.'

'And thanks for *your* concern, sir,' I said in turn. 'I don't suppose — and this is just a wild guess, you understand — that this change would involve a little audit work?'

Collins smiled — a rare, and portentous, event.

'Cheers,' he said.

* * *

I could have refused of course. But a combination of factors stopped me.

First, Collins was a friend. Good friend and bad acquaintance?

Second, I was in his debt. He had saved my life. Not once. But twice.

Third, it wouldn't have done the slightest good. There was a greater probability of altering the orbit of a distant planet with a pocket magnet than of deflecting Collins from a chosen course. And, if the truth be known, I was only too happy to go along with his scheme. I didn't just appreciate his sense of frustration; I shared it. Lack of progress on Prospekt was grinding us all down.

All this went through my mind as I sat listening to Collins morally blackmailing some unlucky person over the telephone. Whoever it was on the other end of the line didn't seem to be putting up much of a fight. Maybe it was the mixture of excitement, tension and determination in Collins's voice. Or perhaps I wasn't the only one in his debt.

'Spot of lunch, Shannon?' Collins asked as he replaced the receiver.

I'd experienced his choice of eating establishments before. He usually frequented the type of place depicted in guidebooks by a knife and fork glistening with congealed grease.

A noncommittal shrug seemed the safest response. With luck, and lack of encouragement, he might go off the idea.

'How's your appetite?' he pressed.

'As good as the next man, I suppose.'

'That's a shame,' he said with a smile. 'Considering the next man will have spent his morning carrying out a post-mortem.'

CHAPTER THREE

It doesn't always pay to make assumptions. I had been expecting to meet, across a Formica-topped table shrouded in a noxious mist of chip fat, a dour-faced vegetarian who sliced his food with robotic precision — and then left it untouched. Instead, here I was sitting in a theatrically propped Italianate basement watching a jolly trencherman heave great forkfuls of meat into his smiling mouth.

The food was described as 'authentic Tuscan peasant cuisine'. The price of a meal would have kept an authentic Tuscan peasant fed and clothed for a month. The menu was printed on that hard shiny paper that is supposed to look like vellum but only served to remind me of the inside of school lavatories. It ran for ten pages — usually a sign that the chef prefers to order in bulk by telephone rather than scouring the markets at the crack of dawn for the freshest produce. Still, there was a veritable carnivore's cornucopia of choice: robust stews, roast lamb 'infused with mountain herbs', chicken, grilled steaks or veal, plain or covered in a bewildering variety of sauces. And at least a dozen varieties of fish. So why did Collins's guest have to order *liver*?

I pushed aside my barely touched plate of baked sea bass. Leaned back in my chair to avoid the full blast of some pickled-onion-smelling chemical that wafted across from the rough cloth of the man's tweed jacket. Sipped at my red wine. Stared around the restaurant so that I wouldn't catch another glimpse of the pink cross-section of his flash-fried offal.

The room was full of advertising executives and other assorted marketing folk entertaining clients and reliving the culinary joys of last year's holidays in between vital conversations on this month's model of mobile phone. (What a marvellous invention: it is now possible to be disturbed absolutely anywhere at any time of day or night.) The walls were white emulsion over a stippled plaster; in seemingly random places were dotted large tiles hand-painted with pictures of tiny birds that your average Tuscan probably traps in small-weave nets and eats as a treat on special occasions. Wooden beams ran lengthways across the high ceiling; beneath them hung a collection of highly polished, heavy copper pots and pans. The plates were intentionally crude examples of the rustic art of the potter — and ideal for the microwave. The glasses were chunky and utilitarian, green-tinged and bubbled like the carafes. They sat on tablecloths of precisely the same shade as the inside of the bloody liver.

Collins grinned across at me.

'Eat up, Shannon,' he said. 'Polenta's good for you. Must be. What other reason could there be for its existence?'

The trencherman finally polished off the last morsel. Wiped his mouth on the pink napkin. Settled back in his seat. Rubbed his stomach slowly and appreciatively.

He had introduced himself as 'Davies. Trefor. With one "f", that is.'

There are about fifty recognised forensic pathologists on call to the police forces of England and Wales. Historically — which usually means for no good reason — this 'Home Office list' does not include the many eminent pathologists, based in the capital's medical colleges, who serve the Met and the City of London police force. Professor Davies, since the forced retirement of his predecessor, was regarded as *the* expert on murder.

'What do you want to know?' he asked in a deep sing-song voice that had probably been the pride of the baritone section of some Welsh Methodist choir. His face was round and bore a permanent smile. It lit up the table like the full moon on a December night. I estimated his age as fifty, his weight at fifteen stone — plus a couple of pounds added in the last half-hour by the polenta.

'Anything — everything — that's not in the newspapers,' Collins said, bending forward attentively.

'Not official, then, this enquiry?' Davies said.

'Not exactly,' Collins replied. 'Let's just say we have an interest in the death.'

'Fascinating world, Fraud Squad, is it?' the professor asked perceptively.

'Is it?' Collins said unenthusiastically.

Davies laughed, a deep rich sonorous boom that caused heads to turn in his direction. He gestured with an unexpectedly slim-fingered hand around the restaurant. 'Living proof,' he lectured Collins, 'that there's no such thing as a free lunch. Tell me, how many years have we known each other?'

'I don't know,' Collins replied, a suspicious look on his face. 'Ten? Twelve?'

'Whatever,' Davies said with a dismissive wave of his hand. 'And how many times have you bought me lunch?'

'Well . . .' Collins said. It was the evasive utterance of someone playing for time rather than searching his memory.

'Let me give you a clue,' Davies said. 'Count them on the fingers of my hand.' He raised a clenched fist in the air.

'You know how it is,' Collins said, raising his eyebrows hopefully.

'Yes. One hand washes the other. Isn't that what you policemen say? You helped me get a new job by exposing the crass inefficiency of my predecessor, the late but unlamented Winstanley. Now it's my turn. Am I right?'

Collins shrugged. 'Something like that, Trefor.'

'He was stabbed,' Davies pronounced.

'What a surprise,' Collins said, shaking his head.

He turned to me to explain his remark — and show off his knowledge.

'Over six hundred murders a year in Great Britain, and the majority are committed with knives. As far as gangland culture is concerned, carrying a knife is now an integral part. Endemic, you might say.'

Endemic. He didn't have to show off that much.

'Before going out at night,' Collins continued, 'every villain — big or small, young or old — checks that he's got his knife, wallet, comb and condom. But always knife first.'

The prevalence of knives was not a revelation to me. My friend, and former cellmate in Brixton, Arthur, was a bouncer at a nightclub. He accepted it as an occupational hazard that at least once a week some drunk would take exception at being asked to leave and pull a knife on him. Fortunately, Arthur was an ex-wrestler and knew how to handle himself. The dead man wasn't, and didn't.

'But,' Collins said, rubbing his hands together, 'if someone has to be murdered, we like a stabbing, don't we, Trefor?'

'Lots of evidence,' Trefor said, nodding vigorously.

'Lots of the old claret,' Collins said with relish. 'A knife is what we in the trade call "a contact weapon". Unlike a gun, with a knife the victim and the attacker have to be within touching distance. That makes it almost impossible for the attacker to get away without being marked by the victim's spurting blood.'

I summoned a waiter and ordered a double espresso — somehow the red wine had lost its appeal. Collins thirstily emptied his glass. Davies took a mouthful of his mineral water — strong drink and scalpels not being a good combination in his line of work.

'But it's not just the blood, you know,' he said. 'You can deduce a great deal about the attack from the type of wound. Whether it is incised, the blade cutting gashes across the body; or a stab, where the point and a length of blade penetrate the body.'

'Any defensive marks on the victim?' Collins asked.

'None.'

'You've ruled out suicide, I suppose?' I said, risking demonstrating my naivety in order to gain entry into this arcane conversation.

Davies humoured me. 'It can be difficult, of course,' he said, without a hint of condescension, 'to differentiate murder from suicide in these circumstances. But it's rare for suicides to be by such violent methods. People prefer a less painful death, and there's plenty of pills readily available nowadays to make that possible. Plus the fact that the weapon itself was not found at the scene. Bit of a giveaway, that, you see. Considering the victim died instantly: one deep wound that punctured the heart. He would have had no chance of throwing the instrument away.'

'What else can you tell us?' Collins said.

'From the angle of entry, the attacker was right-handed.'

'Terrific,' Collins groaned. 'Must be my lucky day.' He rolled his eyes in disgust. 'What's happened to all the left-handed murderers? Been taking lessons in ambidexterity to make life difficult for us coppers.'

'Wallet was missing,' Davies continued, more helpfully. 'Probability, therefore, of a mugging.'

'Time and place of death?'

'Victim found by a security guard in the company car park at half past ten yesterday evening. Hadn't been dead long at that stage, I'd say. An hour at the most — could be a lot less. But I can be more precise when I get the results from the analysis of vitreous humour.'

'What's that?' asked Collins, to my horror.

'Recent development,' Davies said. 'We draw a little fluid from the eye. Following death, you see, the red blood cells break down. The potassium in them enters the vitreous fluid at a slow but predictable rate. Most accurate method of determining time of death. Unaffected by temperature, isn't it?'

'Had the victim been drinking?' I said, switching for reasons of my own to a different tack.

'Good question, Shannon,' Collins said with a ghoulish grin. 'Tell us about the stomach contents.'

'Urine analysis,' Davies corrected, 'showed no trace of alcohol. Or, before you ask, drugs. No clues from the stomach, either — empty in fact. Surprising that.'

Not to me, it wasn't. The dead man had probably had lunch with a forensic pathologist.

'He had an ulcer, you see,' Davies explained. 'Small one, granted; but he would have been in some pain with no food inside him.'

Collins shrugged disinterestedly. 'What about the weapon? What sort of knife was it? Switch-blade? Flick-knife?'

Davies grinned. 'That's the trouble with policemen, isn't it, Nick?' he said. 'Always jumping to conclusions.'

'The modern trend,' Collins said, trying to redeem himself, 'is a Stanley. But from what you said about the depth of wound that doesn't seem possible.'

'That's a better guess,' Davies said. 'But only in the sense that it demonstrates a little more imagination. Want to try again?'

'Stiletto?' Collins ventured.

Davies shook his head, his increasing pleasure showing in the widening smile.

'Angler's knife?' I chipped in.

'No.'

'Kitchen knife?' Collins said.

'No.'

'Then, put us out of our misery,' Collins said, tired of the game. 'What the bloody hell was it?'

'Chisel,' Davies said, beaming from ear to ear.

'How the bloody hell were we supposed to guess that?' Collins said with a huff. 'That's hardly fair.'

'In my line of business — and yours, I would have thought — one soon learns that life is rarely fair.'

'But you said a knife,' Collins protested.

'No,' Davies corrected, '*you* said a knife. I only said the man was stabbed.'

'Huh.'

'How can you tell?' I said. 'That it was a chisel, I mean.'

'It's tricky, I admit. When a blade is pushed into the body there is a certain amount of stretching of the skin before it is pierced. Then the skin — elastic stuff, you know — springs back to leave a hole that is actually smaller than the weapon. But it's not the size that's important. It's the shape. A chisel,' he said with a wink, 'if one's mind is open sufficiently to contemplate such a possibility, is unmistakable.'

Davies paused. Retrieved a battered brown leather briefcase from the floor. Rooted around inside.

'I brought along a photograph,' he said.

'That's OK,' I said quickly. 'If you say it's a chisel, I believe you.'

'It's not a picture of the wound,' he said. 'Something much more interesting.'

Collins stopped sulking and bounced in his chair with uncontrolled interest. I sat still and concentrated on reining in my imagination.

'This is the victim's back,' Davies said, passing a grainy black-and-white photograph across the table.

Collins stared uncomprehendingly at the haphazard collection of tiny bruises that peppered the area below the dead man's shoulder blades.

'This time,' he said, throwing Davies an accusing look, 'I'm not even going to bother to guess.'

'I will,' I said, to their surprise.

But it wasn't a guess.

I'd seen the marks before.

'It's a scourge,' I said.

Davies clapped his hands.

'Bravo,' he said. 'There speaks a man with the dubious benefit of a strict religious education. Always assuming you're not a sexual deviant, that is.'

CHAPTER FOUR

Prison psychiatrists are busy people. They can't be expected to spot every psychopath.

For one thing, they have hundreds of prisoners in their charge, the majority necessitating an interview and report on entry, and then again prior to release or parole application. The demands on their time are heavy, the questioning and testing of inmates consequently cursory.

For another, their job is complicated by two factors. The number of sane prisoners who claim to be mad in order to justify their past crimes without having to accept guilt, or in the hope of being transferred to one of the special hospitals where they believe, mistakenly, the regime will be more liberal and open to abuse. And, on the other side of the coin, the truly deranged who firmly believe themselves to be sane. Maybe they are, much of the time — or simply clever, or crafty, enough to adopt convincingly the persona of the mentally balanced as and when it suits their ends. Whatever they might be.

But Tully should never have slipped through the net.

The other inmates recognised him immediately for what he was. It wasn't just that he was a murderer — that term covers a multitude of sins and a diversity of motives, and can be applied to a sizeable proportion behind the bars of Brixton. Nor that his victims were all prostitutes, both male and female, some as young as fourteen. One look at his eyes, burning with a manic inner fire, told you all you needed to know about Tully.

So we kept our distance.

Which wasn't difficult, since Tully was generally — but not *normally* — withdrawn. He preferred to watch proceedings from a distant corner. Sitting perched on a chair like a bird of prey, shoulders hunched, hands wrapped round his knees, feet tucked against his bottom. Muttering under his breath. Thinking dark thoughts. Casting sly glances heavenward.

In Brixton, during my time there on remand, every inmate showered once a week — whether they needed it or not, as the old and sick joke went. The shower complex is not a row of individually screened cubicles — the denial of privacy being one of the prime objectives and main punishments of prison — but a communal area resembling that found in coal mines. Down the pits the reason for such an arrangement is not cost or security but pure functionality — each man can scrub another's back. In prison that is the last thing you want. For prison is like Jurassic Park, but infinitely more dangerous: a single-sex society where some specimens, through a freak of genes, can mutate to the opposite sex. And others, through an excess of libido, willingly lose the ability to differentiate.

So you can understand how I — twenty-one years young at the time, tall, slim, fair of face and ripe for the picking — could accomplish taking a shower without ever getting soap in my watchful eyes. And complete the weekly peepshow in less than two minutes.

The day I saw Tully's back it didn't even take that long.

I caught the briefest glimpse, and my stomach churned.

The random pattern of marks was the same as that depicted in the photograph of the dead man. But, instead of being the proud possessor of a collection of bruises, Tully had scars. Deep, puckered, ugly welts that might have been easily mistaken for the impact of shotgun pellets at close range — except that no one could have survived such a blast. Tully, in his mania, as we learned later, had scourged himself.

Not once or twice. But every day. For years.

Not with the listless flick of the wrist of the transgressor going through the motions of penance. But with a ferocity that cared nothing for pain — and only for pain.

For his crimes, he bore a stigma; for his madness, a stigmata. He would carry both for the rest of his days.

Which were not to be many.

Tully's mistake had been to show emotion.

The profanities of Standard Prison English — where it is obligatory for every sentence to contain at least three four-letter words or their longer adjectival derivatives — didn't seem to bother him. But if someone should dare to take the name of the Lord in vain, then it was time to stand back and wait for the eruption. Tully's mouth spouting warnings of eternal damnation. His eyes blazing with religious fervour.

Once his weak spot had been revealed, of course, they taunted him, from a respectful distance, at every opportunity — rubbed salt into his wounds. You don't get many laughs in prison; perhaps that's why I tend to overcompensate now that I'm on the outside. Opportunities for sport are somewhat limited. Baiting Tully became the latest team game.

And if God would not punish the blasphemers by sending down a thunderbolt, then Tully knew it was only because he was destined to be His chosen instrument.

If Ladbrokes had run a book on which of the inmates would act as the ultimate spark to light Tully's short fuse, you would have got long odds on it being Tippett. But outsiders do sometimes romp in.

Tippett, a pale, thin, inoffensive little man, who didn't have the heart to say 'Boo' to a hearing-impaired goose, was awaiting trial for a series of break-ins at office premises. As usual during the precious time-slot allowed for 'association', he was absorbed in the television. Part of a boisterous partisan crowd, swathed in a sweet-smelling cloud of smoke from anorexically thin roll-ups, watching England take on some third-rate nation at football. And made to look fourth-rate in the process.

Despite all the inherent advantages — our team's strip was better tailored than theirs, the players' haircuts more professionally coiffured — we were nil-one down with ten minutes to play. Then along comes the golden opportunity to scrape a face-saving draw. Long through-ball somehow lands at the feet of our razor-sharp striker. Opposition goal-keeper out of his area. Net undefended. Result: total panic. Three million pounds' worth of footballer skys his shot into the stands.

Tippett, in frustration rather than in surprise, let out an involuntary cry of 'Jesus Christ'.

And deep inside Tully the thin thread holding together his sanity finally snapped.

The day of retribution had arrived.

Tully went about his appointed task with a vengeance. With the last vestige of control abandoned, he became a killing machine in overdrive.

They say that a madman has the strength of ten; with Tully it was certainly true. For that was how many he took on.

He punched with flailing arms. Kicked wildly in all directions. Spat from a distance. Clawed at eyes, bit at any exposed part of the body when at close range. Suffered blows in return that would have finished any normal man. And all just to get at Tippett.

Tully fought his way through the mêlée of fleeing prisoners until he reached his prey and had him cornered. A wild uncoordinated haymaker connected with the unlucky burglar's chin and sent him sprawling to the floor. Tully followed his victim down. Straddled his body. Threw punches into the terrified face that stared up at him.

Until a better idea crossed his mind.

Wrapping trembling fingers around Tippett's neck, Tully squeezed tightly.

All I can remember of that moment is hearing the strangled screams, and thinking that if Arthur had been there he wouldn't have hesitated to pitch in and help out.

It was a salutary lesson in non-involvement — one I hope to master at some stage in the future, if I live that long.

Dropping my book, I leaped from my chair. Sprinted across the room. Used bony elbows to clear a path through the tight circle of cheering onlookers.

Arthur, when tutoring me on how to survive in Brixton, had given me two pieces of advice about prison fights. Don't get into one. And, if you do, don't even think for a second about fighting fair. No one else will.

I kicked Tully in the ribs.

He grunted, swayed a little unsteadily, but the grip didn't loosen. Tippett's tongue was poking out of the corner of his mouth, a thin trickle of blood running from it in a vampirish line down his chin.

I sank down beside Tully and grabbed his hair. Yanked upwards. His elbow shot back. Smashed into my right eye. Sent my head spinning, and my body smacking into the concrete.

Tippett's face was turning blue; Tully's was beaming.

I tried to knock the smile off with a left jab, awkwardly delivered while still lying there half-sprawled. The punch glanced off his nose, producing a momentary blink of the staring eyes but achieving nothing in the race to relieve the unremitting pressure on Tippett's neck.

I raised myself to my knees. Interlocked my fingers. Delivered a double-handed chop in between Tully's shoulder blades.

He didn't even flinch.

It was then that I realised the futility of further punches or kicks. He would simply absorb all the pain I could inflict. I might as well go out and head-butt an oncoming steamroller for all the effect I was having. Tully's mind would permit nothing to interfere with the prime objective. Tippett must die. Tippett *would* die. Unless I thought of something fast.

I pressed my mouth to Tully's ear.

'God does not exist,' I shouted. 'Only the devil. He is the master. And I am his servant.'

The roar of rage split the air.

I jumped back with a start.

But was too slow, too close to him, to avoid the blow. He clubbed me with a sledgehammer swing of his closed fist. I spun in the air and landed back on the floor. Tully was above me now.

He stabbed the heel of his boot into the tender flesh of my stomach. Then, as I doubled up with pain, moved in for the kill.

His left hand clamped over my blasphemous mouth; his right covered my nose. He was screaming incoherently. Somewhere in the background, I heard agonising rasps as Tippett caught his breath.

I took hold of Tully's wrists. Tried to free myself by forcing upwards and outwards. Succeeded only in spurring him on to summon extra strength. The downward thrust increased. I could feel his fingernails digging into my cheek. My lungs cried out for air.

A mist drifted across my brain.

I looked up into Tully's eyes. Saw nothing there but hate.

The mist thickened into a fog.

My eyes gave up the struggle and closed.

Maybe that was why my other senses became more acute.

I felt the vibrations run through my body.

Heard the sickening thuds.

As the warder brought his stick down on Tully's skull.

Once. Twice. Third time lucky.

* * *

They put him in solitary confinement. Where he supposedly could do no harm.

But they reckoned without the ingenuity of the insane mind.

At first it appeared he would starve himself to death. Trays of food were returned untouched at each meal. Tully lay silent and still on the bed, blanket wrapped tightly around him. Only his head was visible, his eyes staring blankly at the ceiling.

Nobody noticed the missing spoon.

Until they found it in Tully's hand.

In the last few years prisons have switched to using plastic cutlery — the sort you get with your airline meal and is seemingly designed to self-destruct at the slightest pressure. At that time, though, a spoon was the only eating implement, knife and fork representing too much of a hazard.

Tully had taken the metal spoon, bent it backwards and forwards until it snapped in two. And used the jagged edge to slit his wrists and throat.

No one mourned the death of Tully.

Not even his Maker, I suspect.

* * *

'So you're *that* Nick Shannon,' Davies said with a frown of realisation when I finished recounting the story. 'I'm sorry.'

Apart from the three of us, the restaurant was empty now, the clarion call of political correctness despatching the other diners back to their offices. Waiters hovered in the background, mumbling discontentedly among themselves and peering ostentatiously at their watches. Tables had been stripped and relaid for the evening trade. The bill came, unrequested. Collins glanced at it, put it aside without any hint of movement towards his wallet and flamboyantly examined the inside of his empty wine glass.

The Mexican stand-off didn't last long. Three large grappas arrived to the accompaniment of an exaggerated sigh from the waiter. Collins smiled triumphantly. And greedily, as Davies pushed his glass across the table.

'I'm sorry,' the forensic pathologist repeated.

Collins probably mistook the remark as sympathy. But I knew what Davies meant. The penny had dropped on the reason for my lack of appetite.

It had hurt once.

A lifetime ago.

That Fate had not been satisfied that my sister should be crippled in life, but had also decreed that she must be defiled in death, her body cut and plundered. Just because the stupid laws of our land demanded a post-mortem. And even though I had never denied what I had done.

I couldn't forget her.

That would have been hard for anyone who had known Susie, however fleetingly. Absolutely impossible for a big brother.

But I tried to remember her beauty, her vibrancy, and the infectious laugh of the teenager in the days before the hit-and-run driver turned her into a pitiful apology for her former self.

And, most of all, I held the memory of the forgiving, thankful smile on her pale lips as I injected her with the fatal dose of morphine.

If I hadn't managed to keep that vision intact, I would have gone as mad as Tully. And probably taken the same course of action.

I sipped at the grappa. It was as smooth as sandpaper. Made Collins's Scotch taste like holy water.

'It was all a very long time ago,' I said with a shrug. 'You learn to live with the memories.' Well, most of the time.

'Now would be a good moment to pay up and look big, Chris,' Davies said. 'If you're finished, that is.'

'With the dead man, yes. But there's another matter. Can you do me a favour, Trefor?'

'I thought I already was,' Davies replied.

He watched as I lit a cigarette. Seemed to notice for the first time the two missing fingers of my left hand — deliberately sliced off in the jamb of a sharp-edged steel door.

Another permanent reminder of the past. And a constant stimulus to my determination never to do anything that would result in a return to prison.

'Ask,' Davies said without a hint of consideration. 'For some strange reason I seem to be in a giving mood.'

'I have a file,' Collins said.

My heart missed a beat. And sank. How far? Down to the boots.

'A file,' he continued, 'that someone, somewhere, went out of his way to make it very difficult for me to obtain. The file on the hit-and-run.'

'Let it drop, Chris,' I said. 'Haven't we got enough on our plate already?'

For two months now, since the first moment I had set eyes on the damned file, I had been in a state of turmoil. Schizophrenically split in two. Half of me desperately wanting to ask questions, examine inconsistencies, find a lead to the driver who had crippled my sister and killed her boyfriend. The other, more rational, half ordering me to let the matter rest: warning me that I might not be satisfied with the knowledge alone; that revenge is not a dish best eaten cold but one that should never be tasted at all.

I had managed to negotiate these two warring factions into an uneasy truce. But, as with Bosnia or Northern Ireland, I remained unconvinced of how long the cease-fire might last — or whether the two sides were merely taking the opportunity to regroup and rearm, preparing for one last battle whose outcome I couldn't predict. And didn't wish to contemplate.

'I'm not asking this favour for *you*, Shannon,' Collins said forcefully. 'Something here smells wrong. I need to find out what it is, why it stinks, and who is responsible.'

'It's been nearly nine years,' I said, trying to deter him with practicalities. 'There isn't a hope in hell of finding the driver. Look, sir, I've learned to cope with the fading whiff of injustice. But dig up old ground and the stench could be too much to bear.'

'Excuse me,' Davies said, gingerly raising his hand. 'But why not let me decide? Tell me exactly where I fit in. After all, I might not be able to help. That would resolve the argument.'

I shrugged, agreeing to his mediation. Deep inside, my fear was that Collins, in typical bulldog fashion, would not let the matter rest. If Davies couldn't help, Collins would simply find another way round the problem.

'When I asked officially for the file,' he explained to Davies, 'my request was denied. Politely, but firmly. OK, so it was none of my business — old cases are the responsibility of the Reserve Squad. But a detective superintendent's whims are usually humoured. Rank has its privileges.' He frowned. 'But not, apparently, where this particular file is concerned.'

'Yet you still managed to come by it?' Davies said. 'Whoever is putting obstacles in your way doesn't know you very well.'

'Or knows me only too well,' Collins said, his eyebrows creased with suspicion. 'And took extra precautions. When I did manage, via the back door, to get a copy of the file, there was a page missing. Page nine, to be exact. Of the forensic report.'

'I see,' said Davies thoughtfully. 'Where I fit in, that is. And what you're hinting at.'

'This has all the signs of a cover-up, Trefor. One that does no credit to the police force. Or the forensic people. Your forensic people, perhaps.'

'So you want me to dig around? See what I can find out? After nine years.' He managed a half-hearted smile. 'When you ask favours, Collins boy,' he said, 'you don't bugger about with small ones, do you?'

'Is it possible?' I asked, not knowing what answer I wanted. 'After all this time.'

'It's possible,' Davies said. 'And necessary. Evidence should be presented in its totality, not selectively.' He turned to Collins. 'I'll make some discreet inquiries. But I can't guarantee the result.'

He sat back. His fingers ran over his lips and chin, quietly worrying away at them in contemplation.

'Rotten apples,' Davies said with a sigh and a sad shake of his head. 'The trouble is, if you don't search them out, you never know how far the contamination has spread.'

'My sentiments entirely,' Collins said. 'Thanks.'

'Don't thank me yet,' Davies said. 'It might lead nowhere.'

Fingers crossed, I thought. But on which hand?

CHAPTER FIVE

I left my old Lancia in the car park at Holborn police station — well, if it wasn't safe there, then what hope was there for the fight against crime? — and braved the Tube for the journey home. Never my first choice of mode of transport. I preferred the car, bus, walking — even crawling along the pavement with my legs tied together — anything to avoid the tunnels with their enveloping blackness, the narrow winding passageways, the oppressive crowds bearing in on all sides. But, once a month, I forced myself down into Hades in a stupidly macho proof that my claustrophobia was still in check.

For the one-station first leg of my journey from Holborn I squeezed into a carriage that even sardines would have considered to be grossly overcrowded. I progressed about three inches inside. Stood wedged up against the curvature of the sliding doors by a throng of people intent on maximising their personal space. My back was contorted into an uncomfortable arc. My head touched the roof. One of those little cream-painted steel rivets dug into my skull. Underground trains, it appeared, had been designed long ago by a race of engineering pygmies who failed to visualise that anyone could grow to a height of six foot three.

Emerging at Tottenham Court Road like Quasimodo with a bad case of sciatica, I was swept along by a tidal rush of passengers desperately fleeing central London. Mental note: Must listen to the radio more — obviously I was the only person down here who had not heard the news that a nuclear holocaust was scheduled to occur at any moment.

On the Northern Line I found a spare seat. My surprise didn't last long. On my left was a man waging a personal crusade against the insidious spread of deodorants in society, on my right was a Scandinavian backpacker who must have spent the day chewing pickled herrings. I sighed heavily, moving my head from side to side and exhaling a slow stream of grappa fumes. Childish, but satisfying.

For the remainder of the journey I concentrated on reading the *Evening Standard*, it being taboo in this environment to actually look at one's fellow travellers — some ancient tribal superstition, I imagine, like having your soul captured by a camera if your picture is taken. My eyes struggled to focus on the report of the murder, the speeding train throwing me violently about as it rounded each bend in the tunnel — even the driver must be anxious to reach the safety of his fallout shelter.

The police, so the correspondent said, were following several lines of inquiry — usually a public-relations metaphor for running around in different directions like headless chickens. A 'spokesperson' — therefore female — for a firm of estate agents charged with the challenging task of disposing of office space in Docklands (where the body had been found) defensively presented statistics demonstrating the relatively low crime rate in the area. The case was based on the ratio of offences to square foot of premises. Even without the advantage of having studied mathematics and statistics at university I could have spotted the weasel: much of the property was unoccupied — of interest, maybe, to squatters looking for a quiet life but offering little temptation to your average burglar.

At Archway I alighted with relief, leaving behind the well-dressed secretaries of Finchley and the drably suited stockbrokers of High Barnet, walked up the hill and into the land of imposing houses subdivided into 'individual letting units'. I shared a two-bedroom furnished ground-floor flat with Norman. The arrangement suited both of us. For Norman, it provided a base during those periods when his tax-exile status permitted him to be in England — if the wages of sin are death, the profits of embezzlement are tax exile — and allowed him to keep a fatherly eye on his pupil. For me, his contribution to the rent and running costs made the place affordable — and I didn't always have to come home to the echoing silence of an empty flat.

'"See, the conquering hero comes!"' Norman proclaimed as I stepped through the door, a broad welcoming smile on his lips. '"Sound the trumpets, beat the drums!"'

He was sitting in one of the pair of battered armchairs either side of the fireplace. A few months ago he would have been hunched forward on one of the straight-backed dining chairs, glued to the screen of his computer. But Norman, like Mr Toad, flits in and out of hobbies, changing corresponding identities with a fickleness that belies his constancy when it comes to the two things that matter to him: money and friends. Today, for some unaccountable reason, he seemed to be trying out for size the persona of a worldly-wise grandparent. He was wearing a knitted cardigan and a pair of those tartan slippers you can only buy if you show the shop assistant your bus pass or pension book. Arthur, decked out in his working clothes of dinner suit, black patent shoes and bow-tie, sat opposite. He had a mug of tea clamped in his huge hand. And a face like a blues singer about to break into 'Woke up this morning . . .'

'Late tonight, aren't you?' Norman said as if, given another five minutes, he would have started to ring round the local hospitals.

'One of those days,' I said.

'Sounds like another client for Norman's Tea and Sympathy Clinic. Pour yourself the cup that cheers, Nick,' he said, gesturing to the tray on the dining table, 'and join the queue.'

'Have you got problems, Arthur?' I said, studying the lines on his face with deep concern.

I sat down on the lumpy settee with my tea, lit a cigarette and stretched my legs out on the rug that covered the worst of the worn patches of the threadbare carpet.

Arthur unclipped his bow-tie (no one has ever been strangled by a clip-on bow-tie), placed it on the coffee table, undid his top button, and shook a melancholy head.

'I'm getting too old for this lark,' he said. His voice, naturally deep and low, now seemed to be rising up from the soles of leaden boots.

'Nonsense,' I said. 'You can't be much more than fifty. And you're still in good shape. There's plenty of time before you need to consider a career move.'

My words were intended as reassurance. What I had left unsaid was that he should stick to the devil he knew; there weren't many alternative jobs for someone like Arthur. Not legal ones, at least.

Arthur was a bouncer — sorry, *security executive* — at a West End nightclub. He was six feet five inches tall, and built like he'd just stepped straight out of the rockface of Mount Rushmore. Wasn't the world's quickest thinker, though — a trait that had forced him to abandon professional wrestling (too many opponents unfortunately injured when he failed to remember the pre-arranged moves) and landed him in prison for demanding money with menaces (innocently collecting a debt that did not exist). Arthur's brain, like the man himself, was slow but steady. It could be relied upon to come to the right conclusion given enough time — enough time to grow a beard, that usually meant.

'What's the problem, Arthur?' I said.

'Excuse me,' Norman chided. 'But who is running this counselling session?'

I shrugged my shoulders. 'Carry on.'

'Right,' Norman said. 'What's the problem, Arthur?'

Norman sat back in the chair, interlocked his bony fingers, placed them on his thin stomach, and inclined his head enquiringly. Any moment now, I thought, he would adopt a Germanic accent and ask questions about Arthur's relationship with his mother and the details of her method of potty training.

'It's the bloody music, for one thing,' Arthur complained. 'A few years ago, at least I could recognise some of the songs — hum along a bit, even. Now it's all this gabba techno House stuff. I can't tell when one record has finished and the next one has started.'

'Pining for "Hi Ho Silver Lining", eh?' I said, smiling ruefully.

'And the kids,' he said, ignoring the interruption and edging his way, I presumed, towards the real source of his dissatisfaction. 'Not bloody natural. Bouncing up and down all night. Too much energy for their own good. And all they drink is gallons of water. That doesn't help the profits. The management's talking about making redundancies.'

'Rest easy in your size-twelve boots, my friend,' Norman said. 'You would be the very last to go. There can't be anyone who is better at the job. Or with more years of experience.'

'Thanks a lot,' said Arthur huffily. 'Like I said, I'm getting too old for this lark.'

Norman frowned. Ran his fingers thoughtfully through thinning hair. Leaned close to Arthur. Then smiled encouragingly. 'Come on,' he said softly. 'Music and Adam's ale haven't produced this mood.'

'I could murder a drink,' Arthur replied, shuffling his huge boots in tight nervous circles on the carpet.

'Beer?' I asked. 'Red wine?'

'What sort is it?' Arthur enquired.

A year ago, I'd needed to cajole him to try red wine; now he was a budding Jancis Robinson.

'Bulgarian,' I said.

'Yeah, OK,' he said. 'Packs a punch, does your Bulgarian. Has it been breathing?'

I rolled my eyes. Hurried out to the kitchen to fetch a bottle and glasses before Arthur could start to ask about grape variety, region and whether the sun shone on the south slopes of the particular vineyard.

He was sitting silent and motionless when I returned, his eyes gazing broodily at some fixed point on the ceiling. He took the glass and sipped experimentally.

'Well?' Norman pressed him. 'Tell us all about it.'

'It's all right,' Arthur said. 'Not as good as the Australian you served last Sunday, but all right.'

Norman emitted a strangled cry, part snigger, part groan.

'I don't think that was quite what Norman meant,' I said.

'Oh, I see,' Arthur said, his face turning red. 'Sorry.'

He stared into the glass mournfully.

'Last night,' he said. 'Well, about three this morning, to be exact. There was this young girl. Typical customer. All legs and Lycra. Arms pounding away like the pistons on a Porsche. Not a care in the bleeding world. Then, all of a sudden, *thud*. Down she goes. White as a sheet, Lies there in a heap on the dance floor. I had to drag her out of the crowd before she got trampled on — the rest of the kids were all still jogging about like maniacs.' He took a fortifying gulp of wine. 'She was in a coma by the time the ambulance arrived.'

'Ecstasy,' I said. It wasn't a question, just a grim statement of fact.

Arthur stared at the floor. Couldn't seem to make up his mind whether to nod his head as confirmation or shake it in disbelief.

'So they reckon,' he mumbled. He gazed searchingly into my eyes. 'Christ, Nick,' he said, frustration raising the level of his voice. 'What are we supposed to do? Can't frisk everyone at the door. Pointless, in any case. Bloody tabs are so small we'd never find them. And, anyway, most of the kids swallow them while they're waiting to come in. Bloody hopeless.'

'It's not your fault, Arthur,' I assured him. 'Half a million kids are reckoned to be regular users of Ecstasy in this country alone. Blame the dealers for making the stuff so readily available. Blame society. Peer-group pressure. The parents, even, for lack of control or watchfulness. But, Arthur, the one thing you mustn't do is blame yourself.'

'You forget,' he said sharply, 'I'm a parent, too. Well, sort of. I've got a kid, at least. Although I hardly ever see her anymore. Not since Brixton and the divorce. It could just as well have been my daughter lying there last night. Tell me this,' he said, a tear forming in his eye, 'what sort of father have I been?'

So this was the root of the problem. Wasn't just delayed shock or some mid-life identity crisis.

'You love her,' I said simply, for that much was undeniable. 'And she knows you'll always be there if she needs you. Perhaps that's all a father can ever hope for.'

'Maybe,' he said grudgingly. 'It's just that I keep asking myself what kind of example I've set for her. You know? Prison. And a job where everyone sniggers behind your back and says things like "How do you make a bouncer laugh on a Sunday? Tell him a joke on a Wednesday."' He shrugged his heavily muscled shoulders, but couldn't seem to shake off the hopelessness and despair that rested upon them. 'It would be nice to make something of my life, that's all. Do something to make her proud.'

'Have you ever intentionally hurt anybody?' I asked. 'Who didn't deserve it,' I added quickly.

'S'pose not.'

'And who,' Norman said, 'do we always turn to when we need a helping hand?'

'Me?' he said uncertainly.

'Of course,' we replied in unison.

'And . . .' he said with a deep sigh, before petering out.

'And what?' I asked.

'No pension. No prospects.' He looked at me sadly. 'I'd like to know where I'm going. What the future has in store.'

'Cross my palm with silver,' I said.

'Go on, joke,' he said, as if I needed any encouragement. 'You're all right. You've got Arlene.'

'Yes,' I agreed. 'But life isn't that simple.'

Arlene knew exactly what she wanted. That was a help, I suppose. And a hefty burden, too. Her plans for us were mapped out — with a little dotted line to show each step on the path to be followed. I would emigrate to America; settle down in her house in New England; make my peace with her eighteen-year-old daughter, Mary Jo (who idolised her late father and vilified me as a money-grabbing gigolo); we'd have a child while she was still able (at thirty-seven, Arlene could hear the biological clock ticking away loudly in the background); and we'd all live happily ever after.

The trouble was that the first link in the chain was emigrating to America. And that looked like being nigh on impossible.

According to the strict rules and regulations controlling immigration, I was classed as someone who had been convicted of 'a crime involving moral turpitude'. I'd had to look it up in the dictionary. *Base wickedness*. It seemed like Mary Jo and the US government held the same high opinion of me — the word *high* being used in the olfactory sense.

What this all boiled down to was that, in theory — and probably in practice, too — I had as much chance of acquiring a permanent-residence visa as overtaking Concorde while riding side-saddle on the back of an airborne pig.

Still, I was trying to pull whatever strings I could: both Collins and the Commander had written long letters supporting my application, explaining the extenuating circumstances of my crime, giving details of my current posting to the world-famous Metropolitan Police Force. But, to be honest, no one was particularly hopeful that it would do any good.

At some stage in the not-too-distant future I was going to have to come clean with Arlene. Bite the bullet. Destroy all those well-laid plans.

'She's coming over,' Norman said absentmindedly. 'On Sunday actually.'

I gave him a piercing look.

It wasn't that I didn't yearn to see Arlene: I had simply been hoping to postpone the inevitable for a little while longer. How I'd changed. A year or so ago I would have jumped in with both feet, blurted everything out. But this needed thinking about. Perhaps there was still a way to make the dreams come true. Don't give up, Shannon. Not until every avenue has been explored. Only then turn your mind to how best to sugar the pill. In the meantime, keep whistling 'Always Look on the Bright Side of Life'.

'I don't suppose,' I asked Norman, 'that you would have anything to do with this?'

'I thought you needed a break,' he said.

'O Lord,' I pleaded, 'spare me from people who think I need a break.'

'What have I done now?' he asked. 'All I did was arrange for her to attend a meeting in London. And suggest she stay on for a couple of weeks. Little holiday for both of you, I thought.'

'Does she know yet?' I asked.

'About what?' he asked innocently.

'About you owning the company that employs her.'

Norman was — had been, I suppose — an embezzler. That was how fate had contrived to bring us together. And how I had been railroaded into studying for the accountancy exams. Norman, my bullying tutor, had been the one to think of my future at a time when I cared only for the past. He had taught me all he knew. Which gave me the distinct advantage over the conventionally trained accountants of being able to think like a professional swindler. Norman, so he would protest, was straight now. Or as straight as he ever would — could — be. He had a fifty-per-cent share in a thriving London restaurant, owned a real-estate project on Cape Cod — Arlene ran the sales side of the operation — and never relished questions about whence the money had come. If there was ever a fast buck to be made, you had to get up early in the day to beat Norman to it. Faults he may have — don't we all? — but he meant well.

'No, she doesn't know,' he said sternly. 'And don't you let on, either. People can be very funny about these things. Too proud for their own good sometimes. I wouldn't want her to see what I did as some sort of charity.'

'Don't panic,' I said. 'I won't tell. Arlene might start worrying about the company I keep.'

'I think it's time,' he said dismissively, waving his empty glass at me, 'for a refill of wine and an explanation of your remark about it being "one of those days".'

My turn on the couch, it seemed.

I drained the remains of the first bottle into our glasses. Opened a second to breathe, Arthur smiling like an *aficionado*. Settled back to recount the story of the day. Précised, and simplified, as much as was possible so as not to lose Arthur. Omitted — for my own benefit as much as theirs — some of the more grisly pearls of forensic wisdom.

'Arlene's not going to be too pleased,' was Arthur's verdict.

'Why?' I asked.

'Well, you getting involved in a company where someone is pulling a scam, and the finance director just happens to have finished up with a chisel in his heart. Sounds to me like you're putting yourself in danger of becoming the next victim.'

'There isn't any danger,' I said confidently.

'How can you say that?' he said.

'Because there isn't any scam.'

'How do you know?'

'Because the sum involved is fifty-four pounds,' I said.

'Huh,' he said scornfully. 'Could be the tip of the iceberg. And, anyway, plenty of people have been killed for a lot less than that.'

'You don't understand,' I said. 'If it was fifty-three pounds or fifty-five, I might be concerned. But not fifty-four.'

'Can't see the bloody difference,' he grunted.

'Let me explain,' Norman said. 'Fifty-four is divisible by nine.'

Arthur's brow creased in puzzlement. 'And the world is just a great big onion. What the hell is that supposed to mean?'

'It means,' Norman continued, 'that it is a virtual certainty that the difference is a simple bookkeeping error. Whenever you have a difference that is divisible by nine, it is almost always down to two digits being transposed: sixty-three being put down instead of thirty-six, ninety-five instead of fifty-nine. You try it. Works every time.'

'I'll take your word for it,' Arthur said. 'So there's no scam, then? No danger if you dig around inside this company?'

'Of course not,' Norman said.

I nodded my head in reinforcement.

'You're sure?' Arthur pressed.

'When have I ever been wrong?' asked Norman immodestly.

'Always a first time,' Arthur said. 'Specially when Nick is involved.'

'I know I'll regret this,' I said, 'but would you be so kind as to explain that last remark?'

Arthur held up his hands. 'This is you,' he said, showing me his left palm. 'Covered in Velcro. Right?'

I shook a bewildered head in his direction.

'And this,' he showed me the other palm, 'is your old sparring partner, Mr Trouble. Also covered in Velcro. Right?'

He put his palms together. Made great play of trying to separate them. Gave a broad smile.

'Well, Nick,' Arthur chuckled, 'thanks for cheering me up.'

'Are you being sarcastic, Arthur?'

'No. Straight up,' he said, offended. 'I mean it. It's good to talk. Makes you realise that problems are all bleeding relative.'

CHAPTER SIX

I wasn't the only one who was up with the lark that morning — or, as they say less poetically in London, in time to hear the sparrows take their first cough of the day. As I walked across the car park towards the Lancia, Walker emerged from the back door of the building. She blinked in the sunshine, gave me a peremptory nod and sashayed over the tarmac, swinging a briefcase in time with the inner music of her steps.

To say that my relationship with Cherry Walker was strained was like calling the Crusades 'a slight difference of opinion between two bodies with contrasting theological views'. Whenever the two of us were together the atmosphere was electrically charged, threatening to shoot a spark of static into air composed of a combustible mixture of minds that could never meet and bodies that once had.

'You're early, Shannon,' she said, interrupting my trip down Memory Lane. That dispiriting time when Arlene and I had been going nowhere — Shannon sacrificed on the altar of the mother-daughter bond. That uplifting night when Cherry and I had formed an entirely different bond.

'Early, yes,' I said. 'But can still only manage second place, it seems.' Subconsciously I had dropped back into the role she expected of me. Where Walker was concerned, on top was the only place to be. Without exception.

'You really mustn't be so competitive,' she said. Her voice, even when laced with such condescension, was deep and smooth, never failing to conjure up in my convoluted brain visions of molten chocolate.

'That's rich,' I said, 'coming from you.'

'If I'm competitive, Shannon,' she said, 'it is not out of choice, but out of necessity.'

'That makes it all right, then,' I said, smiling sweetly. 'The ends justify the means? You and Collins would make a good team. You share the same expedient Jesuit philosophy.'

Except that Collins has a sense of loyalty, I thought. That puts a brake on the worst excesses of his behaviour. Walker allowed no such constraints to hinder her.

'How many officers in the Fraud Squad, Shannon?' she said, her tone flat and bored.

'A hundred and fifty-five,' I replied with a sigh. We'd been through this many times before. It was the much-practised central core of our double act.

'And how many women?' she continued, bang on script.

'Four,' I said, giving the stock reply.

'And how many in senior positions?'

'None,' I said.

'Yet,' she said with a broad smile. 'Just give me a little while. And spare me the moralising in the meantime.'

As usual, our conversation had degenerated into argument.

We never intended it to happen. But it always did. And it wasn't that there was too little understanding between us. The exact opposite: too damned much.

'OK,' I said, recognising futility when I saw it. We were both too set in our ways to change. 'Let this be the dawn of a new era.'

She narrowed her eyes and peered at me with obvious distrust. 'Didn't we say that last week? And the one before that?'

'Third time lucky, then.'

I winked at her.

'I like the suit,' I said.

'And what is that supposed to mean?' she said.

'It means I like the suit. Nothing more, nothing less.'

'Oh.' Her voice carried a hint of uncertainty, as if her brain was still suspiciously searching for a hidden motive. 'Thanks. It's new.' She frowned, and quickly added: 'Only mail order.'

'But perfect,' I said. 'For you, that is.'

It was the truth, not flattery. The superlatives didn't exist to make it possible to flatter Walker. Not physically, that is. Personality was a whole different ball game, as Arlene would say. Had said, in fact.

The suit was sheer simplicity — probably designed that way for reasons of economy and ease of mass-production — but on Walker it was raised to the height of elegance that only usually comes with the hefty price tag of classic styling. The material was lightweight cotton, its soft pastel yellow stolen from Van Gogh's palette. The skirt was discreetly cut to brush her knees: the jacket, long and straight, hiding her delicious curves, finished three inches above the hem of the skirt. The lapels, meeting at a single button at waist level, formed a long narrow wedge that showed a tantalising section of black scalloped top. Around her neck was a thin gold chain — a present, no doubt, from one of her many admirers.

'You look like a million dollars,' I concluded.

'That's nice to know,' she said, her lips parting in a wide smile. She gazed deep into my eyes, head tilted thoughtfully. Nostalgically, perhaps?

Then she destroyed the moment.

Shrugged her shoulders at me.

'Shame about us, Shannon.'

Cherry Walker turned on her heels and started towards her car.

'Wait,' I said.

'Can't,' she called over her shoulder. 'No time.'

I ran after her.

'What's so important?' I asked. 'I need to talk. Ask a favour.'

'Sorry,' she said. 'But you've got me mixed up with someone else. I don't do favours.'

'For me you do,' I said.

She came to an abrupt halt. Placed the briefcase on the floor and her hands on her hips. Looked at me with fire smouldering in her dark brown eyes.

'Are you threatening me, Shannon?'

'I wouldn't dream of it, Cherry. Unless I had to, of course.'

'I'm disappointed in you, Shannon,' she said sadly. 'Very disappointed.'

'But not altogether surprised, eh?'

'Listen,' she said sternly. 'This situation won't last. You know that, don't you?' She wagged a slender finger in my face. The nail had been bitten to the quick. 'At the moment, you and I are finely balanced. Mutually dependent, shall we say? You can make life very awkward for me — and vice versa. One day it will change. I'll have the upper hand. But until then,' she sighed wistfully, 'I suppose I do you favours. What the bloody hell do you want? As if I can't guess.'

'I'm off for a while. But I'm sure you knew that already. Not to mention the where and the why. That's the favour. Don't mention the where and the why. Is that clear?'

'Perfectly,' she said sharply. 'Now, if you don't mind, I've got to go. Important visitor to pick up. Big meeting this afternoon. The phones will be red hot in an hour — every member of the Liaison Group has to be there. Pity you'll miss it.'

She moved past me and marched off in the direction of her car.

'Something happening on Prospekt?' I called after her. 'A break in the case?'

'Who knows?' she said, throwing the briefcase into the back and slipping into the driver's seat, shapely knees pressed tight together.

You do, I thought.

And in advance of everybody else. That was for sure.

Yes, I liked the suit. I hoped the VIP would, too. After all, she'd dressed in his honour this morning.

* * *

Brooding on Walker helped pass the time as I crawled out of the City and along Commercial Road on my way to Docklands. Even going against the main flow of traffic, it was a slow journey. And a depressing one: the delights of places like Shadwell and Limehouse are few and far between. Turner had painted many scenes of London; 'Slums by Sunlight' was not one of them. The Lancia wasn't impressed, either. She coughed and spluttered her disapproval as the points of the two-litre engine clogged up with the incessant staccato rhythm of the stop-start motoring.

I had tried to give Walker the benefit of the doubt on numerous occasions, but she always managed to do something to spoil the gesture. I understood only too well that she had to overcompensate, prove time and again to the world at large that she was strong enough to bear the heavy cross that dug into the silky skin of her shoulders. Cherry Walker's cross — like all others, when you come to think of it — had four sections: she was black; a woman in a man's world; marked for special envy by a leap-frogging progress along the graduate-entry fast-track; and was saddled with a name that provided a rich source of material for the nickname compilers — 'Street' being the least offensive of the puerile puns. Constantly lifting that combined weight makes for hard muscles. Shouldn't necessarily make for a hard heart, though.

It wasn't that I minded her stepping over other people. It was stepping *on* them that rankled.

Walker was a user.

Better that than *being* used, Shannon, she would counter.

Best to be neither, I would reply. If you have a choice.

What I could not forgive was her duplicity. Her willing role in the setting-up of Collins. Agreeing — volunteering, for all I knew — to act as the Commander's mole in 'C' Squad. Watching Collins's every move; straining her ears for every word that drifted through the thin partitions of his office. Diligently building a damning dossier of rules bent and marks overstretched. And when it was time for the Collins experiment to end, for the old religion to return, it would be Walker who would administer the Judas kiss on his cheek.

And I couldn't warn him.

If I told Collins about the spy in his midst, or the Commander about the baby Walker had given up because it got in the way of her driving ambition, then she would return the compliment.

Good deeds can get you into bad trouble. As a favour to Collins, and because I liked Louise, I'd tried to tip off his ex-wife that both the police and Prospekt were searching for her. I'd tracked her down to the Grand Hotel in Eastbourne. But so had Prospekt. Not only had I not been able to save her, but I had also given Prospekt the perfect opportunity to issue their second warning to me to keep my nose out of their business. Louise had finished up in a burnt-out car at the bottom of a cliff; my fate was to be incriminated in her death. Prospekt had planted a tea cup bearing my fingerprints in her hotel room. Walker, by some devious route or other, had managed to acquire this piece of forensic evidence. She had thwarted Prospekt's plans for me. And achieved her objective of bringing about a state of uneasy equilibrium between the two of us. An ongoing duel, more like. Matched pistols loaded with mutual blackmail.

Collins, via selfishness and serendipity, had been right.

So had the well-intentioned Norman.

I did need a break. Badly.

Somewhere out of the firing line for a change. Away from political machinations, never daring to turn a back in case someone stabbed a knife in the exposed shoulder blades.

A week or two of ticking figures and gazing at spreadsheets in the safe haven of the insurance company.

I'd go through the motions, of course. Ask a few questions. Delve into the far reaches of the accounts. Reassure everyone that there was no fraud, no motive for murder.

As long as I had something to report back, then Collins couldn't grumble.

And, meanwhile, the local CID could get on with the job of finding the murderer without threat of interference.

It was a happy Shannon that slipped a cassette of Fats Waller into the stereo, sang along to 'Ain't Misbehavin', and drove on to the Isle of Dogs.

Bye-bye, police Alsatian and sniffing bloodhound, I said to myself. From now on, Shannon, you're a poodle at Cruft's. Your presence here is just for show.

CHAPTER SEVEN

Say what you like about the buildings of London Docklands — everybody else has — the one word that is guaranteed never to crop up is *understatement.* Each of the new structures — screaming out over the mournful sigh of the decaying old — is an individual monument to the unrestrained creativity and flamboyance of the Beau Brummels of the architectural profession. The gleaming offices of the *Financial Times,* the pagoda facade of China Wharf, the brickwork and tiling of the multi-coloured colonnaded Storm Water Pumping Station, you can't move among them without tripping over a self-congratulatory award of some sort. And the prime example of this trend for rampant egocentricity was Assurance House.

Assurance Hive would have been a more fitting name.

Weird!

I sat in the Monte Carlo and gazed through the windscreen in stunned amazement. Before me was a collection of seven regular hexagons — one in the middle, the other six forming the exterior borders — all welded together to resemble a giant steel honeycomb. It was either absolutely brilliant or totally monstrous. When my brain eventually recovered from the visual onslaught, it would make a decision. But, for the moment, the only instruction my mouth received was to utter: 'Jesus Christ!'

I climbed from the car and was hit by a vortex of wind that swirled around the building in a man-made demonstration of the principles of aerodynamics. By leaning hard against the dragging air I managed to weave my way unsteadily across the car park. Two wall-mounted cameras tracked my erratic progress, providing some small level of amusement to whoever might be watching. I was willing to bet that the female staff here wore either trousers or tight skirts — or were Marilyn Monroe wannabes.

Dramatically — like a character in *The Tempest*? — I blew through the automatic doors and into the shelter of the main entrance. From behind a long pale-wood reception desk a pretty girl greeted me with a mechanical smile. To her right sat a green-uniformed guard staring intently at a row of closed-circuit TV monitors. He fiddled with a joystick, tutted to himself and made a note on his clipboard.

'Good morning, sir,' said the pretty girl.

The words were delivered in that slightly high-pitched robotic tone of voice that is pre-programmed to follow up the greeting with 'May I help you?' (receptionists) or 'Soup of the day is oxtail' (steak-bar waitresses).

'May I help you?' she said. I'd never gone much on oxtail anyway.

'Shannon,' I announced.

A badge pinned to the breast pocket of her orange blouse said 'Pat'. 'Auditors,' I continued quickly, before my brain caught terminal frivolity and started wondering if the word was appellation or invitation. 'I am expected.'

Pat consulted a list, nodded approvingly, inserted a piece of plastic into a slot on an elaborate machine, and started tapping at her terminal. She input my surname, forenames, company, car registration number, whom I was visiting, time of arrival and expected departure date. Forgot about blood group and religion, though. Maybe that came later.

'This is your pass, Mr Shannon,' she said, fixing a chain through a hole in the plastic card and handing it to me. 'As a visitor, your security clearance is only Level One — access to Computing is not possible. Please carry this card with you at all times. It provides entry to the permitted cells.'

'Sorry,' I said, my mind flashing back in time. 'But did you say *cells*?'

'It's our name,' she said patiently, regretting now the lapse into jargon, 'for the seven units that make up the building. Because of the shape, you see. Each one resembles the cell of a honeycomb.'

'As long as it's not a prison,' I said cheerily.

'There are some who . . .' she began to say, and then checked herself. 'If you'd like to take a seat, Mr Shannon, I'll arrange for someone to collect you.'

I hung the chain around my neck, the word VISITOR glaring out from the card in the same bold red letters that once would have been used to identify lepers, and sat down as instructed. The chair was too low for comfort, unless you slid down, laid back and stretched your legs right out. Somehow I didn't think that would create quite the right first impression when my guide arrived. So I sat with my knees pointing at the recessed lights of the false ceiling and gazed self-consciously about me.

The reception area occupied about half the total floor space of the first cell; two glass-sided turnstiles provided access to the riveting world of insurance beyond. The walls were covered in hessian; the colour chosen was the same vivid shade of orange as Pat's blouse (which, I now deduced, must be a company-issued uniform — unless she was chromatically challenged in the taste department, of course). Behind the reception desk was mounted a circular slab of dark, highly polished wood four feet in diameter. Around the top edge ran the supposedly reassuring words 'Future Assurance PLC'; in my mind they conjured up the monogram FA. Still, the associations could have been worse: before the company's elevation to PLC status it would have been known as Future

Assurance Limited. In the centre was a highly stylised coat of arms complete with shields, scimitars and securely closed portcullis. In a curving scroll at the bottom ran the legend *Ad utrumque paratus* — whatever that meant. 'Over the top' was my non-classicist's guess.

One of the turnstiles clicked.

I looked up to see a woman in her late forties. She was wearing a dark blue knitted twin set, a long grey skirt in a heavy weave, and a nervous smile. She strode purposefully towards me on the leather soles of sensible brown shoes. Looked the type who thought nothing of taking the dog for a four-mile route march each morning; I didn't think much of it, either. Her hair was light brown streaked with grey — or grey streaked with light brown, whichever way you like to look at it, for the proportions were pretty much equal; it was shoulder-length, the left side straggly as if she had been distractedly running the fingers of her free hand through it. A pair of spectacles dangled on a cord around her neck and bounced on her low-slung bosom with each step.

'Mr Shannon?' she enquired hesitantly.

Here was a lady who didn't take any chances. There was no one else perched uncomfortably in the reception area. I was tempted to peer Cleese-fashion behind the chairs to check for lurking visitors.

'I'm Meg Wilson,' she said, not a moment too soon. 'Accounts manager.'

'Nick Shannon,' I said, shaking her extended hand. It was cold, limp and damp, a freshly filleted piece of plaice briefly in my grasp before being quickly withdrawn.

'If you would like to follow me,' she said, 'I'll take you through to Accounts.'

She walked to one of the turnstiles and signalled me to take the other. Swiping her card across the slot, she waited for the red light to turn to green, then squeezed her pear-shaped bottom through.

I followed her example precisely. Apart from the pear-shaped bit, that is.

Pull yourself together, Shannon. This is a change of scene, just a short break, not a holiday; there's no reason to get demob happy.

We entered a small antechamber-style area whose sole function seemed to be the housing of three more sets of double turnstiles. Whoever had bought this system suffered from a bad case of paranoia.

It was catching, too. The thought occurred to me that somewhere in the forbidden zone of Computing a specially written program would be logging my every move from one part of the building to another.

'To your right,' Meg said, waving a hand in an easterly direction, 'is the cell for senior staff, together with meeting rooms and conference facility. That leads on to Sales and Marketing, and then to the Computer Department and the record archive. Here' — this time she pointed to a one o'clock position — 'is the central cell. This can be accessed directly from all the other cells. It contains the restaurant, recreational area and a room for people who must smoke.'

No prizes for guessing what that would be like. Small, insufficiently ventilated and with all the comforts of your average betting shop (i.e. none) — a token gesture designed to extract from unrepentant sinners the maximum guilt and degradation. I'd rather stand outside in the force-ten gale, windblown but proud.

'This way,' she said, leading me through the turnstiles set at eleven o'clock.

We stepped into a large area that housed the main administrative centre for the company. The walls were covered in yellow hessian this time. It was a clever choice of colour. So dazzlingly bright that eyes were forced to turn away and take refuge in the work on the desks. And there were lots of desks. But only half as many people.

Meg raised her voice against the background noise of a battery of printers churning out personalised letters, proposal forms and an infinity of direct mail shots destined for impersonal bins across the length and breadth of the country.

'Nearly there,' she said.

We passed through another set of bloody turnstiles and entered the sanctuary of Accounts.

The walls were ice blue.

I shivered involuntarily.

Meg laughed, the natural movement dissolving the lines on her face and revealing a brief glimpse of a pretty face concealed below the drab make-up.

'It has that effect on everybody at first,' she said. 'I think the intention was to induce in us a cool, calm, collected air. But all it accomplishes is to make us wear an extra layer of clothing.'

'Industrial psychologists,' I said with a sigh. 'Don't you just love 'em?'

She smiled at me. 'Come and sit down,' she said. 'I expect you have some questions before you start work. Coffee?'

I nodded, and returned the smile with gratitude.

'Black. Two sugars, please.'

We walked across the room, like its predecessor half-deserted. Inquisitive heads peered around computer screens, examining me critically. Meg paused to relay my coffee order to a young girl in a peach-coloured tight skirt — told you so — and fluffy pink jumper who scurried off like a conscientious milk-monitor in the direction of the central cell. We sat ourselves down at a large L-shaped desk set in the top corner of this hexagon. It faced out, proprietorially, into the room, a window behind on each flank.

My eyes were drawn magnetically to the screen saver on her terminal: a large tropical fish, electric blue and exceedingly ugly, nibbled destructively with a hooked bill at a clump of coral.

'Horrible, isn't it?' she said. 'I'd like to change over to something a little less grotesque but . . .'

'I could do it for you,' I offered. 'I know my way round computers. It wouldn't take a moment.'

'Another day, maybe,' she replied, frowning deeply. 'This was David's desk — his computer — you see?'

'Ah,' I said, understanding her reluctance to erase any memory of her late boss. Such haste would appear unseemly at the very least.

'You've come at a bad time,' she said gravely. 'You must excuse us if we seem a little distant or unfriendly. It's not that we don't like outsiders, but we've all had a great shock. We haven't had a chance to adjust properly yet. Aren't quite sure how to react. Half the staff don't want to talk about it, the other half want to do nothing but.' She looked at me uncertainly. 'You do know about David — Mr Whitley — I take it?'

I nodded sympathetically. Wondered what to say to ease the strain that showed on her pale face.

'I understand,' I said soothingly. 'It can't be easy. Must be very unsettling for you all. Not just his death, I mean. The loss of a colleague — a friend? — must be bad enough on its own. But knowing that there's still a murderer on the loose . . .'

The coffee arrived, providing a welcome interruption, a merciful distraction.

The young girl registered the pained expression on Meg's face.

'Are you all right, Miss Wilson?' she said, fixing me with an accusatory stare.

Brilliant start, Shannon.

'Yes, thank you, Sandra,' Meg said bravely, trying to set a good example. 'You mustn't worry. I'm fine. Really.' She forced a smile. 'Now, back to your desk. Business as normal, you know.'

'Yes, Miss Wilson,' the girl said politely.

She turned on the low heels of a pair of slingbacks and walked back across the room. But not before flashing me a stern-eyed warning.

Which I chose to ignore.

Well, the damage was done. I'd make my peace with Sandra later. I had to seize this moment. There were questions to pose.

'Do you know,' I asked Meg innocently, 'if the police are making any progress?'

She shrugged.

'I haven't heard anything,' she said. 'But, then, I'd probably be the last to be told. They've finished with us here, though. I know that much. We've given all the help we can. Provided statements as to our whereabouts at the time — established our alibis, I suppose. And Security have handed over the tapes from the closed-circuit TV cameras. Nothing to do now but cross our fingers and hope they catch him quickly.'

I sipped the coffee. It tasted as if it had been freshly brewed — a week ago last Wednesday was my estimate — from an industrial blend that was predominantly chicory and guaranteed by its makers to put hairs on your chest. Meg, I noticed, was drinking tea.

'At least you are all safe inside this building,' I said. 'Hard to imagine anywhere more secure. Fort Knox, maybe.'

'Good analogy,' she said. 'Our computers are connected to those at the bank.' She said the word with awe, as if it demanded to be spelled with a capital letter. 'That's why we're so careful. Access to the Computer Department is very strictly restricted.'

What she said sounded reasonable enough — Norman, for one, would be licking his lips if he ever found out there was direct link from here into the bank's main computer. But something niggled at my brain — just didn't add up.

I was reminded of that old song — the knee bone connected to the thigh bone, the thigh bone connected to the hip bone, and so on. The terminals on these desks were connected to some server (mainframe, mini, whatever) in the computer room. That in turn was connected to the bank. If someone wanted to infiltrate the bank's computer, then it should theoretically be possible to do so without moving from this chair. If one knew the right procedures and passwords, that is.

There seemed to be two possibilities.

The first — requiring an act of faith on my part — was that the over-elaborate security system had indeed been designed to protect the computer. I could be wrong — OK, so it wouldn't be the first time — about the ease with which one could follow the chain from terminal to its very end. Or maybe I was right — infinitely more likely — but it was simply an oversight on their part, the thought never occurring to anyone before. After all, I did have the dubious benefit of a Norman-trained criminal mind.

The second possibility, however, was more intriguing; perhaps that was why I found it so much more appealing. What if the purpose of the security was not to prevent access to the computer, but to the room itself? Was there something else in there that needed to be hidden from prying eyes?

Only one way to find out.

'Isn't it a bit inconvenient, though?' I asked. 'All this swiping cards to pass through barrier after barrier. And doesn't it pose a danger to staff? What do you do, say, if there's an emergency?'

Meg gave me a condescending smile. I had the distinct impression I hadn't asked a very original question.

'Did you notice our motto in reception?'

'Noticed, yes. Understood, no. My knowledge of Latin only extends to Catholic masses, *caveat emptor* and *sic transit Gloria Hunniford*.'

'*Ad utrumque paratus*,' she said, regarding me uncertainly. 'It means "ready for any eventuality". "Prepared for the worst", if you prefer. The turnstiles are wired directly into the alarm system. Set off any alarm and every turnstile opens automatically. And, as belt and braces, there is an emergency exit in each of the outside cells.' She pointed over my left shoulder in evidence. 'We have regular fire drills. There's never any problem. No danger whatsoever for the staff.'

Meg finished her tea and pushed the cup aside.

'This is for you,' she said, extracting a large manila envelope from the desk drawer. 'From Jameson Browns. All the working papers on the audit to date.' She stood up. 'I expect you want to get down to work.'

Not especially. But it looked like I didn't have much option.

I took the parcel from her, deftly turning it over as I did so. The layer of sticky tape on the flap appeared to be undisturbed.

'Thanks for the coffee,' I said, rising in turn from my chair.

'If there's anything you need,' she said, 'just come and ask. Now, pick a desk. As you can see, there's plenty of choice.'

She made a sweeping motion with her hand.

I was supposed to be looking at the sea of desks. But something else drew my attention.

The cardigan of her twin set was unbuttoned.

It had drawn aside with the expansive movement of her arm.

My eyes had caught a flash of an ornate piece of costume jewellery. Some sort of shiny silvery metal. Studded with opalescent deep blue stones.

A brooch.

In the shape of a crucifix.

Hold tight, Shannon. Don't get carried away.

One swallow doesn't make a summer.

And one crucifix pinned to her chest doesn't mean there's a scourge in her bedroom. And everything else that implies.

CHAPTER EIGHT

The envelope contained good news and bad news. The good news was that the audit was almost complete; the bad news was . . . the audit was almost complete. A couple of days of reasonably hard work and I could — should — be out of here. That didn't fit in with anybody's plans.

Collins expected me to stay until I could provide him with concrete leads to the identity of the murderer or, less satisfactorily, prove to him that this was not an inside job. And I wanted to hang on to this cushy little number for all the while Arlene would be in London. That way I could come and go as I pleased (using 'called back to the office' as an all-encompassing, suitably vague excuse) and spend the maximum time with her. Somehow I would have to come up with a convincing reason that would allow me to spin out the remainder of the audit for an extra couple of weeks.

I parked the problem — there was no rush to do anything after all — and turned back to the manila envelope containing the file of background papers. Leaning back in the chair, I looked over the top of the file. The desk I had chosen was next to the emergency exit — old habits die hard. It provided me with a view of Meg hard at work on my left, the turnstiles to the Computer Department straight ahead, and the thinly populated arctic waste of Accounts all around me.

The room contained about thirty desks, each equipped with a computer terminal. I counted only twelve people in the department. Apart from Meg, the rest were young girls aged between seventeen and twenty. I wondered if Meg felt the same way as I: accounts clerks are like policemen — when they start to look young, you know you're getting old.

Sandra caught my roving eye, frowned and set me a virtuous example by tapping away furiously at her keyboard. Shamed, I took out a pencil, bent over the desk and started to examine the papers.

Future Assurance was less than ten years old. Started by its four directors — including the late lamented Mr Whitley — in the mid-eighties, it had enjoyed spectacular growth by concentrating on a niche market of 'low risk-takers' — teachers, civil servants, middle managers with one eye on retirement — that sub-set of the population whose motto is 'Who dares, loses' and who either drive a Volvo or aspire to one.

I yawned, and turned the page.

With five years of rising profits behind them, and the need for an injection of capital to keep the ever-demanding treadmill of growth turning, thoughts had turned to the benefits of being acquired. Good for the future of the firm: greater stability, the resources of a larger company as insurance against a lean year, maybe even turnover benefits from cross-selling of products by the parent — Want a mortgage? Want a loan? Sure. But we'll need some insurance on your life as security. And, on a more personal level, very good for the pockets of the four shareholder-directors.

In the heady — headstrong? — days at the end of the last decade there was no shortage of interest in a company like Future Assurance: cash-rich predators, furiously pedalling at their own treadmills, desperate to expand their empires and their profits, paranoically anxious not to lose ground against their competitors, licked hungry lips at the prospect. Three suitors emerged from the chasing pack, and courted the company by whispering in its ear sweet nothings about funding ('We'll give you all the money you need to grow') and autonomy ('And we won't interfere in the day-to-day running of the company'). Some people will promise anything to get somebody in bed with them.

Jameson Browns — before my time — had been engaged by City & County Bank, the smallest, and therefore the most pressurised, of the Big Five clearing banks, to carry out the 'due diligence' investigations to establish the company's worth. After three months of assiduous checking of all aspects of Future Assurance's business, the price was agreed, the terms of the deal struck, and the contract signed.

At times like those, you wish you'd had a clairvoyant on your team. Jameson Browns, as myopic as all the other perpetual optimists of that decade, had not seen the recession coming round the corner. Until it was too late for City & County to avoid the damaging collision.

Future Assurance — what a joke! — had geared itself up for expansion, used its parent's money to move to bigger premises in Docklands, gone on a spending spree of office furnishers, installed a new computer and security system. And then the market turned.

Outcome: empty desks, profits wiped out and glum faces all round. And not just at City & County. The four original shareholder-directors were losers, too — or, at least, gained a lot less than they had expected.

The contract of sale — thanks to the natural caution of accountants — had set the purchase price according to a formula based on past and future performance, the latter carrying the lion's share of the weight in the equation. The shareholder-directors had been paid a small lump sum on signing the sale agreement and were then due a much larger additional amount (an 'earn-out') for each of the following five years, the precise value of this extra money being dependent on hitting certain profits targets.

I wish I could have given credit to Jameson Browns for coming up with the face-saving (and, ultimately, money-saving) deal, but it was the method of purchase most commonly used then. It, technically, benefited all sides. The buyer was ensured the continuing commitment of the people who had built up the company (who were usually also tied in with long-term contracts of employment) and conserved its cash by paying the annual earn-out money with the profits generated by the company it had acquired. And they say accountants aren't creative. The sellers, for their part, are presented with the opportunity of having a thick layer of jam tomorrow on top of the bread and butter handed over on Day One. And the accountants — we mustn't forget them — reap larger audit fees because of the extra work involved. Wherever there are earn-out targets, there is also a great temptation for the sellers to inflate the profits of the company in order to hit them.

Maybe I'm just plain cynical, or my Irish blood is too diluted, but I've never been able to believe in leprechauns. Or that every rainbow has a pot of gold at its end.

This case proved my point, although I probably wouldn't have mentioned it if it had been otherwise. City & County were saddled with a loss-making company they couldn't give away; the shareholder-directors had seen their dreams of untold riches fade and die, disappearing with the jobs of the teachers, civil servants and middle managers that provided their living.

So much for history.

The whizz-kid financiers had learned their lesson. Wouldn't make the same mistake again. At least, not for ten years or so. By which time a new breed with short memories, rose-coloured designer spectacles, and itchy palms would have risen to the top of the heap.

The present didn't look too promising, either.

As far as I could tell from the results of the audit so far, Future Assurance's income was still insufficient to cover the pared-down overheads and the inconsiderate claims of its policy-holders. Another year of loss rather than profit. Future Assurance was a corporate haemophiliac, without a Rasputin standing by in the wings ready to weave magic spells to stem the fatal loss of blood.

'Lunch, Nick?' Meg said, making me jump.

The ever-watchful Shannon strikes again.

'If you'd like to join me today,' she continued, 'I'll show you the ropes. Then tomorrow you can be a free agent.'

'Always my wish,' I said. 'But never my calling.'

She gave me a puzzled look.

'Sorry,' I said. 'I'm a founder member of the Cryptic Club. You'd do best to ignore me.'

Her frown deepened.

'I meant about being a free agent,' I explained. 'Isn't that what we all dream of?'

'Shall we just eat?' she said. 'I'm not sure I can cope with homespun philosophy on an empty stomach.'

'Lead on, Macduff,' I said.

'A common misconception,' she said.

It was my turn for the puzzled frown.

'Like "Play it again, Sam",' she explained. 'The words were never uttered in the film, but everyone thinks they were. By adopting the phrase, the life of the misquotation is sustained at the expense of the original. In *Macbeth*, the actual saying is "*Lay* on, Macduff; And damned be him that first cries, 'Hold, enough'". Sorry to shatter your illusions.'

'Just as long as I don't have to hand back my O-level certificate. I'd hate to think that all those hours spent studying *The Ancient Mariner* had been wasted.'

Or that I'd learned nothing about the dangers of dicing with Death.

* * *

We swiped our cards through the machine at the turnstiles and then again at the cashier's station in the restaurant. The computer, it seemed, wasn't content simply to know my whereabouts in the building; it wanted to log my eating habits, too. I wondered how far its curiosity extended. Would there be swipe machines in the washrooms? On the top of the wailing wall? Inside the doors of the cubicles? Data collected and input as part of some complex analysis of bladder control. Isn't technology wonderful? Where would we be without it?

'The meals are subsidised,' Meg said, as if to pre-empt any complaints. 'Not as heavily as when we first moved here, of course. Times have changed, I'm afraid. Still, the only alternative within walking distance is to pay five pounds for a drink and a sandwich in one of the yuppie-filled wine bars or "themed" public houses.' She grimaced at the thought. 'And it's such a nice room, don't you think?'

You could see the sky, certainly — a limited advantage in the English climate, of course, but worth the expense of the Plexiglas dome that covered the inner hexagon for rare days like this. Clear blue, dimmed a little by the protective tint of the plastic, and cloudless. I resolved to make time for a walk outside before resuming the arduous task of prolonging the audit. Drink in the sun; feel the air on my face. It's the romantic in me. Absolutely nothing to do with thoughts of a cigarette.

The tables — far too many, not unexpectedly — were stripped pine; the chairs a country-kitchen mixture of the same wood for the frames and wickerwork for the seats. The walls were barley-white (hessian — surprise, surprise). The much-needed colour contrast came from red paper napkins and the clothes of the workers and drones. Young girls (hired for reasons of economy, I now assumed after having read the background papers on the company's parlous state) in summery skirts and blouses or crop-tops of yellow, rose-pink and light blue; plus a lesser number of equally inexperienced lads in vividly patterned shirts and ties — with the odd pair of red braces in evidence among the really thrusting types.

The air-conditioning provided a constant breeze. It wafted across the room, working hard to clear the cheesy smell of overcooked lasagne, and even harder to counteract the all-pervading miasma of gloom and doom. It was like being in a Shrewsbury monastery in the days following the death of Brother Cadfael: long faces, awkward silences and lousy food.

At one table, an island separated from the mainland by a sea of empty chairs, three people older than the rest sat lethargically playing with their pasta.

'They don't look particularly happy,' I said to Meg, pointing to the long-faced group with the prongs of my fork.

'Would *you* be in their place?' she said. 'They're the directors.'

That explained why they weren't exactly spraying everybody in the room with champagne.

'The one with the dark hair,' she said, 'is Robert Tresor. He's our managing director.'

'Where the buck stops,' I said. 'No wonder he looks worried.'

The man's brow was creased with a railway network of lines as he talked earnestly to his colleagues. The jacket of his sombre — respectful? — dark grey suit hung limply over the back of the chair. His shirt was crisp white, the knot of his red-and-blue-striped tie deliberately small to fit inside the gap of the button-down collar.

'The other man is Toby Beaumont — Sales and Marketing.'

I could have guessed that much: he had a mobile phone next to his right hand. His shirt was light green, his tie the unfortunate victim of an explosion in a paint factory — that psychedelic mix of colours that only looks right if you're on the same LSD trip as the wearer. I averted my eyes and let them settle on the final member of the trio.

'And the woman?' I asked.

'Stephanie,' Meg said. 'Stephanie Williams. Administration. Her job is to keep the wheels turning. And hiring and firing.'

Mostly firing for the last few years, I thought. I wondered how she coped with such a depressing job: easing out the experienced and costly, replacing as few of them as possible with the young and cheap. Would she have moved on to a brighter world without the chains of a long-term contract?

Stephanie rose from the table and walked across the room. Heads turned to watch her. And no one breathed.

The girls cast admiring glances at the tightly fitting red wool dress. The lads concentrated on the curves beneath.

A series of thoughts crossed my mind. Three of them were even relevant to the job in hand.

'He stoppeth one of three' — Samuel Taylor Coleridge. Not often you can quote from *The Ancient Mariner* twice in one day.

'Cherchez la femme' — Alexandre Dumas. Wow, only been here a few hours and my French was already coming on by leaps and bounds.

And 'shake that tree' — Spenser (Robert B Parker's private eye, not the *Faerie Queene* man). His theory was that detection was pretty much like walking through an unfamiliar orchard at dead of night — unlikely, I admit, but it's the metaphor that's important. In order to discover what kind of tree you're standing next to, you have to shake it. Then examine the fruit that falls to the ground.

'Tea, Meg?' I said, already moving on an interception course towards the queue at the counter.

Immediately in front of Stephanie was a short, pimply youth who looked like he'd chosen his clothes that morning by spraying himself with glue and walking through a wardrobe. He was waiting self-consciously for a glass of warm milk, shuffling from foot to foot with all the elegance of a hippopotamus walking on coals.

'Three coffees,' Stephanie said, watching the lad warily.

'Hi,' I said cheerily. 'Nick Shannon. Auditors.'

'Yes?' she said, examining me through long lashes with eyes as green as my own. She was aged somewhere in the indeterminate zone of the mid-thirties, wearing a little too much make-up for my taste, but I wasn't going to grumble. It couldn't hide the sensuality that oozed from every pore.

'Just to say,' I smiled reassuringly, 'that I'll keep any disruption from the audit to the very minimum.'

'I would hope that goes without saying,' she replied with a curt shake of her head that caused barely a movement of her hair. It was cut into one of those ultra-short styles that always reminded me of childhood pictures of pixies with petalled hats.

I tried to think of my next line. It wasn't easy. I was enjoying watching each movement of her lips. Wide, full lips made wider and fuller by a deep pink lipstick inside the perfectly drawn outline of a deeper pink lip-pen.

I knew one thing. Whatever I said would have to be a question. That way I could carry on indulging myself voyeuristically.

'When would it be most convenient for us to talk? Discuss systems and so on?'

'I'll let you know,' she said, picking up the tray of coffee and turning away.

The lad in front of her chose that precise moment to pick up his glass of milk, discover it was hot rather than warm, and drop it on the floor. The glass shattered, the milk splashed up.

Stephanie stepped back hurriedly. Too hurriedly. Turned her ankle and stumbled.

Shannon to the rescue. I steadied her by grabbing hold of her arm and taking her weight with my hand.

My left hand.

She looked at it with abject horror as it rested on her elbow. Shuddered. Mumbled something that might have been 'Thanks' or 'Eek!' Then walked swiftly away.

I felt like a Boy Scout who had mistakenly helped an old lady back across a road she had just taken fifteen minutes to negotiate herself. I shrugged, not totally unused to the reaction of distaste. It didn't hurt much anymore. Thanks to Cherry and Arlene.

Stephanie recovered her composure quickly. Switched back to her role of flame among the assembled moths. She walked unfalteringly back to the table on three-inch heels in that manner fashion models favour — you know, very deliberately, as if traversing a narrow beam across a deep gorge, each foot planted in a perfect straight line that brought the utmost movement of her hips.

She reached the table. Leaned forward slightly in a move that must have been sending the lads wild with delirium. Slowly placed the tray down. Said something inaudible. Tresor looked in my direction and scowled.

'Two teas, please,' I said with a sigh to the lady in a green overall.

She smiled at me. Part humour at my plight, part pity for its source.

'Anyway, love,' she said, nodding at Stephanie, 'you'd only be wasting your time. She's spoken for.'

'No harm trying,' I said, only a little sheepishly.

'Two teas,' she said, shaking her head. 'And don't say I didn't warn you.'

* * *

I needed a cigarette.

Not strictly true. I craved a cigarette.

I was giving up. Doing well at giving up, too. In fact, on average, I was giving up about fifteen times a day.

Meg finished her tea and strode back to her desk — Whitley's desk as was. I briefly inspected the smoking room — as squalid as I had imagined, furnished in those orange 'leatherette' chairs that are as pitiless on the eye as on the backside — and made my way outside. Sandra was there, leaning against the wall, a pack of Silk Cut and box of matches in her left hand.

I joined her. We lit up simultaneously.

'Nice day,' I said, turning my face to the sun.

She blew the smoke through her nostrils — and to think they used to say that smoking gave a woman an air of sophistication! The wind whipped the two grey plumes away. She pulled the fluffy cardigan tightly around her.

'How long you gonna be here?' she said, seemingly thrilled at my presence.

'How long would you like?' I replied with a wasted smile.

She shrugged, her brown plastic shoulder-bag rising and falling with the economical couldn't-care-less gesture.

'Depends,' she said.

I leaned against the wall, mirroring her body language. The new trendy science of neurolinguistics said — as had Desmond Morris barely twenty years earlier — that it helped to build rapport.

'On what?' I said.

'On whether you're gonna upset Miss Wilson again.'

'It wasn't intentional,' I said contritely. 'How about making allowances for me being a new boy? I won't make the same mistake again, don't worry.'

She gave me the same shrug.

Must practise a lot in front of the mirror during her spare time. Otherwise how could she get it exactly identical each time?

I bit back a sigh. Drew on the cigarette instead. Jesus, this was hard going.

'How long have you worked here, Sandra?' I asked, choosing a sentence she couldn't shrug at.

'Year.'

What a great conversationalist! Trained at the Trappist school. Graduated with honours, no doubt.

'Do you like it?' I said.

'It's all right, I s'pose.'

Enthusiastic as well as gabby.

'Meg seems like a good boss,' I said, trying to draw her out.

'Yeah,' she said, grinding the butt of the cigarette under the toe of her shoe. 'I gotta go.'

'Nice talking to you,' I said. Not *with* you, but *to* you.

Sandra looked at me dubiously. Undid the catch on her bag. Dropped the pack of cigarettes and box of matches among the other clutter.

'That's beautiful,' I said, pointing inside the bag. 'May I have a closer look? Please.'

With reluctance, she withdrew the object that had caught my attention. Passed it to me.

It was a remarkable piece of workmanship. Lovingly made. The surface silky-smooth to the touch. The grain of the wood catching the light like ripples on a pond. The joints of the arms of the cross perfectly mitred. With the aid of a chisel.

'I'd love to buy one of these,' I said. 'A present for someone very special. Tell me, where did you get it?'

'Mr Whitley gave it to me,' Sandra said, her voice shaky with emotion. 'He made it himself.'

'Oh,' I said.

'If you really want one,' she said, seeing the look of disappointment on my face, 'you'll have to go to St Jerome's.'

'I think I will,' I said. 'Where is this church?'

'It's not a church exactly,' she said. 'More like a mission, I suppose. They make the crosses to raise money. Mr Whitley used to help out there. It's only a few hundred yards up the road. Right on the waterfront. You can't miss it.'

'You don't know my sense of direction,' I said with a smile. 'If I'm not back in an hour, send out a search party.'

CHAPTER NINE

I walked down Westferry Road towards Mudchute, following the signs for Island Gardens and the Greenwich Foot Tunnel and a party of carefree schoolkids who were overdosing on ice creams and Mars bars. I slowed my pace to a casual saunter and lingered behind them, my jacket slung over my shoulder James Dean style, shirtsleeves turned over a couple of times, tie off, collar unbuttoned, feeding off their infectious laughter and drinking in the warm rays of the summer sun. Shame about the scenery, though. A vast modern public house, acres of glass held together by eyeball-stabbing brand-new bricks, stood overlooking — and selfishly obscuring — *Cutty Sark*.

In the tarmac ocean of the car park there was a flotilla of company cars protected by three flagships in the garish fluorescent livery of police Rovers. Directly abutting the road sat two large Portakabins. A white board with blue lettering said 'Police Incident Centre'. Beside it, a notice chalked on a blackboard in meandering capitals gave details of the time and place of the murder and requested anyone with information to step inside. I strode hurriedly past. The prospect of a cup of stewed tea and spotlights in my eyes didn't tempt me. Not that I knew anything. Yet.

Coming out of the lee of the pub, I felt a warm breeze drifting in from the west, bringing with it that seemingly impossible, oxymoronic, muddy-fresh smell of the river, tainted by the odd whiff of diesel from the slowly chugging pleasure boats plying their trade between Westminster and Greenwich. And, with the view no longer obstructed, I was suddenly transported a hundred years back in time.

Sandra was right. You couldn't miss St Jerome's.

It was one of a row of six old Dutch-style warehouses perched on the Thames. Not next to, or at, the water's edge, but on.

They were built on ash-grey wooden pilings, as straight as poplars and as solid as oaks, driven directly into the river bed. Each warehouse was slightly different in shape and colour; and yet this added to, rather than detracted from, the overall visual appeal. When watercolour artists died and went to heaven, this was the sort of scene they painted.

Some had sharply pointed roofs, the two sides sweeping down at acute angles; others were flatter, the roof sections made up of six separate planes with gentle sloping pitches. On two, the peeling wood had once been painted black, another two were faded yellow, one was sunset red weathered down to a dull fuchsia, one the colour of bronze. In the middle of each, running top to bottom at every level, were large double doors for swinging through the goods pulled up by the block and tackle fixed at the very top. The tallest, in the middle of the row, was six storeys high; its pilings were more widely spaced, allowing entry for narrow boats to dock directly underneath.

They were ripe for conversion. Ripe for spoiling. Only spared this long by the glut of empty property, both business and residential, and the vanishing fortunes of the developers. The recession had brought some good after all.

It would take a labour of love to restore them. And more cash than I could earn in a lifetime.

Dream on, Shannon, I thought, as I stepped onto the jetty.

St Jerome's, the handmade sign told me, was the one in the middle with the boathouse. On the deck outside sat the most beautiful girl I had ever seen. Forgive me, Sis, but I have to tell it like it is.

Her hair was a waterfall of molten copper. It flowed from under a wide-brimmed straw hat and cascaded down to her waist. Her skin looked like it had never felt make-up: it was clear and fresh, with a dotting of freckles on her cheeks and along the sides of the little button nose. Eyes as dark as bitter chocolate. Lips as red as the sweetest strawberries.

Around her slim neck was a blue-tinged Spanish silver Celtic cross on a long chain. It hung outside a man's white long-sleeved shirt which was tucked into a pair of blue jeans bleached to ice by the sun. On her feet was a tiny pair of peach-coloured ballet shoes.

She was sitting, straight-backed and cross-legged, on a large cushion, sewing. The pink tip of her tongue poked through her lips in concentration. At her side was a heavily pregnant black cat dozing peacefully, a brown beret containing a handful of pound coins anchoring a thin pile of notes, and a large black cloth. Over the surface of the cloth was spread a carefully arranged display of crucifixes of various styles, brooches, rings, necklaces, earrings, bracelets and cufflinks.

'Welcome,' she said, smiling serenely up at me.

'You know,' I said, returning the smile, 'that's the nicest thing anyone has said to me all day.'

'If you have need of comfort,' she said with a look of deep concern, 'Brother James will be back at five. Please stay. If you wish, that is.'

Her voice was soft and melodic, the accent slow and full of the long slurred vowels that hinted at West Country origins.

I didn't ask where exactly.

The answer would have shattered my fantasy.

Camelot was my guess.

'Thanks for the kind offer,' I said. 'Another time, perhaps.'

She nodded understandingly, a strand of hair flicking over her face to brush a dimpled chin.

'Brother James's door is always open,' she said, the warmth of her eyes emphasising the invitation.

I went down on my haunches and examined the wares. The materials were cheap — wood, fake stones, thinly plated metal — but the designs showed an eye for creativity and originality, and the execution was finely and patiently worked. My fingers indulged in the tactile pleasure of running along the smooth surface of a white metal torc etched with a cornucopia at each finial end. I wondered if Arlene would like it — and whether it would make her neck turn green.

Hell, nothing ventured, nothing gained.

I made two decisions. It was time to take a couple of risks.

First, I'd have the torc — a green neck might look quite fetching.

Second, it was the moment to shake a tree again. What would fall to earth this time? An apple containing the sweet juice of knowledge, or merely hiding a maggot within.

I checked my watch. Frowned. 'Work calls,' I sighed. 'Still, what better day for the short stroll back to Future Assurance.'

'Then, you knew David,' she said, a cloud of sadness passing across her face.

I shook my head.

'Only started there today,' I explained. 'So I never had the chance to meet him. What was he like?'

'David,' she said, staring up at the sky as if she could see him there, 'was a good man. Gentle and kind. And giving. He taught us how to work with our hands. Paid for our machinery and tools. We all miss him. And we pray for his soul.'

'Did he make any of these?' I asked, pointing to the jewellery.

'No,' she said. 'All David's work has been sold.'

'That was quick,' I said, thinking of a queue of macabre bargain-hunters swooping down here ahead of me.

'David's work was much prized,' she said. 'He was a true craftsman, taking trouble and time, and injecting a little of himself into each piece. And over the last month he produced little. David was in pain.'

'Physical?' I asked, remembering the ulcer revealed by Professor Davies and puzzling over how that might stop him carving. 'Or spiritual?'

A voice rang out from the doorway.

'What do you want?'

Thud.

Back to reality.

Or maybe it was still Arthurian legend and the Black Knight had just arrived on the scene.

'I came to buy,' I said, moving my eyes with a show of reluctance away from the torc.

'So buy,' a young man said. 'Then go.'

The girl frowned at him. But it lacked any bite. There was too much love in her eyes for that.

'Mickey,' she admonished, immediately extending a forgiving hand to him.

Mickey didn't move.

Just stared at me, hands on his hips, jaw jutting out pugnaciously.

He was about nineteen, I estimated: a year or two older than his girlfriend. A little under six foot. Scrawny. Complexion unhealthily pale with contrasting red blotches. Long mousey hair matted into rats' tails. He was wearing a pair of trainers that had seen better days — England winning the World Cup, probably — dirty blue jeans, and a black sweatshirt with the sleeves chopped off just below the elbows. He looked like the bookies' favourite for the Scruff of the Decade competition, odds-on with the thin layer of sawdust that radiated out from his right hip to smear the dark clothes and white skin.

The girl stood up. Her jeans hid slim legs, but not the tell-tale bulge of the baby she was carrying. She floated across to him, gracefully and silently on the cushioned leather soles of the ballet shoes. Stared up longingly into his eyes. Reached out with her left arm and took him by the hand. Brushed tenderly at the dust on his forearm, more for the feel of the contact than for effect, for the tiny particles of wood were caked firmly on with sweat. Then she pulled him towards her and planted a light but loving kiss on his cheek.

Throughout this show of affection, his eyes, lined and bloodshot, never wavered from me.

'How much is this?' I said to the girl, picking up the torc and holding it in the air.

'Twenty-five pounds,' Mickey said.

Her lips turned down.

'Twenty,' she corrected.

'And the matching ring,' I said on impulse.

'Ten,' she said.

'I'll take both.'

I stood my ground so that she had to unclasp her hand and walk back towards me. Mickey's face hardened; dust-flecked eyebrows knotted, eyes narrowed and lips tightened.

Not much room for doubt there. Someone else spoken for.

She took a paper bag from underneath the beret and placed the torc and ring inside.

I extracted thirty pounds from a now much-depleted wallet and passed it to her.

'I hope these are for someone close to you,' she said with a smile.

'Very,' I said.

'May the cornucopia work its magic for you both.'

'I'm sorry,' I said, puzzled, 'but I don't understand.'

'The cornucopia — the horn of plenty — is the symbol of Fortuna. Roman goddess of prosperity. And,' she added with a coy laugh, 'of fertility.'

'Can you have one without the other?' I asked with a smile.

'Would she want one without the other?'

I shrugged.

'Come on, Rhee,' Mickey snapped impatiently. 'Pack everything up. Now. I need your help inside.'

She bent down and began to bundle up the cloth.

'Unusual name,' I said. 'Rhee.'

'It's short for Rhiannon,' she said.

'And I'm Shannon,' I said. 'Easy to remember. Shannon. And Rhiannon. Together we make a rhyming couplet.'

Mickey's chest rose and fell as he breathed deeply through his nose like an enraged bull. His face became dark and brooding. And his eyes, deciding that the situation required more than bulk-standard Beano daggers, sent a steady stream of Kalashnikov bullets in my direction.

If looks could kill, I thought, I would be lying in my grave now.

Alongside Whitley, maybe?

CHAPTER TEN

The cell containing the offices of the directors was hessianed in green. Heavy-handed symbolism again. Spring. Growth. Julie Andrews running through lush grass and edelweiss singing, 'The tills are alive . . .'

It's OK, you can stop your fingers drifting towards the back of your throat. Times had changed at Future Assurance. 'Autumn Leaves' was now the company's signature tune. A harsh wind was blowing over the corporate tree, stripping it of more leaves with each passing day; and those that still clung on were dry and brittle, prone to crumble at the slightest touch.

I knocked on Tresor's door, answering his summons.

On my return to Accounts, Meg had been twiddling her nervous fingers through her hair. 'Tresor wants to see you,' she had said in anxious tones. 'And then I'm next.' She touched the crucifix brooch through the fabric of the cardigan as if she could hear the tumbrils coming to take us away. 'Don't put him in a bad mood. Please. For my sake.'

'Come,' rang out the pedantic instruction.

Why do people do that? *Come in* is so much more inviting. What's wrong with a bit of tautology every now and again? Life's not 'Just a Minute'; I mean, even if the rules were changed to allow repetition and hesitation the buzzer would still be perpetually sounding for deviation.

Tresor stood up as I entered. Not out of politeness, I'm sure. More like a childish attempt to intimidate me physically. I must introduce him to Arthur some time. Show him what intimidation really means. Might stop him bullying poor Meg.

I smiled at him.

The smile was supposed to be disarming.

His look told me he took it as further evidence that I was an idiot. Making what could be construed as a pass at his woman, or whatever; an hour late back from lunch. Maybe he had a point, after all.

Tresor was forty-something; my guess was somewhere on the downward slope towards the Big Five-O and the obligatory identity crisis. Stood five foot ten in his shiny black lace-ups. Thickset, a larger chunk of the former muscle (rugby full-back? football central defender?) than he would have liked turned to fat by the sedentary lifestyle. Waistline broadened by too much beer and calorific subsidised meals. His brow was creased into exactly the same network of lines I had noticed in the restaurant. (Tattoo? I wondered frivolously. Result of some moment of drunken impetuosity, perhaps?) There were bags under his eyes, but that could have been due to Stephanie rather than worry. His chin was dark with the premature arrival of a five o'clock shadow. His hair, smartly cut to flick over his ears, was black. Impossibly black. Vainly black. Still, I suppose if you have to resort to a bottle for comfort, then Grecian 2000 is less harmful than whisky. Probably tastes smoother than Collins's whisky, too.

'Sit,' he said, waving at a chair with a large hairy hand.

I thought of saying, 'Woof,' but decided to hold that in reserve for the subsequent orders of 'Roll over' and 'Die for England'.

The chair was uncomfortable, designed like the room itself — dark hard-edged desk, harsh fluorescent lighting — as a deterrent to inconvenient interruptions. There were conference rooms available for proper discursive meetings. Tresor's office was for quick in-and-out MD-style pats on the back or kicks up the backside. I didn't need a Tarot deck to tell which I was in for.

'How much longer before you finish the audit?' he said.

So nice to feel wanted.

'Just a couple of days,' I said.

The lines on his brow flattened a touch. Wasn't a tattoo, after all. Silly me.

'Then,' I continued, 'I can send all the papers to the office for typing, printing and binding.'

'Good,' he said. 'City and County are pressing me for the results. They need our figures for consolidation into their accounts. I've got enough on my plate at the moment without them chasing me every day.'

'You can tell them middle of next week,' I said. 'Without fail.'

He gave a satisfied nod.

'So,' he said, 'you'll be gone in another couple of days?'

I was going to enjoy this. Outstaying a welcome I'd never actually had.

'More like a couple of weeks, I'm afraid.'

'But I thought you said you were nearly finished,' he said, voice raised a semitone and brow returning to the familiar crease.

'On the audit, yes,' I said, trying not to smile. 'Just the usual list of queries there. Won't take long to go through them with the relevant members of staff. Yourself. Mr Beaumont. And Stephanie Williams, of course.'

Blue veins stood out on his forehead. You could almost see the blood pulsing through them.

Go for it, Shannon.

'Then there's the fixed-asset schedule,' I said. 'It will take a day or so to check your equipment against the list.' I paused. 'I'll need my access changed so I can inspect the Computer Department.'

His dark eyes examined my face.

Not much joy there for him. I'd spent — wasted? — too much of my youth playing poker to allow the inner bluff to seep through to the outside.

None the wiser, he looked away and wrote a note to himself on the right-hand page of an impressive black leather diary. I studied the framed photograph on his walnut-topped desk. Tresor with smiling wife and two boys. The picture was heavily posed, as if the resident *paparazzi* for *Hello!* magazine had freelanced the session for Walt Disney studios. Soft focus, Vaseline-smeared lens, so grainy as to be almost pointillistic. Tresor in blazer and tie. Wife, glittering gold necklace and earrings, hair coiffured to perfection, in designer black dress. Two boys, hair slicked down, in the formal uniform of some expensive public school. The four of them seated on a long, low chesterfield. Parents in the middle, holding hands. Kids on the flanks, gazing at the camera as innocent — and as unreal — as a pair of cherubs. It was all so sweet I thought my teeth would drop out at any moment.

'See Pat on Reception in the morning,' Tresor grunted. 'Can't fix it before then.'

Can't? Or won't?

He inclined his head slightly to one side and peered uncertainly at me.

'Still doesn't sound like two weeks' work,' he said. 'Counting a few computers. Even allowing for the amount of time you spend away from your desk.'

Ouch.

'You're not trying to spin this out, are you?'

Who — me?

'Because there's no point. The audit fee was agreed in advance. Can't be increased now.'

'No,' I said, giving him my affronted look. 'It's the FRA that takes the extra time.'

'FRA?' he asked. 'What's that?'

'Fraud Risk Analysis,' I explained. The idea had come to me while walking back from St Jerome's. Something like the FRA provided me with a perfect excuse to snoop around and ask awkward questions, while at the same time allowing me ample opportunity to slope off and spend time with Arlene. The more I'd thought about it, the more advantages there seemed to be: 'Fraud Risk Analysis' sounded impressive, was sufficiently vague to cover most actions, and the report didn't need to be written at Future Assurance. Might not even need writing at all — an oral statement of 'all clear' would bring grateful sighs of relief from all concerned. 'It should by rights have been done last year,' I lied. 'But somehow it seems to have slipped through the net.'

I sucked in breath through clenched teeth and shook my head in the never-known-anything-like-it manner of a motor mechanic or service engineer who has a mug punter dead centre in his sights.

'What does it involve, this FRA?' Tresor asked.

'Hard to explain,' I said, trying to deter him from probing too deeply. No sense limiting myself by being too specific. Maybe Tresor wouldn't press me.

'Try,' he pressed me.

'An audit,' I said, nodding my head sagely, 'as I'm sure you must know, is a detailed examination of the company's records and systems. Fraud Risk Analysis — FRA in our shorthand — is more like an overview of the company itself.'

He looked at me blankly.

'Think of fraud like any other crime: the three necessary ingredients are means, motive and opportunity. The existence of these three factors depends very much on the company's ambience.' Good word, Shannon, I thought. I didn't know about *him*, but *I* was pretty impressed. 'Ambience,' I repeated for good measure. 'That's what the FRA concentrates on.'

'Give me an example,' he said.

Swine! Didn't he ever give up?

'Well,' I said, switching tack and borrowing from Metcalfe's Book of Boredom, 'we divide up the risk of a fraud occurring into four source categories: Cultural — management demanding results at any cost, poor commitment to control, no code of business ethics, unquestioning obedience of staff, for example; Structural — complex responsibility chains, several firms of auditors working in isolation, remote locations poorly supervised, etc.; Business — liquidity problems, mismatch between growth and systems development, that sort of thing; and, finally, Personnel — poor-quality staff, low morale, untaken holidays, unusual behaviour, expensive lifestyles and so on.'

Tresor nodded, as if, at last, it was making sense.

So my grandfather dangling me by the ankles to kiss the Blarney Stone had been worth it after all.

'So,' I continued, while on a winning streak, 'the FRA makes recommendations for the future — changing the underlying policies or procedures that give rise to fraud, tightening up where necessary. We often find,' I said with a frown, 'that when management or staff have been in the same job for a while they fall into sloppy habits. The FRA is a good discipline to go through. Re-emphasises the guidelines.'

Tresor wrote the last three words in his diary alongside the heading 'FRA'.

'Mr Whitley had been with you a long time, hadn't he?' I asked.

'He wasn't sloppy at his job, if that's what you're implying.'

'No,' I said, so wounded by the accusation. 'I didn't mean that. God forbid. It's just that his death must leave a big hole in the running of the company. And where there's a hole a fraudster will climb in. I'd advise you to act quickly, Mr Tresor. Yet I would have thought it was hard to replace someone with David Whitley's knowledge and experience.'

'It's hard to replace a friend, Shannon. Knowledge and experience you can buy off the shelf. Friendship takes time to build.'

'I'm sorry,' I said. 'I didn't mean to sound heartless. Comes from being a professional bean-counter. We're supposed to be impartial, uninfluenced by emotions. I should have realised how much his death has affected everybody.'

'Can you imagine what it is like, Shannon?' he said, his voice raised in angry accusation. 'There you are, relaxing after a hard day, cold beer in your hand. Then your mobile phone rings. You curse a little, tell yourself it's probably something minor. Instead, what do you get? Security guard stammering out that your best friend has been murdered. Just like that.'

I nodded sympathetically. Pictured the security guard going through the break-it-gently routine: 'All those with best friends one pace forward — not you, Tresor.' Maybe I'd been too harsh on the man. Shouldn't judge a book by its cover. What the hell did it really matter that he dyed his hair and got his kicks from intimidating people?

'And it doesn't stop there,' he said, waving his finger like a sword at me. There he goes again — just as I was softening, too. 'As managing director, I was the first to hear the news. It fell to me to relay it to the others. Tell Stephanie. Call Toby — knowing he would be thundering up the M1 making for a conference the following morning and might drive off the road when he heard what I had to say. Then I had to work out how I was going to break it to the staff.'

He shook his head sadly.

'I didn't sleep much that night,' he said. 'Haven't done since, for that matter.'

'That's understandable,' I said.

His eyes flared at me.

'If I wanted understanding, Shannon,' he said ungraciously, 'I'd call the Samaritans. What I want from you is simple. Get on with your job. Do it as quickly as possible. And don't make waves. Don't go around looking for oil on which to pour troubled waters. That's the last thing we need right now.'

He rose from the chair, signalling the end of the interview. Turned his broad back towards me. Stared out of the window.

'Understood,' I said, leaving the room.

He gave no sign of having heard me.

As I walked back to Accounts, his words echoed in my ears.

Call the Samaritans.

Call Toby.

But *tell* Stephanie.

He had been with her on the night of the murder.

I hoped Tresor chose his words more carefully when talking to his wife. Otherwise his troubles were only just starting.

* * *

Meg returned, hot and flushed, from her meeting with Tresor. Started to peel off her cardigan, changed her mind, and slumped down in the chair behind her desk.

Sandra and I gathered round anxiously.

'Tea, I think, Sandra,' I said. 'Hot and sweet. Would you? I'll look after Meg. Don't worry.'

I sat down opposite Meg. She was gazing out across the room, eyes unfocused.

'What's the matter?' I said.

'I can't believe it,' she said. Her hair swung lankly as she shook her head. A lock stuck to the perspiration on her forehead. She dragged it aside with her right hand.

'What did Tresor say to you?' I asked, my anger rising and my conscience pricking as I remembered her request not to upset him. 'You haven't been fired, have you?'

'Bless you, no,' she said, smiling. 'Just the opposite. They've made me finance director.'

I sighed with relief.

'I should have sent Sandra for champagne, not tea,' I said. 'Celebrations are in order.'

'That doesn't seem right,' she said. 'Not in the circumstances. The staff would think it callous. I wouldn't want that.'

'Then, let me buy you a drink after work. Toast your future. How about it? What do you say?'

'Just you and me?' she said uncertainly.

'Unless you want to bring along a chaperon.'

'Yes,' she said. Then blushed. 'Not about the chaperon. The drink, I mean. Yes,' she said decisively. 'I need to make a phone call. Change my arrangements. But, yes, I'd be delighted.'

Sandra brought the tea. Registered the improvement in Meg's expression. Asked no questions. Just turned her face towards me. And beamed.

Progress at last.

* * *

We walked the short distance to the pub. Without my long legs I would have found it difficult to keep up. I suppose, if you're going to be pedantic, Tresor-style, without my long legs I would have needed a wheelchair; but you know what I mean. Meg strode along like a paratrooper yomping under the beady eye of his sergeant major.

The pub, the Cox and Eight — very Henley, all pull together, chaps — was no better inside than out. It was like being on the moon — no atmosphere.

The barman, decked out in a Cambridge Blue vest and matching kerchief tied round his neck, acknowledged us with a wave of his hand as we entered. Meg asked me for a small sherry and headed for a quiet table in the conservatory. I walked across the blue carpet to the bar. It had a pair of crossed oars on the front.

The bar top had more pumps than a chorus line. And none of your Stella Tortoise or Australian amber nectar mass-produced stuff. Real ales only. All made by the same age-old process and traditionally stored — every one guaranteed to be as warm, flat and unappetising as its neighbour.

I ordered a dry white wine. A group of men — plain-clothes policemen, taking a breather from the Incident Room, judging by the obviously large size of their boots and the assumed small size of their brains — sniggered in their beer.

'And a sherry,' I said.

The sniggers grew louder. All I needed to do now was add a Babycham — with cherry and umbrella — to the order and they'd be falling off their stools convulsed with hysterical laughter.

'Hang on,' I said to the barman, 'I forgot to ask whether it was sweet or dry.'

'Dry,' he said with authority. 'The lady you're with always drinks dry sherry.'

Don't read too much into it, Shannon.

So she was a regular. What of it? One Tio Pepe doesn't make her a lush. Still, it was interesting. Unexpected. Worth probing later. At this rate my arms would ache from all this tree-shaking. Spenser had never mentioned that drawback.

'One small sherry,' I said, placing the glass on the white-wood table in front of Meg and seating myself on a none-too-stable bentwood chair.

The conservatory was warm. Meg had already stripped off her cardigan, exposing the crucifix to the world for the first time that day. I removed my jacket and tie. Placed them on the chair beside me. Glanced round as I did so.

The enormous picture windows were draped with over-powering ersatz Laura-Ashley-on-speed flowery print curtains; they were symmetrically ruched up and tied back with specially themed light blue corded ropes. Potted plants had been meticulously positioned about the room, the edges of their square tubs lined up exactly with each other, and with each table. Whatever had been the desired effect, it wasn't very homely or relaxing. You felt that if you moved one of the tubs by just the merest fraction of an inch a distraught interior designer would come running out of the wings tearing at her hair and screaming maniacally: 'Put that back where it belongs!'

I shuddered at the thought. Then slipped my mind into gear, running down the checklist of topics to be covered: Meg, Whitley and St Jerome's. Then Any Other Business.

I raised my glass. 'Congratulations. Here's to you. And your promotion.'

'Thank you,' she said. 'You know, I still can't get over the shock. I never imagined the day would come.'

'Why didn't you move on, then?' I asked. 'If you couldn't see any prospect of promotion.'

'To tell you the truth,' she said, taking a minute sip of sherry, 'I never saw myself as finance director material. Or gained the impression that the directors did, either. My annual staff appraisals lauded me as a doer, but then damned me in the same breath for lack of imagination.'

'That can be a bit of a limitation in a finance director,' I said, thinking of the consequences if the boss couldn't keep one step ahead of his staff.

'But,' she said, 'recently I've begun to think that I could do the job. Almost *have* done the job in fact. Poor David was pretty much a passenger lately.'

In my curiosity, I almost revealed myself by asking whether that was due to the ulcer. 'Was there any specific reason for that?' I said instead. 'Or had he simply become bored with the job?'

'I suppose,' she said thoughtfully, 'that the rot set in about eighteen months ago. He was involved in a bad car accident, you see. That seemed to change his whole personality.'

'Head injury, was it?'

'No,' she said. 'David wasn't hurt in the accident. Perhaps it would have been better for him if he had.'

My eyes narrowed in puzzlement.

'His young son was a passenger in the car. Wasn't strapped in properly. The poor child broke his neck. At least he didn't suffer. Killed outright.' She looked across at me with a deep sadness in her eyes. 'David blamed himself. For getting involved in the accident in the first place — he was drowsy, not really concentrating. And again for not checking the boy's seatbelt. David felt that he should have been the one to die. He lost all heart after that.'

'Did he seek any professional help? Trick cyclist? Therapy?'

'Not professional. No,' she said, shaking her head in sorrowful reinforcement. 'I used to come here with David after work. Try to get him to talk. Act as a sort of escape valve. And it was better than him drinking alone.'

She sipped again at the sherry. Another tiny amount that wouldn't have wetted the whistle of a hummingbird. I reckoned she could make it last all night at this rate.

'Then there was Brother James,' she said, dabbing needlessly at her lips with a nervous finger.

'Brother James?'

'He runs a sort of hostel — St Jerome's — a little way up the road from here. Youngsters mainly. Runaways. Dropouts. Provides them with a home. An address so they can claim social security benefit. And tries to talk some sense into them.'

'Did he manage to talk some sense into David?'

'I would think so,' she said. 'David managed to get the drinking under control. He enjoyed working with the kids. Making things with his hands. Teaching them to do the same. He spent most of his time at St Jerome's in the end.'

'What did David's wife think of that?'

'Huh,' Meg said derisively. '*She'd* left him a year back. They reached a settlement — which I expect meant that she took David for every last penny.'

'Not a great fan of hers?'

Her cheeks flushed with embarrassment at her accusation. 'I only know one half of the story, so maybe I shouldn't jump to conclusions. Condemn her out of hand.'

'But . . .' I said.

'But,' she said, 'it seems to me that, after a tragedy like that, a marriage must experience tremendous stress. Couples need to support each other even more if the relationship is to survive. She didn't give him one ounce of support. On the contrary, she drew further away from him. Blamed David for what had happened. And let him know it. Maternal revenge and paternal angst are a powerful combination.'

'The other thing that results from tragedy,' I said, as if giving her the benefit of my experience, 'is that people either lose their faith or find a religion — sometimes it doesn't even matter what sort. That's how some of these weird cults get their converts. David found his religion at St Jerome's, I take it.'

'As long as he died happy,' she said philosophically, 'does it matter what he found?'

CHAPTER ELEVEN

Arthur's van was parked in the street outside my flat. I hoped it was a social call and not another consultation with Norman 'Sigmund' Timpkins. I was willing to bet that he, after just one session with Arthur, was already growing a beard and had spent much of the day in front of the mirror practising the pronunciation of words like *catharsis* in a heavy Germanic accent.

As I unlocked the door I heard a burst of bear-like guttural laughter. Arthur had cheered up. Normal service had been resumed.

Norman, one of his very best wedge-of-Edam grins plastered all over his thin face, had a glass of red wine in his hand. Arthur stood up from the rickety armchair and raised his glass. From behind me came the creak of the bedroom door opening.

'Welcome home,' Arlene said.

If we had been on a beach, it would have been a replay of one of those corny scenes: running in slow motion along the sand, the distance between us narrowing with each joyous step, until finally we threw ourselves into each other's arms. Sentimental nonsense.

I took a pace forward.

She took a pace forward.

Then we threw ourselves into each other's arms.

Arlene hugged me tight. Very tight. I could feel the warmth of her body, the beating of her heart, through the sheer material of the sleeveless dress. And goosebumps of emotion standing proud between the soft downy hairs on her arms.

I transferred my hands to her head. Ran my fingers through her hair. Smelt the familiar fresh aromas of her peach-scented shampoo and flowery perfume. Turned her face to mine. Felt her raise herself on the toes of high-heeled strappy sandals the better to press her lips to mine.

Arthur coughed.

He could have detonated a thermonuclear device for all we cared. We had our own chain reaction taking place — meltdown imminent.

'Er hum,' Norman said loudly.

I heard the soft pad of his carpet-slippered feet crossing the room and the sound of the back door being opened to let out some of the heat that was being generated inside.

Reluctantly — politely — we broke our kiss. Stepped back to stare at each other.

She looked even better than I remembered — dared to remember, given the external pressures on the future of our relationship. The dress was cream, some smooth and sensual material — satin, silk, shantung, I could never tell the difference and, anyway, the electrifying effects on me were all the same; it was high-waisted, shaped to her storm-in-a-C-cup body at the top, then flowing out over her full hips to finish a few inches above the delicate shoes. Her face and arms were tanned, her auburn hair streaked with the New England sun. Hazel eyes sparkled at me.

Arlene ran a hand self-consciously over the front of her dress, swivelled nervously on the spike of a high-heel.

'I couldn't wait any longer, Nick,' she said.

'Don't ever apologise for being early,' I said. 'It's good to see you. Very good. You look great.'

‘Let the lady sit down,’ Norman interrupted. ‘She’s had a long day.’

He placed a glass of red wine for me, and what looked like a long cool spritzer for Arlene, on the coffee table by the sofa. Waved his arm imperiously.

‘Everything’s arranged,’ he said, as we sat down. Arlene drew close, placed a hand on my leg and smiled up at me. ‘Arthur and I will stay for a quick drink. Then we’ll leave you in peace to enjoy’ — Norman grinned — ‘your meal. There’s some oak-smoked salmon and a freshly cooked lobster in the fridge. Salad, mayonnaise, brown bread. Even wedges of lemon. And, of course, a bottle of the finest Chablis.’

‘You haven’t actually been shopping, have you, Norman?’ I asked, stunned by the idea. Norman’s knowledge of supermarkets was so limited he thought Safeway was a well-lit road with heavy police presence.

‘You can be very hurtful at times, Nick,’ he said.

Arthur gave a scornful grunt.

‘Oh, well,’ Norman said with a sigh, ‘I suppose I can’t complain. I’ve always told you to trust your instincts, Nick. That’s because they are generally right. While Arthur was collecting Arlene from the airport, I picked everything up from Toddy’s.’

Toddy and Norman co-owned a restaurant. A very good and very successful restaurant. Norman supplied the business acumen to make lots of money and pay virtually no tax; Toddy excelled in the kitchen — just as he had done in HM Prison Chelmsford. Only now he had the use of the very best ingredients — and never committed the cardinal sin of spoiling through over-elaboration.

Toddy was a talented man. Not only were his culinary skills second to none, but he was also one of the best forgers of the twentieth century. Ex-forger, I should say. Although his record on giving up forgery was a little like mine and smoking — he lapsed a little too frequently for his own good.

I sipped the wine. Norman had stinted on nothing tonight, it seemed. It was one of his favourite Pomerols. Had been breathing for a good many hours by the exquisite taste of it. Ultra-smooth, rich, and concentrated with the flavours of fruit and vanilla.

I squeezed Arlene's hand.

Life was good.

I took out a pack of cigarettes from my jacket pocket and offered one to Arlene.

'No, thanks,' she said. 'I'm trying to give up.'

'You should, too,' Norman said disapprovingly.

'A cigarette saved my life once,' I reminded him defensively. But, the potential enjoyment diminished, I put the pack and lighter down on to the table.

'Tell us your news,' Norman said to Arlene. 'How's the job? Windsor Club thriving?'

The Windsor Club was a purpose-built resort complex on Cape Cod — golf courses, tennis courts by the dozen, riding stables, gymnasium, long sandy beaches, water sports, the works. Norman had picked it up for a song ('You Got to Pick a Pocket or Two', I think it was) from the American equivalent of the Official Receiver. It was a shady deal, of course; but, then, again, all Norman's deals make an Icelandic six-month night look like noon in Africa.

'Just great,' she enthused. 'Plenty of interest in the property from the retirement market. And people are buying second homes again. The local economy's good and strong.'

Arthur took a glug of wine — his philosophy was 'the better the wine, the bigger the swig' — and went off in a rapturous trance.

'Not much unemployment, then?' Norman asked. 'I bet even Nick could find a job over there.'

'Well,' Arlene said, 'it just so happens that one of the local firms is crying out for qualified accountants.'

'You'll be qualified in a few weeks, won't you, Nick?' Norman asked.

'Well,' I said, smelling the rat of a set-up, 'isn't that a coincidence?'

'Offer of a job might help your visa application,' he said, nodding wisely.

Arthur, sitting stiff and silent, examined the colour of his wine.

'The American accounting regulations,' I reminded him, 'are very different from those in this country. I'm not sure that an English qualification would carry much weight over there.'

'Wouldn't take more than a couple of months to catch up,' Arlene said encouragingly. 'Not for someone with your talent. And being English would be a big advantage. Billy says it would give the firm a touch of class.'

'Billy?' I asked.

'Runs the biggest accountancy practice on the Cape.'

'Business associate, is he?'

Arlene nodded. 'Old friend of Cy's, too,' she said casually.

Cy was Arlene's late husband. And Mary Jo's demigod of a late father.

'And Billy came up with this job offer spontaneously, did he?'

'Yes,' said Arlene, almost without hesitation.

'And how's Mary Jo?' Norman asked quickly.

Even he couldn't keep the tension out of his voice.

Arthur consulted his watch, then distanced himself from the pre-arranged conversation by staring out of the back door to examine the piece of scrub land the landlord mendaciously called a garden.

'Mary Jo's really looking forward to seeing Nick again,' Arlene said unconvincingly.

'Just like the folks of Hamelin were really looking forward to seeing the rats come back to town,' I said.

'Don't be hard on her,' she said. 'Given time, she'll see you for what you are. A good man. Who makes me very happy.'

Arlene turned her eyes towards me. There was a hint of moisture among the hazel.

'I want her to get to know you better,' she said, reaching down out of habit to the pack of cigarettes. At the very last moment she pulled her hand away. 'That's why I've asked her to join me over here on Sunday. Stay for a couple of weeks.'

'Good idea,' Norman interjected at a rate of knots before the silence could build to oppressive levels. 'Home territory and all that. I don't mind moving out for the duration. In a good cause.'

'That's very kind, Norman,' Arlene said, 'but I've booked her a room at the Savoy. More central for the sights, I thought.'

Not to mention that a two-bedroom flat in Archway was not Mary Jo's style. That was stretching the concept of home territory a little too far.

'So it's all arranged, then,' I said huffily.

Arthur looked across at me and shrugged his shoulders, deliberately dissociating himself from the charade that had taken place.

Arlene picked up my glass and went through to the kitchen to pour a refill.

'Now, make a bloody effort, will you?' Norman said, when she was out of earshot. 'Swallow your pride. Arlene's gone to a lot of trouble lining you up a job. And orchestrating a situation that gives you the best chance of making your peace with Mary Jo. Don't spoil it.'

'What happens,' I said, 'if Mary Jo doesn't change her tune? And what if I don't get the immigration visa?'

'For a bloody optimist,' Norman said angrily, 'you sure know how to pour cold water on someone's dreams.'

'I'm only trying to be practical,' I said in my own defence.

'Look,' Norman said, wagging a paternal finger at me, 'the important thing is to do your best. Be nice to Mary Jo. If she still insists on regarding you as the devil incarnate, then that's her hard luck. At least you will have the satisfaction of knowing you tried. And Arlene will feel free to do what is necessary.' He looked warily towards the kitchen to see that the coast was still clear. 'And, as far as the visa goes, we can sort that out for you. Toddy can knock up a fake passport, easy as pie. Whole new identity. All we need to do is go through the death certificates to find someone of your age and—'

'Yes, I know,' I said, cutting off his germ of an idea before it could take root. 'I *have* read *The Day of the Jackal*. Do you think either Arlene or I would be happy living under a cloud? Forever looking over our shoulder waiting for some English tourist who has read the reports of my trial to show up and point the finger? Thanks for the offer, Norman. But, as they say in the movies, no thanks.'

'Bear it in mind,' he said persistently.

'Bear what in mind?' Arlene said re-entering the room. Her eyes were red.

I felt a heel.

'Nothing,' I said. 'Nothing that is of any importance. Come here.'

I took her hand, interlocking my fingers with hers.

'Norman and Arthur are just going,' I said.

Arthur swigged down the last of his wine and rose overhastily.

'Will you do me a favour?' I said to him, knowing that in the circumstances he could hardly refuse.

'Of course,' he said with a wry smile. 'Don't hurry back. Is that it?'

'That, and something else,' I said. 'I'd like you to have a drink in a pub tomorrow.'

'You call that a favour? I'll join you for a jar any day.'

'Unfortunately, I can't be there,' I said. 'I have something else to do.'

He looked at me suspiciously.

'The pub is in Docklands,' I said.

'I see,' he said dubiously.

It was Arlene's turn to give me the suspicious look.

'I'll explain later,' I said to her. 'The pub is called the Cox and Eight.'

'Doesn't sound very promising,' Arthur grunted.

'There's a police incident centre in the car park. And thirsty policemen drinking inside.'

'Coppers?' Arthur said, aghast at the thought.

'Just enjoy the odd pint, Arthur,' I said, using the word *odd* as a private joke about the real ale, 'and keep your ears pinned back. See what you can pick up. Anything would be useful.'

'I'll come,' Arlene volunteered. 'Keep you company. It's the least I can do. And I've always wanted to see your Docklands.' She put the accent on the last syllable.

'Well, all right, then,' Arthur said grudgingly to me. 'I'll call about eleven thirty, Arlene.'

'Let's go,' Norman said, leading the way to the door. 'And' — he shot me a warning glance — 'remember what I said, Nick.'

Arlene looked at me enquiringly, her head tilted to one side.

'Don't bloody spoil anything,' Norman mouthed silently behind her back.

* * *

'Sorry,' Arlene said.

We were in the kitchen taking plates of Toddy's food from the fridge before transferring them to the dining table.

'I should be the one apologising,' I said. 'Two months since we've seen each other and I act like a bear in need of an aspirin. I appreciate what you're doing for me. For us.'

'But I shouldn't have sprung it all on you like that. Or involved Norman and poor Arthur. I should have had the guts to tell you everything myself. It just seemed so important.'

Her voice trailed away.

I took the platter of smoked salmon from out of her hands and placed it on the worktop. Scooped her into my arms. Held her body close to mine. Felt a tension within.

'Are you hungry?' I asked.

'Not much,' she said, getting interested. 'Not yet.'

'I am,' I said.

'Oh,' she said, disappointed.

'For you,' I added.

'You limeys are so damn corny,' she said with sparkling eyes. 'But I love you.'

'And you colonials are so damn pushy,' I said, 'but I love you, too. And need you.'

She let her head fall on to my shoulder and clung on to me desperately.

'You know,' I whispered in her ear, 'in trendy restaurants nowadays, before your meal you have a little appetiser. It's called an *amuse bouche*.'

'What are we waiting for, then?' she said, kissing my neck. 'Let's go and amuse our bouches.'

* * *

'I've forgotten something,' I said.

'It's a bit late now,' Arlene said.

Her voice was muffled. She was lying with her head on my chest, long hair tickling my stomach, her hand tracing lines along my ribs.

'Just give me a minute,' I said, easing my body from under her.

Naked, I padded out of the bedroom and across to my briefcase. Retrieved the paper bag containing the torc and ring. Padded back, cursing myself for not having bought some decent wrapping paper.

'I have a present for you,' I said, sliding back into bed.

She sat up and pulled the sheet around her. 'What is it?' she said excitedly.

I handed her the bag, kissed her gently on the lips and said: 'Welcome back. To England. And to me.'

She took the torc from the bag, and ran her fingers over the fine etching on the smooth metal.

'It's beautiful,' she said, looking from it to me and back again.

'The cornucopia is a sort of charm. Symbol of the goddess Fortuna apparently. She's supposed to bring prosperity. And,' I said with a typical limey blush, 'fertility.'

She laughed.

'I have a present for you, too,' she said.

'Shall I get it?' I said excitedly. 'Save you climbing out of this cosy warm bed. Where is it?'

She took my hand. And placed it on her stomach.

'Here,' she said.

Christ, I'd been stunned before in my life — once by a heavy hand bringing a hard object down like a ton of bricks on to the back of my skull — but this was a whole new dimension.

My mind went into overload. I was back on that beach again, not running along the sand this time but in the water — deep water? — being pounded by a series of emotional breakers.

Stupidity was the easiest to identify and admit. Arlene arriving early, unable to contain herself or her news any longer. Giving up smoking. The weak spritzer. Job lined up. Mary Jo coming over for peace talks. All the clues were there, as Loyd Grossman was prone to say. But it was wood and trees. Too damned close to make the obvious logical deductions. Bloody fine detective you are, Shannon.

Then there was pride. God knows why. Not the most difficult — or least pleasurable — thing in the world, launching a few tadpole torpedoes. Yet the result was the ultimate achievement. The creation of life. Maybe all men feel that way; I don't know. I didn't know anything at this moment. It's just that, for me — well, I suppose the feeling went deeper, had extra significance. Hope for a girl, Shannon. Call her Susie after your sister. The equation balanced at last.

'What are you thinking?' Arlene asked anxiously.

'That your present to me is more beautifully wrapped than mine to you,' I said. 'How long before . . . ?'

'Before the wrapping comes off?' she said with a smile. 'A little over six months. Our plans for Christmas may have to be a little flexible this year.'

'So you're nearly three months pregnant?' I asked with a worried frown. I wished I'd studied harder in biology lessons. 'Should we have . . . you know?'

'You're a bit late again, Nick,' she said, sniggering. 'Three months ago was the time for thought.'

'No, I meant just now,' I said sheepishly.

'Sure, it's fine,' she said, a reassuring smile on her face. 'If I had a history of miscarriage, then it would be different. But I don't. And with every week the risks to the baby get less. I'll soon be in the second trimester.'

'Sounds like some phrase from an American high school. "Gee, Mom, I'm gonna be in the second trimester."'

Arlene didn't laugh.

'Nick,' she said, her voice taut and tremulous, 'you still haven't told me how you feel. About the baby. And me, too, I guess.'

'You've only had half my present,' I said. 'Look again in the bag.'

She peered inside. Drew out the ring. And waited for me to speak.

'I know it's not a diamond,' I said, shrugging my shoulders, 'but it's the thought that counts. Arlene . . . will you marry me?'

'No,' she said.

'What?' I said, shocked.

'Not unless you do it properly,' she said with a smile. 'Bended knees and all that jazz.'

What could I do?

All that jazz.

I got out of bed, bent down on one knee, took her hand between mine.

'Arlene,' I said with due solemnity, 'will you marry me?'

'Yes,' she said, her lips twitching. 'I will marry you. Thanks, darling Nick. For the proposal. And,' she added, giving a deep and throaty laugh, 'for a moment I will never forget. You can put your clothes on now.'

* * *

Arlene laid the table. On her insistence — 'Enjoy your last days of freedom, buddy boy' — I took a dining chair outside into the garden and sat with a glass of Chablis and a much-needed cigarette. The sun was no more than the narrowest of arcs visibly sinking in a crimson sky; Mercury was already shining brightly, other stars hard on its heels in the race to twinkle in the fading light.

I inhaled, very long and very slow, on the cigarette. Blew the smoke out in an elongated stream that vanished before my eyes in the warm breeze.

Well, Shannon, I thought. If you're going to change your life, there's no point just fiddling around at the edges. All or nothing is the only way. Marriage, baby, new job, new home, new country.

All you need is that damned visa.

CHAPTER TWELVE

As I left the flat the following morning for Docklands, Arlene was debating with herself over what was the most appropriate outfit to wear for eavesdropping on policemen; Norman was loudly humming 'Making Whoopee' for the umpteenth time. We agreed to meet at Toddy's at eight o'clock for a celebration meal and to compare notes.

Arriving at Assurance House, I parked the Lancia in the same spot at the deserted outer reaches of the car park. I could have parked a lot closer to the building, but wherever possible I played safe and selected parking bays clear of the dangers posed by other drivers. The old Monte Carlo was a breeding ground for rust: if the door of another car was carelessly flung open, knocking against mine, a snowstorm of red oxidised flakes of metal fluttered to the ground. Like all good things, the car would not last for ever, but the least I could do was postpone as long as possible the journey to that great multi-storey car park in the sky.

I climbed out of the bucket seat and into the turbulence. Gently patted the bonnet of my trusty but totally impractical two-seater, mid-engined sports car. I loved the car. Had sweated blood — lost blood, more accurately — to acquire her. It would be a sad day when we parted company. I wondered what I would be driving in six months' time. A Nissan Dorma, the footballers' favourite people-carrier? A 'station wagon', perhaps? If Arlene insisted on some such yawn-inducing vehicle, then I'd have to show her who was boss. Put my foot down. Draw the line at one of those miniaturised fir trees that emit a smell like a Norwegian pimp's aftershave. Even the odour of rancid nappies had to be better than that.

In Reception, the security guard was busy peering at his monitors. Pat was reading a half-hidden copy of one of the tabloids — I could swear her lips were moving. She broke off to go through the 'Good morning' routine — today's soup minestrone? — and exchange my personal identity card. With the self-importance of someone with 'enhanced security privileges', I swiped my way through to Accounts.

Meg was already at her desk, surrounded by a pile of papers and a pungent cloud of lavender toilet water. She was swaddled against the psychosomatic chill of the ice-blue environment in the sort of tweed jacket that should have had brown leather patches on the elbows and a shotgun tucked under an armpit. She greeted me with a wide smile.

So did Sandra. Who volunteered to get me a coffee. I took it as an olive branch rather than the actions of a Lucrezia Borgia impersonator.

First on my list of priorities for the day was the unreconciled Sales Ledger. Apart from a few minor queries, this was the only task holding up the completion of the audit. Once that was out of the way, I could turn my attention to the more interesting prospect of snooping in earnest. I pulled the thick printout from the desk drawer and started running my eyes over it.

I checked for obvious errors — the same amount input twice, an end-of-month adjustment debited instead of credited, that sort of thing. There was none. Whichever way I looked at it, the total on the Sales Ledger, as Metcalfe had told us in his own in-im-it-a-ble way, disagreed with the sum of receipts by fifty-four pounds. My money was still on a transposition error being the culprit.

It was the kind of simple mistake that should have been spotted long before the audit, but Whitley's mind had presumably been on other matters and — if Meg was to be believed — his heart was elsewhere. There was nothing to do but check each individual sales entry with what should be the corresponding item in cash received until the difference was discovered.

A needle in a haystack?

No, not that bad.

A needle somewhere in one of twelve smaller haystacks.

With monthly accounts, if a mistake is made it will carry over to the next month, and the one after that, and so on until finally detected. By checking backwards on the totals on the trial balance for each month it was possible to determine when the original error had been made. Only then was it necessary to enter the mindless zone of comparing entries in the two separate listings of sales and cash received.

It took less than thirty minutes to pinpoint the offending item. It was buried within the accounts for three months back. That meant Whitley had missed it three times in a row. Three strikes and you're out would have been the American verdict on his sloppiness.

I explained the problem to Meg.

'So I need to go right back to the original sales record,' I said. 'If the amount shown there ties in with the cash received, then that proves the error to be a transposition, and that's the end of the matter. Where do you keep the original documents?'

'In Central Storage,' she answered. 'That's located in the same cell as Computing.'

'Two birds with one stone, then,' I said. 'I was planning to go there to tick off the equipment against the fixed-asset register.'

'You'll need Stephanie if you want to enter the storage area,' she said.

'Diplomatic to ask her permission?' I asked.

'Not just that,' Meg said. 'Central Storage is locked. Stephanie has the combination.'

Well, what a shame. Looks like I would be forced to recommence my study of the movements of Stephanie's perfectly lipsticked mouth.

* * *

The half of the cell occupied by Computing resembled the bridge of the Starship Enterprise during an attack by the Romulans. The walls were lined with red-alert hessian; a handful of operators sat on swivel chairs, fingers blurring over the keyboards of terminals; everywhere, lights flashed with an insistent urgency on the control panels of serried ranks of impressive-looking hardware. Stephanie was supposed to meet me here. She was late. A woman's prerogative, I suppose. Or an overt demonstration of our relative status in the pecking order.

The remainder of the cell was hidden from view by a brick wall. In its exact centre was set a steel door with keypad combination lock and one of those heavy rotating handles you usually only see on the airlocks of submarines. The whole construction was purposefully designed to be fireproof — bombproof even, for all I knew, considering that the whole Docklands area was a prime terrorist target — to protect the records stored within.

A thin man in a suit and tie came over to me and introduced himself as Brackley, head of the department. 'You must be Shannon,' he said.

My fame had preceded me.

'Come to make sure we haven't sold off any of the equipment, I hear,' he added belligerently.

I must get a new publicity agent.

'Just a routine check,' I said. 'If you'd line everybody up with their hands against the wall, I'll do a quick spot check. We can leave the strip-search for silicone chips until later.'

His jaw dropped. 'But I thought . . .' he stammered.

'Just a joke,' I said with an apologetic smile. 'If you'd be kind enough to call out the serial numbers on each piece of equipment, I'll tick them off the list. Let's start with that big machine over there.'

'That's a tape drive,' he said, shaking his head condescendingly.

I knew very well what it was. The hardware was similar to that I had played around with in the computer complex at university — more modern, granted, but bulk-standard DEC (Digital Equipment Corporation) machinery. Still, I played dumb so that he could demonstrate his knowledge and I could conceal mine. You never know when being underestimated will come in useful.

Everything was there, of course. I hadn't expected otherwise. The point of the exercise was to provide cover for a quick snoop, not to find a tape drive slipped into an operator's back pocket. As we went from machine to machine, and terminal to terminal, I spent as much time as possible keeping him talking while taking mental notes on all I saw.

'That looks complicated,' I said, pointing to the display on one of the screens.

'Actuarial tables,' Brackley explained. 'Plimpson is our actuary. He can tell you the chance of any individual event occurring, and the associated average claim cost to the company. Death, car accident or theft, household fire, burglary — you name it, and Plimpson knows it by heart.'

But, I thought from a quick character summary of Plimpson, not who is the current England cricket captain, or which political party was in power — still, that's forgivable given that it didn't seem to make much difference to performance in either case.

Actuaries are statisticians in anoraks. They gravitate into the profession because accountancy is too scarifyingly exciting. They spend their lives constructing, and then constantly revising, tables of probabilities so that, like a bookmaker or a casino operator, the odds are always in the company's favour.

If you think your car insurance is too high, or can't get medical insurance, now you know who to blame.

Plimpson, the butter-fingered hot-milk juggler from the staff restaurant, grinned up at me inanely. He was mid-twenties going on twelve. Pimpled face, thick boyish lips and school-swot glasses. He was wearing a hand-knitted tank top in rusty brown that had either shrunk in the wash or had been hand-knitted for someone with a chest two sizes smaller — if that was possible. Grey trousers, a chequered shirt in blue and red, and scuffed brown suede Hush Puppies completed today's ensemble. I had the distinct feeling that if I stayed by his side any longer he would launch into a thousand 'interesting' facts, all prefaced by the words 'Did you know . . . ?'

'What about these modem thingies?' I said to Brackley, pointing to a row of black boxes on the floor. 'Why do you need those?'

Brackley bristled, and went into automatic rebuttal mode. 'Vitally important,' he said firmly, his voice adopting the clipped manner of a general facing defence cuts. 'They link our computer with those at City and County. Electronic mail, data transfers, all taking place at the speed of light between us and the bank's head office and branches. City and County provide about a third of our new business, you know. Sales leads are flashed to us, and we respond the same day, while the prospect is still hot and hasn't had an opportunity to get alternative quotes. Modems beat snail-mail every time.'

I raised an eyebrow, the non-verbal communication equivalent of flinging down a gauntlet in challenge.

'I'll tell you something,' he said. 'I used to be sales manager here before I was given the responsibility of forming and running the computer department. You can't *imagine* the number of bits of paper that were circulating around the offices. And the number that got mislaid somewhere on their travels. That meant lost sales. Those days have passed.'

'But isn't it a security risk?' I asked. 'For City and County, that is. Staff here being able to access their computer?'

Brackley scratched his head, pondering how best to explain the intricacies of computer security. 'Look,' he said, 'being able to send a memo or read one's own electronic mail is as far as we can get into the bank's system. We can't pry into a customer's account details or authorise transfers, if that's what's worrying you.'

'But,' I said, switching tack, 'what about internally? What's to stop someone reading Mr Tresor's mail? That could be dangerous surely. Or, at the very least, embarrassing.'

'Individual passwords are closely guarded secrets to each user. And they're changed weekly. The system's foolproof.'

I shrugged, and looked at him with as much scepticism as I could muster.

'I'll show you,' he said wearily.

He took me over to his terminal. Motioned me to sit down. Clicked the mouse on a telephone number from the autodialler's list. Waited for the screen to flash its message.

WELCOME TO CITY & COUNTY BANK.

LOGIN:

'Type my name,' Brackley said.

I did as he requested. Hit ENTER.

ENTER YOUR PASSWORD:

Brackley handed me a printout.

'There you go,' he said. 'That's the file of all current passwords.'

Against the name of each authorised user was a string of gobbledegook letters, numbers and symbols. I typed in the entry against Brackley's name.

SORRY TRY AGAIN.

I did. Three more times.

INVALID PASSWORD. DISCONNECTING AFTER 4 TRIES.

The screen went blank.

'Why doesn't it work?' I asked, as he expected of me.

'The passwords are encrypted. The first time a user logs on he chooses a password. Let's say it is FUTURE. The computer scrambles the letters into an encrypted string

— "psndhy5k@gh" for instance — that is unique to the original word selected. It is the encrypted passwords that are stored and used for verification at each subsequent log-in. Even if someone manages to get hold of this file, it's of no earthly use. As you have just proved. The program used is called a "trapdoor" — only works one way. You can't derive a user's password from the encrypted version. The code is unbreakable.'

'You've proved your point,' I said. And shown me that the basic system had not changed one iota since my university days.

Behind me I heard the click of the turnstile. Brackley's face softened, and his pupils went starry. I didn't need eyes in the back of my head to know that Stephanie had arrived.

'Good morning,' I said, turning round.

She was dressed less blatantly today. Still had on a pair of high heels, but the pure white skirt was a couple of inches lower down her thighs, the tight black Lycra body mostly hidden by the jacket of the suit.

'Good morning, Shannon,' she said, somehow managing to restrain her long lashes from fluttering at me. Her pale-pink lips danced an oral lambada, though. 'Shall we get on with it?'

A million wisecracks scudded through my brain. I resisted them all. Simply nodded at her.

She sashayed over to the safe. Blocked my view with her back as she tapped out the combination on the number-pad. Spun the handle. Swung open the hydraulically assisted door with an effortless movement of her right hand. A light flicked on automatically, illuminating the cavern within.

I stared inside. Into my worst nightmare. It was that damned cell in Brixton all over again. But ten times worse — not even a window. And a bloody steel door that could swish shut in an instant.

A steel door.

Like the one that had been used to chop off two fingers on my left hand.

I could feel a tidal wave of panic rising from deep within me. Sweeping through my brain, it detonated an explosion of uncontrollable instinctive fear-response reactions. My stomach churned hollowly, then performed a series of somersaults. Sweat began to break out all over my body. There was an ache in my groin as my testicles shrivelled and tried to beat a hasty retreat inside my body.

From some point in the dim distance Stephanie's voice was wittering away — something about files being in number sequence starting to the left of the door and working anti-clockwise from there.

Her arm was a blur as it waved me inside.

'It would be a lot quicker if you found the files,' I said shakily.

'And get this white suit covered in dust,' she said. 'You must be joking.'

Run, Shannon, run, screamed the coward in me.

If you run, said the voice of sanity, will you ever stop? Give in now and the cancer of fear takes hold. Spreads throughout your mind. Unstoppable. Irreversible. Go inside, Shannon. Prove to yourself that the progress you've made was part of a long-term cure, not simply a short-term remission.

Run, Shannon, run.

I ran.

Straight past Stephanie, brushing against her body with my only thought being to get inside and back out again in a new world-record time.

The place was spinning as I looked around frantically. Focusing as best I could on the wall-mounted metal racking, I grabbed an armful of files which hopefully included the one I wanted. Turned unsteadily on my heels. And almost threw myself out of the door.

I stumbled to a free chair. Dropped the files on the desk. Sat there breathing deeply.

'You're claustrophobic,' Stephanie said, her voice a mixture of surprise and — I suspected, but wasn't in a fit state to judge — contempt.

Well bloody spotted, I thought angrily. Give the lady the I-Spy Phobia-Recognition badge. And stitch it on her forehead.

The anger helped. It gave me something else to concentrate on. Kicked my mind back into gear. OK, I wasn't exactly functioning on all cylinders but at least I could splutter forward.

'Just a teensy bit,' I said, forcing a smile. 'Bad experience before birth. Womb with no view.'

Stephanie looked at me without expression. Better than a sneer, I suppose.

'The files can't leave this area,' she said. 'Examine them here and let me know when you're finished. I've things to discuss with Brackley and Plimpson.'

She turned her back on me and walked — even more haughtily, even more pneumatically, it seemed — across to Brackley.

I shrugged to myself. What the hell! You did it, Shannon. Not the most convincing performance. But you did it.

There is, of course, my brain reminded me, the little matter of putting the files back.

* * *

They could have been replaced in their stacks immediately. But I was loath to send up a flare signalling that, in my panic, I had taken the wrong bloody ones.

I sat there for a while cursing myself and simultaneously flicking through the files in an effort to cover my gaffe.

Each record contained a complete dossier on an individual policy. All correspondence. Claims forms. Notices of Interest in houses where a mortgage was linked to an endowment — hence the combination lock and fireproof safe. Death certificates. Copy grants of probate impressed with the authenticating seal of the Probate Registry, or signed indemnities certifying that the estate of the deceased was less than twenty thousand pounds — either of these alternative documents necessary before the money could be released. And proposal forms.

The proposal forms were a real mess. To give some fastidious person his due, I did come across one that was still in virgin condition, creaseless and clean, but the rest indicated that a member of the population could not put pen to paper without a cup of coffee or a jam doughnut in the other hand. A variety of stains — some of unimaginable origin — decorated the forms, making it even more difficult to decipher the handwriting.

But all that is *en passant*. A little diversion undertaken solely to eat up the time before re-entering Dante's personally customised inferno. I got up from the chair and headed towards the desk where Stephanie was engaging Brackley and Plimpson in heated debate. Stood politely back and hovered till one of them acknowledged my existence.

Stephanie saw Brackley looking over her shoulder. Using the sharp tips of her heels, she swivelled her chair slowly round to face me. The skirt rode up with the movement, giving everyone a flash of milky thigh. Brackley leered. Plimpson blushed.

'Give Shannon a hand,' she ordered Plimpson. 'I think he needs some files replaced. I'll be over to close up in a moment.'

'Thanks,' I said to her back, as she swung round.

Plimpson walked with me to the desk where the files lay in a pile.

'While you're in there,' I said, 'there's one last file I need to check.'

I gave him a slip of paper with the serial number of the record I should have taken in the first place. He trudged bravely into the safe — go on, Shannon, make sarcastic comments about him now, if you dare — carrying the heavy bundle, and reappeared a minute later. I took the file from him. Flicked directly to the proposal form. Inspected the amount of premium paid. Verified that the error was indeed a transposition. And handed it back.

Simple as that. It could have saved a whole lot of time, not to mention angst, if Stephanie had volunteered Plimpson's services at the outset.

I thanked him. Shook his hand heartily. Gave him a warm smile.

He shuffled his feet in embarrassment. Then managed a toothy grin.

From the effort it took, it didn't look like something he did very often.

Friend for life, from now on.

* * *

I'd had enough for one morning. I needed fresh air, a cigarette and a slow walk to St Jerome's. Not necessarily in that order.

I took an exploratory route via Sales and Marketing (dark blue colour scheme), passed through the Senior Staff and conference cell (as green and tasteless as an imported Golden Delicious), and stopped at Reception. Depositing my notes for safe-keeping with Pat, I borrowed her phone and rang Meg to let her know I was taking an early lunch. While doing so, I idly watched the screens in front of the guard as they panned slowly across the car park.

Another wave of panic hit me.

I dropped the receiver back in its cradle and ran round the desk to take a closer look. There was no doubt about it. My heart thumped.

'Where's my car?' I shouted. 'Someone's stolen my car.'

The guard looked at me impassively.

'Where did you leave it?' he asked patiently.

'In the car park, of course,' I said with mounting frustration. 'It's not there any more.'

'Bet you a tenner it is,' he said.

'What do you mean?' I snapped.

'It's there,' he said casually, 'but it's simply not showing up on the cameras. No need to panic. There's a blind spot, that's all. I ask you, how do they expect us to do our job properly? How can you spot the car thieves and undesirables when you can't see the whole picture? Tell me that. And all because the motor on one of the cameras is jamming. Been waiting for a replacement part for three weeks. Do you call that service?'

I must have still looked puzzled.

'Look at this,' he said helpfully.

He showed me a diagram of the building and the surrounding area. There were two hand-drawn arcs radiating out from black circles which indicated the position of the front-facing cameras mounted to either side of the doors to Reception. The left arc was smaller than that emanating from the right.

Net result?

The arcs didn't cross.

There was a narrow corridor that was not subject to scanning by either camera.

'As a matter of interest,' I asked, trying to keep the excitement from my voice, 'where was Mr Whitley's body found?'

'Judging by the evidence of the videos,' the guard said, 'or lack of it, pretty close to where your car must be.'

CHAPTER TWELVE (B)

Bad luck?

Unhelpful coincidence?

Or just the way the world weaves its wearisome web?

First, a right-handed murderer. And now a blind spot. I couldn't wait to see Collins's reaction when I gave him the news. On second thoughts he probably wouldn't be too displeased. At least it meant that the official investigation didn't have the distinct advantage of possessing Tarantinoesque footage of the murder being committed.

How many people inside the company, I wondered, knew about the blind spot? And outside the company, for that matter. Staff talk. Are prone to grumble. Especially where security is lacking in an area marked by a bull's-eye on the terrorists' map. Over the course of the past three weeks, the information could have been spread far and wide. Someone might have heard the sound of opportunity knocking.

I decided to postpone my trip to St Jerome's for a little while. Check on something in Accounts first.

'Purchase orders,' I said to Meg. 'I'd like to test the system.'

'Why?' she asked. 'Something wrong?'

'All part of this Fraud Risk Analysis I'm conducting. No stone left unturned, you know?'

'What exactly do you want to do?'

'I understand one of the security cameras is on the blink.'

'Is it?' she said.

'A replacement motor has been ordered. I thought I might check that the procedures have been followed correctly. Make sure that the purchase order has been signed.'

Almost all companies operate some sort of purchase order system. Whenever a member of staff requests goods or services, the supplier is sent a piece of paper — part of a duplicate or triplicate set — bearing the signature of a director confirming the order to be official. Without a signed purchase order the supplier does not get paid. This has two benefits. First, it protects the company from staff secretly ordering goods that are then spirited away. Second — and here my cynic's hat sits squarely on my head — it allows the company to delay payment. Deal with a supplier regularly and the company can make what appear to be urgent but reasonable demands: the supplier feels constrained, for the sake of the relationship, to supply on the oral instruction alone. Then the company is purposefully lax in sending out the appropriate purchase order. Result: helpful supplier waits three months or more for his money. And the company gains extended, and unintended, credit.

'When was this motor ordered?' Meg asked.

'About three weeks ago, I'm told.'

She left her desk and walked, long skirt swirling around her ankles like a pack of beagles, to a row of loose-leaf binders lined up on top of a filing cabinet. Selected one, and brought it over to me.

She opened the binder and started working her way through the pink copies of the purchase orders.

'Here you are,' she said with satisfaction. 'All shipshape and Bristol fashion. Duly signed. Satisfied?'

'Yes,' I said.

Satisfied, but not helped much.

The signature was Whitley's.

* * *

I drove to St Jerome's. Well, I was going to have to repark the car in a spot where the guard could watch over it and ensure its safety, so I thought I might as well use it in the meantime.

Rhiannon, disappointingly, was not outside today. I crossed the jetty and knocked on the heavy wooden door. My planned cover was the purchase of another gift. Something suitable for dear sweet Mary Jo — scold's bridle perhaps?

There was no answer. I knocked again, wishing for Tippett (special skill: burglary) to appear like magic and effect an illicit entry.

The wish didn't come true. But it didn't need to. The door wasn't locked. Just like Rhiannon had said: Brother James's door is always open.

'Hello,' I called, just in case someone was on the top floor and hadn't heard my knocking. 'Anybody there?'

My voice echoed back to me. I strained my ears but heard no sound, no evidence of any other presence in the building. I sniffed at the air, trying to get a handle on the strange smell that was tickling my nostrils. Woven into the general air of age, damp and mustiness was some kind of exotic sweet perfume.

No, not perfume. Too aromatic for that. Too spicy.

Incense. That's what it was.

Curiouser and curiouser, as Alice once said.

In front of me was a long dark corridor. There were doorways to my left and right, and a flight of steep wooden stairs disappearing in the gloom to the floors above.

I tried the door on the right.

It led into a large oblong room. Black as night.

I flicked the light switch. Nothing happened.

Clicking my lighter, I examined the room by its flickering flame. In one corner was a long refectory table, its top scrubbed to whiteness; six chairs were lined up on each long side, and one positioned at the head. Thirteen in all — someone here isn't superstitious.

The floor was bare boards, smoothed down and painted dark green. Not a traditionally lucky colour, but the overall effect was not unpleasant, somehow in sympathy with the waterfront setting. Around the room was scattered a collection of floor cushions, each about three feet square and decorated with hand-sewn designs of eastern influence — geometric patterns in deep maroon and brown on a background of sandy beige. The pregnant black cat was nestled on one of the cushions. It opened one eye, squinted suspiciously at me, thought briefly about stirring, rejected the idea as far too energetic, and went back to sleep.

There were windows to the front, but these had been covered by a heavy tie-dyed material that may well have been sacking in a previous existence. Short squat candles stood on saucers on the table and at random points on the floor. I lit one, and carried it through to the next room.

The light blinded me. Two large, wide, multi-paned, south-facing windows were awash with the early afternoon sun. The room overlooked the river. I could hear the gentle lapping of the Thames around the pilings. Past the glinting water I could see Greenwich Pier, matchstick figures standing on its rough planking waiting for the next boat upstream or down to the Thames Barrier. To its right, the grey-slabbed Victorian monolith of the southern entrance/exit to the Foot Tunnel. On the left, the twin towers of Wren's Royal Naval College. Further back, the red ball (still lowered at one o'clock each day as a time check for shipping) of the now defunct Royal Observatory (the London haze obscured the telescope's view!) and the dome of the Queen's House, both sitting imperiously among the manicured lawns of Greenwich Park. Bloody sensational. Evocative — that's the word. Of the peace and serenity of a bygone era. A feast for the eyes, and the heart.

Which you could not say for the interior of the room.

It was a kitchen. Of sorts. Butler sink. Two-burner flat-bed Calor gas stove in the middle of an old table, blue cylinder on the floor beneath, rubber tube running up through a neatly drilled hole. Two other tables — both also second-hand shop rejects by their sorry appearance. One bearing piles of plates and bowls, mugs — no two the same — a box of assorted cutlery and an earthenware pot with a miniature rainforest of lush green mixed herbs; the other weighted down by economy-sized bags of rice, lentils, nuts, flour, salt and suchlike. A garish red plastic — so sacrilegiously out of keeping — three-tiered rack on castors contained onions, carrots, tomatoes and root vegetables caked with organic earth. All the ingredients for the construction of a healthy vegetarian meal. Yummy, yummy.

Carrying the candle, I left the kitchen, crossed the corridor past a door leading to a rear landing-stage and into the room opposite.

The workshop.

Repository of more chisels than a convention of confidence tricksters. All different shapes and sizes from narrow and thin to broad and sturdy. All neatly lined up in clips screwed to the wall so that it was easy for anyone to select the precise one required. For whatever purpose.

There were also a variety of saws, planes and other esoterica that meant little to someone like myself who had been expelled from woodwork as a danger to myself and others. In one corner was an antique foot-operated treadle lathe that would have graced any craft museum. In another, a table with a single gas burner and three small copper saucepans which, judging by their interiors, were used for smelting down metals.

There was no connecting door from the workshop to the room opposite the refectory at the front of the warehouse, so it was back into the corridor and past the stairs. Opening the door to this final room on the ground floor, the smell of incense hit me like a nasal piledriver. So much had been burned here on so many occasions that the heady aroma seemed to permeate deep within the wooden walls and floor, springing out to ambush me from all directions.

The room was creepy. Cushions — thirteen again, I counted — arranged in a tight circle so everyone could sit and hold hands, seance-style. Heavy oaken cross suspended on one wall from a blacksmith's thick iron nail. More candles. Sprigs of incense poking out of jam jars like a poor man's entry in a dried-flower-arrangement competition. On the back of the door hung a long flowing purple robe.

A cupboard, two feet high, had been fixed at eye level in one corner. I walked across and opened the two doors gingerly, unsure of what I would find. Trepanned skull for the drinking of virgin's blood? Goat's head complete with devil's horns?

Imagination. Useful in context — right time, right place — but best not let run riot. Inside was a harmless statue of the Madonna and child, fifteen inches or so high. I closed the cupboard doors with a sigh.

Then opened them again.

Something was wrong. The doors were too long. Five or six inches more than was necessary to encase the shrine.

I put the candle on the floor. Carefully took hold of the statue with both hands and lifted it out. Set it down out of harm's way in the centre of one of the cushions. Turned back to examine the bottom of the cupboard. Rapped it with my knuckle. Listened acutely.

A hollow ring.

I felt along the base with my fingertips. Found a raised edge. Eased upwards with my nails till it came free. Propped the short length of wood on its end. Retrieved the candle and peered inside the false bottom.

A scourge: brown sweat-stained wooden handle, black leather knotted thongs.

It nestled on a bed of small transparent plastic bags. Some containing little cubes of hardened brown resin. Others full of white powder. A few containing small squares of blotting paper.

It wasn't someone's spare hoard of Oxo cubes, icing sugar and stationery at which I was staring open-mouthed. Another bag with five needles, protective caps on their points, told me that much. Pretty unequivocally.

I didn't speculate on the discovery. There wasn't time. Not with the sound of the front door banging shut triggering the clanging of alarm bells in my ears.

I replaced the shelf. Grabbed the statue. Placed it back in its original position. Left the doors conspicuously open.

Just had time to get down on my knees, head bent, hands clasped in prayer, as the door to the room swung open.

I concentrated on slowing my breathing. And listening to the sound of two sets of footsteps approaching.

Till, at my right, stood the unmistakable sawdust-flecked jeans of Mickey.

And, on my left, a long brown habit.

Brother James, I presume.

So we meet at last.

CHAPTER FOURTEEN

They kneeled beside me. Prayed with me in a silence that was aching in its intensity.

After what I hoped was a decent and respectful interval, I crossed myself and stood up. Mickey jumped to his feet and placed a restraining callused hand on my shoulder. 'Wait,' he whispered, nodding his head at Brother James.

Brother James rose, bowed his head at the Madonna, and turned to me.

He was tall and, from what I could tell from the knotted cord around his waist and the way the brown habit draped baggily from his shoulders, very thin. But his body seemed unimportant, was merely a backdrop, a canvas on which to paint the face that sent me mentally reeling, and physically taking a pace backwards. Long and narrow. Straggly goatee beard. Straight nose. High arched eyebrows above dark mesmerising eyes. And all surrounded — framed, I suppose — by shoulder-length black hair. It was the Turin shroud come to life. Looking at Brother James was like staring into the face of Christ himself, an eerie confrontation with the distinctive and familiar features from a thousand paintings, sculptures and icons. A knee-jerk reaction would have been to genuflect and kiss his feet. I simply stared.

'What is your name, my son?' he asked, his voice soft and soothing.

'He's called Shannon,' Mickey interjected sharply. 'I caught him sniffing around Rhiannon yesterday.'

'I wasn't sniffing around Rhiannon,' I protested, annoyed at both the content and delivery of his remark, but none the less grateful to him for the reintroduction of reality. 'I came here to buy some presents and was simply being polite and friendly.'

'"Rhiannon and Shannon,"' he mimicked whiningly. '"Together we make a rhyming couplet."'

It wasn't a very good impression. Entirely missed the depth of character in my voice: strong yet gentle, manly but sensitive, intelligent yet approachable — need I go on? But he made his point. And wore his heart on his sleeve, his jealousy in his eyes like hard contact lenses, while doing so.

'Look,' I said, 'it didn't mean anything. Not in the way you seem to think, at least. I say things like that sometimes.'

'And what else do you say, Mr Shannon?' Brother James asked. 'Shall we find out? Mickey, some tea for our guest. While he and I talk.'

Mickey trooped off sullenly. Brother James seated himself on the floor. Motioned to the cushion next to him.

'What order are you?' I asked, sitting down and crossing my legs.

'I am of no order,' he said, 'and yet every order.'

'What religion, then?'

'No religion, yet every religion.'

'Another question,' I said.

He nodded.

'Who writes your scripts, Brother?'

He smiled. It had all the appearance of being completely natural.

'I'll explain everything later,' he said. 'Meanwhile, what were you doing here, Mr Shannon?'

'Call me Nick,' I said.

'Not a very auspicious name,' he said.

'Call me Young Nick, if it helps,' I said.

'That won't be necessary,' he said. 'Just my little joke. Forgive me, I thought it was my turn.' He looked at me — inside me? — studying my reactions by the light of the candle. The flame reflected from his pupils. 'So tell me, Nick, why are you here?'

'The presents I bought yesterday — a torc and a ring — went down so well I thought I'd come back today and buy another gift.'

'You are a generous man, Nick. Perhaps I should call you Saint Nick?' Another joke? Or knowing sarcasm. 'We are grateful to you; all contributions to our cause are welcome.' He tilted his head to one side and asked: 'And what were you doing in this room?'

'Well,' I said, 'there was no answer when I knocked. The front door was unlocked, so I thought I might wait inside, out of the heat of the sun. Then I heard a noise from this room. I opened the door to find it was just a cat. Must have got itself shut in. It seemed so peaceful here I . . .' I cast my eyes downwards like a true penitent. 'It's been a long time since I prayed,' I said to the floor. 'I didn't think anyone would mind.'

'I have no objections to you praying,' he said.

I had the feeling he knew what was going on in my mind, and had omitted the words *if that was what you were really doing*. Maybe it was just my imagination getting out of hand again. Wouldn't have been surprising, given the atmosphere and the man's disquieting appearance.

'Give me your hands, Nick,' he said, holding out his own.

What was this — palmistry time?

But I did as he asked, some quality of the voice, the eyes, effectively lowering my resistance.

His touch was gentle as he examined my hands, turning them over as he did so.

'You are troubled,' he said.

Not a very difficult guess to make, I thought. Two missing fingers must give him scope for a shot in the dark.

I kept silent. Yet wanted to say: 'Tell me more.'

'I can help — if you will let me. Trust me, Nick.'

'Maybe if you told me more about yourself, and St Jerome's.'

'Would that, then, be trust?' he asked.

'No,' I shrugged. 'But, when you're searching for your faith, trust comes a poor second.'

Mickey entered with two mugs of tea. Placed them with a grunt on the floor at our feet. Exited stage left, scowling.

The tea was milkless, sugarless, but not tasteless. Unfortunately.

'A mixture of herbs and spices,' he said, seeing me struggling to place the flavour. 'Our own blend. To soothe the inner man.'

'St Jerome's?' I persisted. 'What is it? What do you do here? Who are you? What is *your* faith?'

'So many questions, Nick.' He shook his head. 'Don't you know the danger of seeking after truth? You may find it.'

'Whatever happened to enlightenment, Brother James?'

He ignored the question. 'You are — were — a Catholic,' he said. 'You crossed yourself after praying.'

Good detective work. If it wasn't for the lack of electricity, I would have put him down as an avid viewer of *Retired Country Policeman Forensic Vet-Chef* or whatever the programme was called.

'Both my parents were Catholic,' I said. Another unintended clue for him — *were*. 'My father was Irish — well, half Irish — my mother English. Hers was the stronger faith. She made sure I was educated as a Catholic.'

'And St Jerome means nothing to you?'

'Flunked RE,' I said. 'Too busy solving equations. Too interested in answers, even then.'

'St Jerome,' he said thoughtfully. 'Cussed man, by all accounts. Disagreed with just about everyone.

'There were two prevailing, and therefore opposing, doctrines at the time — sixteen hundred years ago. One propounded by Pelagius, the other by St Augustine.' Now I remembered: *he* was the 'Lord, give me chastity' saint. 'The Pelagians believed in free will, and the denial of the need for divine grace and redemption — you reach heaven by your own efforts and righteousness, not through any particular faith or rigid adherence to dogma.'

'Sounds reasonable to me,' I said.

'But it was heresy at the time. The Augustinians — who held the power — believed in original sin. Transmitted from Adam to every succeeding generation by the act of procreation. Only the irresistible grace of God could free His creation from the power of sin. And that grace is made accessible to Man through the Church.'

'Logical, I suppose.' I was beginning to sound like a *Guardian* reader, agreeing as I just had with both sides in the debate. 'If you accept the original premise, that is.'

'Which St Jerome did not. He argued against both Pelagius and St Augustine. That is why I say we have no order. And he drew his influences not just from Christianity, but also from the East — hence my words about having no religion. And yet St Jerome's greatest work was the Vulgate translation of the Bible. So, like St Jerome, we are, shall we say, eclectic — embracing all orders and all religions.'

For eclectic, I thought, substitute having the best of all worlds.

'It allows us,' Brother James said, 'to reject no one for inclusion in our little community. There is a home here for anyone in need. That is where the other story about St Jerome fits in. It is probably apocryphal, just an unreliable fable passed on by word of mouth, but the story goes that it was St Jerome who pulled the thorn from the lion's paw. Join us, Nick, and we will draw out what troubles you. We limit our community to myself and twelve others, but we happen to have an unexpected vacancy at the moment.'

'David Whitley?' I said. 'Rhiannon mentioned him. Did he stay here?'

'Sometimes,' he said. 'When the need for support was at its greatest. He was a man of conscience. You understand that, I think, Nick.' His eyes snatched hold of mine. 'Let us hope poor David was at peace with himself at the moment of death.'

Unlikely, given he'd just had a chisel plunged into his heart.

'Your community,' I asked, 'how did David fit in?'

'Each of our members has a past. I simply provide the environment necessary to come to terms with that past. Only when that is achieved is it possible to build a better future.'

'It's hard to believe that Rhiannon has a past.'

'Appearances can be deceptive, Nick. Join us tomorrow. Six o'clock. Then you can learn more about Rhiannon. And Mickey, and the others. Will you do that?'

'Yes,' I said. Well, you can't shake the Tree of Knowledge if you're not in the orchard.

He reached out and took hold of my left hand.

'I can't heal your hand,' he said. 'But I can heal your mind. Go now. Soon all your questions will be answered. Even those you dare not frame. Tomorrow we will talk. About your sister.'

'What are you?' I asked, amazed. 'Some kind of mystic or something? Do you read minds?'

'No. I read hearts. And,' he said with a laugh, 'also *The Times*.'

* * *

I sat in the car for a while before heading back to Assurance House. I lit a cigarette. It helped assuage the nicotine craving, but did nothing for my embarrassment over being so foolish. *Some kind of mystic or something? Do you read minds*? I'd behaved like some credulous fan of *The X-Files*. And all because of a few cheap trappings of the occult — thirteen chairs and cushions, smelly incense — and Brother James's startling appearance. He probably cultivated the resemblance to Christ anyway — easy enough to grow a beard and dispense with visits to the barber's. What I should have focused on was finding answers to practical, not theological, questions. Forget about how many angels can dance on a pinhead, Shannon. How about why were there drugs hidden in the house? And what exactly was Whitley's involvement with St Jerome's? Did it stretch beyond being carpenter-in-chief? Had he learned some secret — also found the drugs cache, perhaps — that provided a motive for his death?

Tomorrow, Shannon, I counselled myself, make sure you keep your mouth shut and your eyes and ears open.

And bring along a flask of real coffee.

Whatever was in that herbal tea, you can bet caffeine wasn't included on the list of ingredients.

How was a man supposed to concentrate?

Or was that the whole bloody point?

CHAPTER FIFTEEN

I spent the afternoon on mundane accounting matters. Which is identical to spending the morning on mundane accounting matters except — if, like me, you've missed lunch — your stomach rumbles more.

I had all the information to put together a first pass at a set of audited accounts, but without a spreadsheet to make life easy I would have to resort to paper, pencil and calculator. And devote three times as many hours as was really necessary.

It was a good excuse to switch on the terminal on my desk, curiosity more than laziness drawing my finger to the button. If anyone asked what I was doing, I had those trusty words 'Fraud Risk Analysis' poised on the tip of my tongue. And if that proved inadequate I would have to embrace fully the tried and tested management technique known as the Three B's: Bullshit Baffles Brains. Blind them with 'firewall penetration' and 'intruder simulation' and other impressive phrases.

The computer requested my name. A paranoiac would have wondered if it was a trick question. I typed in 'Shannon' with hardly a pause. The computer was unimpressed. Gave a virtual frown and doggedly repeated its question.

'You'll have to guest,' Meg said from behind me.

Of course. Should have tried that at the outset. The computer's operating system was VMS, the same as the one at university. A guest facility is built in to provide for the needs of visitors. Just type in 'guest' when asked for your name, and again as a password, and you are allowed access. But very restricted, unfortunately. Only to standard programs like word processing, spreadsheets and database. And for a very limited time period. At university it had been five minutes.

'How long can I remain logged on as a guest?' I said.

'Only five minutes,' she answered. In the fast-moving world of computing, some things are too basic to bother about changing, it seems. 'But, if you keep saving your work, there's nothing to stop you repeatedly logging back on. Bit of a bind, I'm afraid. But there's no other option unless you can persuade Brackley to issue you with a password.'

Meg didn't sound too confident about the effects of my powers of persuasion on Brackley, so I decided to go with the guest facility. I took off my watch, laid it next to the keyboard as a reminder to save before I was disconnected, and called up the spreadsheet program.

It was slow work, but still a lot faster than the manual alternative. The first time I saved my file the computer showed me a list of all the other spreadsheet files so that I wouldn't overwrite some other user's work by duplicating a name. The files appeared on the screen in light grey, rubbing it in that they were inaccessible for someone constrained by lowly guest status.

After a little over an hour — and twelve separate, and increasingly irritating, disconnections and log-on procedures — I had completed the Profit and Loss Account. Or, in Future Assurance's case, the Loss Account. I pressed the Print icon and walked over to the printer to collect my output. Nothing emerged. Except a groan from me.

'Meg,' I said, elongating her name and mixing it with a liberal helping of helpless sigh.

'Yes?' she said, walking over to where I was bent double examining the printer for red lights warning me too late about lack of paper or some other annoying malfunction.

'Nothing printed out,' I said.

'Well, it wouldn't, would it?'

'At the risk of appearing a complete numskull,' I said, 'you couldn't explain that last remark, could you?'

'This printer is purely for Accounts use.'

'Silly me,' I said, staring about me. 'I must have wandered into the restaurant in a trance.'

'No,' she said, with more patience than perhaps I deserved. 'This particular printer is set up for continuous stationery. It's only used for cheque runs, payroll slips and trial balances. Anything else — everything else — is routed to one of the lasers in Administration. You'll have to go there to collect your output.'

'All part of a Keep Fit regime, is it? Break up the sedentary lifestyle by getting everyone to walk round the building each time they print something?'

'It's more economical, that's all,' she said. 'By print-sharing throughout all the offices we can get away with fewer printers. No sense replicating facilities in each of the cells.'

'I suppose not,' I said, seeing the sense of the argument but ruminating cynically about the hidden cost of people trudging from cell to cell.

I went back to my desk and collected the fixed-asset schedule. While in peripatetic mode I might as well tick some more equipment off my list.

Leaving my jacket draped ostentatiously over the back of my chair in a pre-emptive strike in case Tresor came by while I was absent, I stepped through the turnstiles, leaving behind the polar region of ice blue Accounts and entering the tropical zone of bright yellow Administration.

To make life easy for me, there were six different printers from which to choose in the hunt for my single sheet of printout. The first was churning out a fresh batch of proposal forms. The second, labels. One of the army of young, pretty female operatives — did the men have to pay to work here? — was engaged in the production-line process of folding the forms, stuffing them in envelopes, sealing them, peeling labels from the sheet, sticking them on the front and placing the finished product in a tray marked 'Post'. She was chewing gum, a task that required, I guessed, the employment of more brain cells than the work she was actually involved in.

My spreadsheet was sitting by a printer that was now engaged in disgorging a pile of memos addressed to 'All Staff'. It was the official news of Meg's promotion, two copies of the short memo produced on each A4 sheet. Another girl was helping to save more money by slicing the paper in half with the aid of one of those old-fashioned guillotines that make Health and Safety Inspectors turn ashen and go wobbly at the knees: it was basically just a machete on a hinge — twist off the little nut and you could hack your way through a jungle, no problem.

For a while I provided everyone with a welcome distraction by going about my equipment check: peering at the backs of terminals; upending a large flatbed scanner used for copying images and artwork such as the company coat-of-arms logo, and editing them before inserting in sales literature or whatever; manoeuvring printers into positions where I could see their serial numbers. Having done my bit to lower temporarily the boredom level of humanity, I left the Amazon for the safety of the arctic.

Toby Beaumont was standing at Meg's desk, exchanging an expenses sheet for a wad of notes and some loose change. He placed the former in a zippered compartment of a bulging personal organiser, the latter in his trouser pocket. As he chatted, he jangled the coins with a subconscious movement of his right hand.

'May I talk procedures?' I said to him as he was about to walk past my desk without even acknowledging my existence.

He looked at his watch and screwed up his lips.

'Won't take a minute,' I said, getting up and dragging a chair across for him.

Beaumont sat down. Leaned back in the chair. Placed one elbow on the armrest. Crossed his legs so that one ankle rested on a knee. Grasped the ankle, pulled it back slightly towards him and smiled casually at me.

One of us had been watching too many old movies about American private investigators. 'Shoot,' he said.

Philip Marlowe couldn't have been cooler if he'd had each foot in an ice bucket. Except that Marlowe — or Spenser, or Sam Spade, or any of the others — would rather have played Russian roulette with bullets in all six chambers of a Colt Python than wear a tie like Beaumont's.

It was like a design sample for Joseph's dreamcoat before they decided to whittle down the number of colours. My eyes wanted to sue for assault and battery yet, in their disbelief, kept coming back for another pounding. I dragged them away and on to his face. His skin had that reddy-brown tan that usually indicates the wearer's hobby is sailing along some breezy coast, or running on a treadmill in a wind tunnel while facing a sun lamp. I reckoned it was the former, but you never know nowadays — there are some funny people about, what with Care in the Community being the latest panacea for all known ills. His eyes were a disconcerting mixture of small grey pupils set within large white spheres, giving him a look of constant surprise.

'Part of my job,' I said, 'is to examine the risk of fraud.'

'Robert told me,' he said, nodding his head of blond hair.

'What precautions do you take when selling policies?'

'Every one possible,' he said, sounding somewhat affronted by the question. He stared up as if consulting a checklist projected onto the ceiling. His slim fingers moved like a child's as he counted down the bullet points. 'There's a detailed questionnaire on every type of proposal form — any question not answered fully and truthfully negates cover. For all life policies we insist on seeing a certified copy of a birth certificate as proof of age — that being the principal factor in the cost of the premium. Those where cover is a hundred thousand pounds or more are subject to a full medical before acceptance. And as far as actually paying out' — his startled-rabbit look changed to one of somebody who had inadvertently swallowed a spider — 'we insist on incontrovertible documentation for household or motor claims; doctor's reports for permanent health insurance; and, for life policies, grants of probate so as not to fall foul of the taxman, and original death certificates — not photocopies, because they can be altered. In addition, any claim over ten thousand pounds needs the signature of two directors on the settlement cheque.'

'And what about expenditure?' I asked, edging along the path of real interest. 'Large items like advertising and promotion, for instance?'

'All budgets are agreed each year by the board, with a revision after six months if necessary. Purchase orders are needed for every item of expenditure. Any deviations from budget are examined critically by the financial director and discussed, where action is deemed necessary, at our monthly board meetings.'

'And small amounts?' I said, arriving finally at the intended destination. 'Expenses, say?'

'All expenses,' he intoned in a bored voice, 'must be approved and countersigned by a director before being reclaimed.'

'And who guards the guards?' I asked.

'What do you mean?' he asked with a touching naivety.

'Who signs the directors' expenses?'

'We each sign our own.'

'Well, that's all right, then,' I said.

'Is it? Oh, good.'

So much for the subtle deployment of sarcasm.

'Sorry,' I said. 'It was meant as tongue-in-cheek.'

'Oh,' he said. He thought for a while, unsure whether to smile or frown. 'Well,' he said defensively, 'there has to be some element of trust, you know. And, anyway, David used to run his eye over our expense claims. I presume that you, as auditor, also check them all in any case.'

I shook my head in an overt and very unsubtle — I had him sussed now — demonstration of dissatisfaction. 'But the trouble is,' I said, 'that by the time I check, it's well after the event. Stable doors and horses, you know? Then there's the tax problem.' I sucked air portentously into my mouth while at the same time stoking my lungs to give him a blast of the Three B's. 'Your personal liability under the new Section 35 amendments.'

'What's that?' he asked, worried.

'Hard to explain,' I said. Especially as no such section existed. 'Perhaps if I were to go through your last set of expenses. That way I could see that you're not transgressing any of the new rules. Laying yourself open to the automatic fines.'

'Would you?' he said eagerly.

'Only be too glad to be of assistance.'

'Thanks,' he said, getting up and borrowing back his expenses sheet from Meg.

I ran my eyes down the list while he sat hunched forward twitching with anxious interest.

'This journey here,' I said, tapping my finger against an item on the list. 'Monday. What was the purpose?'

'I was travelling to a conference that started first thing on the Tuesday,' he said. 'Local branch of the National Union of Teachers. I was going to give them a talk about the benefits of contracted-out pensions. Utilising insurance-linked investments, of course.'

'That's fine, then,' I said. 'You're covered if the inspector does a complicity check.' Nice phrase that, don't you think? *Complicity* conjures up worrying visions of being in the dock on some conspiracy charge. Plus, any use of jargon is also very convincing — no matter that it might be meaningless. 'Plenty of people to verify you were there.'

'But I wasn't,' he said.

'You weren't?' I shook my head slowly from side to side. 'Oh dear,' I said, placing the point of my pen threateningly by the side of the offending item as if to strike it out.

'It was the evening that David was killed,' he stammered out, his voice half an octave higher than normal. 'Robert phoned me while I was *en route*, and I turned straight round and headed back. Couldn't have kept on going in the circumstances. Surely that must be all right?'

I turned to look at the receipts stapled to the back of the form. There was one for petrol and another for a coffee and a preposterously expensive Danish pastry. The date coincided; the times fitted in. Beaumont had an unbreakable alibi, too. That put all three directors in the clear.

'The receipts prove intent,' I said reassuringly. 'Gives you a waiver under the *pro bono* defence in Section 39b.' I gave him a broad smile. 'So I wouldn't worry, then, if I were you.' I rose from the chair, his expense form in my hand. 'I'll take this back to Meg for you. I wanted to have a word with her anyway. Thanks for your time, Mr Beaumont.'

'No,' he said. 'Thank *you*.'

'It was nothing,' I said. 'Honestly.'

* * *

'Shall I fix that screen saver now, Meg?' I said.

'Well . . .' she said uncertainly.

'Be done in a flash,' I said. 'And the terminal, the desk, everything, is yours by right now.'

'Oh, very well,' she said, vacating her seat. 'Why not?'

I disabled the sourpussed fish with a couple of clicks of the mouse. Then sat there looking pensive.

'What shall we put in its place?' I said, drumming my fingers on the desk. 'I know. How about something personal.'

I stared at the list of possibilities on the screen.

'What are your hobbies, Meg?' I asked, still avoiding eye contact. 'What do you like to do for relaxation? When you get home from work in these long summer evenings?'

'Gardening is my love, I suppose. There's always something to do in a garden. You can lose yourself in a garden. The hours just seem to fly by.'

I busied myself testing some of the more promising options.

'So peaceful, so quiet,' she said wistfully.

'Must have made it worse,' I said, pausing to look at her sympathetically.

'What do you mean?'

'I was just thinking, that's all. You in the garden, working away so happily — pruning, weeding, whatever — on Monday evening. And having that peace and quiet shattered when Mr Tresor phoned with the news about David.'

'He didn't phone,' Meg said. 'At least, I don't think he did. If I'm at the bottom of the garden, I don't always hear the telephone.'

'On second thoughts,' I said, still probing, 'if Tresor did phone, it was probably later.'

'In that case,' she said, 'I was probably in the bath, easing away the aches and pains of gardening. What with the door shut and the radio playing in the background, I doubt if I would have heard the phone then, either.'

'All done,' I said. 'I'm afraid there wasn't much choice. I discounted clouds drifting across the screen, fires spreading, and a hand that magically appeared to spray corny graffiti — the best of which seemed to be "Oedipus is a nervous Rex".'

'So what did you settle on?' she asked dubiously.

'Autumn Fall,' I said. 'I've set it at an interval of two minutes before the screen saver cuts in. Take your seat, Miss Financial Director, and wait.'

We changed places.

After the promised two minutes, a succession of leaves in the russets and yellowy-browns of autumn began to flutter slowly down the screen.

'Very soothing,' she said approvingly. 'Very relaxing.'

Just like a nice hot bath after an evening of gardening, I thought.

I prefer a shower to a bath myself. Still, shower or bath, it doesn't make much difference really. They are both pretty inadequate when it comes to establishing an alibi.

CHAPTER SIXTEEN

There are restaurants, and there are restaurants. Some are like temples: the cuisine — *cooking* is too secular a term — there to be worshipped, conversation frowned upon, laughter an excommunicable offence. Some are simply venues for the beautiful people to see and admire each other, the food inconsequential and served in minute portions so as not to distress overly the bulimics and the anorexics. Some are 'concepts', easily spotted by the multi-coloured cocktails, waitresses wearing tiny tea towels knotted at the waist in lieu of skirts, twenty-seven variants of expensive hamburger and the queue for tables — no reservations permitted, unless the theme is Cowboys and Indians. There are those places where speed is all: the lighting harsh, the music loud and frenetic, and the food regarded as fuel to be stoked hastily into the furnace so that the engine can — and jolly well should — move on as soon as a full head of steam has been built up. Others where the staff, from mightiest chef to lowliest everybody else, are perfectly happy in their work — or would be if it were not for the damned inconvenience of having customers. And then there is Toddy's.

Walk through the door and it's like heaven on God's birthday. Sighs of contentment rise up from every table — well, almost every table, it being some unwritten law that every restaurant in the world must always contain one red-faced couple arguing in hushed voices and threatening each other with the points of their knives. People smile, customers and staff alike. In Toddy's it is always Happy Hour, spiritually speaking — Norman doesn't hold with price-cutting gimmicks.

Some might say that the décor is a little on the macho side — oak panelling, plain wooden tables, thick table-mats rather than cloths, heavy cutlery — but that would be finding fault for fault's sake. And it's true that the place lacked an open fire; but if it had one, then nobody would ever leave. Toddy's has atmosphere, not ambience. Like all simple ideas, it worked. Convivial surroundings, attentive service and fine cooking. And that, in Toddy's view, meant taking the very best ingredients and letting the flavours shine through.

I walked over to Norman's table in the corner. Kissed a radiant — blooming? — Arlene on the cheek. She was wearing a midnight-blue dress, long and wispy, sleeveless with scooped top; her hair was drawn back with tortoiseshell combs. The white metal of the torc gleamed around her neck. She toyed with it conspicuously with the ring finger of her left hand. I took a seat next to her. Arthur smiled at me with a soppy-schoolgirl moony expression that telegraphed the fact that Arlene had told him the news — our news. Norman reached for the bottle of champagne and poured me a glass. Collins held his out for a refill.

'This must be a first for you,' I said to him. 'Two meals in one week. And it's still only Thursday.'

'Hope you don't mind me joining you. But when Norman told me the good news I couldn't miss an opportunity to help you celebrate.'

'And to get a progress report?'

'Only as a spin-off,' he said.

'Spin-off?'

'Sorry,' he said, rolling his eyes. 'Too many liaison meetings. If I start using words like "proactive" and "facilitation", you have my permission to slap me round the face.'

'Can I have that in writing?'

'When have you ever had anything in writing from me?'

'Silly question,' I said.

'Congratulations to you both,' he said, raising his glass in the air.

Arthur and Norman joined in the toast.

'And, Shannon,' Collins said sternly, 'look after this lady. Or you'll have me to reckon with. Understand?'

I nodded. Understood only too well. *Don't make the same mistake as me*, he was saying. Once he had been a father-to-be. His pregnant wife had fallen down the stairs. Lain there neglected for too many hours until a workaholic Collins finally returned home. It had cost them the child, the marriage and eventually, through a twist of fate, her life. A life we had both sworn to avenge. My terms of reference were to bring the culprits to justice; Collins had a preference for the rough variety.

'Talking about looking after me,' Arlene said, 'can we order? I'm ravenous.'

'I'll second that,' Arthur chipped in. 'All we've had to eat today is bloody quiche' — he pronounced the start of the word as in *queen* — 'and salad. What sort of grub is that for a grown man, not to mention someone who is supposed to be eating for two. Quiche! Egg-and-bacon pie, my old mum used to call it. And bloody awful it was, too. Crust like the bodywork on a panzer tank.'

Arthur shuddered at the memory, then brightened as the waiter arrived to announce the specials of the day. He chose grilled giant prawns followed by a rib steak, barely able to enunciate the words for the anticipatory licking of his lips. Collins and I echoed his selection. Norman plumped for oysters and rack of lamb. Arlene ordered calf's liver and spinach as her iron-rich main course, and as a starter — she blushed deeply — 'a peanut butter and jelly sandwich, if that's possible?'

'You can have the moon on a stick, madam, if that's what you would like,' the waiter said without blinking. 'Wholemeal bread?'

'Have you got any of that pre-sliced, soft and squidgy bread you British excel at?'

Still didn't blink. That's training for you.

'And what kind of "jelly" would you like, madam?'

'Strawberry?'

'Excellent choice. Consider it done.' He collected up the menus and started towards the kitchen. 'And,' he added, over his shoulder, 'best wishes for the baby.'

'Well?' Arlene said, her hazel eyes roving challengingly around the table.

'Could be worse,' I shrugged. Never let it be said that Nick Shannon baulks at a challenge. 'Pickled gherkin and chocolate sauce, for instance.'

'Damn,' she said, winking at me. 'I was saving that for dessert.'

Collins squirmed in his seat. Searched in his pockets for a pack of cigarettes and a lighter, only to be pounced upon by Norman.

'Smoking's not permitted at this table,' he announced stern-faced.

Collins looked aghast. 'I was going to ask Nick to put me out of my misery, but it now seems that's impossible.' He leaned forward eagerly, unable to contain his curiosity any longer. 'So how have you been getting on? Do I need to oil the handcuffs yet?'

'Not exactly,' I said.

'I know your *not exactly*s,' he said with a sigh. '*Not at all*, you mean.'

'There are some interesting leads,' I said positively, 'but what we really need is a breakthrough.'

'You haven't got anywhere, have you?' he sighed.

'I've been able to eliminate some suspects.'

'Look, Nick,' he said wearily, 'there are around forty million adults in this country, thirty-six million of whom are right-handed. I don't have time for eliminating suspects.'

'Perhaps,' Norman interjected, 'if you recap everything for us, Nick. And Arthur and Arlene can chip in with any information they managed to pick up today. If we all put our heads together, maybe we can come up with some ideas. Tell us first about Future Assurance.'

If Collins hadn't been there, I would have extracted a promise from Norman about not using anything I might say for his own purposes. But, as far as the detective superintendent was concerned, Norman was as straight as a die — the sort where the plural is *dice* was my personal opinion, judging by the number of faces he seemed to possess.

'Weird building,' I said.

'Can we skip the scene-setting?' Norman said single-mindedly. 'Clouds scudding across the sky, the sun a crimson orb in a violet sky, all that Barbara Cartland stuff. Just fast-forward to the interesting financial details.'

'Future Assurance has been in existence about ten years,' I said. 'The last five years as part of City and County Bank. The four original directors — down to three now, of course — were equal shareholders. Sold the company under an earn-out agreement.'

'So they've been inflating the profits to bump up the money they receive?' Norman said with a wise nod of his head.

'No,' I replied. 'The company's making losses. No chance of reaching the profit targets set in the original agreement.'

'Then, they must be skimming off the top.'

'Don't appear to be,' I said. 'The audit was almost complete when I came on the scene, but the guy who did all the legwork before I took over seems to have checked everything thoroughly. The figures appear to be correct.'

'You don't mean to say,' a horrified Norman said, 'that the accounts are an accurate reflection of the company's position? No one on the fiddle? Not even depriving the taxman of his ill-gotten gains?'

'All above board,' I said.

He shook his head sadly. Waved his hands helplessly in the air.

'Some people have no creativity,' he said.

I tried hard to suppress a grin. Failed miserably.

'Don't laugh,' he said with a frown. 'This is bad. It has consequences. It's the thin edge of the wedge. If other companies follow this despicable trend, then Collins here is out of a job for a start. You, too, Nick. And all the City analysts who make their living by interpreting the profits printed in the annual reports for the benefit of the masses. Unemployment soars. Social security budget goes through the roof. Money taken out of circulation by increased Corporation Tax receipts. This fine country of ours will never pull out of the recession.'

'I shouldn't worry,' I said. 'I don't think anyone is going to follow this company's example. I give it a year at the most before City and County bite the bullet and cut their losses.'

The first course arrived. The smell of the sea wafted over the table before being sucked away by the air-conditioning. Arlene stared in wonder at her plate. Some well-meaning wag in the kitchen had used a pastry-cutter on her sandwiches: two hearts had been stencilled out of the bread and arranged to overlap slightly. A fresh strawberry, juicy red with green stalk attached, garnished the plate.

'Looks too good to eat,' she declared.

'You don't want to offend Toddy,' I said.

'You're right,' she said, snatching up a sandwich and taking a bite. 'Heaven.'

And they say the way to a *man's* heart is through his stomach.

'What about the three directors?' Collins asked, dipping a prawn in garlic mayonnaise and raising it towards his mouth. 'Any friction,' he said, as a blob of mayonnaise dripped unnoticed on to his tie, landing equidistant between the OK sauce and the grease from a bacon sandwich, 'between them and the dead man?'

'Whitley,' I reminded him, ignoring the distraction of Arlene placing the corner of her napkin in the fingerbowl and dabbing away at the mess. 'Not that I've heard. No obvious motive. And they all have alibis. I can place Toby Beaumont — he's Sales and Marketing, and this year's main contender for Mr Gullible — a hundred-odd miles away when the murder took place. And the other two — Robert Tresor, managing director, and Stephanie Williams, Administration — were together at the time. In bed, I wouldn't be surprised.'

Collins was writing down names, presumably to run through criminal records in the morning. 'You seem pretty sure of that.'

'You haven't seen Stephanie,' I said.

'Oh yeah?' said Arlene.

'Don't get excited,' I said. 'She's not my type. And, anyway, I'm almost a married man.'

'And don't you forget it, buster,' she said.

'This Stephanie bird?' Arthur asked with that pained expression on his face that usually implied deep thought. 'Stunner, is she? Tall? Slim? All legs, lashes and lips?'

'Sounds about right. Although I've hardly paid the slightest attention to her.'

'Huh,' grunted Arlene.

'And this Tresor bloke,' Arthur persisted. 'He got shares in Grecian 2000?'

'What *are* you, Arthur?' I said, my eyes narrowed in puzzlement. 'Psychic?'

'No,' he said, 'Church of England.'

He said it so deadpan that nobody at the table laughed, just in case it was an innocent remark rather than a joke.

'They were in the pub,' he explained. 'At lunchtime. Having a drink.'

'And the rest,' Arlene exclaimed. 'If it had been a movie, the censors would have cut it to ribbons. Not your type, huh?'

'I've got you, Arlene,' I said, smiling sweetly. 'And I never did go a lot on lashes. Except for yours, that is.'

'Sweet-talker,' she said. Then realised the omission. 'Hey, what about legs and lips?'

I squeezed her hand.

'And if you think you can get round me like that,' she said, 'then you're damned right.'

'Anyone else?' Collins interrupted with characteristic lack of patience and abundance of persistence.

'Well, there's Meg Wilson.'

'If you say legs, lashes and lips again,' Arlene said, 'I'm gonna kill you.'

'Hardly,' I said. '*Homely*, you would say. Late forties. Very county. More Norman's type really.'

'Thanks a bunch,' he said. 'So when did I lose my taste?'

'She's the new finance director,' I said.

'Nothing wrong with county,' he said, nodding his head with interest. 'Can't beat a nice twin set, I reckon.'

'So she's got a motive,' Collins said. 'Promoted into Whitley's job, I mean.'

'I can think of better jobs to be promoted into,' I said. 'This one could be about as enduring as a vodka franchise in a mosque.'

'Is she right-handed?' Collins asked.

'Well, I do believe she is,' I said. 'Looking pretty conclusive is it, Mr Detective Superintendent, sir?'

'Any alibi?'

'Nope. Not one that would stand up in court. She was home alone all evening. At the time of the murder she was either in the bath or in the garden.'

'Funny, that,' Norman said. 'I was only thinking today about taking up gardening.'

'I'll check her out,' Collins said.

'What?' I said, feigning astonishment. 'You mean *before* you strap her in a chair and rearrange her features with a truncheon?'

'We don't do that anymore, Shannon,' he said with an emphatic groan. 'Got to be careful about repetitive strain injury. Especially with these new spring-loaded batons. Very heavy, they are. Play havoc with the wrist.'

Two waiters approached the table and set down our main courses. The white wine was cleared away and replaced by bottles of Californian Cabernet Sauvignon.

Arthur looked at the label circumspectly.

'I've never had an American,' he said. 'What's it like?'

'Think very hard before you answer that question, buster,' Arlene warned me.

I kept my silence.

'Um,' said Arthur, swirling the wine around his mouth before swallowing. 'Full-bodied, fruity, and luscious on the tongue.'

A broad grin crossed my face.

Arlene started to giggle.

'I didn't say a word,' I said.

'You didn't have to,' she said. 'Your face is a picture. And a picture, dear Nick, is worth a thousand words.'

* * *

We concentrated on eating and drinking for a while. It was all too good to spoil with the real-life story *Death by Chisel.* The beef rib had been perfectly hung, then char-grilled to pick up the appetising distinctive crisscross markings and special aroma of a barbecue. Arthur ate his with mouth-searing fresh English mustard which didn't seem to affect his appreciation of the wine. Collins and I had *béarnaise* — there was hope for the man, after all. Norman's rack of lamb was covered in a herb crust, and as pink and tender as the steaks. Arlene made a valiant effort at her liver and spinach before deciding that there's only so much iron a person can eat without being in danger of kidnap by anyone with a magnet. She tried some of the rib, then the lamb — purely to check that Toddy was maintaining his standards, of course.

'Did you overhear anything of interest in the pub?' I asked as Arthur set down his knife and fork in the middle of the clean plate and smiled in contentment.

'Mr Plod — Sorry,' he said to Collins, 'the police don't have a clue. Got it down as a random mugging. Waiting for someone to use the credit cards that were in Whitley's wallet.'

'It didn't sound like the police were having much luck, to be fair,' Arlene said. 'There was a lot of grumbling and head-shaking going on. Apparently they've got a video of the car park, but that doesn't show anything useful.'

'There's a malfunction on one of the cameras,' I explained, watching Collins carefully. 'A blind spot. Well, more like a corridor really. Which neither camera can cover.'

'What a shame,' Collins said insincerely. 'No snaps of Whitley and the murderer, then.'

'The video,' Arlene said, 'shows Whitley going to his car, taking something from the trunk — the boot? — and then walking out of shot. The pictures were too fuzzy, it seems, for anyone to be able to make out exactly what it was. Several of the cops were speculating — no, make that *arguing* — about it. But they haven't reached any conclusions.'

'Anything else?' I asked.

'There was a lot of talk about the directors,' Arthur said vaguely.

'About Stephanie, you mean,' Arlene corrected.

'They reckon that, if they have to interview her again, they'll either have to hire an auditorium or draw lots.'

'*Basic Instinct* with a raffle scene?' I said.

Collins shrugged. 'It's a dull job much of the time,' he said philosophically. 'Don't deny them a little pleasure with the pain.'

'Sexist pig,' Arlene said.

'Don't call me sexist,' Collins said, with a smile and a grunt.

'So is that the lot?' I said. 'Nothing more to add?'

Arthur shook his head. 'You don't want us to go back again, do you?' he said, panic-stricken. 'Not another day of warm beer and quiche. And a barman wearing a bleeding scarf. I made him put my change on the counter and not in my hand, I can tell you.'

'No,' I said with a smile. 'I'm not going to ask you to go back. I wouldn't have the heart.'

I turned to Collins. 'I've another name for your list. Brother James.'

'What is he? Medieval monk or trade unionist?'

'He wears a habit, if that's anything to go by.'

'Don't talk about habits,' he said.

'I need to use the ladies' room,' Arlene said, patting his hand sympathetically.

Even as she was rising from her chair, Collins had his cigarettes out. I kept him company — didn't want him feeling bad all on his own.

'So what's with this Brother James?' Collins asked, punctuating the words with puffs of smoke.

'He runs a sort of hostel — *mission*, he would call it. St Jerome's. Whitley was somehow involved in it.'

'Interesting,' he said.

'They raise funds by making and selling crucifixes and costume jewellery — that's where I bought Arlene's torc and ring. Whitley helped with money to fund their workshop.'

'Getting more interesting.'

'The workshop is well equipped,' I said, saving the best till last. 'Especially in the chisel department.'

Arthur frowned.

Collins didn't.

'My cup runneth over,' he said, rubbing his hands together.

'Save a little room,' I cautioned. 'I found some drugs hidden under a figure of the Madonna. Pot, cocaine and/or heroin, LSD — as far as I can tell.'

'Ah ha,' he said loudly and gleefully. 'Time to dust off the truncheon after all.'

'Not yet,' I said. 'Too soon and too circumstantial for one of your *Go, go, go* jobs. Anyway, I'm returning there tomorrow.'

'Where are you returning tomorrow?' Arlene said, sitting back down and watching us self-righteously as we stubbed out our cigarettes.

'Place called St Jerome's. Where I got your presents.'

'Oh, we passed it this afternoon,' she said.

'Pub on wheels, was it?' I said. 'Funny. Hadn't noticed when I was in there.'

'It would have looked suspicious to sit there all afternoon,' she said logically. 'And we were bored. So we took a little walk. Sat in the sun for a while at a place called Mudchute. Did you know they've got a park and farm there? Would you believe it? And then we strolled back past Island Gardens — you can see all the way to Greenwich, you know.'

I thought briefly of informing her that it was pronounced to rhyme with porridge but I liked the way she said it — kinda cute.

'And there's this old tunnel, too,' she enthused, as if she'd taken a temporary job with the Docklands Tourist Board. 'You can walk all the way under the Thames.'

'Wonderful,' I said, with just the merest hint of irony. A stroll through a tunnel under the Thames. Just what we claustrophobics dream about when in flights of pure fancy.

'But St Jerome's is really something, isn't it?' she said, sounding as awestruck as I had been on first seeing it. 'What a building. History, but in a folksy way. And what a view. Just think of waking up to that every morning. Or sipping a drink while watching the sun sink slowly in the west.'

'It usually does,' I said.

'What?' she said.

'Sink slowly in the west.'

'Oh, you know what I mean.'

'Just teasing,' I said. 'It's a great place. But the wrong price, and in the wrong country.'

'We'll find somewhere like it on the Cape,' she said, patting my arm.

'Anything you can tell me about Brother James?' Collins asked. 'I don't hold out much hope for CRO without a second name. I could try "Brother" as an alias, but . . .' His shoulders rose and fell in resignation.

'He bears an uncanny resemblance to Christ,' I said.

'What, *the* Christ?' Arthur interrupted.

'No, the other one,' I said.

Arlene slapped me on the wrist.

I moved quickly on.

'He wears a brown habit,' I said, 'and has a purple one for Sunday best.'

'Not purple,' Arlene asked, an anxious look spreading across her face.

'I admit it's not my automatic choice,' I said, raising my eyebrows. 'A little on the garish side for my liking. But who are we mere mortals to cast the first stone against the colour-blind? And if it's good enough for bishops and royalty . . .'

'Purple,' she persisted, screwing up her mouth. 'I don't like it. It's spooky.'

'Are you serious?' I asked. It was a redundant question: the frown was evidence of that. And the way she was tightly gripping my arm.

'Don't laugh,' she said, 'but colours have great significance.'

'So what does purple signify?'

'It's a flashing colour.'

Blank looks all round.

'You take a piece of paper, OK?' she said. 'Paint a bright yellow sun in the middle. Finish off by covering the whole background with purple. Then you stare at it. The purple and the yellow flash — the colours change places. The yellow sun has turned to purple.'

It sounded like one of Plimpson's Thousand Most Amazing Facts.

'I still don't understand,' I said.

'Yellow is the holiest of colours. Central to countless myths and religions through the ages. Forget about royalty and bishops; that's just a modern trend. It's yellow that has always represented good. And purple is its antithesis.' Her nails dug into my flesh as she shivered involuntarily. 'It's the colour of evil.'

CHAPTER SEVENTEEN

We laughed it off. Or made a jolly good stab at it for the sake of reassuring Arlene about any possible danger. Put it down as a load of mumbo-jumbo. Psychological claptrap. But that didn't stop Arthur pounding on my door to rouse me at six o'clock the next morning.

I tucked the sheet around the shoulders of a slowly stirring Arlene and went to investigate.

'I'm not happy,' he said as he entered.

I yawned. Rubbed the sleep from my eyes. Examined my watch disbelievingly. Shook it against my ear.

'I'm not exactly over the proverbial moon at this very moment, either,' I said, with what I thought was admirable restraint.

'Bit touchy, aren't we?' he said unreasonably.

'Arthur,' I said, sighing, 'it's six o'-bloody-clock in the morning. I'm tired. Confused. And full of no coffee. What do you expect?'

'Didn't Philip Marlowe say that?'

'What?' I said irritably.

'"Full of no coffee."'

'Maybe,' I said, having to employ my first shrug of the day to cover the 'Damn!' that was trying to escape from my mouth.

'Not that tired and confused, then, are you?'

'Can we get to the point, please, Arthur?' I said.

'I'm sorry,' he said, 'but I can't let you do it.'

I groaned. Sometimes I wondered if he said things like that on purpose, just to test the limits of my patience.

'What can't you let me do?'

'Can I talk you out of going back to St Jerome's?'

'No.'

'Thought not,' he said solemnly. 'In that case, I can't let you go in there unprepared.'

'Good preparation this is, Arthur,' I said. 'I'm likely to walk through the door, curl up on the first piece of empty floor and fall fast asleep. The Big Sleep.'

'It could be a trap,' he said earnestly.

'Frankly, my dear, I don't give a damn.'

'Rhett Butler,' he said proudly.

'I suggest we dispense with the three-in-a-row-and-a-bonus-mark routine and move straight on to the next round.'

'Right,' he said purposefully. 'What I want you to do is slip on a pair of jeans, some trainers and an old white T-shirt. Oh, and fetch me a towel before you do. And a saucer and a pastry brush.'

I pinched myself.

Ouch.

Not a bad dream after all.

I accepted my fate. Padded out to the kitchen mumbling to myself. Took a tea towel from the hook by the sink, a pastry brush from the drawer and a saucer from the cupboard. Carried all three mystery items back. Handed Arthur the former, and placed the latter two down with peevish bangs on the dining table next to his holdall. Went to get dressed, as per instructions.

'What are you doing?' Arlene asked, peering at me through one half-open eye.

'You wouldn't believe it,' I said, shaking my head. 'Go back to sleep, sweetheart. I'll join you a little later. Hopefully.'

When I re-entered the room, the back door was open. Arthur was standing outside in the garden, beckoning me.

On one of the rusted chairs he had placed the saucer. Next to it was a bottle of red ink. I blinked my eyes as he poured the ink into the saucer, picked up the pastry brush and started to paint the tip and lowest two inches of a thick wooden ruler.

I walked across to him. He lunged at me with the ruler, stabbing my chest and leaving a red line on the T-shirt as proof.

'You'll have to do better than that,' he said. 'If this had been a real chisel, you'd be dead by now.'

He repainted the ruler.

'Right,' he said. 'Let's try again, shall we?'

* * *

Thirty minutes later I collapsed on the grass, exhausted and soaked with sweat.

Arthur looked down at me. There wasn't a bead of bloody perspiration on him.

'I'll make some tea,' he said.

I lay there, groaning loudly, staring up at the sky.

'Can you fetch my cigarettes and lighter?' I said self-pityingly. 'They're on the mantelpiece.'

'No cigarettes for you,' he said. 'You're in training.'

'Don't I know it.'

Lunge, parry.

Feint, lunge and parry.

Feint, kick, lunge and parry.

Feint, kick, slash, parry, lunge.

Perm any combination you like. Arthur had put me through it.

'Not bad,' he said, handing me a mug of tea.

I sat up and took a sip. It was so strong, contained so much sugar, you could have stood a bargepole in it and climbed up. Magic.

'Thanks,' I said. 'Very reassuring. I can rest secure in the knowledge that if ever anybody attacks me armed with a ruler dipped in red ink I'll take 'em apart.'

He frowned at me.

'Sorry,' I said. 'I appreciate what you're trying to do. Thanks for taking the trouble.'

He leaned back in the chair and gave me an embarrassed smile.

'S'all right,' he said. 'Got to consider the baby. Don't want it born into a one-parent family, do we? Arlene's not the only one who needs looking after from now on.'

'I'm scared,' I admitted.

'Wouldn't be natural if you weren't. Somewhere out there a murderer is on the loose, and you're going the right way about setting yourself up as his next victim.'

'No, not that,' I said, shrugging. 'Well, that, too, I suppose.'

He let out a bellow of a laugh.

'It's the baby, isn't it?' he said, shaking a reproving finger at me. 'You big wet Nellie!'

'Well,' I said glumly, 'after a vote of confidence like that I feel so much better.'

'You'll cope,' he said. 'You're adaptable, Nick. The way you survived prison proved that. And you know right from wrong. Teach your kid that, and you won't be doing too bad.'

'Any other tips?'

'Three,' he said. 'First, get as much sleep now as you can.'

'I think you'd better go straight on to number two.'

'Second, don't listen to other parents. Whatever age your kid is, all they ever say is: "If you think the kid's a problem now, you just wait till next year." And then they'll go on about teething, or the terrible twos, or starting school, or changing schools, or the first boyfriend, or—'

'Third?'

'You're part of a team. You won't be on your own. You've got Arlene. Think of her for a moment. If *you* are worried about the responsibility, then think how *she* must feel. Especially right now. Carrying a kid round inside her. Trying to keep it safe. And not knowing for another six months or so whether . . . Well, you know.'

'Thanks, Arthur,' I said, feeling ashamed but better. 'I don't know what to say.'

'Try "How many fried eggs would you like with your bacon and sausages?" But you'd better get a move on. You need a shower before going to work. Look at the state of you.'

The T-shirt was covered in red marks from where the pretend chisel had penetrated my defences. So were my bare forearms and hands from fending it off.

'Jesus,' I said, staring at my hands.

'Instinctive reaction,' Arthur said. 'If someone comes at you with a blade, you use your hands to defend yourself. Doesn't matter that they're gonna get cut to ribbons. It's the most vulnerable parts — eyes, chest and stomach — you have to protect. At any cost. It's only natural.'

'Not for everyone, it seems.'

'Rubbish,' he said dismissively. 'It's the only rule with no exceptions.'

'Whitley,' I said pensively. 'He was an exception. Apart from the wound that killed him, there wasn't a mark on the man. Not one single cut on his clothes or his hands.'

'Doesn't make sense,' Arthur said, frowning.

'Then, we have to make sense of it, Arthur. Try to find a reason. The answer to one question. Why didn't Whitley defend himself?'

CHAPTER EIGHTEEN

'Making up for lost time, Shannon?' Tresor said.

We were in the car park at Assurance House. I was early. Only ten minutes, I admit, but you would think it more a cause for celebration than confrontation, especially considering that Tresor had given every impression of wanting me out of his jet-black hair as soon as possible.

He must have had a bad start to the day. Maybe his breakfast cereal hadn't snapped, crackled and popped to the exact beat of his baton. Or was the pressure getting to him? Mounting losses couldn't be tolerated for ever after all. Something had to give. Was he experiencing some premonition? A mental picture of the guillotine being sharpened for the bloodletting?

Whatever the reason for his mood, it takes two for an argument. Roll over, Shannon. Don't let him bait you.

I prised my long legs out of the cockpit of the two-seater and climbed ungracefully from the bucket seat. Tresor watched me disdainfully, standing erect with puffed-out chest in the long shadow cast by his top-of-the-range, all knobs and whistles, turbo-driven black Saab. I didn't covet it. Much.

'What can you do in that thing?' he said, waving his hand dismissively at my Lancia.

Thing!

'About one twenty-five,' I said, controlling myself — and omitting the rider about downhill with a gale blowing from behind.

'Really,' he said with contrived amazement and simultaneous disbelieving shake of head. 'And there was I thinking it would be fast.'

Watch it, Tresor. You're on very dangerous territory. You can criticise a man's wife, his kids, school, university, job, even his football team, and get away with it — but make snide remarks about his car and it's considered sufficient grounds for justifiable homicide (by male jurors, at least).

I stopped myself — just — from saying: 'Only goes to show that looks can be deceptive.' And from putting the boot in with an accompanying gesture of running my fingers through my hair. I gave him a shrug instead, and basked in the inner warmth of those who know that blessed are the meek.

The puffed-out chest deflated a little. 'Well,' he said, sounding frustrated and disappointed by my refusal to match him verbal blow by verbal blow, 'I can't stand here all day; I've got work to do. And so have you, Shannon. You've got the audit to wrap up.'

'All in hand,' I said.

'And talking of hands,' he said, brightening up when he noticed the state of mine. (Good old Arthur, not the world's best forward-thinker, had used *permanent* ink: vigorous scrubbing with the nail brush in the shower had achieved nothing but make my skin sore.) 'Occupational hazard of the pen-pusher, I presume?'

I could have told him that if I had been pushing a pen, then he should be grateful. That it could only have been for the benefit of his accounts — the ink was *red*. But passive resistance seemed to be doing a pretty good job of spoiling his fun.

'We tap keys nowadays,' I said matter-of-factly.

'How very satisfying for you,' he replied, turning on his heel and heading for the entrance while he retained the high ground of having had the last word.

But he'd reckoned without my experience of the cut and thrust of repartee.

I raised two fingers to his back.

* * *

I sat down at my desk and switched on the terminal, retribution on my mind. Pen-pusher indeed. I'll show you, Tresor. I'll give you something to think about in my Fraud Risk Analysis report.

The Accounts Department was deserted — made a pleasant change from half-deserted. Simply too good an opportunity to waste.

Computer security is only as good as the person in charge of it. If the systems manager lacks knowledge, experience or imagination, then he may as well not bother with passwords. Not that the software designers make life easy. There is many a computer department that has pinned on its wall a notice consisting of a four-letter acronym: RTFM. It stands for Read The Flipping Manual — approximately. Somewhere in the twelve volumes that describe the workings of the operating system is the answer to every conceivable question. The problem is the near-physical impossibility of finding any specific answer — always providing you can come up with the question in the first place.

Imagine the plight of the poor systems manager. Having bought his mini or mainframe computer, removed it from the crate and switched it on, he's got to be able to use it. If the machine is protected by passwords, then he won't be able to log on that very first time. So it comes complete with three 'accounts', each with its own password. The accounts are SYSTEM (for which the password is MANAGER), FIELD (password: SERVICE) and USER (password: USER — how very creative). And these are all 'privileged' accounts, allowing unrestricted access to the system for legitimate purposes such as maintaining the software, changing the internal clock in spring and autumn, fine-tuning the parameters (to improve performance — for example, when the system is overloaded and giving a good imitation of an arthritic tortoise) and letting people use the computer (adding new users). Once the system is up and running, these pre-set passwords should be changed. Many systems managers don't bother — no specific, convenient instructions are included with the machine, and RTFM is a powerful disincentive. Brackley, I was willing to bet from his background and inexperience when transferred from Sales to set up the department, would fall into this category — or might not even have considered the existence of a problem (and its resulting dangers).

I tried FIELD first, SYSTEM being too risky — Brackley might have kept that account for himself. If he happened to attempt to log on while I was using SYSTEM, then he would get the big elbow from the computer together with a tell-tale error message, in essence saying 'Hacker at Work'.

It was as easy as shooting heavily sedated fish in a narrow barrel with a machine-gun. The computer welcomed me like a long-lost friend. I almost expected it to say: 'Hi there, FIELD. Where you been, old buddy? Wasn't something I said, was it?'

Over the course of the next fifteen minutes I copied a selection of files across to three floppy disks. With little discrimination, I chose everything included in document and spreadsheet folders marked with the names of Tresor, Toby Beaumont, Stephanie and the late David Whitley, plus a couple of databases for good measure — staff personal details and the main policy-holder file. Over the course of the weekend, in the comfort of my own home, using Norman's once-beloved PC, I would choose some suitably blush-inducing examples for inclusion in the FRA.

Before logging off, I went to the gateway that would take me through to the main computer at City and County. Tried to enter using the three magic 'Open Sesame!' passwords in turn. No joy.

Still, you can't win them all. (Why not? I want to know.) And it was somehow reassuring to know that the lurid details of my current account — and its embarrassingly inadequate contents — were well protected from prying eyes and itchy fingers.

The rest of the working day was a matter of killing time before the main event: the return visit to St Jerome's. At eleven o'clock I called Arlene to see how she was coping with her daily bout of morning sickness ('Ugh, don't talk about it!') and to remind her I'd be a little late home that evening ('Take care, Nick'). At one o'clock I did my good deed for the day by having lunch with Plimpson.

He was sitting all alone, eating sausage, chips and beans, and peering myopically through his thick glasses at a book on chess endgames.

'Do you play?' he asked hopefully, as he caught my glance at the book.

'No,' I lied, not wishing to get dragged into a boring conversation on the relative efficiencies of Spassky, Fischer and Petrosian in finishing off their opponents. 'Bridge is my game.'

'Did you know,' he said excitedly, 'that there are 635 billion possible hands that any named player can pick up?'

There were two ways to play this — dumb or educated. But which stood the better chance of stopping him going through each of the 635 billion in turn?

'But only eight billion permutations for a second named player,' I said. 'Since thirteen cards have already been allocated.'

'Wow,' he said, looking at me as if I had a big S on my shirt and my underpants outside my trousers. 'Not many people know that.'

'I read Maths at university. Games theory was my speciality. At one stage I was going to do a doctorate, write a thesis on the subject. But . . .'

'Shame,' he said, shaking his head sadly. 'You could have been an actuary.'

'I've often thought that myself,' I said. 'Still, you can't have everything in life.'

He nodded sagely. 'You wouldn't fancy a game some time?'

'I'm a bit committed at the moment,' I said. His face fell. 'But,' I relented, 'in a couple of weeks. How's that?'

'Great,' he said. 'Thanks.'

I left him on a high. Went outdoors. Shared a cigarette break with Sandra — quite a chatterbox today, said a couple of dozen words.

During the long afternoon I put the finishing touches to the audit, gave Meg a list of adjustments to make to the accounts, and set a new world record for the number of cups of tea drunk at a single session. And all this using only my right hand, my left being reserved for the impatient drumming of fingers on the desk.

At twenty to six I and my sore nails could stand it no longer. I climbed into my car, gunned the engine to give anyone who was listening — hopefully Tresor — an ear-shattering duet from the throaty exhausts, and set off. Warp factor eight.

* * *

'Shannon,' Rhiannon said, opening the door and smiling warmly. 'Nick. Come in.'

She was wearing the same peach-coloured ballet shoes and ice-blue jeans as when I first saw her, but today teamed with a faded pink T-shirt and a blue-and-white-striped butcher's apron. There was a thin black band around her forehead and a red ribbon tying back her long copper hair into a bunch. She took me by the hand. 'I am your angel,' she said.

I gave her a puzzled look. It wasn't difficult. I was getting plenty of practice lately.

'When someone is about to join the circle,' she explained, 'they are assigned a helper — an angel — to guide them. Come.'

She led me through the refectory with its table set for thirteen, and into the kitchen.

'You're early,' she said.

Unlike Tresor, Rhiannon made the statement sound as if I'd just given her an unexpected birthday present.

She let go of my hand, depositing me by the side of the table, and moved with light soundless steps to the little stove. A large saucepan of water was bubbling away on one of the gas rings. On the other was a frying pan with onions and garlic sweating down and a tantalising sweet aroma rising up. Rhiannon picked up a large measuring jug filled with rice and tipped it into the water. Stirred the mixture in the frying pan, then joined me at the table. She picked up a heavy long-bladed knife and started to slice the large caps of a pile of field mushrooms into neat strips.

'Dinner in fifteen minutes,' she said.

'Anything I can do to help?'

'No,' she said. 'Everything is under control.'

That makes a change. I held the view that Chaos Theory had been conceived and developed solely for the purpose of explaining my unpredictable progress through life.

'Who was *your* angel, Rhiannon?' I asked, as casually as possible.

'David,' she said.

'And what brought you here? From your accent, you're a long way from home.'

'This is my home now,' she said, her eyes fixed on the chopping board. 'I came to be healed.'

'Uh huh?' I said. Not exactly a Jeremy Paxman no-holds-barred, *now-come-on* line of questioning, but softly-softly seemed more appropriate.

'It's a long story,' she said.

'Dinner in fifteen minutes,' I reminded her.

'My father walked out when I was ten. Left us for another woman, and with enough insecurities to fill a psychiatrist's casebook. I didn't understand — how can you at that age? Thought it was something I'd done. My mother felt rejected. Spent her time searching for love. And overcompensating. Throwing herself at everything in trousers. Without success.

Used and dumped. Time after time. Went on for years like that. Then she met Jem.'

Her grip on the knife stiffened. She seemed to attack the mushrooms with extra vigour.

'I was fifteen at the time. Didn't like him from the very first moment I set eyes on him.' Rhiannon shrugged her shoulders. 'Nothing specific. Just creepy, I suppose. I told Mum how I felt, but she had her claws in real deep and wasn't going to let this one escape. He was ten years younger than her — a boost for her ego, I suppose. Had the body of a mountain gorilla, and the brain to match. He didn't suspect a thing when Mum got pregnant. Readily agreed to the marriage. It was all so easy.' She looked up at me, her dark eyes strangely cold. 'Are you sure you want to hear this?'

'Go on,' I said, although I had the hollow feeling in the pit of my stomach that I would be shocked but not surprised.

'He started to come into my room at night. When Mum was asleep. Or pretending to be asleep; I don't know.'

I walked over and stirred the onions, turned the gas down low. It was something to do, that's all, something to take my mind off what was inevitably to come.

'The first time,' she continued, pausing briefly and weighing the knife in her tiny hand, 'was horrible. His big hairy hand clamped over my mouth to stifle my screams. His hot sweaty body crushing me. It took all my effort, all my will, just to breathe. That suited him fine. While I was fighting for air, he could do whatever he wanted.'

The knife — *chop, chop, chop* — took her revenge on the mushrooms.

'And, as if that wasn't painful enough, he beat me afterwards. Told me I'd get another helping if I said anything to Mum. Kept his word, too.'

Rhiannon raised her right hand, knife still clutched tight, and wiped away a tear with her knuckles.

'I told Mum. And she refused to believe me! Said I was making it up because I didn't like him — or because I was jealous. That I was a spiteful and wicked girl. And no wonder Dad went away.'

'Didn't you show her the bruises?'

'Of course,' she said bitterly. 'But Mum was too afraid of losing Jem — even more so now that she was expecting. Couldn't admit the evidence of her own eyes. She said I'd done it myself. Can you believe it? Self-inflicted to make my lies look more convincing. She said she didn't want to hear another word: that was to be the end of it.'

Poor kid. Abandoned by her mother to a thug who had now been given *carte blanche* to rape her whenever he wished.

'But it didn't stop there, I take it?'

'For a while. Just long enough to make me wonder whether he'd regretted what he'd done, or had got too scared for a second attempt. Just long enough for me to learn how to sleep again at night. And then it happened again. And again, and again.'

'Was there no one you could tell?'

'What was the use? Mum would take his side, I knew. Either refuse to believe me again, or say I'd egged him on. No, there was no point. So I decided to run away to London. Packed my bags and waited for the right moment. That was four months ago. Brother James found me sobbing my heart out on Paddington station. One look at his eyes and I knew I could trust him. He brought me here. A place of safety. Where I could come to terms with the guilt.'

'There's no reason for you to feel guilty.'

'Oh, but you're wrong, Nick,' she said calmly. 'I told you I was waiting for the right moment. For Jem to come again. I lay there with a carving knife hidden under the bedclothes. I stabbed him.'

The knife in her right hand jerked as she said the words, nicking her thumb. She winced, stuck her thumb childlike into her mouth and sucked at the blood.

I walked round the table, placed my arms on her shoulders, led her to the sink and held her thumb under the cold water.

'You didn't kill Jem, did you?' I asked, my voice trembling.

'No,' she said without emotion. 'But I intended to. I wasn't strong enough, that's all. Still, he'll think twice before trying the same thing on some other girl. And have a hell of a job explaining the scar.'

I took her thumb from the water and examined it. The cut was superficial. I kept hold of her hand and stared into her dark eyes.

'How old are you now, Rhiannon?' I said softly.

'Just turned sixteen,' she said.

She looked older; but, then, I suppose that wasn't surprising.

'The baby?' I said apprehensively.

'Mickey's. Thank God.' She turned her eyes heavenward. 'I know what you're thinking,' she said. 'That we're too young for a child. But we love each other. And where there is love everything will be all right.'

'I hope so,' I said, squeezing her hand.

'What are you doing, Shannon?' came a voice from behind me.

Chaos Theory strikes again. This time in the person of Mickey.

He saw me holding Rhiannon's hand. Put two and two together. And made a million.

'Rhiannon's cut herself,' I said.

'I'll take care of her,' he said, brushing past me with steam hissing out of his ears. 'Come on, Rhiannon. There's a first-aid box in the workshop.'

He took her by the arm — none too gently, I thought — and whisked her from the room.

I made myself useful. Discarded those mushrooms tainted by the accident, scraped the rest into the frying pan, added salt and pepper, gave a small sigh and a large stir.

I walked through to the workshop, anxious to clear up the misunderstanding if only for Rhiannon's sake. Mickey was placing a bright orange plaster on her thumb. His face made the Grim Reaper look like a Maplin's Yellowcoat on Comedy Night.

Maybe this wasn't such a good idea after all. Mickey didn't look the type who believed in the principle of being innocent till proved guilty. I hovered by one wall, examining the neat row of chisels for a second time and trying to think of the right words.

'Nice tools,' I said, playing for time and hoping that, meanwhile, the compliment would smooth the way.

'Don't touch them,' he shouted protectively. Mickey clenched his fists and glared at me. 'Don't touch anything of mine, Shannon. Not ever again.'

CHAPTER NINETEEN

'The food of the gods,' Brother James said, spearing a piece of mushroom and waving it at the assembled company before popping it in his mouth with a knowing smile.

We were seated, the thirteen of us, around the large scrubbed-top wooden table, short stubby candles glowing in saucers, plates of ersatz risotto-cum-biryani in front of us, mugs of what the Trades Descriptions Act would require to be called 'tea-style beverage' steaming at our sides. The atmosphere was heavy, the pungent aroma of the unidentifiable herbs and spices mingled with a general air of suspicion. Maybe they were always like this with strangers. Or, more likely, Mickey — as biased a judge as the one I had encountered nine years ago — had directed the jury as to the verdict they should reach on Mr Nicholas Shannon.

Just before six o'clock, the inhabitants of St Jerome's had begun to gather, entering the room either individually or in pairs. Some carried bundled-up cloths with jewellery wrapped inside, others toted thin boards where the items for sale had been pinned in a neat display. Wearily — almost mechanically — they went through what I assumed was the pre-dinner ritual. Pockets were emptied of the proceeds of the day's labours, the coins and notes deposited in a large biscuit-tin. Then through to the kitchen to wash hands and faces in the butler sink before dinner. Back to take pre-arranged places at the table. The passing of the communal pot of food, the wooden bowl of salad, the basket of bread. A moment's silence while Brother James stood at the head of the table and said grace (in Latin). A reverential chorus of 'Amen' in response.

I had been positioned, my back to the kitchen door, at his right hand. In profile, his appearance was somewhat less striking. Perhaps, I theorised, it was simply because the visual link to art was weaker, Jesus invariably being portrayed facing the viewer. Further up the table they would be getting the more familiar full-frontal iconic image.

Rhiannon, on his insistence, and much to Mickey's obvious displeasure, was on my other side. She had disappeared for a little while before dinner. Returned in a plain white ankle-length cotton dress, the black ribbon still round her forehead but her hair untied and flowing down in tiny curls like ripples on a lake. A dark wooden cross hung from a thick leather thong around her neck.

'Do you know why mushrooms are known as the food of the gods, Nick?' Brother James asked.

'Because of the taste?' I said, scooping together a forkful of the mixture. 'Like manna from heaven?'

Brother James grinned and shook his head. 'Tell Nick, please, Rhiannon.'

'When Agrippinilla, wife of the emperor Claudius, wanted to dispose of her husband she fed him a poisonous mushroom. After he died he was deified by the Romans. So eating a mushroom made Claudius a god.'

'Good story,' I said, my fork poised in mid-air. 'But lousy timing.'

Brother James laughed. 'We are all eating from the same pot, Nick,' he said. 'You have nothing to fear here.'

I could feel everyone's eyes on me.

Here goes, then.

I placed the forkful of food in my mouth and smiled at the audience. Chewed on the grains of rice and the slices of mushroom.

Yuk.

It was far too salty for my liking. Either Rhiannon's hand had slipped when salting the rice, or we had both seasoned the mixture in the frying pan. I sipped the tea, slaking my instant thirst and giving a different taste bud a hammering.

'You promised . . .' I started to say.

'To answer your questions,' Brother James interrupted, completing my intended sentence. He turned to the others at the table. 'Nick is curious about St Jerome's. If we want him to trust us, we must first show him our trust. What do you wish to know, Nick?'

'I'm puzzled as to what you actually do here.'

'We heal the mind and the spirit,' he said.

'What of?' I pressed, determined not to let him give me the cryptically phrased run-around again.

'You know Rhiannon's story, I understand,' Brother James said, looking at Mickey and Rhiannon in turn. She nodded at the rest of the group in confirmation. 'Everyone at this table has a similar tale to tell. A reason for running away. A reason why they joined the circle. Who would like to start?' His eyes roved around the table. 'Mickey,' he said, 'why not show Nick your arm.'

Mickey, sitting opposite me — best position for maximum impact from the scowls and glowers — pulled up the chopped sleeve of his sweatshirt. Brandished his right arm at me.

In the crook of his elbow was an unsightly pattern of dull red puncture-marks and brown scabs in a variety of stages of healing. My appetite diminished in inverse proportion to my growing revulsion.

Brother James inclined his head at Mickey, silently commanding him to explain.

'Heroin,' he said, his voice challenging me to make something of it.

A small sigh came from Brother James. He looked into my eyes and gave a weak smile. 'You must excuse Mickey,' he said. 'Irritability is one of the many symptoms of withdrawal; that's why he reacted so strongly when you threatened to touch his tools. To any craftsman, they're very personal.' And the rest, I thought. 'But Mickey is a credit to us. Four months ago I fished him out of this very river. He was too high to care if he drowned, too incapable to put up a fight. Now he has something to live for. Something to fight for.'

Brother James placed his hand on top of Mickey's. Patted it tenderly. 'Almost there, my son,' he said.

Supportive nods came from the others. A couple of people echoed the words like a chant. 'Almost there, Mickey.'

A hollow-cheeked girl at the other end of the table raised her arm politely in the air and, receiving teacher's approval, told her story: broken home, anorexia nervosa, started to take amphetamines as an appetite suppressant, got well and truly hooked, indulged in some necessary shoplifting to pay for the habit, taken into care, did a runner.

The others followed her example. Each history, each confession, coming hard on the heels of the last. Some spoke softly and with heads bowed in shame, others with the loudness of defiance or the confidence of restored pride. And always to the accompaniment of a supportive nod or sympathetic touch.

I listened absorbed but saddened, sipping away at the mug of tea. I was growing accustomed to the taste. It reminded me of drinking retsina: the first mouthful seems indescribably awful, but once you've managed to swallow a whole glass — nose held, if necessary — the rest of the bottle slips down without touching the sides.

Of the eleven 'disciples' — four girls, including Rhiannon, and seven males, their ages ranging from about fifteen to early twenties — there were six more drug addicts, two alcoholics, the anorexic and three who had been physically and/or sexually abused; some — the most unfortunate — qualified for more than one category.

'And does everyone leave here cured?' I asked. 'Healed in body as well as in mind and spirit?'

'We don't work miracles,' he said. 'But our success rate is probably about eighty per cent.'

'That sounds pretty miraculous to me. Conventional treatments for addiction' — better to leave 'psychosis' unsaid — 'don't achieve a fraction of that figure.'

'What you have to remember, Nick, is that we are a self-selective group. No one is forced to join — or, for that matter, to remain. Simply by being part of the circle, a person has demonstrated commitment. The will to change. That is the first step in winning the battle.'

'And how do you work your cure?'

'St Jerome's provides food and shelter, and a stable environment. The circle provides the all-important mutual support and common source of strength. Then we use prayer and meditation.' He paused to wink at me, before adding: 'Not to mention a little methadone. It helps to smooth the process of weaning off heroin. All legally obtained via prescriptions: we register all our addicts as a matter of course.'

'What about money?' I said. 'The proverbial root of all evil? You fund your programme from the proceeds of the workshop sales?'

'That, and other sources. Because we can provide members of the circle with an address, they can claim social security. And then we accept donations from those who can afford it. David was one of our benefactors. By the way,' he said, 'you misquote the Bible. Money is not the root of all evil. St Paul said: "*The love of money* is the root of all evils." There is a world of difference.'

'I told you I flunked RE,' I said. 'But I do know a little Genesis. "In the beginning . . ." How did St Jerome's come into existence?'

'I was a member of the Order of Friars Minor,' he said, his voice tinged with boredom as if he had recounted this history many times. 'You would know them better, perhaps, as the Franciscans. The Order is based on preaching, charitable work and a devotion to learning. I was sent to London to study. What I saw here — the widespread drug problem, the violence and prostitution so inextricably linked with it, the despair that results — convinced me that my time would be better spent helping society's undesirables, life's unfortunates. So I founded St Jerome's. And, like St Francis, gathered round me twelve disciples. Not out of imitative vanity, but because it is the maximum number I can handle. Maybe one day,' he said, giving a small sigh and gazing longingly heavenward, 'with more resources and more help, we can expand. But, until then, it is sufficient reward to change some lives each year. To remove despondency from a few hearts, and put hope in its place.'

Brother James rose from his chair.

'I must prepare for our meditation,' he said. 'Stay here, Nick. Relax. Drink more tea. Rhiannon will bring you through in a while.'

He left the room, signalling a reluctant Mickey to follow. The others set about clearing away the dishes, leaving Rhiannon and myself sitting there. She topped up our mugs, sipped, and waited for me to do the same. It wasn't difficult to oblige; my mouth felt drier than if I had just eaten a dozen large boxes of muesli — packets and all.

'I forgot to ask you earlier,' she said, 'were your gifts — the torc and the ring — well received?'

'An instant success, one might say.'

'I'll tell Mickey,' she said. 'He likes his work to be appreciated.'

'Don't we all?' I replied. 'But I hardly think he cares much for what I, or anyone connected with me, thinks.'

'Mickey is struggling at the moment. He's been on a reduced dosage of methadone for the last week. And then there's David's death, and having to bear the brunt of the responsibility for the workshop now. It's a bad time for him all round.'

'He'll pull through,' I said, 'if he's got any sense in that jealous head of his, that is. With you at his side, what bigger incentive could he have?'

'Thank you,' she said blushing. 'Come. It is time for us to join the circle.'

She stood up. Placed her hands on the leather thong. Lifted the crucifix over her head. Placed it around my neck. And led me from the room.

My watch said a quarter past seven.

My heart said thump.

* * *

The smell of incense was overpowering: it pounded at my nose like a succession of straight lefts from a boxing glove with a horseshoe inside. I shook my head vigorously in an effort to clear my brain and concentrate on anything other than the suffocating, intoxicating aroma. Blinked my eyes to adjust to the paucity of light. The refectory hadn't exactly been lit up like Blackpool illuminations, but this room was dimmer than a *Blind Date* contestant. One candle sat in the middle of the circle, its flame flickering in response to the synchronised controlled breathing of the silent disciples. Another glowed at the foot of the Madonna, making the small figure appear to be suspended in mid-air, floating like a bird of prey on the invisible thermal currents of the collective aura.

Brother James stepped from the darkness at the far side of the room. He was wearing the purple robe. It rustled softly as he walked across to one of the free cushions. He gathered it up at the knees and sat down in the cross-legged guru pose, his back to the statue. I wouldn't have been surprised if it had flown across the room and perched on his shoulder.

Get a grip on yourself, Shannon. It's just a load of mumbo-jumbo, OK? Don't be taken in by it. Detach yourself. Watch. Listen. Learn.

Rhiannon guided me through the gloom to the two remaining cushions; she positioned me opposite Brother James and sat herself on my right.

'This is our time for meditation,' Brother James said, his voice so quiet that it was almost as if the heavy incensed air, like the Red Sea, had to part for the words to reach me. 'Join hands, my children.'

The anorexic's bony fingers took hold of my left hand, Rhiannon tenderly clasped my right. A signal nod from Brother James caught my eye.

Uneasy, I looked away and down at the candle. Mentally prepared myself to join in a slow rhythmic chanting of 'Ommmmm'. Tried hard to decide whether the more appropriate comment would be 'Nice tune, shame about the lyrics' or vice versa. What I heard wiped any burgeoning smile from my face. Rhiannon's angelic voice ringing in my ears. Soft, gentle, moving and soothing, she sang:

'Such love, pure as the whitest snow
Such love weeps for the shame I know
Such love, paying the debt I owe
O Jesus, such love.'

I fought against the tide of words. Told myself there was no dam to break, no flow of emotion to flood out.

Rhiannon — sensing my resistance? — tightened her grip on my hand.

Brother James's voice drifted over the top of the hymn.

'Tell us, Nick,' he said. 'Tell us your story. Share the burden.'

I looked into his eyes. I swear they were green now.

No, Shannon, it's just a trick of the light. Something to do with the candle. See how the flame moves and changes as it reflects from his pupils.

Other voices, low and plaintive, joined Rhiannon's. The music swelled and swirled about me as Brother James held my eyes.

He said — or was it whispered, or merely mouthed? — 'Share.'

No one gets inside my brain. Its thoughts are mine and mine alone. Yet maybe I should give them a little peep inside.

Just enough to make it seem natural that I should be here. Play along with the game.

A shake of my head. Uncertainty? Defiant declining of Brother James's offer? Both? Neither? I wasn't sure. All I knew was that the singing had stopped while I had been debating with myself.

Rhiannon stood up and helped me to my feet. The show was over. And what had I achieved? Aching knees from the unaccustomed sitting position, sore and dry eyes from the effects of the candles and incense, and a zero increase in knowledge.

She led me from the room. In the hallway she placed her arms round my body, her head on my chest and clutched me tight. 'Oh, Nick,' she said, a tremble in her voice.

'I must go,' I said urgently, pulling away from her.

All I needed now was for Mickey to arrive on the scene and it would be pistols at dawn.

And Arlene would be waiting. I didn't want her worrying.

I opened the door and stepped outside.

Into the dark.

* * *

I stood on the narrow jetty outside St Jerome's, barely registering the lazy sound of the water lapping at the edge of my consciousness. I stared about me. Saw streetlights twinkling against the night sky. Felt the chill that had crept into the air — or was it just into me?

I shook my head. Knew the reason this time: utter disbelief. I fumbled a cigarette into my mouth while trying to make sense of the impossible. Lit it, eventually, with a masterful feat of co-ordination of shaking hands and quivering lips. By the light of the flame I consulted my watch.

It told me the bare facts: ten-thirty.

I wanted to shout at it: 'Liar.' But you shouldn't shoot the messenger. The bad news was my fault alone.

A cold sweat broke out on my body as the questions bounced around my confused brain. What had I said? What the hell had I done? In those missing three hours.

I tried to tell myself that perhaps the amnesia would only be temporary. But I wasn't very convincing. If my theory was right, then I wasn't ever going to remember the events of the evening. And yet my panic at the loss of control, and the fear of uncertainty that grew from it, was tempered by a most peculiar feeling. I couldn't place it, but it was almost as if a small voice was whispering soothingly inside me.

As if to prove the point, I felt hot breath on my ear.

In the instant before my head was suddenly and roughly jerked back.

The cigarette fell from my mouth and gave a splutter as it dropped into the river.

Isn't it always the way of the world? You practise countering a bloody knife attack, and then what happens? Someone tries to *strangle* you.

The wooden crucifix that had been dangling loosely around my neck was now up against my windpipe, its top digging sharply into my Adam's apple. The leather thong had been pulled back and was now being twisted relentlessly. It bit deep into my skin as it tightened.

I gasped for breath. Raised my hands to the thick strip of leather and tried to ease my fingers between thong and neck to relieve the pressure. It was an instinctive reaction — focusing on the point of attack rather than on the attacker himself — and, as such, absolutely futile. The assailant has all the advantages: the element of surprise, a perfectly balanced stance, the use of your body as a fulcrum to concentrate his strength. Defence is a losing strategy, resulting only in a gradual decline in resistance through lack of air until the moment inevitably arrives when you are overpowered.

With an effort of will I told instinct to take a hike. Dropped my hands from the constricting strip of leather and switched to attack while I still had the strength.

I leaned my head backwards and arched my spine, creating a gap between the attacker's body and my own. It was taken as a sign of weakness. I heard Mickey hissing triumphantly in my ear: 'You should have left us alone, Shannon. And kept your big mouth shut. This is what happens to spies. And coppers.'

I brought my right elbow up behind my body and into Mickey's stomach. He staggered back, dragging me with him, the sharp movement increasing the pressure of the thong on my neck. There was a bump followed by a judder as he collided with the guard rail of the jetty. For a moment we hovered on the brink of the Thames. Another backward thrust by me would take us both down through the swirling waters of the river into the cloying mud beneath. But doing nothing would be as good as surrender.

And, just as you think things can't get any worse, they do.

A shot rang out in the darkness.

A tall figure ran towards us, gun in hand.

My brain flashed out a series of questions that would have been better left till later. Who? Why? And why now? The *who* could only be Prospekt. No one else bore me a big enough grudge to engage an armed killer. As for the *why*, maybe there had been some breakthrough in the case and Prospekt had assumed I was behind it, their patience not stretching to a third warning to mind my own business. *Why now?* No sense of bloody timing, I suppose. The hit man must have followed me here, or spotted my singular car, and lain in wait for me to come out of the building. What other explanation could there be? And what the hell does it matter, Shannon?

I tried to manoeuvre Mickey around so that he was between me and the new source of danger. We whirled around like contestants in the Dervish Pairs Final. The man stopped, balanced himself professionally on the soles of his feet, legs spread wide, gun held in that two-hand grip you usually only see in movies. The gun swivelled uncertainly in the general direction of the erratic struggle taking place.

A bullet might be a swifter death than strangulation, but I wasn't overly keen on either alternative. The sound of another set of footsteps told me that the odds were getting worse by the second.

I kicked back, scraping the heel of my shoe down the length of Mickey's shin. There was a rewarding cry of pain in response. And an even more welcome relaxation of the grip on the biting leather. I reached behind me, grabbed his head, jerked forward, bending my back horizontal to the ground, and tossed his lightweight body over my shoulders. It hit the wooden planks with a force that caused him to bounce up a few inches and brought his head in contact with the jetty a second time. A groan escaped from Mickey's mouth. Then he was silent and still.

One down, one to go.

I turned my attention to the tall figure with the gun.

He heard the footsteps for the first time. Looked behind. And felt the full force of Arthur's fist on his chin.

Arthur was breathing hard. I was breathing desperately, my body greedily sucking in the air it had been denied by the noose. The man on the floor was breathing — just.

'Let's get the hell out of here,' Arthur said, placing a hand under my armpit and leading me along the jetty.

'Wait,' I said, bending down to the inanimate figure. 'Let's find out who he is. Maybe we can prove a link to Prospekt. This could be just the break we need.'

'Come on, Nick,' he implored. 'There may be more where he came from.'

I reached inside the man's jacket. Took out his wallet. Ran over to the nearest streetlamp. Examined the contents in the downward beam of harsh light.

'Are you bleeding mad?' Arthur shouted angrily. 'Get out of the light, for crissake. You're a sitting duck.'

'I'm not mad,' I replied. 'But he certainly will be.'

I showed Arthur the card I had found in the wallet.

'Shit,' he said.

That's the thing about Arthur. Not the world's quickest thinker, but somehow always finds the right word.

The card said: 'Agent Toomey. United States Drug Enforcement Administration.'

CHAPTER TWENTY

'Groan,' said Agent Toomey with feeling.

He was sprawled on the small sofa in my flat, one knee pointing at the ceiling, the other out into the room. An ice pack was balanced precariously on his forehead. As it melted, drips of water ran down his cheek in a steady trickle. Pearl-shaped droplets formed on his ear before gravity claimed its due and sent them plopping on to the tartan car rug. He reached up a hand, clutched at his head and groaned again. He'd done little else since we'd carried him in from Arthur's van. It was beginning to get a tad monotonous by now. Maybe if he varied the groan a little, either pitch or length, added the occasional whimper even — I didn't care — it wouldn't have grated so much on our nerves; but none of us felt too justified in grumbling.

Arlene's relief at seeing me walk through the door in one piece — her anxieties at my failure to arrive home had prompted the swift despatch of Arthur to search me out — had been quickly replaced by puzzlement and then a sigh of weary resignation.

'What have you two been up to this time?' she had said. 'Who is he' — one hand raised from her hips so as to point an accusing finger at the semi-conscious figure in our arms — 'and why have you brought him here?'

'He sort of walked into Arthur's fist,' I'd replied evasively, sensing I was in enough trouble already. 'His name is Agent Toomey, Drug Enforcement Administration. And he's here because I didn't think we could leave him spreadeagled across the pavement in Docklands, prey to any passing mugger. Plus, not being a great believer in coincidences, I want to find out what he was doing at St Jerome's.'

Toomey groaned again. Arthur rolled his eyes and reached for another beer to help relieve the monotony, or at least deaden its effects. 'What's with this Drug Enforcement Administration?' he asked Arlene.

'The DEA,' she said, 'is our equivalent of your Drug Squad.'

'Except we don't actually have one central Drug Squad: there's eight in London and others spread across the country. Maybe if we did, then—'

'Honey,' she interrupted, 'not now, huh?'

'Sorry,' I mumbled with added contrition.

'The DEA,' she continued, 'works with the FBI. Together they share responsibility for reducing the supply of illicit drugs produced domestically or entering the States from abroad. They have offices in over forty countries, and operate in an undercover role elsewhere. That's the official information.'

'And unofficially?' I asked.

'Mean bunch of guys, by all accounts.'

'And getting meaner by the minute,' Toomey said, tossing the ice pack on the floor and dragging himself up into an unsteady sitting position. He drilled Arthur with cold grey eyes. 'You've got some explaining to do, buster,' he said.

'And you, too,' I said, gingerly picking up the gun from the table and waving it at him. 'Is this legal?'

He ignored the question. Scanned the drinks on the table. 'Got any Bourbon?' he asked.

Bourbon. The only sort we had came in packets and was made by McVities.

'Oh, sure,' I said tetchily. 'Any particular brand?'

'We've got some Bushmills,' Arlene said, adopting a more sensible, pacifying approach. 'Would that do?'

Toomey nodded his head and winced with the movement.

I smiled. Serve him right for his cheek. Made a welcome change from a groan, too.

'What's with the gun?' I said.

'You expect me to walk around naked?' he said.

'It can be arranged . . . buster,' Arthur threatened.

'I'm here after Prospekt,' Toomey said, turning his eyes on to me. 'Does that answer your question?'

I examined the man closely. He was tall, lean and fit. Close-cropped hair. Hard face. Eyes so strongly hooded it looked like he could crack walnuts with one blink. Rugged jaw — bruising nicely at this moment. Black jeans. Ankle boots, non-slip rubber soles with a tread like a Pirelli tyre. White sweatshirt — stained with the dirt of London streets and the grime from the back of Arthur's van.

'So you're the one Walker dresses up for,' I said, thinking back to our conversation in the car park and making sense of it for the first time. 'And, I take it, for whom she arranges the provision of a gun.'

He shrugged.

It didn't fool anyone. Even Arthur.

'We'd do the same for any of your cops in our country,' he said casually. 'It's only neighbourly.'

Toomey stretched his hand out towards the gun.

'Say "pretty please",' I said.

'Do you have to, Nick?' Arlene chided.

'Yup,' I replied. 'I have the awful feeling that this is the last time I hold any power over our new buddy. Isn't that right, Agent Toomey?'

'I wanna do you a favour, that's all,' he said, smiling.

'Why is it that my heart sinks whenever anyone says that? Especially when the words come with such a sincere smile.'

'I ain't your therapist, Shannon. Stick to questions I can answer.'

'Like what were you doing at St Jerome's? As if I can't guess. Which leads me on to what do you want with me?'

'I wanna help you, Nick.'

'It gets worse,' I said.

Toomey sipped at the Bushmills, rolling it around his tongue with obvious pleasure before swallowing. 'OK, so I followed you. I wanted to talk. Walker told me all about you.'

'And yet you still sought me out?' I replied with feigned astonishment.

'She said you were a wisecracking smartass.'

'No marks for flattery,' I said.

'But otherwise pretty accurate,' Arlene chipped in.

'You are allowed to disagree,' I said to Arthur.

Silence.

'But,' Toomey continued, 'she also said that you were good at your job. Damn good.'

I blew on my nails and buffed them on my shirt.

'So what's your problem?' I said.

'Prospekt is my problem.'

'Welcome to the club,' I said gloomily.

'I don't intend my membership to be permanent,' he said, his voice stern and resolute. 'That's where you come in, Nick.'

'How, precisely?' Arlene said anxiously.

'Ain't the British police wonderful, lady?' Toomey said to her, his tongue almost visibly poking through his cheek. 'So damn wonderful that in three months of working on the Prospekt case they ain't gained a yard. Gone backwards in fact. Telegraphed their play so successfully that Prospekt is quitting this country and transferring its business elsewhere. Do you need three guesses as to the exact location?'

'The good old US of A, I take it.'

'Now, I'm a Republican,' Toomey began.

So was Nixon. 'Good of you to admit it,' I butted in.

'And,' he continued, shaking his head at me, 'I don't hold with free trade. Never have, never will. Don't like imports much. Especially when it's your drug dealers.'

I shrugged. 'What am I supposed to do?' I said, waving my hands helplessly in the air. 'If the combined might of the Metropolitan Police Force can't catch Prospekt, well . . .'

'But you have one advantage, Nick,' Toomey said. 'You ain't expected to act within the letter of the law.'

'Now, hang on a minute,' I said.

Toomey raised his hand to cut off my protest.

'Shut 'em down, Nick,' he said unequivocally. 'Get 'em out of my backyard.'

'And how exactly am I supposed to do that?'

'Hell,' he said, shrugging uncaringly, 'I'm only on planning. You're on execution.'

'Thanks a bunch.'

'I'll do what I can. But this is your show.'

'Forgive me,' I said, 'but I thought *you* were going to do *me* a favour. Is this another example of two nations separated by a common language, or have I missed something? From where I sit, the arrangement would appear a little one-sided.'

'Don't want to get an immigration visa, then?' he said, taking a long pull at the drink so that the sentence hung in the air.

'Of course Nick does,' Arlene interrupted. 'The application's currently being considered.'

'Lady, he don't stand a hope in hell. Not without some kind words from an influential friend.'

'Like you?' I said.

'Like me,' he replied.

'What's he talking about, Nick? I thought it was a formality.'

Toomey frowned and shook his head in mock sadness. 'Not in Nick's case.'

'I don't understand,' she said, her voice tense.

'Moral turpitude, ma'am,' he said.

Arlene blinked at him uncomprehendingly.

'The conviction for murder,' I explained. 'Technically that precludes me from being given an immigration visa.'

'But wasn't the Commander sending a reference to support your application?'

'Won't do any good,' Toomey said, a smug twist to his lips.

'You're a real Job's comforter,' I said.

'Only speaking the truth,' Toomey said unapologetically.

Arlene's face dropped. She sat down heavily in one of the armchairs. Pulled the thin material of the cream floor-length waistcoat-cum-jacket around her in a search for comfort rather than warmth. Placed her hands on the bulge in her blue satin pants and gazed at the floor.

I walked over and put an arm round her shoulder.

'All our plans, Nick,' Arlene said, staring up at me questioningly with tears in her eyes. 'Tell me it's not true.'

'He's bluffing,' I said. 'Just playing up his hand to get me to do what he wants. Take no notice. The Commander will see things right.'

'Let me tell you something for nothing,' Toomey said. 'Do you know what we in the DEA and the FBI think of your Metropolitan Police?' He didn't give me a chance to answer. 'Stuck-up sons of bitches who ain't worth diddlysquat.'

'Do you have any basis for this lofty and erudite opinion?' I asked Toomey.

'Remember Brinks-Mat?' he asked.

'Remember it?' I said haughtily, thinking of the many hours Norman and I had spent in prison poring over the facts of the case. 'You're talking to an expert. I've studied it inside out. Brinks-Mat is *the* classic case study in money laundering. And how ineffective the controls are at putting a stop to it.' I rubbed Arlene's shoulder. 'Listen to this,' I said, hoping to take her mind off visas for a while.

'In 1983 the Brinks-Mat warehouse at Heathrow was robbed of six thousand four hundred gold bars. Now, that's one hell of a lot of gold. Three and a half tons in fact. The price at that time was two hundred and fifty-eight dollars per ounce. So the total value of the haul was over twenty-six million pounds.'

I glanced across at Toomey to check if he was impressed. His face was impassive. Still, I had the feeling he wouldn't show any emotion if I stood on my head and juggled with four oranges while telling the story.

'Just one problem,' I continued. 'You can't walk into Marks and Sparks and hand over a gold bar for your groceries and lingerie. And you can't plonk one down on the counter of a bank and ask for it to be changed into used fivers. Gold bars carry serial numbers. The ones from the robbery were all identifiable. So how do you launder them — turn unspendable red-hot gold into real cool clean cash?'

Arthur shrugged obligingly.

'This is complex,' I warned him, 'but beautiful. A mixture of the very simple and the extremely intricate.

'The first step was to buy from a Jersey merchant bank eleven legitimate one-kilo gold bars. When buying the gold the launderers insisted on being given a certificate of purchase that didn't state the serial numbers of the bars. Then the same number of stolen bars were taken to a jeweller's in Bristol; they were mixed with copper and silver coins, smelted down and recast into new gold bars that appeared to come from scrap. Next they were sent to the Government Assay Office for authentication. With this official legitimisation they could be sold on. The Jersey certificate was there as back-up if anyone asked any awkward questions. Not that they did, mind you. We British are too polite to ask where money comes from.'

Toomey gave a nod of agreement.

'When it worked once, the launderers simply repeated the operation, the one certificate covering each series of transactions. The cash proceeds of the scrap sales were then deposited in a branch of Barclays Bank in Bedminster, Bristol. So much cash was going through the branch that the bank had to lay on extra tellers to cope with counting it! Yet no one thought to question its provenance or to inform the authorities — as the law relating to disclosures states must be done.

'From Bristol, the money starts to get spread around — the more complex the journey, the less likelihood there is of leaving a trail capable of being followed. Over the course of five months, ten million pounds in cash was transported to London — in black rubbish sacks. One tranche is deposited in the Croydon branch of the Bank of Ireland before being transferred to the bank's Dublin office. One and a half million goes through the same bank's Balham branch and on to Douglas, Isle of Man. Eight hundred thousand or so is paid into an account at the Hong Kong and Shanghai Bank in Zurich, and half a million handed over the counter at their Bishopsgate headquarters in a sports bag — which they kindly left behind.

'And so it goes on. Deposits, transfers, more accounts in more banks. Some of the money is repatriated to Britain for investment purposes. Five and a half million pounds was pumped into property in Docklands. They sold it all at the height of the boom, doubling their money. Clever.'

'So how did they get caught?' Arthur asked. 'If they were so bloody clever.'

'They were unlucky,' I said. 'But they deserved to be. The Jersey merchant bank, uneasy about the insistence of no serial numbers on the certificate for the bars they had sold, alerted the police. Two undercover officers from C-11 — the department of the Met that specialises in close target surveillance — were sent to investigate. One of them, John Fordham, was killed — stabbed eleven times, mostly in the back.'

Toomey gave me a look that said unmistakably: 'And you wonder why I carry a gun?'

'The number of officers working on the case was instantly increased to two hundred. Every stop was pulled out. But they still got nowhere. Until the day they had their first stroke of luck.

'The launderers had an account in Liechtenstein, coincidentally Prospekt's favourite launderette. It was an anonymous "Red Cross" or charitable-foundation account similar to the type favoured by the late Robert Maxwell. They also had an account with Crédit Suisse. Well, a draft on the Swiss account was used to fund one of their property deals. But the entire balance in that account had already been transferred to Liechtenstein before the draft had cleared. Normally any bank would simply refuse to honour the draft. But Crédit Suisse tried to be helpful. They arranged, off their own bat, to transfer sufficient funds back from the Red Cross account to cover the draft. That simple act proved there was a two-way link between the accounts, establishing the ownership of the previously anonymous Liechtenstein account. The trail was finally signposted.'

'Don't forget us Americans,' Toomey prompted.

'The second stroke of luck,' I said, acknowledging his point, 'was the involvement of an American with one of the robbers who was under surveillance. The American was apprehended trying to board a plane while carrying a pair of switchblades. He was pulled in for questioning, exercised his rights to remain silent and not to have his fingerprints taken. Impasse. Until one of the police officers managed to pull the oldest trick in the book — got the Yank's fingerprints on a glass of water. They proved that he was a hired killer with known links to a laundryman for the Colombian drugs cartels. With a proven drugs connection the bank files could be opened at last.'

'This is where I come in,' said Toomey. 'Under the treble damages rule in the United States, we were able to sue the hoods for seventy-eight million pounds, three times the value of the crime with which they were associated. We also seized all the drug-trafficking assets. Netted a grand total of three hundred and eighty million dollars.'

'Smiles all round,' I said.

'Could have been,' he said, shaking his head. 'But you don't know the whole story. The DEA and the FBI operate a scheme called "asset sharing". Its purpose is to encourage countries to take a hard line on drugs. We split the proceeds of any asset seizures equally with the overseas agency involved. Our only condition is that the money is used somehow to fight the war against drugs. We sent a cheque for a hundred and ninety million dollars to the Metropolitan Police.'

Wow.

'And what did the Met do with it?' I asked.

'Sons of bitches,' he said, shaking his head. 'The stupid, arrogant sons of bitches sent the cheque back. Can you believe it? Said they didn't want to be seen to be "bounty hunters"!'

Toomey looked at me, brimming over with self-satisfaction.

'So now you know, Nick,' he said. 'Know exactly why your commander's recommendation ain't gonna cut no ice. Worse than that. Counterproductive, I reckon.' He sucked air in through his teeth to reinforce his point. 'There's only one person who can arrange that visa for you. And that's me. You scratch my back, Nick, and I'll scratch yours. What do you say?'

'If Nick helps you,' Arlene said, frowning, 'you guarantee he gets the visa?'

'You have my word,' Toomey said, extending his hand towards me. 'Shake on it, Nick.'

All eyes turned towards me.

Toomey's were bright with expectation. Arthur's were narrowed into a tight frown. Arlene's were creased with worry. For me, I guessed. And our future.

'It's up to you, honey,' she said.

How could I disappoint her? Spoil her vision of a new life for me and the soon-to-be three of us.

I had no idea as to how I might pull it off. Just knew in my heart that I had to try.

I shook Toomey's outstretched hand. 'It's a deal,' I said.

CHAPTER TWENTY-ONE

'So, Nick,' Arlene said, rubbing at her tired eyes, 'I think it's time you told us just why were you so late. And why you couldn't even phone. What the hell happened at St Jerome's?'

It was two o'clock in the morning, but felt more like four — the day after tomorrow. The bottle of Bushmills had run out, and so had Agent Toomey, wearing the broad smile of someone who had successfully passed on a problem to a new owner. Arthur had trudged off for another night of mind-numbingly repetitive music played at a volume level that could split the atom, let alone the eardrums, and dizzying visions of hyperactive teenagers intent on starting the weekend with a bang of nuclear proportions. Norman had arrived back from Toddy's and been informed of the terms of the deal that had been struck. The three of us now sat drinking thick black coffee with a caffeine content so high it could have kept a member of the House of Lords awake during a debate on — well, *anything* really, since all subjects seem to have equally soporific effects on the Upper House.

'It's a long story,' I said, hoping she might suggest putting it off till after we'd had some sleep and thereby allow me to dodge making the uncomfortable admission for a little longer.

‘I’m not going to like it, am I?’ she said, nestling up against me on the sofa. As she settled down, she wrinkled her nose and sniffed like an analytical chemist at the heavy aroma of incense that had worked its way into the fibres of my clothes.

‘Well . . .’ I prevaricated.

‘You’re not going to like it,’ said Norman. He stretched out his legs, crossed his slippered feet, interlocked his fingers and placed his hands in his lap.

‘It could be worse,’ I said, unsure how.

‘I think you better let us be the judge of that, honey.’

So I recounted the story of the evening. Norman nodded his head wisely from time to time; Arlene shook hers sadly, especially when hearing the tales of Rhiannon and the other disciples.

‘And you say you can’t remember anything after she started singing?’ Arlene asked, trustingly keeping a suspicious grunt from her voice.

‘Nothing,’ I said.

‘He wouldn’t,’ said Norman.

‘So you don’t know what you did?’ Arlene said. I gave a wan smile in answer. ‘Or what you told them?’

‘Everything, I suspect,’ I said, recalling Mickey’s jibes about me being a spy and a copper, and Rhiannon’s hug accompanied by the shaky-voiced ‘Oh, Nick’.

‘He would,’ said Norman.

‘That’s unfair,’ I protested.

‘How do you feel?’ he asked.

‘Strange,’ I said. ‘It’s hard to describe. Sort of light-headed.’ I shrugged my shoulders inconclusively. ‘Every sense amplified as if my mind has just had a twelve-thousand-mile service and it’s bright, shiny and new. Hell,’ I said, having finally found the word that summed up how I felt, ‘reborn, I suppose.’

‘Well, you would,’ he said.

‘Look, Norman,’ Arlene said impatiently. ‘Is there any chance of you explaining yourself or are you gonna sit there all night stuck in would-wouldn’t mode?’

'Catharsis,' he said.

I managed a knowing smile. Nice to be proved right once in a while. He *had* been practising. The German accent still needed a bit of work, though: consonants not quite hard enough at present.

'Catharsis,' Arlene said with a groan. 'Gee, thanks a bunch. It's all crystal clear now.'

'Listen,' he said. 'I've been doing a bit of reading about psychology since Arthur came to consult me.'

Consult him. Any moment now Norman would be pinning a sign on the door of the flat saying: 'The doctor is in.'

'All the mumbo-jumbo,' he said to me, 'the candles, holding hands in a circle, the singing, was simply to lower your defences. Make you receptive. For the process of catharsis.'

Norman put on his glasses. Not to see through, but in order to peer over the top of in an exaggerated professorial manner.

'Freud,' he said, visibly enjoying the opportunity to lecture us, 'in his early work with a man called Breuer, found that if patients could be induced to release all their pent-up emotions and anxieties — the process they named "catharsis" — then they felt better. Bringing all the repressed inner conflicts to the surface — what we call the conscious level — released tensions and reduced the symptoms of illness. Catharsis is now the basis of most modern-day therapy.'

'And how did Freud do this?' Arlene asked.

'Latterly through free association,' Norman said learnedly. 'But the first experiments used hypnosis. It is my opinion' — notice he didn't add a qualifying *humble* — 'that Brother James hypnotised Nick.'

'I'd reached the same conclusion,' I said sheepishly.

'It's nothing to be ashamed of,' he said. 'Most people are susceptible to hypnosis under the right conditions. How do you think Brother James achieves such a high success rate with his oddball collection of addicts and dropouts? You can't simply put it down to herbal tea and sympathy. And, while we're on the subject of tea,' Norman added, 'I'm willing to bet it contained more than just herbs. There's a variety of drugs — codeine is probably the easiest to get hold of — that are termed "enhancers" or "accelerators". Their function is to make the subject more vulnerable to hypnosis.'

I didn't feel quite so stupid now. To reveal all under hypnosis was something I'd previously associated with the weak-willed; doing the same after being drugged was more like being thrust into the pages of a spy thriller. An enigmatic Harry Palmer style smile settled on my lips.

Norman misread it: either he'd never seen *The Ipcress File*, and therefore didn't recognise my faultless impersonation, or he simply reckoned I was still basking in the afterglow of rebirth.

'Don't get carried away, Nick,' he said. 'Catharsis doesn't always work completely, and almost never at the first attempt. Some problems are too deep-rooted. And even when a patient is curable it takes time. Why do you think Mickey, Rhiannon and the others have been there for months? One session will bring superficial relief — that's what you're experiencing at the moment — but to eliminate all guilt and anxiety involves repeated treatment.'

Norman paused. Not for breath or thought, but to see which of Arlene and I would crack first and ask him to explain further. 'Explain further,' I said.

'Think of yourself as an onion,' he said, grinning with pleasure.

'I might have difficulty with this concept,' I said.

'Your mind, Nick, is like an onion. It's built up of many layers. Tonight Brother James stripped off the outer skin. He's got a long way to go yet before he gets right down to the core.'

'No way,' Arlene said firmly. 'Where Nick is concerned, I'm the only one who does any stripping off. And, in any case, the situation won't arise; Nick's not setting foot in that place again.'

My silence betrayed me. She wriggled her body round and stared up into my eyes.

'Oh, no,' she said in amazement. 'You're not thinking of going back, are you? Not after what Mickey tried to do to you tonight.'

I pursed my lips noncommittally. She wasn't fooled.

'Don't you think,' she said, 'that you might not already be taking too many risks? Jeez, agreeing to Toomey's demands to put Prospekt out of action would be enough to satisfy most people's lifetime's intake of adrenaline. But *you*' — she paused to make sure I'd caught every last nuance she'd injected into the word — 'want to waltz back into the lion's den of some wacko cult, too.'

'There's no option, I'm afraid. And, for some reason, my instincts tell me to trust Brother James.'

'I'm not sure you can rely on your own judgement at the moment,' Norman said, frowning deeply. 'Like I said earlier, most people can be hypnotised — but only twenty per cent are susceptible to a deep trance. The fact that you can't remember anything is pretty conclusive evidence that you, Nick, are one of those twenty per cent. That makes you prone to post-hypnotic suggestion. How do you know your mind hasn't been tampered with? Brother James could have planted the desire to return. And reinforced it with a feeling of trust in him. After all, under really deep hypnosis almost anything is possible.'

'That's why I have to go back,' I said.

'I don't understand you, Nick,' Arlene interrupted, raising her voice. 'Aren't you forgetting something? There's still a killer on the loose out there. It could be Brother James. Or one of his crazy band of disciples.'

'That's why I have to go back,' I persisted, raising my hands to quell any further interruptions. 'Let's get a couple of things straight. First, this has nothing to do with a need for another session of catharsis; as far as I'm concerned, there's no guilt or anxiety to rise to the surface. And, second, I accept everything that Norman says about the ability to alter deep emotions. That's the whole point. Look at my hands,' I said, showing them the marks of the red ink. 'Don't you see? Despite the basic instinct for self-preservation we all possess, Whitley made no attempt to defend himself. There wasn't a single cut or scratch on his hands. I need to find out whether Whitley, like me, was a member of the élite twenty-per-cent club.'

CHAPTER TWENTY-TWO

We finally got to bed at three o'clock. I was still awake at four when the dawn chorus began. My brain was reverberating with the loud ticking of a time bomb. The countdown had started. The explosion would not be long coming. Mary Jo was arriving today.

'This town ain't big enough for both of us, Shannon,' I could hear her saying.

'This *world* ain't big enough for both of us, Mary Jo,' I replied, after due consideration. Spontaneity is good, but even better after a rehearsal.

At half past six I waved the white flag of surrender in the face of the enemy of sleep. Slid out of bed, grabbed a pair of jeans and a T-shirt, and tiptoed from the room. Padded out to the kitchen. Made a cup of tea. Carried it through to the living room.

It was a muggy morning, the second day in a July that seemed determined to make up for a dismal June with a vengeance. I opened both the back door and the window. Felt warm sticky air saunter lazily into the room, bringing about as much relief as a misanthropic miser on Red Nose Day. I sat down at Norman's computer, switched on, sipped my tea, lit a cigarette — maybe I should forget about the inner layers of the onion and switch Brother James's therapy to helping me kick the smoking habit — and slid the first of the disks I had copied at Future Assurance into the floppy drive.

The databases were of marginal interest; but, then, again, to find any database riveting you have to possess a nerd rating of astronomic proportions. A bit like the man who preferred reading the dictionary to any work of fiction — not much story, but at least he could understand every word.

Anyway, the first was a listing of customers with all the usual details: names, addresses, phone numbers, age, family circumstances, policies held, mailshots sent and so on. I smiled as I contemplated Tresor's face when he read the Fraud Risk Analysis report and saw just how easily I had obtained the file. An unscrupulous competitor would pay handsomely for such a ready-made marketing tool: the official going rate for the sale of an insurance company's 'book' (the list of policy-holders with its assumed future business) was around two hundred pounds per policy. Come to think of it, given FA's recent track record, selling the list would be more like an act of sabotage on the unwitting buyer's profits.

The second was the personnel file, and that told me more than I ever wanted to know about the employees. Tresor lived in leafy mid-market Surbiton (usually a holding position before advancing to more exclusive territory), Toby Beaumont in fashionable Weybridge (home of those who are easily persuaded, paying over the odds for the prospect of brushing shoulders with ageing rock stars in the twee lounge bar of the local hostelry), Stephanie in cosmopolitan Islington (where anything goes — generally the video and stereo when the burglars call). She was thirty-four years old, unmarried, and must have had a fling in the past with someone of influence at British Telecom: her phone number was one of those unforgettable combinations usually reserved for Freefone advertisers or helplines. Meg and Plimpson, coincidentally, both lived in the no-man's-land of Ilford, an unleafy suburb (no, that's unfair, there are trees in Ilford — I think they are both sycamores) that suffers from schizophrenia, being undecided as to whether its allegiance should be given to London or Essex.

Whitley's word-processing files were the normal accountant's collection of intense memos, stiltedly worded, concerning the 'paramount' need for cost control ('No avenue must be left unexplored, no overhead unquestioned, in the search for any reduction, however small'), the importance of submitting expense claims on time and stamping out the sin of making private calls on company lines.

I had reached the point where I was scrolling through them more quickly, paying increasingly scant attention, when Norman entered the room in dressing gown and slippers. He glanced over my shoulder at the screen, yawned perceptively, picked up my empty cup and walked liked a house-trained zombie into the kitchen.

'There you go,' he said, a minute or two later, placing a fresh cup beside the rapidly filling ashtray.

'Thanks,' I said distractedly.

He disappeared briefly to pick up the paper from the mat in the hall and eased his bony body into the armchair for the morning ritual of checking the company news, noting significant movements in share prices and studying the obituaries ('It's not the deaths I take pleasure in, Nick, but still being alive to read about them').

I clicked on an unpromising file labelled 'LAWLET. DOC', and paused to sip at the tea.

'Jesus Christ,' I said, working rapidly through the letter.

'Did I forget the sugar again?' Norman said distractedly. 'Help yourself, eh, Nick? There's a good lad. I've just got nicely settled.'

'And I've just got nicely unsettled. Come and look at this.'

'Do I have to?' he sighed. 'You know how much I enjoy this time of day.'

'It doesn't matter, then,' I said casually. 'You just sit back and relax. Later will do.' I heard the paper begin to rustle. 'Let me know when you're finished, Norman. You probably wouldn't be interested anyway. After all, it's only the instructions for the drawing-up of Whitley's will.'

Norman may not have been able to leap buildings at a single bound, but he could certainly move faster than a speeding bullet when the need arose.

'What's it say? What's it say?'

'All the usual stuff,' I said, feigning apathy. 'Being of sound mind and such. This revokes all previous wills, blah, blah, blah.'

'All right,' he said, sighing through gritted teeth. 'I'm sorry. I should have come when you first asked. Satisfied? Now, get on to the juicy bit. Who bloody inherits?'

'The sum of five thousand pounds goes to Rhiannon Pengelly.'

'And?' he said, his voice indicating that his interest had waned with the smallness of the bequest.

'The balance of the estate is settled upon . . .' I paused for dramatic effect. 'Let's hear it for everyone's favourite hypnotist — Brother James.'

'*Cui bono*?' Norman said. '*Cui* bloody *bono*?'

'Translation, please.'

'Who stands to gain?' he said, nodding his head wisely. 'Who bloody stands to gain?'

* * *

I replaced the receiver of the telephone.

Collins had been his usual charming self, obviously thrilled to hear from me.

'What the hell do you want, Shannon?' he'd barked down the line. 'I was in the bloody bath.'

'Sorry,' I'd replied. 'I forgot it was the first Saturday of the month.'

'Don't waste your breath. Better people than you have tried to insult me. Water off a duck's back.'

'But rarely bath water.'

We could have gone on in this happy bantering fashion all day — I with my inexhaustible fund of amusing little quips, Collins with his impressive aptitude for repartee (heavily reliant, it appeared, on the Complete Thesaurus of Profanities and Expletives) — but I was too excited by the discovery to draw out the polite preliminaries.

I'd told him about the will and slipped in a *cui bono* as if it were a phrase that rolled off my tongue every hour of every day. 'A motive,' I had explained condescendingly. 'Brother James has a motive.'

* * *

'Trust you,' Norman said, 'to trust him.'

It takes a big man to admit a big mistake, especially to Norman.

'The evidence is purely circumstantial,' I said stubbornly. 'Innocent until proved guilty, you know. Let's reserve our judgement, eh? See what Collins can dig up when he checks him out.'

'Checks whom out?' Arlene said, emerging from the bedroom.

She drifted across to me, a bath towel stretched tightly round her body, a hand towel wrapped more adequately round her head. Placed a hand lightly on my shoulder. Bent down to kiss me on the cheek.

'You smell of peaches,' I said appreciatively.

'If you don't want my peaches, baby,' she replied, 'don't shake my tree.'

'Brother James,' Norman said, blushing, but still somehow managing to inject a hint of triumphant I-told-you-so into his voice. 'He's the beneficiary of Whitley's will.'

Arlene ran her hands through my hair.

'I think I'll go and get dressed,' Norman said, beating a retreat.

'So you won't be going back there now, honey?' she said in the soft coaxing tones of a sea-nymph luring me to her bidding.

'No,' I said.

She rubbed the nape of my neck in what Norman would have termed 'positive reinforcement' and the rest of us laymen called a carrot.

'At least, not on my own, I won't,' I added.

She dug her nails into my skin — the stick now.

'Ouch. That hurt.'

'Serves you right,' she said. 'How can you be so pig-headed?'

'A man's gotta do what a man's gotta do,' I drawled.

'The hell he has,' she said, improving considerably on my John Wayne impression. She took hold of the chair and swivelled it round so that I was directly facing her. Pointed a finger at me. 'I'll tell you what this man's gotta do today.'

'Beginning to sound interesting,' I said, smiling winsomely.

'Shopping,' she said.

Must have been smiling losesomely by mistake.

'Shopping?' I echoed. 'Is that the best idea you can come up with for a lazy Saturday?'

'Who said it was going to be lazy? We've got a lot to do if we're going to have Mary Jo over to dinner tomorrow.'

'And who said we were going to have Mary Jo over to dinner tomorrow?'

'I did, honey.'

Arlene placed her hands on her hips.

I knew that gesture. And the resolute look that followed rapidly behind.

'Fair enough,' I said, swiftly backing down. Well, it gets boring being a hero all the time. You have to allow yourself a touch of cowardice once in a while. 'On one condition,' I added, going for twice in a while, 'Norman and Arthur are invited, too.'

'On one condition,' she countered.

'What's that?' I asked suspiciously.

'You let me borrow your car so I can collect Mary Jo from the airport.'

Dilemma time. Which was the lesser of two evils — facing Mary Jo without the support of Arthur and Norman, or letting Arlene slip behind the wheel of my beloved Monte Carlo?

'You're not supposed to think about it,' Arlene said reprovingly. 'Your hesitation might be construed as lack of confidence.'

'No, it's not that,' I said. 'I trust your driving implicitly. It was the navigating I was worried about.'

'Diddlysquat, as the eloquent Agent Toomey would put it.'

'OK,' I said. 'You can have the car. On one condition.'

'Haven't we been through this already? I'm getting a strange sensation of *déjà vu*. Are we stuck in a time-loop or something? Destined to spend the rest of our lives forever repeating ourselves?'

'Destined to spend the rest of our lives forever repeating ourselves,' I replied teasingly.

She shook her head in exasperation. 'What's the condition?' she groaned.

'You don't let Mary Jo drive the Monte Carlo.'

I'd had the gross misfortune of experiencing Mary Jo's driving. Only once, I admit, but the occasion was indelibly etched on my brain, the scar tissue still painful. It was so traumatic that I'd given up eating strong cheese in the evening in case it brought on the nightmares.

Mary Jo drove a customised pink Cherokee jeep. *Drove* was the wrong word really. *Terrorised the highways* was a better way of putting it.

It was an ordeal even when the vehicle was stationary: sitting in the passenger seat of this lipstick-pink spoilt-brat-mobile, enduring the jeers, heckles and denigratory hand gestures of streetwise Bostonian kids wearing baseball caps turned back to front. But when the car started to move . . . My God! Mary Jo, it was immediately evident, was a graduate of the Kamikaze School of Motoring. I didn't know which was worse — keeping my eyes open and being scared witless in three dimensions, or clamping them tightly shut and letting my imagination project terrifying scenes on my mind in just two. And the noise. Horns blaring, deafening torrents of invective streaming from the gaping mouths of incredulous motorists forced to take evasive action. Granted the jeep was so solid it was damn near impregnable, but I wouldn't have felt safe inside a Centurion tank if Mary Jo had been at the wheel. The slogan 'Keep death off the roads' could have been dedicated to her.

'Don't worry,' Arlene said understandingly, 'I won't let Mary Jo drive. Or fiddle with any buttons, or retune the radio from Jazz FM. OK? I'll take care of your precious car. You can trust me with it.'

'*It* is a she,' I rebuked her.

'It would be,' she said, sighing.

'Arlene,' I said seriously, 'when are you planning to tell Mary Jo? About us getting married. And the baby.'

'I thought I'd collect her from the airport and drive straight to the Savoy. Get her settled in, wowed by the décor in the room and the view of Ol' Man River rolling along outside, order afternoon tea — all very English, very civilised — wait for her defences to lower, and then break it to her.'

'And the best of British luck,' I said.

'She'll be OK. I'm sure.'

'You don't sound it.'

'Hell,' she said, 'it's something that has to be done. I'll take care of it.'

'You don't have to do it alone,' I said. 'You know that, don't you?'

She squeezed my hand. 'I know,' she said. 'But it's better this way. It will be your turn when I bring her over for dinner. Don't forget the whole point of the exercise. Home territory, remember? Show her what you're really like, Nick.'

'Charm her bobby socks off, eh?'

'You don't have to go that far, honey. Just be natural. Be yourself.'

'For a whole evening?' I gasped, exaggerating shock.

'When it's all over,' Arlene said, taking a lock of my hair and twirling it in her finger, 'we'll get a cab to take her back to the Savoy. Then we can relax. How does that sound?'

'You mean I don't have to wait till heaven to get my reward?'

'No, honey,' she said huskily. 'It'll just seem like heaven.'

'How about showing me the colour of your money?' I said, reaching for the knot of the towel. 'A little down-payment as a show of good faith?'

'On second thoughts, Nick,' Arlene said, 'maybe you shouldn't be too natural tomorrow.'

* * *

The rest of the day disappeared in a flurry of activity. We hit the shops — a little later than originally planned — in a big way. Even took advantage of a sale to buy a gas barbecue. My rationale for this impulse purchase was that the dinner would have more chance of being a resounding success (well, less chance of being a disastrous failure) if it were to be informal. And what could be more informal than a barbecue? It also had the advantage of allowing me to display my culinary talents in full view of an admiring Mary Jo. Or, more realistically, provided a place to cool down if — when — things started to turn nasty.

There were some snags, of course. First, we had to arrange for the barbecue to be delivered: the tiny boot of the Lancia could only just cope with all the bags of groceries. Second, it had to be erected. All you needed for this simple task was a screwdriver and a spanner — plus a postgraduate degree in mechanical engineering and a working knowledge of some obscure Chinese dialect in order to decipher the instructions.

Then there was chicken, pork and lamb to marinate, peppers and onions to chop, potatoes to peel, bulgar wheat to soak as the first step towards a *tabbouleh*, a Greek *horiatiki* salad to construct, *gado-gado* sauce to conjure up from a jar of Arlene's peanut butter, onion, garlic, soy sauce, honey, lemon and so many other assorted ingredients as to make me wonder why I hadn't taken the easy route and bought a bottle instead. But I knew the answer: wouldn't have had the same therapeutic value. Sometimes your mind needs to be on other things.

It was half past eight when we finally collapsed on the sofa. And approximately ten seconds later when the telephone rang.

'Didn't disturb you, did I?' Collins said hopefully.

'Would it make any difference if you had?'

'Nope.'

'Thought not.'

'I've driven three hundred miles today,' he said.

'Be on *News at Ten*, I expect.'

'A place called Cerne Abbas,' he said.

'*Abbas* as in *abbot*?' I asked with growing interest.

'Sort of,' he said. 'Except that the Order of Friars Minor — headquarters Cerne Abbas — don't call their leaders abbots. Apparently they're known as *custodes* — that's *guardians* to you and me. Not many people know that.'

He sounded like Michael Caine, or Plimpson. Except that I guessed there was a purpose behind the trivia.

'What else do not many people know?' I said.

'It seems,' he said, 'that Brother James has been a little economical with the truth. A bit overstocked in the pork pie department, one might say.'

A little later, and a lot wiser, I put down the phone. Stood there, staring out the window lost in contemplation.

'Well?' asked Arlene.

'Let's go in the garden,' I said. 'I need to think.'

'You need a cigarette, you mean.'

'Badly,' I said.

She saw the intense look on my face and followed me outside.

'Brother James wasn't sent to London to study,' I said, exhaling smoke in a long, thoughtful stream. 'He was kicked out of the Order.'

'Reasons?' she said.

'Plenty,' I replied. 'According to Collins — admittedly not the world's most unbiased judge of his fellow man, especially when in pursuit of a murder suspect — Brother James was an oddball. Regarded by the friars — and this might be thought rich, given the Jesus similarities — as a zealot. Extreme fanatical views, rebellious, lack of respect for authority or tradition. He wanted the Order to be more proactive. To climb down from its ivory tower. Go out into the community — the real world — in search of souls to save.'

'Sounds laudable enough,' she said.

'There were doubts over his motives,' I said. 'They suspected him of empire-building, his idea of a new crusade based less on conversion and more on the acquisition of power. Power for the Order through swelled numbers, and power for himself as their new leader.'

'So they got rid of him before he could mount a takeover bid?'

'He almost pulled it off, it seems. Persuaded quite a few friars to support him. And then the guardian discovered how he was doing it.'

'Hypnotism,' she said.

I nodded.

'No second chances?' Arlene asked. 'Doesn't seem very Christian.'

'There was another problem. He was accused of breaking one of the fundamental tenets of the Order. His accuser was a Poor Clare — that's a nun to you and me. The rule was the one governing celibacy.'

CHAPTER TWENTY-THREE

'So why can't the police deal with it?' Arthur asked huffily. 'Why me? Again.'

'Come on, Arthur,' I said, refilling his glass with a suitably bribe-worthy Australian Cabernet Shiraz. 'You know how it is. We're doing this for Collins. Helping him escape the bureaucratic quicksands of the Fraud Squad by trying to steal a march on the official police inquiry. Try thinking of yourself as a sort of special deputy. All I'm asking is that you check out a few addresses. Sniff around a little. See what you can learn about some of the people who work at Future Assurance.'

'No sitting in pubs where the barman twirls his pinkies in his neckerchief?' he asked dubiously.

I shook my head.

'No quiche and salad?' he said.

'No quiche and salad,' I reassured him, smiling with the knowledge that he'd as good as agreed. Once someone starts to talk details of execution, it's a sure sign that the concept has been accepted. 'Play it any way you like, Arthur,' I said.

'I can provide you with a few new identities,' said Norman, in the same nonchalant manner he might use if passing around a box of chocolates for us to select our favourites. 'Gasman. Water Board. Electricity. Even got a nice line in market researchers. Maybe not,' he said, shaking his head at the sight of six and a half feet of Arthur. 'Something blue-collar, I think. Take your pick.'

'Norman,' I scolded, 'what have you been up to now?'

'Some people collect stamps. Others stick pins in butterflies. I happen to have an interest in identity cards. Where's the harm in that? Come on,' he said, moving across the room to his computer, 'I'll show you my collection.'

I followed him, partly out of suspicion and partly out of curiosity, but mostly just plain grateful for any activity that would kill a little time.

The three of us were nervously awaiting Arlene's return from the airport with Mary Jo. The overture was playing, the tension was building. Any moment now the orchestra would move on to the dramatic opening bars of 'The Arrival of the Queen of Sheba' — or should it be 'The Entry of Gladiators'?

Arthur, mindful of the gravity of the situation, was looking distinctly uncomfortable in his only non-working suit, double-breasted and charcoal-dark, a slight whiff of mothballs suggesting it only usually saw the light of day at weddings and funerals. He kept fidgeting with his tie and running a finger between his neck and the stiff collar of his white shirt.

Norman — rehearsing for a date with Meg? — had opted for the country squire look: plain fawn jacket, chequered shirt, brown knitted tie, twill trousers, and highly polished brogues in place of his grandad slippers.

And me?

I'd taken the trouble to dress down, appreciating that it wouldn't make the slightest difference to Mary Jo's attitude if I wore a dinner suit or a wetsuit. Smart but casual, I'd responded to Norman's critical frown. I felt so at ease in my stone-coloured jeans and dark blue T-shirt that I almost fooled myself into believing that my body, brittle from tension, wouldn't snap in two at the sound of the car door slamming shut. And I was convinced that it *would* slam shut.

Norman's computer whirred and hummed. Lights glowed on a range of equipment that made Silicone Valley seem like the site of an archaeological dig. He clicked his way into a sophisticated graphics programme and sat back with pride.

'How did you get hold of all of these?' I asked, staring at a Rogues Gallery of images. There was a reproduction of an identity card from every public-service employee imaginable. With the exception of the bloody Wichita lineman — and maybe that was in a separate file — Norman had a full set.

'Every time someone calls,' he explained, 'I put the chain on the door and make them hand me their card through the narrow gap. Pretend to be a dotty old codger who wants to phone their office and check out they're who they claim to be. Then I simply run it through this little gadget.' He tapped his palm on the flatbed scanner beside the computer.

'Huh,' Arthur grunted derisively while pointing at the screen. 'What's the use of that? I look as much like these people as I do the Queen Mother.'

'Never heard of the white heat of technology, Arthur?' Norman clicked on the photograph of a gasman and selected CUT. 'Look on my works, ye mighty, and despair.'

The photo disappeared from the screen, leaving a blank box on the card.

'Pass me the newspaper, Nick, will you?' Norman said, already beginning to grin at the thought rattling around in his devious brain.

He riffled through the paper with mounting glee, tore out a picture and slipped it into the scanner. A couple more clicks, and the identity card now sported the image of the Pope.

'Well,' Norman said. 'Are you impressed, or are you impressed?'

'I think "gobsmacked" would be more appropriate,' I replied, prompted by Arthur's gaping mouth.

'I can edit all the other information, too,' Norman said proudly. 'Name, address, telephone number. Once the card has been scanned into the programme you can change it however you wish.'

He added a computer-drawn handlebar moustache and a pair of thick glasses to the face of the Pope. Substituted 'John Paul II' for the existing name, 'Vatican City' for the address. Sprawled back in the chair beaming up at us.

'You old rogue.' I bit back the smile that would only serve to encourage him. 'I hope you realise that, as someone released from prison on licence, I cannot possibly condone such deception.'

Norman gave a please-yourself shrug.

'But,' I added, 'I think we'll go for the gasman. Who in their right mind is going to argue with someone searching for a leak?'

'Just let me have a passport photo, Arthur,' Norman said, happy again. 'A few minutes' work, a quick pass through a laminating machine, and Bob's your uncle.'

'And here was I,' I said, 'thinking Toddy was the forger.'

'For a professional job on something like a passport, you can't beat Toddy. He's a real artist. Can fool the most experienced Immigration man. But for anything this simple, that won't ever be subject to close examination' — he waved his hand immodestly in the air — 'then all you need is the services of a gifted amateur.'

Outside, a car door slammed.

'All I need now,' I said, swallowing hard, 'is the services of a passing brain surgeon. Changing Mary Jo's mind is a feat that can only be accomplished by a lobotomy.'

CHAPTER TWENTY-FOUR

Mary Jo stood on the threshold of the living room, taking deep breaths, mentally psyching herself up to step inside. She chewed gum in a desultory fashion while, with even less enthusiasm, taking an inventory of everything and everyone in the room. Her hazel eyes, so like Arlene's and yet so different, flashed at me. Moved quickly on to flit dismissively past Norman and Arthur as if they were inconsequential extras in an epic movie. Roved about in an evaluation of the furniture and fittings: the armchairs that were too utilitarian, the sofa with its too-conspicuous tartan car rug, the carpet that showed the effects of too many feet over too many years, the stereo too inadequate to play anything but the too-laughable collection of jazz CDs and cassettes, the rows of too-plebeian mass-market paperbacks. She turned to give her mother a deprecating look, visibly stifled a sigh, and finally took a pace forward.

Removing her red silk bomber jacket, she folded it deliberately inside out, vaingloriously displaying the Armani label and, at the same time, protecting the outside of the jacket from any risk of contamination by the flat or its occupants. She handed it to me with the same level of courtesy normally reserved for butlers and valets who are working out their notice. I ducked into the bedroom and threw it carelessly on the bed. Came out smiling sweetly.

Mary Jo lowered her eyes and placed her hands on her hips. She was wearing a shiny white Lycra muscle-top which emphasised her shoulders and all points south, and matching leggings tucked into hideously expensive brown leather cavalry boots. Not the most appropriate outfit for the English summer, but it certainly achieved her objective of projecting an Amazonian confrontational stance.

Control yourself, Shannon, I ordered myself. And, for crissake, don't ask her where she left the whip.

Mary Jo tilted her left wrist, glanced down at the man's gold Rolex — Arlene's charge account or gift from a rich admirer? — and tossed her head in an overacted piece of non-verbal communication that unmistakably said: 'Come on. The sooner we start, the sooner we finish.' Her dark hair swung round her neck in that manner you only usually see in shampoo commercials, then returned to nestle on the straining straps of her top. Her face was tanned. Her eyes were red-rimmed. So, I noticed sadly, were Arlene's.

'How was the trip from the airport?' I asked politely, a strained smile on my face.

'My trip was fine,' Mary Jo said. 'How was yours, Mother?'

'I don't understand,' I said anxiously. 'What happened?'

'We couldn't get all Mary Jo's luggage in the car,' Arlene said, rolling her eyes.

'Oh,' I said. 'We should have thought of that, I suppose.'

'That's not all you should have thought of,' Mary Jo said acerbically, 'from what Mother has been telling me.'

Good start.

'I'm Norman,' my friend said with the forced cheerfulness of a bomb-disposal operative. 'Pleased to meet you. We've heard so much about you.'

'I bet you have,' she said. Mary Jo gave him a withering look. 'You're the embezzler, huh?'

'I have that honour,' Norman replied, trying one of his cheesy grins.

It bounced off her invisible armour without effect.

'And this is Arthur,' I said.

He dipped his head in a respectful bow.

'You're the muscle,' she said.

'Yes. Er, no. Well . . .' Arthur stammered uncertainly.

'A drink, Mary Jo?' I asked, coming to his rescue. Christ, *we* all need one even if you don't.

'Yes,' Norman said, unusually straight-faced. 'What's your poison?'

I wish I'd said that. But I'm glad I didn't.

'How about a glass of Chablis?' I leaped in.

She gave a minimal shrug to show maximum indifference.

I fled to the kitchen.

Arlene followed.

'Didn't go to plan, then,' I said sorrowfully.

She fell into my arms. Threw her head on my shoulder. And started to cry.

'Don't worry,' I said soothingly. 'It'll be all right. She'll warm up after a few drinks. And so will Arthur and Norman. We'll turn her round. Who could resist the combined might of the Shannon clan?'

Arlene clung on to me, her body stiff, her shoulders giving little jerks to punctuate the flow of tears. I stroked the nape of her neck, gave her the support of contact, and waited. After a minute or two, I felt her catch her breath. She gave a last snuffle. Drew away. Scraped strands of damp hair away from her eyes. Looked up at me apologetically.

'There's something I have to tell you,' she said.

'You're not changing your mind, are you?'

'No,' she said, forcing a smile. 'It's Mary Jo.' She paused as if summoning up her courage, then blurted out: 'She's gone vegetarian.'

I couldn't stop myself.

I burst out laughing.

Here we were with a ton of assorted meat that had been lovingly cubed, marinated overnight, slid on to skewers and now was only minutes away from being placed over the flames of a barbecue — and we suddenly discover we're entertaining a vegetarian.

It was so totally bloody ridiculous as to be hysterical.

Maybe it was the tension that contributed to my reaction — my reflex over-reaction. I collapsed on to a worktop, clutched my sides in agony and felt the tears rolling uncontrollably down my cheeks.

Arlene stared at me incredulously. Then the infection spread. Her face began to quiver. A grin started to appear on her lips. Her mouth parted. And out came an eruption of laughter that rendered her as incapable as me.

'Norman's going to love this,' I said, as we rocked about in helpless mirth. 'Another Shannon plan bites the dust. And Arthur,' I spluttered. 'This means double helpings for him. It'll be all we can do to stop him sweeping Mary Jo up in his arms and planting a kiss of unending gratitude on her cheeks.'

'But what are we going to do?' Arlene asked, pulling herself together.

'Improvise,' I said, settling on the more prudent alternative than getting drunk to oblivion. 'I'll take in the drinks. Start oiling the wheels. Then we need to unskewer. Sort out the peppers and onions from the meat. Give them a wash, and stick it all back on separate skewers. Oh, and there's some Mozzarella in the fridge. By rights it should be Halloumi, but we can slice that up and grill it. I guarantee she'll be knocked out. Before this evening is over we'll have Mary Jo eating out of our hands.'

'I love you, Nick,' she said. 'So bad it hurts.'

Tears appeared at the corners of her eyes. I wiped them tenderly away with the tips of my thumbs. Kissed her lightly on the lips. Felt a knot forming in my stomach.

'I'm a lucky man,' I said.

And long may the luck hold.

'Right,' I said decisively. Switched to a Bilko voice. Clapped my hands. 'Busy, busy.'

She handed me the bottle of Chablis, stood to attention and gave me one of those crisp, economical American salutes. I swivelled on my heels and marched back on to the battlefield.

'Mary Jo's studying psychology,' Norman said enthusiastically. 'We've been having quite a chat.'

'He's a Freudian,' she said. 'I'm a Jungian.'

Surprise, surprise. Mustn't let oneself be on the same wavelength as an embezzler.

'Fascinating,' I said, pouring the wine. 'What's the difference?'

'Freud,' she said, fixing me with cold eyes, 'focused far too narrowly on one aspect of personality. He was obsessed with sex.'

'Well,' I gulped, 'if you'll excuse me for a moment, there's a few last-minute preparations to make before I start cooking.'

'You cook?' she said. 'Is there no end to your talents?'

'He's a good cook,' Arthur said supportively. 'You should taste his steaks. Pink and juicy. And he does this lamb dish — what do you call it, Nick?'

'*Kleftico*,' I mumbled, at the same time sending Arthur a warning grimace in an effort to persuade him to change the subject.

'The meat just falls off the bone,' he said unheedingly.

'Fascinating,' she said mockingly.

'Of course, cooking wasn't all he learned in prison,' Arthur continued proudly. 'I taught him how to look after himself. And Norman trained him to be an accountant.'

'Isn't that a bit like Hitler taking classes in Human Rights?' she asked.

'Have you seen our garden, Mary Jo?' I said, taking a firm grip on her elbow and manhandling her outside.

I turned her round so her back was to the house. Put on a big smile in case Arlene happened to glance out of the kitchen window. Brought my face close — very close — to Mary Jo's.

'Let's get one thing straight,' I said, my voice thick with menace. 'You can badmouth me as much as you like. But don't insult my friends, Mary Jo. They don't deserve it.' I squeezed her arm and looked unswervingly into her eyes. 'Now, you get back in there and be politeness personified or I'll put you over my knee and give you the biggest damn spanking of your life. In front of everybody. Do I make myself clear? Humiliate them, and I'll pay you back treble. Understand?'

'You'd do it, too, wouldn't you?' she said, seeing me in a different, uncompromising light.

'Right at this moment, Mary Jo,' I said, 'nothing would give me greater pleasure.'

'OK,' she said, raking her hair back with finger and thumb and staring at me defiantly. 'This is strictly between you and me from now on.'

'That suits me fine,' I said. 'Inside, Mary Jo. Act like Pollyanna. Be as sweet as blueberry pie. You could even try a smile. Wouldn't hurt too much, eh? Who knows — with a bit of effort you may even get to like them.'

'Liking them wasn't part of the deal, Shannon.'

I watched her walk back indoors. Lit the gas on the barbecue. Regretted not buying a bigger spit. Still, I doubted if they made them that big — what was she, five foot ten in her cavalry boots? And, in any case, the meat would be far too tough.

* * *

'I'll help,' Mary Jo announced to everyone's surprise.

'Barbecues are normally a man's prerogative,' Norman said.

'Why?' Mary Jo challenged.

'I think,' Arlene said, 'it's something to do with mere women not knowing how to burn food properly.'

'And, apart from that,' Norman said with a smile, 'the general idea is to stand there, glass of wine in hand, getting slowly sozzled while talking about the technicalities of spin bowling.'

'That's a most kind offer, Mary Jo,' I said, hiding my suspicions. 'I'm very grateful.'

But not taken in.

She was up to something. Leopards and spots, you know?

'You boys,' Arlene instructed, 'can set the table. I'm just going to freshen up.'

'Arthur,' Norman said uncertainly, as she walked towards the bedroom, 'is it knives on the left or on the right?'

Mary Jo and I ferried the laden plates out to the garden. I placed the Chinese pork kebabs on the griddle — they'd take the most time to cook — and listened to the sweet sizzle as drops of *hoi sin* marinade hit the white-hot lava rocks.

'Was this baby planned?' Mary Jo asked.

Don't beat about the bush, Mary Jo, I thought. Come on, now. Why don't you tell me what's on your mind?

So much for Norman explaining the rules. Hadn't she understood that we were supposed to discuss Chinamen, googlies and flippers? Contraception wasn't on the agenda.

'Yes,' I said patiently. 'It was planned. But, to be honest, neither of us was expecting such immediate results.'

'Macho man strikes again, huh?'

'I'd rather see it as fate.'

'And what a fate,' she said acidly. 'Especially for you. Sharing my mother's house. And her money.'

'It's not like that,' I protested. 'I'll pay my way. I've got a job lined up.'

'One that my mother arranged for you,' she pointed out.

'Does it make any difference?'

'What's the matter with you, Shannon? Don't you have any pride?'

'Love has no pride,' I said. 'Maybe one day you'll discover that fact for yourself, if . . .' I stopped myself just in time.

'If what, Shannon?'

'It doesn't matter,' I said, concentrating on turning the pork kebabs and adding the chicken satay to the grill.

'If any man will have me? Is that what you were going to say?'

'Maybe I was,' I said shamefully. 'And, if so, it would have been unfair. You would have been due an immediate apology.'

Jesus, I didn't know how much longer I could keep this up. Each new piece of bait she dangled in front of me was becoming increasingly difficult to resist. My temper was flexing its muscles, testing the limits of the gossamer thread that was keeping it in check. Any moment now it would snap — like the jaws of a crocodile.

I took a pace back from the heat. Lit a cigarette. Counted to ten.

'Mary Jo,' I said calmly, seriously, sincerely, 'I know how you must feel.'

'Oh, do you?' she jumped in. 'I very much doubt that.'

'Let me explain something to you. Arlene loves you. Our marriage, the new baby — they aren't going to change her feelings towards you.' I drew on the cigarette, hoping that the pause would allow the words to sink in. 'You're a big girl now, Mary Jo. It's about time you settled for a share of Arlene's love, rather than selfishly demanding all of it. And it's also time you let her lead her own life. However she likes. With whomever she likes.'

'I've got money,' she said. 'How much would it take for you to leave my mother alone?'

I shook my head disbelievingly. Hadn't she listened to a bloody word? Was I just wasting my breath?

'I said you could badmouth me, Mary Jo. Not insult me.'

'Worth a shot,' she said, shrugging her shapely shoulders.

'Not when you hit your own foot, it isn't.'

'So there's nothing I can say or do?'

'Nothing. Why not accept the inevitable with good grace? Give Arlene your best wishes. Make her day.' Punk.

'I'll think about it,' she said magnanimously.

'Don't take too long, Mary Jo. Or it might not be interpreted as an adult's act of due consideration, but as a sulky child's way of inflicting punishment.'

* * *

Mary Jo did think about it. Throughout the entire meal she toyed with the food, from time to time distractedly popping a morsel of grilled cheese or sweet red pepper into her mouth and trying hard not to look like she was enjoying it. Her conversation was limited to a series of noncommittal grunts and ambivalent shrugs. It wasn't my idea of politeness personified, but at least she'd stopped short of actually crossing the boundaries of common decency.

She drank sparingly, as did Arlene. The rest of us altruistically accepted the burden of their share along with our own. Bottles of red wine disappeared with indecent but, bearing in mind the mitigating circumstances, justifiable haste.

Arthur leaned back in his chair, rubbed his stomach appreciatively, took a long slow sip of wine and gave a broad smile. 'Gorgeous,' he said.

Norman nodded his agreement.

Arlene fiddled with her bracelet and waited for the complete set of compliments.

Don't hold your breath, Arlene.

Predictable silence from Mary Jo.

I raised my eyebrows at Arlene to let her know it really didn't matter. Sometimes the best motto is 'Expect little. Be satisfied with less.'

She frowned back. Made a small, and unnecessary, adjustment to the angle of the thin strap of her fuchsia-pink dress. Chewed at her lower lip. Turned her head to address her daughter.

'Well?' she asked. 'Isn't Nick a good cook?'

'Not bad for an accountant,' she replied.

'But we don't think of Nick as a mere accountant,' Norman said. 'I would class him more as a financial problem-solver.'

'I can imagine he's very good at that,' Mary Jo said.

'I'm not so sure at the moment,' I said, pretending not to have noticed the intended offence of the throwaway line.

'Don't be modest, Nick,' Arlene said, proudly continuing her sales pitch for yours truly. 'You've pretty much solved the murder.'

'You're involved in a murder?' Mary Jo asked brightly.

It was the first time I had ever heard even a hint of enthusiasm in her voice. She didn't fool me. I knew what was going through her mind. It wasn't the murder itself that had sparked her interest. It was the thought — the hope — that there might be danger involved. For me.

'Only unofficially,' I said. It was the truth, for one thing. And, for another, the more I played down the role, the less encouragement it would give her. 'I actually work with the Fraud Squad.'

'And with the DEA,' Arlene said. 'Nick's very much in demand.'

'The DEA,' Mary Jo said sceptically. 'Mother, *really*.'

'It's true,' Arlene said angrily. 'The DEA wants Nick to close down a money-laundering operation.'

Whoops. Loud miaow from cat escaping from bag. Arlene closed her eyes and sighed.

'And what do you get out of it?' Mary Jo said to me.

God, she was a bitch. But a perceptive one at times.

There were two ways to play it from now on.

I could say nothing, and give warning looks round the table so that the others remained tight-lipped, too. That was the safe option. But also the one that would make Arlene feel worse about her slip of the tongue. And the one guaranteed to keep Mary Jo in her place as an outsider to our circle.

Or I could give the leopard one last chance to change its spots. Hold nothing back in an overt demonstration of absolute trust. Grant Mary Jo inclusion to our group, our extended family.

Oh, well, Shannon. Go for it. Nothing ventured, nothing gained. And, if Mary Jo flunks this test, surely Arlene will recognise a closed mind when she sees it; and, having accepted the inevitable, Arlene would be set free.

'In return,' I said, bullet bitten, 'the deal is that I'll be granted a visa for permanent residence in the United States.'

'I see,' she said. Hope was springing eternal now in her excitedly heaving breasts. So it wasn't all cut and dried after all. 'And how exactly are you going to keep your side of the bargain? Tell me more. It sounds exciting.'

'Yes, Nick,' Norman said. 'Do tell us more.'

'I have a plan,' I said.

Norman and Arthur groaned.

That was grossly unfair.

They didn't *always* go wrong.

CHAPTER TWENTY-FIVE

'Let's recap for Mary Jo's sake,' I said, sending a clear signal to the others of my intention to trust her. 'What do we know about Prospekt?'

The table had been cleared. Glasses refilled. Body postures changed. It wasn't a dinner party any more — but had it ever been? A full-blown council of war was now in session.

'First,' I said, 'we know they're laundering drugs money.'

'But we can't prove it,' Norman pointed out.

'Second,' I continued, determined not to let him interrupt the flow of the argument, 'the money starts off on the street with the pushers and works its way up the chain until it ends in an anstalt account in Liechtenstein. And, from our previous dealings with Prospekt — their black-market currency scam — we even know the name of the bank and the number of the account.'

'Which is of absolutely no use at all,' Norman countered, 'because the Liechtenstein bank wouldn't let the police or the DEA get their hands on the money even if we could prove they were laundering.'

'Don't hit me with the negative vibes, man,' I said in a hippie monotone.

'May I remind you,' Norman said officiously, 'that the whole basis of the Liechtenstein banking system — their entire bloody economy, for that matter — is founded on the sacred principle that their bank accounts are inviolable. Un-bloody-touchable. Totally safe from the police authorities, and the tax authorities, of any country in the world.'

'In that case,' I said, casually brushing aside his objections, 'we have to move the money to a place where it can be touched. And provide a trail that can be followed.'

'Oh, well,' said Norman, 'that's it, then. Problem solved. We can all relax. Congratulations, Nick.' He raised his glass and peered searchingly at me. 'Just one teeny weeny question. How exactly are you going to perform these two simple tasks?'

'I haven't quite worked out all the details yet,' I said with a dismissive wave of my hands. 'The plan is still pretty much' — I searched for a suitably reassuring phrase that wasn't too far from the truth — 'in embryonic form. But at least we've set our objectives.'

'And what about our constraints?' he said. 'You don't seem to have touched on them so far.'

'What do you mean?'

'Number one: that, however this — for want of a better word — *plan* is executed, it must not involve you in anything illegal. No sense in going to all this effort to obtain a visa for the States only to break the terms of your licence and get hauled back to jail in England.'

'Licence?' Mary Jo asked. 'What licence?'

'Nick is a convicted murderer, Mary Jo,' Norman explained. 'In this country, murderers cannot be paroled like other criminals. But they can be released "on licence" from the Home Secretary. Any breach of the law and the licence is revoked. Wham, bam, slammer time, ma'am.'

Arlene's brow furrowed, her lips pursed as she contemplated the consequences.

'Constraint number two,' Norman said, 'is that none of us must be exposed to the remotest chance of being killed. Or injured. I'd add mildly inconvenienced, but I suppose that's too much to ask.'

'I wouldn't put anyone in danger,' I said, nodding my head in agreement. 'And, as for myself, I won't take any unwarranted risks.'

'Promise,' said Arlene, reaching across to take my hand.

'I promise,' I said, proceeding smartly on. 'Now, let's iron out the details.'

* * *

'Money laundering,' I said, beginning an exposition designed partly for the benefit of Arthur, Arlene and Mary Jo, but also in the hope of putting a creative spark to my own thought processes, 'has three distinct stages: immersion, soaping and spin dry.

'Immersion — the loading of the washing machine, if you like — is the most vulnerable of the three stages. This is where the laundryman has to pump money — cash, traveller's cheques, postal orders — into the banking system without arousing suspicion. Once the money is in place, the soaping can commence — moving it in and out of different bank accounts, dummy or shell companies, anywhere and everywhere, to create a maze so complex that it is virtually impossible to find a route to the clean money from its original dirty source. Finally comes the spin dry — the point where the washed funds are taken out of the machine and put back into circulation.'

I scanned the faces round the table to check that everyone was still with me. Encouraging signs mostly. Arthur was struggling, but he'd get there eventually.

'OK. Let's forget about the middle stage for the moment. Our targets need to be set on the first and the last.'

'I don't understand what you're trying to do,' Arlene said.

'Prospekt have been successful at laundering their ill-gotten gains for two reasons. One, they've locked their money away in a safe haven: Liechtenstein. And, two, they've managed to spirit it there without leaving a trail.'

'So?' asked Arthur.

'We're going to make a trail,' I said. 'A paper trail. From start to finish.'

Norman nodded his head sagely, the teacher and pupil naturally on the same wavelength. 'I get it now,' he announced, grinning from ear to ear.

'Well, I'm glad someone does,' said Arthur. 'Maybe if I had another glass of wine.'

'Maybe,' I said, smiling. I picked up the bottle and held it over his glass. 'Answer a simple question and you win a refill.'

Arthur looked dubious. 'How simple?'

'Who were the Smurfs?' I said.

'That's easy,' he said with relief. 'Donkey's years ago. Kids' TV. Bunch of little people in funny hats.'

'Correct,' I said, topping up his glass.

'Brilliant,' said Norman, slapping me on the back. 'You'll need Toddy's help, of course, but that shouldn't be a problem. You know, Nick, this could actually work.'

'Try not to sound so surprised,' I said.

'Slow down, you two,' Arlene said, shaking her head. 'I'm lost.'

'Think of Prospekt as a sort of chain store with branches across the country.' Immediately I'd finished the sentence, I realised that this was deep water. But I'd started now — might as well swim to the opposite shore. 'Its customers,' I said solemnly, 'are the addicts — the vast proportion of whom are teenagers, some as young as thirteen or fourteen, who have to steal, push a little crack or heroin themselves, or prostitute their bodies to finance their habit. The retailers — stalls set out on the streets — are the drug dealers. But who feeds all the money into the banking system?'

'The smurfs,' said Norman.

Arthur looked perplexed. 'You're having us on, aren't you?' he said. 'Or have you finally flipped?'

I shook my head.

'In the jargon of the money launderer,' I explained, '"smurfs" are the little people. The runners. The foot soldiers in a military-style operation. They collect the cash from the dealers.

'Each smurf has his own route, his own list of banks which he visits daily to make deposits. Smurfs favour large branches where the staff are generally too busy to pay much attention to cash deposits. They work in small geographical areas — city-centre high streets, mainly — where there is a high concentration of branches of different banks: that allows them to visit the maximum number of banks in the minimum amount of time. We, dear friends and accomplices, are going to feed our money to the smurfs. It'll be like a game of Fox and Hounds. We use a smurf as the fox. He scatters our paper to create a trail for the hounds — the police — to follow. All the way to the lair — the earth, I suppose, if we continue the analogy — of Prospekt.'

'OK,' Arlene said, running her fingertip thoughtfully over her lips, 'I think I just about understand the theory. What I don't see is how it works in practice. If these smurfs are dropping so much paper into the system, how will the police know which pieces to follow?'

'Because our paper,' I said, 'will be different.'

'Our money,' Norman chipped in, 'will be funny. Absolutely bloody hilarious. That's where Toddy, master chef and master forger, comes into the picture.'

'We alert a bank to the existence of the forged money and make sure that its progress is tracked along the chain.'

'And how are we going to do that?' Arlene asked.

'We're going to write a memo to all counter staff and plant it on the City and County computer.'

'At the risk of sounding repetitive,' she said, 'how are we going to do that?'

'Good question,' I said. 'And one, I must confess, to which I do not have a good answer. I've made one attempt already to hack into their computer, and failed miserably.

Tried all the stock passwords, but none of them will open the door.' I steepled my fingers, tapped them against my mouth in frustration. Then, with determination, said: 'But there must be a way.'

Arlene smiled at me. 'You'll think of something,' she said encouragingly.

'Let's park that problem for the moment,' I said, touched by her faith in me, 'and proceed to the second part of the plan. Objective number two. Moving Prospekt's assets from Liechtenstein to a place where the police can freeze 'em, and seize 'em.'

'Hey, hold on,' Mary Jo said. 'Didn't someone say something about breaking the law and losing your licence? Moving assets sounds to me very much like a euphemism for stealing money.'

'On the contrary,' I said, before Arlene could panic, 'all we are going to do is move the money held in a Prospekt account in Liechtenstein to a Prospekt account in London. Admittedly they won't actually have sanctioned it, but it isn't technically stealing.'

'OK,' said Mary Jo, her eyes alight with enthusiasm, 'I'll be the stooge this time. How are we going to transfer the money to a new account in London?'

Mary Jo had said *we*. She was actually identifying with us. This was looking distinctly promising.

'We transfer the money,' I said, 'by getting into the City and County computer.'

Norman sighed loudly. 'Which takes us back to square one,' he said.

'Picky, picky,' I said. 'No plan is completely without its weak links.'

'And this one more than most, it seems. Correct me if I'm wrong,' he said confidently, 'but doesn't the entire plan rest on this particular "weak link"? No signpost to the funny-money trail. No new account to be frozen. Nothing works unless we can get into the City and County computer? A computer that has already resisted your best efforts?'

'I'll help you,' Mary Jo said.

I stared at her with utter amazement.

'Pardon me if I seem ungracious,' I said, 'but why would *you* help *me*?'

'I've been thinking,' she said.

What was this? A barbecue-dinner variant of St Paul's conversion on the road to Damascus? Had Mary Jo seen the light?

'You haven't told us everything, have you?' she said perceptively. 'I think you've missed out an important point.'

I looked at her innocently.

'The trail has to go from the very start to the very finish, right?' she said.

Smart cookie. I'd underestimated her.

'But,' she said, 'the smurfs aren't the very start of the trail. The dealers are. To get the money to the smurfs, you have to go via the dealers. You're intending to feed the money to the dealers, aren't you? And there's only one way that can be done. By buying drugs.'

I raised my eyebrows noncommittally. Took a small sip of wine as a delaying manoeuvre.

'It seems to me,' she said, frowning reflectively, 'that you *are* putting yourself — and your licence — at considerable risk.' She paused. Swallowed hard. 'You could have refused this Agent Toomey's deal. Told him to take a hike. But you didn't. You're not going to all this trouble, taking all these chances, for yourself, are you? You're doing this for Mom.'

'We want to live in America,' I said matter-of-factly. 'To do that I need a permanent-residence visa. Once you accept that fact, everything follows from there.'

Mary Jo looked in turn at everyone round the table. 'What I'm gonna say isn't easy for me. So I'm only gonna say it once. I don't want any interruptions, or,' she said, fixing her eyes on me, 'any wisecracks. Is that clear? OK.' She cleared her throat. 'I was wrong about you, Nick. And you were right about me. I have been selfish. I apologise, Nick.

To you, and your friends.' She grabbed hold of Arlene's hand, squeezed it very tight. 'Gee, Mom, I'm so sorry.'

'Oh, honey,' Arlene said, smiling through the onset of tears.

'Let me make it up to you, Mom. And to Nick. Let me help.'

'Thanks for the change of heart, Mary Jo,' I said, 'and for the offer. But I don't see how you can help.'

'I'll get us into the computer,' she said.

I shook my head unbelieving. Maybe she wasn't so smart after all.

'This isn't simply a case,' I said, 'of tapping in your credit-card number and waiting for the computer to say "That'll do nicely".'

'I know that, Nick,' she said. 'In fact I know a helluva lot about computers.'

'I thought you were studying psychology.'

'I dated the Professor of Computing at Taft for a while,' she said.

Trust Mary Jo. Couldn't have been some spotty-faced nerd of a freshman — just had to be the bloody professor.

'He liked to impress me,' she explained. 'Couldn't resist showing me how easy it was to hack into computer systems. I'm sure I could do it. What accounts, what passwords have you tried?'

'The usual,' I said. 'SYSTEM. FIELD. USER.'

'They're all VMS accounts,' she said glibly. 'Did you consider that the operating system at City and County might not be VMS, but UNIX instead?'

'No,' I admitted. Not that it would have done any good. The sum total of my knowledge of UNIX could be written on the back of a cigarette packet — probably had been at one time.

'Of the two operating systems,' Mary Jo said with an annoying air of authority, 'UNIX is the one that has the most security safeguards built in. That's why the banks prefer it.'

'If it has the most safeguards,' I asked, 'then how do you expect to hack in?'

'Because I know a magic password,' she said proudly. 'One buried so deep in the dozen user manuals that only the very dedicated would ever come across it. One so obscure that only the very best hackers would appreciate its significance. And one that I have personally witnessed infiltrating the computer of a top-secret military establishment in the States.'

'OK, then,' I said, trying to ignore her look of superiority. 'I'll buy it. Tell me the magic password.'

'Un-huh,' she said, grinning impishly. 'That's *my* secret. And my insurance that you, or my protective mother, won't exclude me from all the excitement.'

Great. We'd gone from the frying pan to the fire in one mighty bound. The plan didn't now depend simply on getting into the City and County computer; it hinged entirely on Mary Jo getting into the City and County computer. I sighed, appreciating that, even if leopards could change their spots, beggars still couldn't be choosers.

'It looks like you're a fully fledged member of the team, Mary Jo,' I said. 'Welcome.'

'Just hang on a minute,' Arlene said. 'Don't I have a say in this?'

'Of course,' I said. 'Go ahead.'

'You promised you wouldn't take any risks,' Arlene said.

'I promised I wouldn't take any unwarranted risks.'

'Don't be so damned pedantic,' she snapped back at me. 'Any risk to your licence is unwarranted. And any risk to Mary Jo. Tell Agent Toomey the deal is off.'

'But we've almost cracked it,' I protested.

'Nick,' Arlene said earnestly, 'I've sat here listening to you talk about counterfeit money, buying drugs and breaking into computers. And, not content at putting yourself in jeopardy, now you've got my daughter involved, too.'

'OK,' I said calmly, 'I hear what you say.'

'Thank you,' she said triumphantly.

'But—'

'What do you mean, *but*?'

'But,' I said emphatically, 'what if we can come up with a way that doesn't involve any of us buying drugs or passing counterfeit money? Will you compromise on the minor matter of breaking into a computer?'

Arlene hesitated.

'And,' Mary Jo said supportively, 'it would be me actually doing the hacking. Nick wouldn't be doing anything illegal. And I can hotfoot it back to the States if anything goes wrong. Which it won't, Mom.'

'It makes sense,' I said.

'Well,' Arlene said, weakening under the two-pronged assault.

'Go on,' I urged. 'Where's your sense of adventure? And it's all in a good cause. We benefit — you, and me, and the baby. And so would thousands of kids when we put Prospekt out of action. Think of the temptation we would be removing.'

Mary Jo hugged Arlene. 'Say yes for me, Mom. It's the only way I can make up for being so stupid. Please, Mom. Please.'

'No risks?' Arlene said.

'No risks,' I said. 'Unwarranted or otherwise.'

'Very well, then,' she said sighing.

'Thanks, Arlene,' I said gratefully. 'And thanks, Mary Jo.'

* * *

Mary Jo and Arthur shared a cab back into town: she to the opulence of the Savoy, he to the basic one-bedroom flat in Soho where the hot-wok smells from the Chinese restaurants mingled with the cheap scent of the streetwalkers. Norman insisted that Arlene relax with a cup of coffee while he and I tackled the debris in the kitchen and went into Planning Subcommittee mode.

I was dead on my feet, the result of the lethal cocktail of zero sleep, mental exhaustion and the emotional drain of the battle with Mary Jo. The prospect of bed seemed like heaven, but there were still items to tick off the checklist, and one final act of persuasion to achieve, before I could retire with a clear mind.

Norman poured two large brandies and we set about our twin tasks of washing up and filling in the flesh on the bare bones of the plan.

'Mary Jo was right, wasn't she?' he said, as the last plate was stacked away in the cupboard.

'About what?' I said innocently. He was fencing with me. Probably already knew the essence of what was coming. But not the substance of the favour I would ask.

'When she said you had missed something out. But she wasn't completely right, was she? There was one other vital element of the plan that you failed to mention.'

I nodded. It was only fair to let him do all the talking now. In a moment he would be speechless.

'Gaining access to the City and County computer is only half the problem, isn't it?' He stared at the brandy glass as if calculating the trade-off between the benefit of the pleasure of the drink itself and the cost of a befuddled brain. 'That will allow you to set up an account for Prospekt, sure, and to send an instruction to transmit funds to the new account. But the Liechtenstein bank won't transfer one penny without the necessary authority. It's not just the magic password you need, is it?'

'No,' I said. 'We also need the key that unlocks Prospekt's account. The verbal key, that is. Their codeword.'

'And how do you propose to obtain the codeword?'

'There's a man called Tippett who won't object to doing me a little favour. Tippett is a burglar. I'm going to ask him to break into Prospekt's offices.'

'Aren't we stepping into the dangerous realms of illegality again?'

'I don't want him to steal anything. I doubt that someone as smart as Corkscrew would take the risk of writing the codeword down anyway. I want Tippett to bug their phones.

When Prospekt next give instructions to transfer money, the bug will record the codeword. What's theirs becomes ours.'

'Yes,' he said thoughtfully, elongating the word into three dubious syllables. 'But what guarantee do we have that Prospekt will actually transfer funds in the foreseeable future?'

'None whatsoever,' I said, picking up the brandy glass and sipping with tantalising slowness. 'Unless we tempt them to do so, that is.'

'And what appetising titbit do you intend to dangle before Prospekt's avaricious eyes?'

'Have some brandy, Norman,' I said.

'Why?' he said. 'Am I going to need it, Nick?'

'Yes. Undoubtedly. Because I want you to place an advertisement in the *Financial Times*. A very tempting offer for sale. An asset that no company who wants to switch its business interests to America would be able to resist. The Windsor Club.'

'What!' he exclaimed. 'You're asking me to sell the Windsor Club at a mouth-wateringly bargain price — and, therefore, drop a million or two in the process — just so we can learn Prospekt's codeword? Isn't there a better way? By better, I mean one that isn't going to cost me a packet.'

'I'm not asking you sell,' I said. 'That would be too much of a favour. I'm simply asking you to *offer* the club for sale.'

'H'm,' he grunted, interested but reserving his rights.

'My idea is that we cook the books. Make the club look like it's profitable — which it is, so that part won't be difficult — but also make it seem desperately strapped for cash. It has to appear that without an immediate injection of funds the business will fold.'

'You know, Nick,' he said, looking at me searchingly, 'I'm beginning to believe the pupil might have finally surpassed the master.'

'What I thought—'

'Don't tell me,' he said quickly. 'That would spoil the fun. Let me see if I can still predict how your mind ticks.'

He picked up his glass, swirled the brandy, and took a long, slow, contemplative sip.

'We need Prospekt to authorise a transfer of money quickly,' he said, thinking aloud. 'But an outright sale of the club would take too long. The due diligence investigation alone would eat up a couple of months that we don't have.'

I smiled, happy that he was following the same logical path as I had done a couple of hours earlier.

'But the size of the transfer isn't important,' he reasoned. 'The actual sum doesn't have to be large.'

I nodded, my confidence in the scam growing.

'We,' he said, 'correction, *I* am going to sell them not the club, but an option to buy it. At a discount, of course, for committing themselves financially.'

'No risk of you losing any money that way.'

'What do you reckon?' he asked. 'An escrow account?'

'Yes. Guarantees that their money is safe. They pay the option price into an escrow account; that means the money can't be touched without both their signature and yours. But the Windsor Club can use the collateral of the account to borrow from a bank and solve the supposed liquidity crisis.'

'It might work,' he said. 'As far as scams go, it follows all the rules. A high probability of a big gain for Prospekt with no apparent risk.'

'So why the *might*? What's wrong with *will*?'

'Two things,' he said. 'First, there's no guarantee that Corkscrew will see the ad or, if he does, take the bait.'

'All we can do is take a big space. Make it eye-catching — pack it out with lots of pictures of the golf courses, tennis courts, swimming pools and so on. And a large advertisement may help to give the impression that you're desperate to sell.'

'Just have to hope for the best, I suppose.'

'OK, what's the second thing?'

'As I said, the scam follows all the rules. The only trouble is that Prospekt don't play by the rules.'

CHAPTER TWENTY-SIX

I was outside the Savoy on Monday morning at nine o'clock sharp. Mary Jo wasn't.

The black-coated flunkey took a break from hailing taxis to scrutinise the Monte Carlo. A puzzled look crossed his face. I could tell what was ticking away in his calculating mind. Was the car an indication of the owner's eccentricity (and therefore to be tolerated among the waiting Jaguars and Mercedes) or of an inability to afford anything newer or better (in which case a tip for the privilege of parking in the cul-de-sac was out of the question)? He evidently decided to play safe. Contented himself with a nonchalant tug at his gloves, and positioning himself so that the moment my passenger appeared he could leap out and open the car door.

The engine idled. So did I. I riffled through the cassettes in the glove compartment, trying to decide which of my jazz collection Mary Jo would find least offensive. Settled on the MJQ. Cued up the tape so that John Lewis would start playing 'Summertime' at the touch of the button. Climbed out of the car and went through the muscle-straining task of lifting out the roof panel. I was stowing it in the boot when I felt a tap on my shoulder.

‘Just give me ten minutes, huh?’ Mary Jo said, already moving towards the door to the hotel. She was carrying three plastic bags. A response, I assumed, to my plea to dress down for the day at Future Assurance. ‘You’re supposed to be an impoverished trainee, remember,’ I’d cautioned. ‘No Chanel, no Armani, no gold Rolex. OK?’ She’d looked at me horrified, as if I’d suggested she should ride down the Strand on the back of a white horse like Lady Godiva through Coventry. But, anxious to see the site of the crime-to-be and test the magic password, she’d sighed, tossed her head and agreed.

I leaned back against the car and lit a cigarette. Smoked it. And then another. At a quarter to ten she appeared.

Do you ever get the feeling that you should have been more specific with your instructions? Mary Jo was wearing a navy blue pleated miniskirt, white blouse, blue-and-white horizontal-striped tie, and black high-heeled shoes. Her long hair was swept back and arranged into a bouncing ponytail. Give her a hockey stick and she would have been a dead ringer for head prefect at St Trinian’s. Inconspicuous she wasn’t.

I let out a silent groan and opened the door of the Monte Carlo. She slid in like a model in a car commercial: bottom first, long legs pulled in with knees clamped together.

‘Sorry to keep you, Nick,’ she said. ‘How do you like the outfit?’

‘Wonderful,’ I lied, at the same time working hard to blot out the visions of the male employees at FA leering at her, their minds soaring heavenward in flights of erotic fancy.

I swung the car round, nosed out into the traffic and headed east, choosing the more scenic riverside route past the Tower of London. We were late anyway, so what was the point hurrying? Might as well show her the odd sight and see if she said, ‘Gee, ain’t it cute?’

‘Great car,’ Mary Jo said, nestling into the contoured seat. ‘And great music, too.’ She hummed along merrily.

I kept my eyes firmly on the road. Don’t look a gift horse in the mouth, they say.

* * *

Miss Soup of the Day — Pat, the receptionist of orange-blouse fame — stared at Mary Jo, frowned, and deliberated the problem. 'She's not on my list,' she said.

I bent down conspiratorially over the desk. Adopted a so-you-think-you've-got-problems expression. Whispered in her ear. 'Sprung on me at the last minute,' I moaned. 'Trainee from the Boston office. Over here to broaden her experience.' I rolled my eyes. 'I drew the short straw.'

She smiled understandingly at me. 'I'll call Meg,' she said.

Ten minutes later, Mary Jo having shown admirable restraint while being confronted with Pat's long list of questions, we had the necessary card and were swiping our way past the yellow zone of Admin and into the ice blue of Accounts.

'What do you call this?' Mary Jo asked under her breath as her eyes roved over the hessian.

'Sixties retro with individual chromatic boundary delineation,' I said. 'Or, more succinctly, as Arthur would put it, "bloody 'orrible".'

'He's not as dumb as he looks,' she said.

I introduced Mary Jo to a stunned Meg — oh, brave new world that auditors should dress like this — enquired politely about her weekend and made enough small talk to exhaust the available subjects and thus ensure that she wouldn't disturb us for the hour or so remaining before lunchtime. I dragged an extra chair over to the desk I had appropriated by the fire escape. Mary Jo sat down. 'What now?' she said.

'We wait,' I said. 'Give everyone a chance to settle down.' After the excitement of your arrival. 'When their noses are pressed up against screens or eyes focused on the papers on their desks, we'll switch on and test your magic password.'

I took off my jacket. Spread the contents of a randomly chosen file around in a haphazard, but hopefully importantly busy, fashion. Chewed a pencil with an air of deep concentration. And scanned the room, head down, pupils raised. Too many pairs of eyes pointed in Mary Jo's direction. She crossed her legs, displaying an inch of tanned thigh above a stocking-top. Eyeballs hit the floor. At this rate it looked like we would have to skip lunch. Dinner, too, if the novelty of her outfit was slow to wear off.

'Maybe you should come and sit beside me,' I said, deciding the only chance was to screen her from view.

'So what do you actually do?' Mary Jo asked, when she had settled herself again.

I didn't flatter myself that she was seeking initiation into the esoteric world of accounting; killing time was my guess. I reckoned her threshold of boredom was lower than a limbo pole at the world championships.

'I used to be in Acquisitions and Mergers,' I said. 'Kind of like a financial doctor, I suppose. Checking out the health of companies, seeing what nasty diseases lurked under the surface. Producing a diagnosis so that the price for a takeover bid could be set.' I lowered my voice. 'Now I'm mostly concerned with fraud, either as part of the Fraud Squad or, like this current job, in an auditing role.'

Tresor entered the room. Registered our presence — mine with the normal disdain, Mary Jo's with abnormal curiosity. Walked purposefully across to Meg. The eyes in the room had someone else to watch for a while.

'Now's a good time,' I said to Mary Jo.

'You provide the cover,' she said, switching on the terminal. 'And no peeking.'

'Don't you think you're carrying this secrecy stuff a bit too far?'

'Strictly a need-to-know basis,' she said. 'And, as I said before, it's my insurance. I don't want you going it alone. I want to be in at the kill.'

She was already into the FA computer and knocking at the door of the gateway to City and County Bank. The toe of her high-heeled shoe tapped impatiently on the carpet.

'I don't press another damn button until I see you talking to those two.' Her head jerked at Tresor and Meg.

Well, she was only eighteen. Allowed a few childish moments. And who was I to cast the first stone against the infantile glass house?

I walked slowly over to Meg's desk. Hovered in the background while they talked earnestly. Tresor noticed me out of the corner of his eye. Gave me a well-what-do-you-want-now look that made up in unambiguity what it lacked in warmth and tolerance. I took a couple of paces forward. Wittered on about how grateful I was to them for allowing Mary Jo to sit in on the audit and the Fraud Risk Analysis; how it was the only way for trainees to learn the ropes and the tricks of the trade; how we wouldn't get in anybody's way or disrupt proceedings. I was just running out of wordy platitudes when Mary Jo caught my eye and signalled me back with a wink.

'There you are,' she said triumphantly.

The City and County logo blared forth from the screen. A list of menu options glowed appetisingly.

'You're sure this password of yours has system privileges?' I asked. 'We can access any program we like?'

'There's nothing we can't do, Nick,' she said, smiling. 'Absolute power.'

Bloody hell. She'd done it. An eighteen-year-old spoilt brat — well, ex-spoilt brat — had cracked a bank's computer system. The prospect, the consequences, were frightening.

* * *

'Time for lunch,' I declared, wondering what their vegetarian alternative would be. *Vegetables solo*, I suspected.

Mary Jo and I passed through the turnstiles into the barley-white restaurant. She excused herself to use the 'bathroom'. I picked up two trays and surveyed the day's delights on the blackboard. In bold capitals a dyslexic had revealed himself (or herself — mustn't make assumptions) to the world by chalking up 'MATELOAF' and 'VEGTABLE

BEAK'. It was a good job it wasn't a pub: 'BRA MALES' didn't bear thinking about.

Mary Jo returned, her face red, her ears looking like they would emit clouds of steam at any moment. She grabbed a tray from out of my hand and stamped her foot as we waited in the queue.

'What's wrong?' I asked. 'Vegtable beak not to your liking?'

'You British,' she said disdainfully. 'To think you used to say that we Americans were oversexed.'

I blinked at her uncomprehendingly.

'I've just been propositioned,' she said.

Didn't surprise me. Some guys paid good money to see a girl with Mary Jo's body dressed up like a schoolgirl. Whatever turns you on, I suppose. Within reason, of course.

'Who, where and how?' I enquired nosily.

'I don't want to talk about it,' she said unequivocally. 'Subject closed. OK?'

I shrugged. 'Let's join Plimpson,' I said. 'You'll be safe with him, at least.'

Plimpson was sitting alone, looking miserable. He took one look at Mary Jo and instantly fell in love. She thrust out her hand in greeting. He shook it with an awestruck tentativeness as if he considered himself unworthy to touch the flesh of this vision of loveliness, blushed profusely and stammered a greeting which came out something like 'Holog'.

'Hello, Plimmers,' I said jovially in an effort to cheer him up and grab his rapt attention. 'How you diddling?'

He looked down at the grey brick of meatloaf in the lake of thin gravy on his plate. Pushed it aside with a natural lack of enthusiasm. Turned his almost colourless eyes towards me. 'I've been given my notice,' he mumbled.

'Not more redundancies?' I said, shaking my head in sympathy. 'Surely an insurance company can't do without an actuary. Or — don't tell me — is this another one of their misguided economy measures? Decided to replace you with some government-subsidised sixteen-year-old with certificates in knitting and needlework. To hell with it, Plimmers. You'll be better off out of this place.'

'Only if I manage to get another job,' he said gloomily. 'And that depends on what sort of reference I'm given.'

'No problem, surely?'

'They're blaming me.' He looked across at me all doe-eyed and plaintive. 'But it's not my fault. I tried to tell them about the laws of probability. But they wouldn't listen.'

Probably — in all probability, that is — would have fallen asleep if they had.

'I'm listening,' I said. 'You can tell me, Plimmers. What exactly are they blaming you for?'

'The company's losses.'

'That's a bit harsh, isn't it?' I said, sensing a scapegoat being tethered in preparation for the ritual sacrifice.

'They say I got the sums wrong. "Claims exceeding premiums equals financial suicide, Plimpson." But probabilities don't work like that. The laws only apply in the long run.'

The great economist John Maynard Keynes once said, 'In the long run, we're all dead.' I kept the quote to myself. As philosophy goes, it was accurate enough — just not very comforting when you're in Plimpson's shoes.

'I know what you mean,' I said. 'In the short term, as any card player will testify, you can have a run of phenomenally good luck, or abysmally bad. But in the long term the luck evens out. The best player always wins. The fittest survive. The natural order of things is restored.'

'It seems I've run out of time as well as luck,' Plimpson said with a shake of his head. 'Two bad years in a row. They're not intending to take a chance on a third.'

'You know what you ought to do,' Mary Jo said, prodding the bake viciously to see if a piece existed that wasn't shrivelled to fossil fuel. 'Tell 'em to stick their lousy job where the sun don't shine.'

'Mighty fine advice, Mary Jo,' I said, wondering if at any moment the ingenuous actuary would ask what Manchester had to do with it. 'With sweet-talk like that, how could the hardest heart resist giving Plimpson a glowing reference?'

'Yeah,' she said, 'but think of the warm glow of satisfaction instead.'

Stephanie and Tresor entered the restaurant. His shiny black hair caught the beams of the fluorescent light and bounced them around the room with a reflective effect that was like a kind of bizarre snow blindness. Mary Jo stared. 'Damn phoney,' she said angrily. 'Yuk. Let's go. I need a drink to take away the sour taste left by wandering hands.'

I was still working my way through the confusing mixed metaphor when she jumped up from the table. Her chair scraped noisily back. Heads turned. Blends in like a chameleon, does Mary Jo.

She stood there, hands on hips, looking down at me.

I rose hastily.

'Remember,' she said to Plimpson. 'Where the sun don't shine.'

* * *

We walked to the Cox and Eight in silence, Mary Jo still brooding on being the unwitting, and unwilling, boost to Tresor's feel-good factor. She trip-trapped along on the high heels, skirt swaying in the breeze, bringing forth the occasional appreciative toot on the horn from the more sexist of the passing motorists. Even an ambulance, siren wailing urgently, slowed down for a better look.

The conservatory was so hot you could have baked pottery inside. We took our drinks over to a quiet table in an ill-lit corner of the cool main bar. Sat on a pair of those velour-covered ultra-low stools that send people limping off to the nearest osteopath for spinal manipulation. I looked round the room. It was gratifyingly underpopulated — maybe there was some hope for good taste after all: just a few solitary diehard drinkers and a handful of policemen. Not that the two sub-sets of the drinking fraternity are mutually exclusive; far from it usually. Both groups stared mournfully into pint glasses, the diehards without speaking, the policemen in an exchange of grunts which was like the first draft of the script of *Ten Million Years BC*.

'What a dump,' Mary Jo said, sipping at a mean measure of white wine.

'Cheers,' I said.

'No,' she said. '*Cheers* it ain't. As sitcoms go, this is more like *The Munsters*.'

'Not all pubs in England are as bad as this,' I said, defending my country. Most, but not all.

'So,' she said, looking at me with the tilted head of interest, 'you're like a sort of detective? Catching crooks and fraudsters.'

'That makes it sound more exciting than it is,' I replied. 'Much of the job is routine checking, that's all. The requirements are an ability to concentrate and a whole heap of good luck.'

'How do you mean?'

'Take computer fraud, for example. Only one in ten is actually uncovered during a formal audit: over half are discovered by pure accident, some little clue ringing an alarm bell and prompting a deeper investigation.'

'Where do you start, then? What do you look for?'

I took out a cigarette and lit it reflectively. Mary Jo frowned.

'You should try gum,' she said, placing a stick on the table.

'I can't chew gum and drink at the same time.'

'You sound like a polite version of Gerald Ford,' she replied. 'He couldn't talk and—'

'Aren't we straying from the subject?' I interrupted, not wishing to contemplate the ex-President's flatulence problem.

She shrugged. 'Go on,' she said, her eyelashes fluttering. 'Knowing what you do, and how you go about it, helps me understand you better, Nick.'

'Most fraudsters aren't very clever,' I said modestly. 'For instance, they often give themselves away by acting abnormally. An accounts manager who is on the fiddle may not take all his holidays, and just have a few days off at a time because he's frightened that someone else will do his work and spot whatever it is he's up to.'

She nodded, a mixture of understanding and encouragement to keep talking.

'And then there are the stupid mistakes,' I said. 'One of the most popular frauds is the false-invoice racket. Someone in the accounts department, for instance, either on his own or in collusion with others, slips a false invoice from a company he controls into the system and authorises it for payment. The cheque is sent out, and the fraudster pockets the money.'

'What's stupid about that?' Mary Jo asked, finishing her wine.

'Do you want another?' I offered.

'No,' she said, screwing up her nose. 'When you're finished, we'll head back.'

She picked up the stick of gum, unwrapped it, bent it in half and popped it in her mouth.

'Nine times out of ten,' I said, 'all I need to do is flick through the file of invoices, and the phoney one stands out a mile.'

'How's that?'

'Because the fraudster overlooks one blindingly obvious point. Authentic invoices arrive through the post — folded.'

'And the false one,' she said, nodding wisely, 'has been slipped into the pile — unfolded.'

'Exactly.'

'It's that easy?' she said, clearly disappointed with the secrets of my trade.

'Just as long as you keep your wits about you,' I said.

Her jaw moved the gum around with a growing lack of interest, reminding me of the bored girl in Administration robotically going about her production-line job.

'Oh, no,' I said out loud as the thunderbolt of realisation struck inside my mind.

I dropped my head into my hands.

You fool, Shannon.

As long as you keep your wits about you.

How about practising what you preach for a change? And not allowing the claustrophobic nightmares of the safe to distract you.

I grabbed Mary Jo's hand. Nearly yanked her off the stool.

'Come on,' I said. 'We've got to get back.'

'What's the rush all of a sudden?'

'She was folding proposal forms,' I said, pulling a perplexed Mary Jo towards the door. 'Folding bloody proposal forms.'

'Slow down,' she protested as we stepped into the blinding light outside the pub. 'For one thing, I can't keep up in these shoes. For another, I haven't a damn clue what you're talking about.'

'Chewing gum is the clue, Mary Jo,' I said, scooping her into my arms and hugging her in an explosion of gratitude.

She pushed me away. 'Being sexually assaulted twice in one day isn't my idea of fun, Shannon. Even though you win hands down. You better explain yourself. And pretty damned quick.'

'Sorry,' I said. 'But it all makes sense now. Whitley's murder. The motive. Everything slots into place.'

'Not for me, it doesn't.'

'Two things have been bothering me. One is why Whitley didn't defend himself — and I think I have that sussed now. The other is why kill a man who has no money? Whitley was supposedly cleaned out by his ex-wife. Meg told me that. Brother James would certainly have been aware of that fact, too. So, if you're the beneficiary of his empty-coffered will, what is the point of killing him?'

'*None* would seem to be the logical answer,' she replied. 'Although my thought processes are a little disadvantaged by not knowing goddam Whitley or Brother James from Adam.'

'I'm willing to bet that Whitley *did* have money. A lot of money. Enough to kill for.' The adrenalin was pumping through my body as the excitement, the sense of elation, rose inside me. 'Plimpson didn't miscalculate his probabilities, or suffer from a run of bad luck. Whitley was on the bloody fiddle. Only it wasn't phoney invoices. Christ, if it had been, I would have spotted it straight away. It was phoney claims. When I checked through a batch of proposal forms there was one that was as pristine — and as unfolded — as the day it came out of the printer.'

'So what are we going to do now?'

'Get Stephanie to open the safe again. And go through every file, even if it takes all night.'

'Oh, Jeez,' she said, screwing up her face at the prospect. 'Must we? It's not that I'm averse to hard work but—'

'That's the down side of the job, I'm afraid. It's not all instinct, intuition or flashes of inspiration. We need proof. And there's only one way to get it.'

* * *

And get it we did.

Stephanie was absolutely thrilled to open the safe again. Stood there hands on hips, looking daggers at Mary Jo and me. 'I thought you were finished with the records,' she'd said accusingly. 'Weren't going to bother me anymore.' I gave her a shrug, and offered no explanation. That would only have slowed down the investigation. And I wanted Collins to be the next to know. Let him decide what action to take. On the fraud and the murder.

And Mary Jo was positively ecstatic about trooping in and out of the safe carrying bundles of dusty files that left grubby marks all down the front of her white blouse.

We went through the files in tandem. It was easy now we knew exactly what we were looking for. By five-thirty we had a pile of a dozen files, each containing a tell-tale virginal proposal form. Bingo!

By the time Stephanie arrived back, anxious to lock up for the night, Mary Jo had hidden eleven of the files in a separate pile at the back of the safe.

The twelfth I had slipped into my briefcase — evidence for Collins, and an aid for myself when explaining to him exactly how Whitley had defrauded Future Assurance. To the tune of over a million pounds.

CHAPTER TWENTY-SEVEN

There was a note on my desk when we got back from the safe. 'Ring Mr Collins,' it said. The message was timed at four o'clock. The word 'Urgent' had been added, underlined in red, but otherwise ignored by the problem-passer of a message-taker.

I dialled, wondering where he was — not at Holborn or at home, it appeared. An anonymous voice answered by unhelpfully repeating the unfamiliar number (or, more accurately, just the last three digits as if, to save time, she had started speaking before actually picking up the receiver). She put me on hold, that telephonic equivalent of limbo designed to allow the application of nail varnish or the selection of horses to back, depending on the sexual orientation of the operator. The insensitively synthesised sound of 'Air on the G String' jangled discordantly in my ear. Bach spun in his grave. I drummed my fingers on the desktop impatiently. Stopped as soon as I realised I was subconsciously keeping time with the music. Shook my head in shame. Smiled helplessly at Mary Jo.

'You took your time,' Collins barked at me.

'Your patience,' I said, with sufficient pause to let the sarcasm filter slowly through, 'will be rewarded. I've got the name of the murderer.'

'You're too late, Shannon. I'm looking him in the eye right at this moment. Get over here now.'

It wasn't exactly the standing ovation I had been expecting. *Well done, Shannon. Brilliant work. Such insight. Such impeccable logic.*

'Where are you?' I asked, dejected.

Collins laughed.

'The autopsy room,' he said.

* * *

I parked next to Collins's Rover at the rear of the sprawling grey-brick teaching hospital. Pushed open one half of the heavy semi-transparent — would a pessimist say semi-opaque? — plastic double doors, checked in with the head porter and followed the complex set of directions down to the bowels of the building. The stone stairs echoed eerily with each knee-jarring footstep. The walls were painted in an injudicious shade of pale green, which had the seemingly impossible effect of making the building feel even colder than it was. No warming rays of sun ever found their way down here. This was the land of harsh lights and giant refrigerators with long pull-out drawers. I shivered as another layer of the onion peeled away, leaving me feeling sad and alone.

Mary Jo had volunteered to make her own way back to the Savoy. Enquired about the quickest route. Decided to try the foot tunnel from Island Gardens to Greenwich Pier and from there catch one of the river taxis. Maybe take the train another time, she'd said. That way see some different sights.

What sight would I see?

I pushed open the final set of doors, the plastic sheets banging loudly behind me. An intense vinegary smell of industrial-strength chemicals kicked at my nose with all the force of a bad-tempered mule suffering from incurable toothache. I caught my breath and coughed involuntarily as the vapours hit the back of my throat. The receptionist smiled understandingly, handed me a shiny green apron, black plastic overshoes that looked like pixies' bin liners, white mask and paper hat. Led me through to a room where Davies was bent over a stainless-steel table doing indescribable, but unfortunately not unimaginable, things to an unknown body.

'You made it at last,' Collins said from his ghoulish vantage point at the pathologist's left side.

'Good to see you, my boy,' Davies said cheerily, laying down a scalpel. It clanged against the metal of a kidney-shaped receptacle. Why did it have to be kidney-shaped? What was wrong with a plain old unsymbolic rectangle?

I stood lurking by the door and coaxed my lips into a weak smile. Then realised that it was hidden by the mask. Raised my shoulders in an equally weak shrug.

'Don't you want to see Whitley's killer?' Collins asked with the confident challenge of a man with a strong stomach.

'He doesn't have to,' Davies countered. 'We know his identity.'

'It's OK,' I said, taking manly strides towards the steel slab. 'I can handle it.'

Davies and Collins stood back. I looked down at the naked body. Saw a white toe with a green tag on it. The red line of an incision running from the pubis up to the neck, bypassing the navel like it was a major city on a motorway. And then my eyes settled immovably on the face of Mickey. Or, rather, what was left of the face of Mickey.

* * *

I came round in a large leather chair in Davies's office. A distant voice said: 'Drink this.' A blur pressed a small glass into my hand.

I wasn't in any position to argue. The brandy made me choke but brought the swirling walls slowly back into focus.

'Lucky that Chris caught you,' Davies said.

Collins grinned inanely. Lit two cigarettes and passed one to me.

'Jesus,' I said, drawing the smoke into my lungs like a drowning man gasps for air. 'What happened to him? His face?'

'His body was found at lunchtime,' Davies said. 'Washed up on the shore opposite the Pumping Station. Two hikers came across it as they were walking along the Thames Path. Poor souls — they won't be doing much sleeping for a while. Not a pretty sight, even I have to admit. Fish probably had the left eye and the soft tissue of the cheeks and lips. As for the other head injuries, my guess is that at some stage in his travels down-river he was hit by a boat. Or a barge, maybe. Not that it makes any difference. Complicates matters, though.'

'How do you mean?' I asked.

'I can't be absolutely certain of the cause of death.'

'Are you saying he didn't drown?' Collins said.

'I'm saying I can't be absolutely certain. There are too many imponderables, too many possibilities.'

'Terrific,' Collins sighed.

'Sorry to be unhelpful, Chris,' Davies said. 'But the body doesn't show the classic signs of drowning — lungs aren't waterlogged, no presence of choking mucus foam, no stones or waterweeds in his hands or under his fingernails, no algae in the stomach — but, then, again, that's not unusual in a case like this.'

'A case like what?' I said, not getting the drift.

'The man died of a condition known as "reflex cardiac arrest". The question is what brought it on.' He rubbed his chin and contemplated the many options. 'It could be due simply to the shock of hitting the cold water. Or he may have been dead when he entered the water. The condition is also caused by extreme intoxication — either too much alcohol or an overdose of drugs. Judging by the sorry state of this man's arm, I'd plump for the latter. It's possible he had a heart attack and then fell in the river.'

'Mickey was a registered addict. Supposed to have kicked the habit, though.' I paused for thought. 'When did he die?'

'Hard to be precise until I get the results of the test on—'

'I know,' I said, recalling the gruesome conversation in the restaurant, 'the vitreous humour.'

'Late Friday night,' Davies said, screwing up his face to indicate he was punting. 'Or early Saturday morning.'

'He was still alive just after ten on Friday night,' I said.

'I'll try to forget you said that, Shannon,' Collins said with a groan. 'Let's not add any more complications, eh? Keep the information to yourself. The last thing we want is for you to be pulled in for questioning.'

'I thought we were talking off the record,' I said defensively.

'Well, if anyone asks, play a different tune, Shannon.'

'Any fresh needle marks?' I said to Davies, moving back to what should have been the main topic. 'Ones that would coincide with the time of death?'

'Just scabs,' Davies answered.

'Could you have missed one?' I asked, in pursuit of a theory. 'A place where you wouldn't expect, maybe?'

'Hang on a minute,' Davies said, catching my drift and hurrying out of the office. 'I'll check again.'

'What are you thinking, Shannon?' Collins asked with mounting interest. 'The local police are convinced that your friend Mickey is the killer — Whitley's credit cards were found in Mickey's pocket. Are you telling me they might be jumping to the wrong conclusion?'

'Wouldn't be the first time,' I said, raising my eyebrows. 'You had me down as a prime suspect in a murder case once, remember?'

'With good reason,' he grunted.

'It was a bloody hunch,' I said accusingly. 'And you know it.'

'Is that what you've got now? A bloody hunch?'

'Maybe,' I said. 'Let's see what Davies has to say when he gets back.'

'Fresh needle mark,' Davies said obligingly when he returned.

'Which arm?' I said.

'Left,' Davies said, nodding his head sagely. 'Like you thought.'

'Doesn't fit, then,' I said.

'What do you mean?' Collins asked.

'He was left-handed,' Davies explained. 'I can tell from the superior muscle development in his left arm.'

I nodded, thinking back to the first time I had seen Mickey. The coating of sawdust down his right side, arising from the right foot being placed forward to operate the lathe and steady the left hand. And, of course, the brandishing of the right arm at the refectory table.

'A left-handed addict injects himself in the right arm,' I said.

'And Whitley was killed by someone who was right-handed,' Collins said excitedly. 'He couldn't have done it.'

'It doesn't necessarily follow,' I said, feeling the need to play devil's advocate.

They both stared at me.

'Brother James is a hypnotist,' I said. 'Is it possible, Trefor, that Mickey, while in a deep trance, could have been implanted with the suggestion to kill Whitley? And to use his right hand when doing so? That would certainly confuse the forensic evidence. Seemingly put him in the clear.'

'Your imagination knows no bounds,' Collins said.

'It's not totally impossible,' Davies said, 'but I don't buy it. Hypnotism isn't as powerful as the layman believes. It can't be used to force someone to do something that is against their nature. If Mickey didn't want to kill Whitley, I don't think he could have been made to do so. No matter how good a hypnotist this Brother James is.'

That was reassuring news, at least. My anxieties over what I might have done in those missing hours eased back a notch or two.

'Mickey was extremely jealous,' I said, probing further. 'If he thought Whitley was trying to steal his girlfriend . . .'

'I doubt if that would be sufficient stimulus,' Davies said dismissively. 'The important issue is why was Mickey killed? Because the evidence of the needle mark in the left arm suggests that he didn't inject himself. Someone else did it. Someone who didn't know — or perhaps forgot in the heat of the moment — that Mickey was left-handed. Furthermore, the evidence would now also suggest that he was pretty near death when he was given the injection; otherwise there would be signs of a struggle — scratches on the arm, perhaps.'

'Blow to the head?' I ventured.

'Possible,' Davies said. 'But unprovable, given the post-mortem injuries from the boat.'

'Whatever,' I said, 'Mickey was a danger to someone. Had to be removed. For good.'

'OK,' Collins said decisively. 'This is the way I see it. Brother James killed Whitley. Motive: beneficiary of will. Mickey witnesses the murder, or simply puts two and two together. Tries to blackmail Brother James. Finishes up swimming with the fishes — Luca Brazzi fashion.'

Collins looked around for support for his hypothesis. 'So,' he said to me, 'who were *you* going to name as the killer?'

'Brother James,' I said. 'Means: one chisel, plus a touch of hypnotism so that Whitley doesn't put up a fight — no defensive marks, remember? Motive: money. Lots of it.'

* * *

'Whitely was pulling a scam,' I said, taking the file from my briefcase and laying it on the desk next to the tray of tea that had been brought in at the professor's request. 'A big scam. What started off as a search for Metcalfe's difference of fifty-four pounds led me to a pot worth over a million.'

Davies settled back in the chair, sipped his tea and reached for a chocolate biscuit. Collins took possession of my unwanted brandy.

'He was slipping false life assurance policies into the system and claiming on them. It all began with this one.' I handed Collins a proposal form. 'It's a policy on Whitley's son — he was killed in a car accident. Whitley considered himself responsible.'

'How do you know it's not genuine?' Collins asked.

I went through the accountant's lesson about unfolded bits of paper. 'Then there's this,' I said, passing Collins an A4 sheet of paper with FA's logo at the top. 'A letter to another of FA's customers. It says there was an administrative error when issuing his policy, and that the wrong reference number was allocated. Gives the insured person a new number.'

'So?' Collins said.

'Whitley couldn't just write a policy for his son, you see: if he took the next number to be issued in the sequence, then it would show that the proposal form was submitted after the death. That would be spotted when the claim was made. So,' I said proudly, 'he switches numbers with a policy that was in existence prior to his son's death. The false policy now predates the death, a new number is issued to rectify matters, and the claim can be submitted.'

'As easy as that?' Collins said.

'Not quite,' I said. 'Whitley would have needed two supporting pieces of paperwork to substantiate each false claim. A copy of the Grant of Probate — simple enough to forge by altering a genuine one that has been scanned into a computer.' Thanks, Norman, I thought. 'It would need impressing with the seal of the Probate Office — that's trickier, requires the assistance of a person with some skill in metalwork who won't ask any awkward questions. But a large wad of cash would dampen curiosity, I imagine.'

'And the second piece of paper?' Collins asked.

'An original death certificate. But, again, that's not a major problem.'

'Sure,' he said, 'when he was claiming in respect of his son. But how did he get death certificates for the other phoney policies? For people who never existed?'

'My guess is that they did exist,' I said. 'I reckon they were real deaths of real people. As reported in the obituaries of local papers.' Thank you a second time, Norman. 'Whitley reads the when and where of the death, and applies to the local registrar for a death certificate. Must seem an innocent enough request for the finance director of an insurance company to make. Probably looks like he's being caring, sensitively saving the family fuss and bother.

'Of course,' I continued pensively, 'he's still got a lot of covering up to do. The cheques can't be made out to Whitley himself — that would ring deafening alarm bells at the audit. For each claim, the payee would need to be a false name at a false address. Then Whitley removes the envelope containing the cheque from the post tray, and opens a bank account in the name of the payee. But he can use the accompanying letter as proof of identity. All a bit sweaty for Whitley, granted, but you can buy a lot of deodorant for that size of payoff.'

'How many times did Whitley pull this trick?'

'Twelve. Each one for slightly less than a hundred thousand pounds — that's the ceiling where a medical is required before the policy can be issued. I like to think,' I said, 'that his motive at the beginning was based on contrition, not greed.'

'You know your problem, Shannon,' Collins said, sighing loudly. 'You're a bloody romantic.'

'When Whitley's son was killed, just imagine the guilt. And the pressure on his relationship with his wife. I believe he made the false claim in order to use the money as a kind of peace offering, or to help them both in making the difficult transition to a new life without the boy.'

Collins gave me a condescending shake of his head. 'So why pull eleven more swindles?'

'Whitley and his wife split up. She cleans him out. Whitley — a tormented soul — discovers the opiate of the masses: religion. The first swindle was so easy he decides to repeat it. Whitley uses some of the money, penance-style, for the good cause of funding St Jerome's. Keeps the rest hidden in his bank account to leave in his will. That way it's not really stealing — more a redistribution of wealth.'

'Would you believe it?' Collins said to Davies. 'The dead man was a bloody latter-day Robin Hood.' He turned his face towards me, his nose wrinkling as if a nasty smell was coming from my direction. 'And Brother James is Friar Tuck, I suppose?'

Even for a so-called romantic that was stretching my credibility too far. Not that I wouldn't have liked to believe it, I must admit. Brother James's work had a base in morality, and he seemed to be more effective in the fight against the evils of drugs than Collins and I.

'No,' I said. 'I wouldn't go that far. I think he's a man with a mission, though. A personal crusade. One that turned into an obsession and spurred him to kill. Twice now. But he can probably justify it to himself — ends and means. The Jesuits used the same reasoning. Then there were the Franciscans and Dominicans — atrocities committed by the likes of Torquemada and the Spanish Inquisition.'

'So how do we prove it?' Collins said.

'I hope that was a rhetorical question,' I said.

'Unfortunately not,' he sighed. Then he brightened as a thought crossed his mind. 'Is Brother James the sort of man who would give us a confession — if I sweat him a little?'

'I thought you weren't allowed to do that sort of thing anymore.'

'Let's say it's a hypothetical question,' he grinned.

'Wouldn't work,' I said. 'Too much conviction, too much faith. Think back to the Inquisition again. Plenty of so-called heretics burned to death without admitting their sins.'

'Trefor,' Collins said, switching to another tack, 'any chance of proving a connection from the chisels?' He turned to me in clarification. 'CID confiscated all the tools from St Jerome's.'

Davies shook his head. 'Let's suppose there was blood on one of the chisels. We could certainly run a DNA test to match it to Whitley's. But the most that would achieve is to establish the murder weapon. Even if Brother James's fingerprints were found on the same chisel that wouldn't constitute proof that he was the murderer. He could have touched the chisel at any time. Sorry, Chris, but I don't think forensics will be able to help you build a case against him.'

'Are those drugs still hidden in the building?' Collins asked me.

'As far as I know,' I shrugged.

'I'll get him pulled in for possession. What can we lose?'

'No,' I said hastily, seeing the ruination of my plan for Prospekt swimming before my eyes. 'Don't do that.'

'Why not, Shannon?' he asked.

'Like I said before, he won't confess. All you will achieve is to alert him of our suspicions. Brother James isn't going anywhere. It'll be another few weeks before probate is granted on Whitley's will and the money can be paid out. Let Brother James think he's got away with it. Maybe he'll make a mistake.'

'And maybe he'll kill someone else,' Collins said thoughtfully.

'Look,' I said reasonably, 'I have to go back to St Jerome's. Give my condolences to Rhiannon — Mickey's pregnant girlfriend. Let me see what I can find out. Mickey might have told her something.'

'OK,' Collins said, surprisingly easily. 'You try it your way.'

I gave him a suspicious look.

'But, at the same time,' he said, 'we also try it my way.'

'And,' I said, knowing there was something a lot more devious than his arm up his sleeve, 'what might that be?'

'A little blackmail of our own, Shannon,' Collins said with a smile. 'Enough to panic him to show his hand. Tempt him to commit another murder.'

'Sounds dangerous,' I said.

'Don't worry, Shannon,' he said matter-of-factly. 'I'll protect you.'

CHAPTER TWENTY-EIGHT

I knew very well the plan to put Prospekt out of business had more holes than a mindlessly vandalised sieve. (I suppose, when you think about it, you have to be mindless to vandalise a sieve. Or, giving it even more consideration, does a mindlessly vandalised sieve end up with fewer holes than the original?) What the hell. The essence of what I'm trying to say is that I didn't need Agent Toomey to point it out.

'Don't like it,' he said, the economy of his clipped Midwest speech underlining his absence of enthusiasm.

'Thanks for the vote of confidence,' I said touchily. 'Always good for morale to give your troops a stirring speech before they go off to battle.'

Toomey shrugged predictably. Stared around reflectively.

The three of us were sitting on a wooden bench in St James's Park, Arthur taking up one half, Toomey and I squashed together in the other. I reckoned that we looked conspicuously like characters in a John Le Carré novel, especially with Toomey in full Langley outfit of dark blue suit, Ben Sherman button-down-collar shirt and striped tie. Passers-by, justifying my opinion, swerved in their strolling to avoid the unlikely trio.

It was Tuesday, just after midday, and sunny. Englishmen were taking mad dogs for walks. Around us, groups of girls with short summer dresses hoicked up to tan their milky white thighs sat on thin jackets and aerated the grass with coy swivellings of their spiky heels. Packs of young men in sleeveless shirts propped themselves on their elbows and agreed targets in that 'Don't fancy yours' claim-staking manner employed the world over. Under cover of the nibbling of sandwiches or the licking of ice creams, the two halves of the population flirted. An intoxicating cocktail of giggles and coarse laughter filled the air. Except on our bench.

'Let me get this straight,' Toomey said, his thin eyebrows raised in an exaggeration of thought — or maybe it was pure scepticism. 'For this plan of yours to succeed' — he started counting off the drawbacks on his long fingers — 'you need to bug Prospekt's offices? Overhear a codeword? Get them to bite at an ad in the *Financial Times*? Transfer all their funds by hacking into a bank's computer? And organise a bunch of kids to buy drugs with counterfeit money?' He thrust his hand, five fingers erect, in my direction. 'Jeez, Shannon. What do you expect me to say? Its beauty lies in its simplicity?'

'Have you got a better idea?' I said, stamping on the butt of my cigarette and grinding it into the bare patch of earth under the bench.

'Hell, no,' he said, shaking his head as if already accepting defeat.

'Right,' I said. 'Then, we have no choice but to go with what we've got.'

'OK,' he said, smiling. 'But I don't like it.'

I groaned.

He smiled a little wider.

'Shall I thump him?' Arthur said eagerly. 'It can be very conducive to a man's level of commitment, can a good thump.'

'It's like a breakfast of eggs and bacon,' Toomey said enigmatically. 'The chicken's involved, the pig's committed. I'm involved, OK?'

Oink bloody oink, I said to myself.

'So,' I pressed him, 'when can you let us have the telephone bug, the listening equipment and instructions suitable for the non-technically minded?'

'That's easy,' he said. 'I have plenty of contacts in the embassy. Catch my wave, Shannon?'

Probably, I thought: he either meant 'drift', or it was Beach Boys Nostalgia Week and nobody had told me — or maybe they had and I'd forgotten, there being a lot more important things on my mind than California girls. Shows just how stressed I was.

'Tomorrow suit you?' he said, bringing me back from my tangent.

I nodded. 'And in the meantime you drop a word in the collective ear of the Liaison Group. Persuade them you have a cast-iron tip off from an unimpeachable source and that they need to stand by to organise a stake-out.'

'Zero problema, amigo,' he said. As if I wasn't having enough trouble decoding his English. 'After all the talking we've done lately, they'll be only too glad to get off their butts and grab some action.'

'And you'll start on the phone calls?'

'Yeah,' he said half-heartedly.

'Don't let me down, Agent Toomey. I don't want to get in sight of the finishing post only to fall at the final hurdle.'

'Give me a while,' he said.

'So when do I get my visa?'

'When it's all over, Shannon. You deliver on your part of the deal, I'll deliver on mine. We shook on it, didn't we? Hands across the ocean, remember? Don't worry. No sweat. OK?'

'If he welshes on me, Arthur,' I said without emotion, '*then* you can thump him.'

'Be a pleasure, Nick. Any particular type of punch or area of the body you'd like me to concentrate on? Straight left in the kidneys is pretty effective. But if you have any other preferences—'

'These things take time, Shannon,' Toomey said defensively, unsure whether to mark down the exchange as an example of incomprehensible Brit Wit. Nice to get one's own back. 'Wheels turn slow. You know? This is a waiver under Section 212(h) we're talking about. Has to go right up to the Attorney-General. You'll get your visa. Eventually.'

'Don't like it,' I said.

* * *

'Am I doing the right thing?' I asked Arthur, as we drove towards Docklands, the hard suspension dipping and rising in complaint against my friend's weight.

He wriggled in the woefully inadequate bucket seat of the Monte Carlo. Would have shrugged if there had been room.

'You're covering all the angles,' he said, after time for thought. 'That can't be wrong, can it? Don't worry. It'll work out fine.'

'Thanks,' I said, gripping the steering wheel tightly as we bounced up and down from the after-effects of an unavoidable pothole in the road.

'If it doesn't,' he said, raising his voice above the loud drone of the engine, 'and you end up staying in England, will you do something for me?'

'Uh huh?'

'Get a different bloody car, for crissake. Every time we hit a bump another of my fillings drops out.'

* * *

The anorexic, pale and gaunt, as insubstantial as a ghost, opened the door. She was wearing a shapeless dress over a shapeless body. Arthur's shadow fell across her and she stepped back as if afraid its weight might crush her. Looked past me and up at him apprehensively. He smiled. Her eyes flicked quickly away and settled questioningly on me.

'I've come to see Rhiannon,' I said.

A bony arm directed us to the refectory. A weak and worried voice instructed us to wait. I watched her walk from the room. Heard her open the door to the room of rituals. The simple action released the sound of soft chanting, the cloying fragrance of incense and, from within me, the dimmest of memories of my previous visit.

Arthur peered at me through the gloom. Walked purposefully to the windows, reached up and ripped down the sacking.

'That's better,' he said, as light poured in.

'Brother James won't like it,' I said.

'If I'm to protect you, Nick,' he said with an apathetic shrug, 'I have to be able to bloody see you.' He turned his attention to the sash window. Struggled with it like the damn thing had not been budged since Dickens' time when gin-swilling bargemen smoking clay pipes unloaded their cargoes to the tune of 'Oom Pa Pa'. He finally forced it open and sucked in air. 'It also helps if I can breathe,' he said with relief.

The stream of light brought the room to life, banishing the dark corners and flickering shadows to the plywood set of *The Munsters* where they belonged. The table, chairs and cushions fared less well: rustic and ethnic went out the window with the stale air, leaving only tacky behind.

I felt the presence before I saw any movement or heard any sound. Turned to see Brother James standing in the doorway, his arm around Rhiannon.

'What have you done?' he said, looking with horror at the discarded sacking on the floor. An act of sacrilege, his expression said. Or maybe it was the demystification that really upset him.

'We thought it was time to throw a little light on the subject,' I said. 'Let me introduce Arthur.'

In any other circumstances, Arthur would have clamped his eyes on the potential adversary and stared him down. But, matched against Brother James, he restricted himself to a wise dip of his head in acknowledgement, and focused his attention on Rhiannon.

It wasn't hard to do. Her beauty was timeless. Guinevere, Maid Marian, Botticelli's Venus, Mucha's model for his painting of autumn: Rhiannon could have been any of them, or all of them.

But not today, when her eyes were dimmed by the mists of sadness.

'Don't let Arthur's size give you the wrong impression,' I said. '"Out of the strong came forth sweetness."' I may not be the world's authority on biblical quotations, but I was a real expert on golden syrup labels. 'Arthur's a pussycat.' Behind me came a low guttural growl. 'Well, most of the time.'

'What do you want, Nick?' Brother James asked, his composure returning.

'I'd like to talk to Rhiannon. In private.'

He touched her shoulder lightly. She gazed at him in response — in obedience? — and then back at me. 'I have no secrets from Brother James,' she said.

Yes, but what about the converse, eh?

She walked to the table and flopped listlessly into one of the chairs. I bent down beside her and lifted the veil of hair from her face.

'I'm sorry about Mickey,' I said softly. 'Truly sorry. I know the pain. The hurt that's so deep inside it can't be reached. It will lessen.' But never completely go away.

She closed her eyes, and a tear squeezed out. I pulled her towards me and pressed her head to my shoulder. Started to rock her back and forth.

'We can care for Rhiannon,' Brother James said abruptly. 'The community looks after its own.'

The disciples, as if responding to some pre-set cue, filtered into the room. Formed a protective ring about their leader.

I stood up, sighing inwardly. Consulted my mental script — 'Cosy persuasive *tête-à-tête* with Rhiannon,' it read — ripped it to shreds and started rewriting hastily.

'Really?' I said. 'Your record doesn't support that assertion. First Whitley, then Mickey. I think you need a little outside help. And, besides, I'm the only one who can put things right. Settle the account for Mickey's death.'

'"Vengeance is mine saith the Lord,"' Brother James warned.

'Sure,' I said, 'but what did He say about justice?'

Nothing apparently, for Brother James didn't pontificate on the subject.

My confidence grew. 'I came here with a proposition for Rhiannon. But maybe you all ought to hear it. Sit down, please, while I explain.'

I sat myself down. Arthur pulled over a chair so it was at my right shoulder, turned it round, straddled the seat with his knees, and rested his thick forearms along the top, displaying the broad bands of muscles for all to see.

They had two options: evict us — fat chance, not with me handling the anorexic and Arthur the rest — or make themselves comfortable and listen.

'Well, Nick,' Brother James said, as they all took their places around the table, 'what is your proposition?'

'I don't remember much about the other evening,' I said, looking at him very briefly, but very meaningfully, in the eye. 'About what I did, or what I said. So I'll start at the beginning. Forgive me, won't you, if I repeat myself?

'For my sins,' I continued, 'I find myself assisting the police. To be honest with you' — but not totally so: just enough to gain your trust — 'I first came here to investigate Whitley's murder. I apologise for the false pretences.'

'You did tell us this,' Rhiannon said with a pained expression that I thought was probably more to do with memories of Whitley than with my needless repetition.

'I kind of thought I might have,' I replied. 'Mickey didn't take too kindly to it. He reckoned I was a spy. I suppose I was, but only as far as Whitley's death was concerned. How you operate, your histories, your past involvement in drugs — none of that really interested me. Until now, that is.'

Anxious looks were exchanged around the table.

'Mickey died of a drugs overdose,' I said.

'No,' Rhiannon said forcefully. 'He couldn't have. He wouldn't have. He was nearly there.'

'I'm sorry, Rhiannon, but there isn't any doubt. I saw his body myself. There was a needle mark in the crook of his arm.' I gazed around the table to assess their reactions. Mostly shock mingled with sorrow. All very natural — even from Brother James. It looked like I'd have to try harder to flush him out as Collins had directed. 'The overdose triggered a heart attack — reflex cardiac arrest, the pathologist called it. Mickey, it seems, then fell into the river and drowned. Poor Mickey,' I added, shaking my head and going all out for the sympathy vote.

'So what do you call justice?' Brother James asked. 'Are you going to offer us an eye for an eye? Because that's not the sort of death I would wish on anyone. And, anyway, it was suicide. His way of atoning for killing David.'

'Mickey didn't need to atone,' I snapped back at him. 'You're behind the times, Brother James. The police don't believe he killed Whitley any more. Mickey was left-handed, you know. Whitley was stabbed by someone who was right-handed.'

'Thank God,' Rhiannon said breathlessly. 'I knew Mickey wouldn't kill. Couldn't kill. I told you so, didn't I?' She looked pointedly around the table. The other disciples avoided her eyes in shame.

'No,' I said, making the word sound pensive rather than a part of the prepared script, 'Mickey wasn't to blame for Whitley's death. Or his own. All of you here know where the blame really lies.' I paused for dramatic effect, and in the hope that someone might point an accusing finger at Brother James. Silence. Well, it had been worth a shot. 'It's the people who put the drugs on the streets,' I continued, leading them down the chosen path. 'Those who tempt the adventurous innocents to try one tab, one smoke, one syringe. And then hold them prisoner for the rest of their lives. The drug barons, the smugglers, the dealers, the pushers — they killed Mickey. Without having to lift a finger, except to count their money.'

'We do what we can,' Brother James said helplessly. 'Rehabilitation is the first step to a fresh start.'

'I'm not knocking your work,' I said, 'and the success you achieve. But sometimes — like with Mickey — it's too little, too late.' I liked that phrase. Had heard politicians use it often. Didn't mean much, but sounded condemning in a forceful sort of way without actually being specific. 'What you do here, Brother James, is clean up the mess that the drug barons leave behind. I'm going to give you the chance to eliminate the pollution at source. Take drugs off the street.'

'Impossible,' he said with a world-weary shake of his head.

'Maybe,' I said. 'But we'll never know if we don't try. And you have to start somewhere.'

'What are you suggesting, Nick?' Rhiannon asked.

'Nick's not suggesting anything,' Arthur interrupted. 'He can't afford to, otherwise he finds himself back in jail.'

'Let's say I'm theorising,' I said. 'On what might happen if a large anonymous donation was to arrive at St Jerome's. Say a hypothetical twenty thousand pounds.'

Everyone sat up and paid very close attention.

'You might well decide that the best way to use that money — especially as you might discover it to be counterfeit — would be to buy drugs on the streets, thereby taking them out of circulation.'

'And the next day,' Brother James said haughtily, 'another batch would arrive, and we would have achieved nothing.'

'Not if the money you used — this very singular, very traceable money — provided the police with a trail to its ultimate destination. Then a company called Prospekt, the very worst of the drugs barons, could be shut down for good.'

'And this theory,' he said, 'would it work in practice?'

'Yes,' I said with a reassuring certainly. 'But only if one of you is prepared to make a sacrifice. In order to establish the first link in the chain, one of you has to be willing to be caught in the act of buying drugs. Someone has to be arrested. Admit everything. And testify against the dealers.'

'I'll do it,' Rhiannon said quickly. 'For Mickey.'

'No,' Brother James said angrily. 'You don't want the baby to start life in a prison cell.'

'I hope it won't come to that,' I said. 'I can't guarantee what will happen. Can't offer any deals with the police — there can be no risk of Prospekt's lawyers being able to claim "agent provocateur". But if you all do exactly as I say — as the theory says, I mean — then I think Rhiannon has a very good chance of finishing up with just a suspended sentence.'

'I'll do it,' she repeated, her eyes misty no more. Filled with purpose instead. 'I'll take my chances.' She looked at Brother James. 'I have to do something. Please.'

'And will the rest of you help?' I said, before he could start to work at dissuading her. 'The more of the money that can be fed into the pipeline, the greater the chances of success.'

'For Mickey,' Rhiannon said, pleading with the other disciples. 'Help me for Mickey.'

'For Mickey,' they nodded.

'Very well,' Brother James said. 'For Mickey. And all the others like him. In the past, and in the future. You shall have your justice, Nick.'

One can but hope.

'Here's what you do,' I said, smiling gratefully.

CHAPTER TWENTY-NINE

Two weeks later

I don't know what annoyed Tresor more — my continued presence at Future Assurance or my frequent absences. Not that I was losing any sleep over it: there were far more important issues rattling around in my brain and keeping me awake at nights. And not that I was deriving any sadistic pleasure from seeing Tresor's weary Oh-God-not-you-again expression whenever he encountered me in the building. Well, maybe just a little.

For the past fourteen days I had flitted in and out of Assurance Hive like a hyperactive bee with a short attention span. Sometimes I ventured in on my own, sometimes accompanied by Mary Jo, but always for just long enough to maintain the vital bolt-hole that would provide us with access to the computer when the time finally came. If it came at all, I was beginning to think.

Oh, for Alexander's sword to cut the Gordian Knot of a tangled web I had woven for myself. Collins was hassling me with increasing regularity about making some progress on flushing out Brother James. In turn, I was stalling him with excuses of decreasing credibility: I couldn't afford overtly to threaten or blackmail Brother James into revealing his murdering hand until his disciples had carried out their part of the plan; and they couldn't be sent out on to the streets until we were in possession of Prospekt's codeword and had tampered with the City and County computer system. Which meant that I couldn't reveal Whitley's fraud and untie the sacrificial lamb that was Plimpson, because at that point there would be no further reason for me to remain at Future Assurance.

It was during one of my expedient visits to FA that Tresor had actually had the nerve — the perception? — to ask me why I was taking so long.

'Fraud Risk Analysis,' I'd intoned, as if the words were a powerful magic spell that could cure all known ills (excluding mad cow disease, of course) and solve all the world's problems (except how to open one of those bricks of milk without spilling half the contents).

'I hope this is going to be worth it,' he'd replied.

'Oh, yes,' I'd said, thinking of the ease with which I had acquired a copy of the customer database as much as of the tale of Whitley raiding the corporate coffers. 'It'll be worth it.'

Plimpson worked bravely through his official notice, soaking up the accusing stares of those who regarded him as the source of all the company's problems and managing to keep a knowledgeable smile off his face. Softy Shannon strikes again — well, how could I let him agonise over his future when it wasn't necessary? He didn't know a fraction of what I actually had planned, or why it was so essential to keep our secret. And he never asked, trusting me that when the moment was right I would reveal everything and he would be back on the payroll permanently. Perhaps, too, it was Mary Jo's influence. Plimpson became glassy-eyed and dreamy whenever he saw her: if she'd asked him to leap off the top of Canary Wharf while whistling 'Dixie', I think he would simply have said, 'In what key, Mary Jo?'

Fourteen days doesn't sound a lot. And when you look at that span of time on a calendar your eyes only have to move down a couple of lines. But in reality it felt more like a whole millennium, even to someone who had learned the hard way all there was to know about patience. Everyone had done their job: Toddy had strained his eyes and given his artist's fingers a bad case of repetitive strain injury before printing off a batch of fake twenty-pound notes (good enough to fool a drugs dealer when pressed into his hand in one of those fleeting illicit exchanges, but poor enough not to withstand the scrutiny of an alert — and alerted — bank clerk); Tippett had successfully bugged Prospekt's offices and was now routinely recording every telephone call; Norman had placed the eye-catching advertisement in the *Financial Times*, received the hoped-for reply, met with Corkscrew, and laid out the lip-smacking deal; Agent Toomey had a battalion of plain-clothes officers standing on alert, armed with more cameras than MGM. The only thing left for me to do was wait. And pray that the fish swallowed the bait, hook, line and sinker.

If it hadn't been for Arlene, I'd probably have gone crazy.

She organised each day into a frenzy of activity that was designed to stop me thinking, and therefore brooding and worrying. We escorted Mary Jo around the Tower, Greenwich, Hampton Court and Windsor Castle; sat craning our necks at the ceiling of the Planetarium; schlepped around art galleries and museums; even hired a car to accommodate the three of us and drove up to Stratford where we did the unexpurgated Shakespeare tour.

In the evenings the three of us went to the theatre, the cinema, a jazz club over the top of a pub in the King's Road, and twice joined the other members of the clan for cosy meals where the topic of Prospekt was strictly *verboten*. Over a T-bone steak, Arthur reported back on the gullibility of the great British public during his unsurprisingly unsuccessful, and now redundant, snooping expedition in the Home Counties. What little he found backed up my earlier conclusions: Toby Beaumont was viewed as 'good for a laugh', which translated as sufficiently unsuspecting as to be a practical joker's idea of heaven; Tresor made a habit of coming home late to a wife who stretched the definition of shopaholic to new heights; Stephanie entertained regularly — wouldn't you know it? — on what was euphemistically described as a 'one-to-one' basis by a neighbour who took a fancy to Arthur and was lucky to escape with his life; and Meg really did have a garden that made the one at Babylon look like the council tip.

And, when the mornings and evenings were over, that left only the long nights. During these, Arlene concentrated on exhausting me physically then soothing me mentally. Sheer hell. Followed by a few hours of broken sleep.

She did it all willingly — some of it very willingly — and grew more contented as the relationship with Mary Jo continued to improve and the mother-daughter bond re-established itself with a new strength.

Norman had moved out of the flat and installed himself, in his guise of anxious and importuning businessman visiting from America, in the room next to Mary Jo at the Savoy. The two of them were getting on famously together, Mary Jo responding to Norman's grandfather figure. Some days he took over the escort duty of Mary Jo so that Arlene and I had time to ourselves. On the Tuesday, the fourteenth day after my recruitment of the troubled souls of St Jerome's, he received the fax. The deal was agreed, the option signed, and the money (two hundred thousand pounds) would be transferred to an escrow account at City and County.

The fish was hooked.

Now we had to reel it in.

* * *

'We're ready,' I said to Agent Toomey over the phone. Future Assurance's phone. If Whitley had been alive and wearing his finance director's hat, then, according to his hypocritical memos, he would probably have condemned the call as a blatant example of fraudulent use of company property. Pots and kettles.

Mary Jo was sitting in front of the keyboard for the penultimate time, waiting for an opportune moment to hack into the City and County computer. It was four in the afternoon. Too late to be able to open up accounts or transfer funds. But 'tomorrow is another day'. Today's objective was to ensure that our circular to all counter staff was beeping urgently at them, demanding to be read, when the bank opened for business in the morning.

'Arthur's making the delivery now,' I continued, speaking cryptically like George Smiley or Bernard Sampson — and enjoying every bloody second of it. 'Our friends will commence their rounds at one o'clock tomorrow lunchtime. Your special favourite starts at King's Cross. OK? . . . Good . . . You'll also be pleased to know that our plant has borne fruit.'

I sighed as he asked me what the hell I was talking about. 'Pop,' went the bubble of my illusions. Maybe I wasn't cut out to be a spook.

'The plant in the office,' I said, enunciating the words clearly and slowly for all the difference it made. 'The one near the telephone . . . Well, thank goodness for that.'

Mary Jo smoothed the skirt of the conservative knee-length plain grey suit she had taken to wearing in the office in order to minimise the risks of arousing Tresor's ardour. She looked across at me, smiled and mouthed: 'Damn Yankees.'

'Any words of wisdom for me?' I asked Toomey.

I listened for a while, gazed casually round the room, rolled my eyes demonstratively at Mary Jo and then had to interrupt.

'Don't tell me about the labour pains, Toomey,' I said, 'show me the damned baby . . . Thank you. It's much appreciated. Brevity is the soul of wit, you know? . . . Of course, I'm grateful. If you were here, I'd kiss your feet, all right? . . . No, I wouldn't go that far, Toomey. Not even for you.'

I replaced the receiver, checked the room once more, and nodded to Mary Jo. She switched on the computer and leaned very close to the screen with the effect that my view was now pretty much obscured. 'Turn your back,' she said, still not taking any risks on me seeing the magic password.

I felt like giving her a lecture on trust, and the benefits that come from putting yourself in someone else's hands. Or reassuring her that I didn't intend to jump in at the last moment, usurp her role and spoil her chance at making amends for the past. But now wasn't the time. I swivelled round in the chair. Let my eyes drift past the fluorescent green pictogram of a running man above the fire exit. Stared out of the window. Listened to Mary Jo's fingers hit the keyboard: once, twice, three times, four times.

'I'm in,' she said, simultaneously loading our file and selecting the SEND option.

I watched the light on the floppy drive blink rapidly, heard it clatter and whirr as the fake circular sped along the wires.

'All done,' she declared, switching off. 'Mission accomplished.'

'Let's hope it goes as smoothly tomorrow,' I said, crossing the fingers of my right hand.

'Quit worrying, Shannon,' she said. 'Everything will go according to plan.'

I crossed my toes, too.

It doesn't hurt to play safe.

CHAPTER THIRTY

Timing. How does it go? Don'tcha just love it? Keep taking the tabloids, Shannon.

Each individual element of the plan needed to take place exactly on schedule: Norman's call to Liechtenstein to give the codeword that would initiate the transfer of all the funds in the Prospekt account had to be made at one minute to twelve British Summer Time (one minute to one Central European Time) so that the actual transaction would be postponed until after the Continentals had worked their way through their three-course set menus and a bottle or two of *vin ordinaire*; immediately after making the call, Norman was due to pick up Corkscrew, the warped brains behind Prospekt, for a lunch to celebrate their deal, and then keep him occupied till three-thirty when normal banking business closed for the day (just in case the Liechtenstein bank took the unusual step of telephoning him for confirmation of the transfer); at four o'clock, Collins and the Commander would meet with a High Court judge and obtain a Mareva order freezing all Prospekt's assets; meanwhile, at two o'clock, Mary Jo would perform her final act of hacking and open up the new account for Prospekt at City and County. Everyone involved in the operation knew precisely what to do, and precisely when to do it.

It was a good plan.

Would have been a great one, if we'd allowed for the bloody case against Rhiannon being put back.

I looked nervously at my watch. Glanced along our row of schoolroom-style tubular-framed chairs where Arlene, Arthur, Norman and Mary Jo sat. Then back at my watch. Over to my right where Collins, Walker and Agent Toomey huddled around the arresting officer. To my left at Brother James, incongruous in his brown habit, and his disciples. Down at my watch again because the time hadn't registered on either of the other occasions.

It was eleven fifteen. In police stations across London, dealers and smurfs sweated in basement cells waiting for charges to be brought against them; on the outside, the power of drugs money was being spent employing glib tongued solicitors and sweetening bent coppers who might be able to pull a string or two, or try the old chestnut about 'snout's privileges'. As soon as Rhiannon was found guilty, the button would be pressed and the courts would be chock-a-block with the capital's crawling maggots. But, until then, the clock ticked away relentlessly.

'Come on,' I said under my breath.

'Too bloody right,' Norman whispered in my ear.

Arlene placed her hand on mine, and smiled reassuringly.

The Liaison Group had chosen this particular court deliberately. The charge of possession is a 'hybrid' offence, capable of being heard at a county court (too long a delay for our purposes) or by magistrates. Out of the four possible magistrate's courts under whose jurisdiction Rhiannon's widespread offences might fall, this court had a reputation for leniency that normally caused police officers to explode and social workers to smile triumphantly into their beards. Apart from that, it had little going for it.

The court occupied half of a single-storey annexe to the borough council's offices. It wasn't a very well thought out arrangement since the other half was allocated to the register office: in a common waiting-area, smartly dressed wedding parties mingled like oil and water with fly-boys in zippy suits, nervous youths with darting eyes, and unshaven men with the stale smell of the cells clinging to the creased clothes they had worn throughout the night.

The annexe had been built — if that is not too flattering a term — in the 1960s when unemployment was low and available skilled craftsmen had obviously been thin on the ground. Pythagoras would have hated the place — there wasn't a right-angle to be found anywhere. Pairs of large metal-framed picture windows were set at a gentle slope into the plasterboard, forming a wide V where they came together: disconcertingly, it was like being spied upon by the slightly quizzical square eyes of a couch potato who regularly watched too much television and was too lazy to change the channel from *University Challenge*. The walls, thinly emulsioned in a shade of grey more commonly associated with battleships, joined each other at inclinations that opticians would diagnose as severe astigmatism.

Collins left the room for a smoke. Agent Toomey followed Collins. I followed both of them.

'Hello, sir,' I said casually, offering Collins a cigarette. 'I don't believe we've met,' I said to Agent Toomey.

'Toomey. DEA,' he said in a voice as clipped as his hair.

It was warm outside. I took off my jacket. Collins did the same. Toomey kept his on. His hooded eyes roamed up and down the road, examining passers-by, peering inside parked cars. Collins sidled up to me.

'Nice of you to come along and show an interest, Shannon,' he said.

'She's a friend,' I said with a shrug. 'What's the hold-up, sir?'

Toomey rolled his eyes. 'They can't find the evidence,' he said.

I stifled a groan.

It wasn't bloody possible. How can something so simple go wrong? Rhiannon, along with the other disciples, passes the drugs to Brother James. He secretes the assorted tiny packages in the folds of his habit, takes them back to St Jerome's, stuffs them in a bin-liner, weights it down with a brick and drops it into the water at the back of the building by a prominent upright post. That way it supports Rhiannon's story that the drugs were never intended to be used. And that way it was a piece of cake for the police divers to find. Short of painting a giant fluorescent X on the top of the water, there wasn't much more we could have done.

'There's a lot of mud in that river,' Collins said.

'Would you believe it?' I said. 'A river with lots of mud in it.'

'She did tell you the drugs were dumped in the river, I take it?' Collins asked. 'Strange, eh, Shannon? If I didn't know to the contrary, I'd say this bloody fiasco had your hallmark on it. But that couldn't be, could it? Too much at stake for you to get involved. Even though you still owe me settlement on a promise as far as Prospekt is concerned.'

'You'll just have to carry around that rain check a little longer, sir.'

'But not much longer, I hope.'

'You can say that again.'

'But not much longer, I hope.'

The joke wasn't funny the first time I'd heard it. Groucho Marx? *Duck Soup?* In the soup, more like it.

Walker pushed her way through the swing doors. 'We're on, sir,' she said. 'The stash has been found.'

I sighed with relief. Took one last fortifying drag on the cigarette before throwing it in the gutter and joining the line that was filing back into court. I paused at the door to let Norman pass.

'Sorry, Nick,' he said. 'But I can't wait any longer. The wily Corskscrew awaits.'

'Good luck,' I said. 'Keep your wits about you.'

'Same to you,' he said. 'In both respects.'

He looked up into my eyes, opened his mouth, and hesitated. 'Dinner at Toddy's, eight o'clock,' he finally said, slapping me on the arm. 'Make sure you're there, Nick.'

* * *

'Rhiannon Pengelly,' the clerk of the court commanded in a stentorian voice that ricocheted off the walls.

She walked soundlessly across the room floating on the thin soles of the ballet shoes, her long white dress flowing behind, her hair shining like burnished copper in the rays of light from the windows. Flanked by the two burly officers, she looked waif-like and vulnerable. There wasn't a person in the room who didn't want to scoop her up, cuddle her protectively and say, 'There, there, my dear. Everything will be all right.' She climbed the three wooden steps to the dock, stood respectfully erect, placed one hand for support on the handrail, the other for reassurance on the small bulge of her stomach, and turned her beautiful face towards the bench.

There were two magistrates sitting today: a rather large lady in her late fifties with grey-flecked dark hair ruffled at the crown as if she had just removed her hat, and a grey-suited man of a similar age who looked like his next appointment was a meeting of his masonic lodge or the local chamber of commerce — not that there's much difference.

'You may sit, Miss Pengelly,' the lady said, smiling sympathetically.

The charges — twelve counts — were read one by one.

After each, Rhiannon was asked how she pleaded.

'Guilty,' she replied, staring straight ahead.

'Is there anything you wish to say before we pass sentence?'

You betcha. Give it to them, Rhiannon. Just like we rehearsed.

'What I did was wrong,' she said, shaking her head contritely and sending the long tresses swirling around her neck like the flicker of flames from a fire. 'I can't deny that. But I had my reasons. Misguided, you may think.' Does no harm to drop an auto-suggestive prompt. 'Please, let me explain.'

She spoke in a voice so soft that the magistrates had to crane forward to hear. It was as if she were drawing them towards her on invisible silken threads. She gave an abridged version of the tear-jerking story about how she had come to run away from home and find shelter at St Jerome's; told them of the good work that Brother James was doing to rebuild the lives of unfortunates like herself; how she had fallen in love with Mickey. And how he had died, a victim of a drugs overdose.

'I've been stupid,' she said, her head bowed. 'Stupid and naıve. I bought the drugs simply so that others could not buy them. A drop in the ocean — I realise that now. But' — she shrugged her shoulders helplessly — 'I needed to do something. Someone has to do something. Or what hope is there for the future?' Her body, heedless of the script, began to shake uncontrollably. Tears welled up in her eyes. 'I'm sorry,' she cried. 'I'm so sorry.'

The two magistrates gulped. Huddled close together, their faces strained and serious. I thought I saw the woman whisper: 'Poor child.'

Detective Superintendent Patterson, the officer in charge of the case, rose to his feet. He was a tall man, built more substantially than the courthouse itself, and difficult to ignore.

'If I may crave the Court's indulgence,' he said.

The magistrates were grateful for any interruption. A nod came from the woman.

'The police are inclined to believe Miss Pengelly's story: the drugs that she purchased have been found at the bottom of the river. We don't consider there was ever any intention of using them, or selling them on.' He turned to face Rhiannon. 'This young girl,' he said, 'has co-operated fully with us, and with the Court by pleading guilty to all the charges. She has even agreed to appear as a prosecution witness against the dealers from whom she purchased the drugs. When all is said and done' — he paused and looked the woman in the eye — 'it seems that this child may have been more successful in taking drugs off the streets than she could have ever imagined.'

The magistrates retired to a small room at the back of the court to take succour in an economy-sized box of tissues and consider their sentence. Reappeared just two minutes later.

We listened to a chastening monologue, delivered in grave tones by the tousled-haired woman, about the serious nature of any and all charges connected to the growing menace posed by drugs.

'We sentence you to six months' imprisonment,' she said.

A low rebellious rumbling ran round the court.

'Suspended for five years,' she added with a broad smile.

* * *

We gathered outside on the pavement, jostling around Rhiannon and taking it in turns to hug her and offer congratulations. Toomey hovered on the edge of the crowd.

'I wish I could stay,' I said apologetically to Rhiannon. 'Thanks for all your help.' I kissed her on the cheek. 'I'll come and see you when it's all over. Look after yourself. And the baby.'

'Good luck, Nick,' she said.

'What better omen could I have?'

I kissed Arlene goodbye, signalled to Mary Jo, and started to head for the car park. A man, half-hidden behind a ludicrously large bouquet of flowers, bumped into me as he hurried towards the register office.

Turning to check on Mary Jo, I saw the man push his way through the crowd and approach Rhiannon. Noticed her expression change from joy to puzzlement and then to the blood-drained whiteness of shock.

I ran back to her, sensing the danger, an adrenaline surge driving me on.

Collins leaped into action, too.

Toomey stood stock-still.

I was still three or four strides away from Rhiannon when the shot rang out.

The man with the bouquet spun round. The flowers dropped from his left hand. The gun wavered in his right.

His head twisted towards me. His eyes stared sightlessly. All three of them. Two of chestnut brown, and one of blood red.

He took a final pace forward before the autonomic reactions ceased and his knees buckled, pitching him to the ground.

The crowd became a circle. It spread back in crying, gasping ripples from the body. Stunned people clutched at each other and stared into disbelieving eyes.

Toomey stepped forward, gun in hand, a wisp of smoke drifting from the barrel. He bent down. Rolled the man over. Gripped him by the chin, turned the bloody face towards the sky. Then released his hold, and watched dispassionately as the head flopped to one side.

Satisfied, he stood up. Retrieved the bouquet. Threw it on to the man's chest.

From somewhere in the scrum I heard the fast clicking of a motor drive as an opportunistic ghoul captured the image on film to sell to the highest bidder.

Collins went berserk. Wrenched the gun from Toomey's hand. Pressed the catch to jettison the clip of bullets, and slipped both clip and gun in his pocket.

'What the hell do you think you're doing, Toomey?' he shouted.

'Covering all the angles,' Toomey replied calmly. He flicked his cold grey eyes in Rhiannon's direction. 'Sure, she made a lot of friends in court today,' he said. 'But she also acquired a whole damned bunch of enemies.'

My stomach sank.

Oh, Shannon. What have you done now?

CHAPTER THIRTY-ONE

It was thirteen minutes to two when we blew through the doors of Future Assurance. That made it thirteen minutes to three in Liechtenstein. As we walked through Reception, the motto on the wall caught my eye. *Ad utrumque paratus*, it mocked me. Prepared for the worst, Shannon? I don't think so.

Maybe, with the benefit of twenty-twenty hindsight, I should have foreseen that one of the drug dealers languishing in the cells would try to take out the prime witness. With Rhiannon dead, the prosecution case would be reduced to the circumstantial evidence of fuzzy blown-up photographs and jerky video footage. Still, for a while she would be safe. After today's attempt on her life she would at least be guaranteed round-the-clock police protection. But what about the long term? For her, and for me.

I didn't mind Keynes — 'in the long term we're all dead' — being right; I just didn't want him to be proved right too quickly. Judging by past performance, it would be at least a year before Prospekt was brought to trial, and another year while the legal machinery ground small and slow. During that time anyone involved in the case against them was at risk. And it wouldn't stop there. Prospekt had long memories: they didn't forget, and they certainly didn't forgive.

I shuddered: Prospekt had just walked over my grave. They'd warned me twice before to keep my nose out of their business. I tried to visualise the camera angle of the photographer who had snapped away outside the court. Was I in shot, standing head and shoulders above the others in the crowd? What if someone on Prospekt's payroll — the two henchmen I'd crossed while they were calmly drinking tea and waiting for the right moment to kill Collins's ex-wife, perhaps — recognised me? Nick Shannon would be a marked man, that's what.

This was personal now.

Prospekt or me.

The only glimmer of hope was to put everyone involved in the organisation away for a long time. Use prison bars to restrict their freedom to manoeuvre.

'Come on, Nick,' Mary Jo said urgently from the other side of the turnstile.

The green light was flashing, commanding me to pass through. I snapped out of worrying about the future. Switched to worrying about the present. Pushed at the bar and headed for Accounts.

Mary Jo, flat-soled Gucci loafers replacing the high heels of her first visit here, positively darted through Administration. I lengthened my stride to keep up with her. Glanced around and saw the gum-chewing girl — the unwitting catalyst to uncovering Whitley's frauds. She was on memo-chopping duty today. The machete blade of the guillotine rose and fell, rose and fell, with a metronomic rhythm. I flashed her a smile. She looked back at me, head tilted questioningly. Must have sensed both the empathy and sympathy in my eyes. She shrugged, shifted the gum into her right cheek, and smiled back.

Another minute had fallen into history by the time we took our seats at the desk. Mary Jo, in pole position in front of the screen, switched on the terminal.

'You know what you have to do?' I asked her anxiously.

'Better than you,' she replied. 'I've lived this moment in my mind over and over again.'

Her fingers were poised over the keyboard.

'Nick,' said Meg, loping towards me, long skirt flapping round her ankles, sheet of paper in hand. 'Can I have your opinion on this?'

Anything, I sighed to myself. The merits of merger accounting as a possible source of tax avoidance, the destruction of the ozone layer, even who should bat first wicket down in the poisoned-chalice number-three slot in the England team. Whatever you wish. But not right now, please.

I jumped up quickly to try to head her off.

Too late. The sheet of paper was already on the desk, and Meg was bent over it jabbing at a figure in a spreadsheet with the point of a propelling pencil.

'Tresor has received the audited accounts for last year,' she said.

Well, bully for Tresor. Probably not the happiest bee in the hive right now, I would guess. But wait till he hears that the accounts have to be scrapped because of the discovery of a fraud costing the company more than a million pounds. How would he react then? Take the honourable course by falling on his own sting? Somehow I doubted it.

Under cover of the modesty panel of the desk, Mary Jo kicked me impatiently on the heel. As if I needed a reminder that *tempus* was bloody *fugit*ing!

'He's asked me to recast the budget,' Meg continued. 'Suggested that we decrease this figure quite substantially. The way I see it is . . .'

There followed a technical question as to whether budgets should assume the continuance of past performance, however poor, or be allowed an optimistic latitude by postulating a change in market behaviour. I gave the problem as much consideration as it deserved in the circumstances.

'How many angels can dance on a pinhead?' I said in answer.

'What?'

'You pays your money, and you takes your choice,' I paraphrased.

'And that's your professional opinion?' she said, disgusted.

'Professional, yes. Personally, I would temper optimism with caution. Be prudent as well as being prepared. The past is there for a reason. Learn from it. Try not to make the same mistakes again. But always have a fall-back position, an exit route, just in case.'

'Thank you very much,' she said. 'You've been a great help.'

I looked at the figure again. Relented. 'If I were you,' I said, 'I'd let Tresor have his way. I have a feeling history isn't going to repeat itself as far as Future Assurance is concerned. You can tell him I said that, if it helps. On second thoughts, I'll tell him myself. Why don't you set up a meeting for me — yourself, Tresor, Beaumont and Stephanie? Tomorrow morning.'

She nodded her head and set off, much to my relief, back to her desk.

'Aren't you the philosopher all of a sudden?' Mary Jo said, beginning to tap out the first password. 'Do you believe in what you said? The past is there for a reason?'

'Does it matter?' I said, thinking how easy it was to give advice — and how much more difficult it generally was to take it. I consulted my watch. 'At least I got rid of her. With two minutes to spare.'

'Close your eyes,' Mary Jo said.

'What if I don't?' I teased.

'Tricky question,' she said, pursing her lips. 'Might take me two minutes to think of an answer.'

I shut my eyes.

Four quick taps on the keyboard.

'OK,' she said.

The screen showed a line of four asterisks where she'd typed in the password.

She unfolded the slip of paper on which I had written down all the details of our chosen account — number, name, address, sort code and so on. 'Come on,' she snarled impatiently at the computer.

'What's the matter?' I asked anxiously, staring at the inert screen.

'System's slow. Too many users sharing too little processing power.'

'Wonderful news, Mary Jo.'

'Don't shoot the messenger, Nick,' she said. 'And don't panic. Once we're in, our privileges give us priority over everybody else.'

The screen flashed. Gave us the usual polite greeting. Mary Jo leaned forward excitedly. Planted a big kiss on the word 'welcome', leaving a perfect lipstick impression.

Dexterously, she pointed and clicked the mouse, rapidly moving through menus with the self-confident ease of Michael Winner.

'You type,' I said, taking the slip of paper from her, 'I'll dictate.'

Enunciating perfectly, I read out the account number. Followed it up with the answers to each of the questions indicated by the flashing cursor.

In the top right-hand corner of the screen the system clock blinked as a single digit changed: 13.58 became 13.59.

'SALES ACTION LIST . . .' moved slowly across the top of the screen. A list of the bank's 'added value' — i.e. extra cost — products and services, seemingly endless, shone out down a column on the left.

'What shall I do?' Mary Jo asked, unprepared for this eventuality.

'Click the lot,' I said. 'That should ensure Prospekt Holdings doesn't go unnoticed for long.'

'Don't push your luck, Nick,' she said, highlighting the first option and then selecting 'DONE'.

'CORPORATE MANAGER . . .'

Mary Jo sighed and typed in 'Yes'.

'SPECIFY . . .'

'It wants a name,' I said. 'Someone responsible for chasing up sales activity on the account. Give it A. A. Aardvark.'

'Shannon,' she hissed.

'Well,' I said defensively, 'Aardvark never hurt anybody.'

She groaned.

And typed in 'G. Lutton' instead.

'For punishment,' she explained. Rather unnecessarily, I thought. My suggestion may have been a particularly painful pun — a pun in the neck? — but it was a lot more subtle than hers.

There was a brief pause as the computer gulped down the final piece of information. The screen changed. In a separate window, up popped the new account.

And not a moment too soon. Three digits on the clock changed this time: 14.00. A line of letters and numbers started to fill in spaces on Prospekt's account as the transfer from Liechtenstein arrived. The date I knew. The transmission reference I couldn't have cared less about. It was the amount I was waiting for.

'Jeez,' Mary Jo spluttered.

'And that's Jeez in pounds sterling,' I said.

'What is it in dollars?' she asked.

'About sixty million,' I said. 'Give or take a few cents.'

She slumped back in the chair like a victim of mental exhaustion or brain overload. Her hands were shaking. 'Now I understand why you smoke,' she said. 'I need a coffee, Nick. A very strong coffee. Would you get me one while I log off?'

'After what you've just done, your wish is my command.'

I left her to complete her task. Moved through to the central cell. Pushed buttons on the vending machine with trembling fingers. Carried the two polystyrene beakers carefully into the smoking room. Lingered there for a while, calming my jangling nerves.

'There you are,' I said, ten minutes later, handing the coffee to Mary Jo.

She was sitting at the desk, terminal switched off, refreshing her lipstick. She smiled up at me. 'Thanks,' she said.

'Thanks,' I echoed, raising my beaker at her. 'For everything. We couldn't have done it without you.'

'Think nothing of it,' she said, sipping at the coffee and pulling a face. She pushed the beaker as far away as possible across the desk. 'Hell, I can't remember the last time I had so much fun.'

'And the day's still young. More excitement yet to come.'

'Huh?' she said.

'Toddy's tonight,' I reminded her.

'Yeh,' she said. 'Celebration time. You know, I reckon I'll go buy myself a new outfit.'

Mary Jo picked up her bag and rose from the chair.

'I'll make my own way back, Nick. You must have a million things to do.'

'A bit of an exaggeration,' I said. 'But, yes.'

She moved round the desk. Stood in front of me. Raised herself on tiptoe. Put her hands on my shoulders. Looked into my eyes. And kissed me on the lips.

'Goodbye, Shannon,' she said, breaking the moment.

* * *

Well, Mary Jo, I thought, watching the confident sway of hips as she moved towards the turnstile, if I've misjudged you, I apologise profusely. If you passed the test with flying colours, you have my admiration and respect for ever and a day. Yet somehow I really don't think so.

There was only one way to find out. I switched on the terminal and went through the now familiar procedure that would transport me to the gateway to the City and County computer.

'PASSWORD . . .' it challenged.

This had better work, Toomey.

'UUCP' I typed. It was the same number of keystrokes as Mary Jo had made. But would it have the same magic effect?

'WELCOME . . .'

Toomey's labour pains had been worth it. All his phone calls to military establishments, enquiring about problems caused by hackers and obtaining the passwords they had used, had given birth to this bouncing baby: UUCP. The most obscure account and password in the whole operating system.

When one machine wanted to talk to another, it logged in to an account named UUCP (UNIX to UNIX Communications Program). Mere people should never be able to use this account. The systems manager should disable it from human log-ins. But only one in a hundred systems managers even knows about it. To learn about UUCP, it wasn't just a case of RTFM: it was Read The Flipping Twelve Volumes of the Manual. FCTC: From Cover To Cover. Till you came to the one paragraph buried away among the graveyard of esoterica.

I consulted the slip of paper and typed in the number for Prospekt Holdings. Examined the statement of transactions. The leopard hadn't changed its — her — spots after all. Simply lain in wait for the right moment to pounce on the prey. Mary Jo had transferred the sum of one million pounds from Prospekt's account. Nick Shannon was now a rich man.

But not for long.

Well, money can't buy you love, can it? On the other hand, love don't cut much ice when you're in the Ferrari showroom.

Get thee behind me, Satan. You're wasting your time against the pure in heart — and the soft in the head.

I reversed the transfer. And, when the million pounds was back where it belonged, deleted both transactions from the records so that no trace remained of either.

No one would ever know.

Arlene need never know.

This would be a secret — rich in potential blackmail — shared by Mary Jo and me alone. That's why, despite my doubts, I'd had to let her enter the City and County computer today when I could just as easily have done it myself. And why I'd had to leave her alone. If she was on the level, I lost nothing. If she was betraying my trust, doing an *Et tu*

Brute impression by stabbing me in the back, then she lost everything. Mary Jo and I were going to get along like the proverbial house on fire from now on. Or else the proverbial fan would be pointed in her direction — in full view of Arlene.

I was as high as a — No, not a kite: enough clichés for one day. An Everest mountaineer on Prozac. Yup. The heights had been scaled. Hell, what's one more battered-to-death cliché among friends? The plan had worked. It had bloody worked!

I planted my lips alongside Mary Jo's imprint on the screen. Grinned inanely. Then impishly, as an idea entered my mind and the temptation grew too strong to resist. This was a day for putting everything right. How did the quote go? I could remember the beginning, if not the end! 'Justice is such a fine thing . . .' Well, justice would prevail. So what if we didn't have any evidence against Brother James? The least I could do while logged on to the bank's computer was make sure he didn't profit from the murder. I would clear Whitley's account, except for Rhiannon's promised five thousand pounds. Transfer the remainder of the money somewhere — surely there had to be a deserving charity who banked with City and County. What was it Mary Jo had said? 'I can't remember the last time I had so much fun.' Too damned right.

It would have been quicker if I'd known Whitley's account number. I set up a global search and leaned back in a warm glow of anticipated self-satisfaction while the computer did my bidding by scouring the records. Meg was busy with her spreadsheets, playing with a set of *what if* scenarios no doubt. The rest of the department was hard at work, fuelled by the calories of the chef's dyslexic dish of the day. There must be a lot of Whitleys — this was taking longer than I had expected. But there was no rush. Three-thirty and close of banking business was still a while away yet.

I picked up the phone and dialled Toomey's number. A dismal voice answered.

'Cheer up, Toomey,' I said. 'Zip-a-dee-doo-dah. Wonderful feeling, wonderful day. For everyone bar Prospekt, that is.'

'I've been hauled over the carpet,' he groaned, 'by my balls.'

I winced. 'Didn't get a medal, then? Pity. You deserve it for saving Rhiannon's life. But that's the trouble with a civilised country, Toomey. No tickertape parade for gunning someone down in cold blood in the middle of the high street.'

'Diddlysquat,' he replied. Or words to that effect.

'This visa?' I ventured.

'Change the record, Shannon,' he moaned.

'That's what I wanted to talk to you about,' I said. 'Changing the record.'

I explained my thinking, my fears about possible retribution from Prospekt, and what it was I now wanted.

'Look, Shannon,' he said, 'the deal was for one visa. Whatever name is on it makes no difference to me.'

I gave him the name I'd settled on.

'What about a passport?' he said.

'I have a friend who can handle that. But thanks for the offer.'

'I wasn't offering,' he said. 'I was just asking.'

'You're a hard man, Toomey.'

'But fair,' he said, on cue. 'I'll drop off the visa before I get manhandled on to the plane. And, Shannon,' he said, his voice softening, 'you're a fair man.'

'But not hard, I know.'

'The perfect choice for the job. Even if I do say so myself. Well done, Shannon. And best of luck for the future.'

'You, too, Toomey. May you always be in the right place at the right time.'

'With a Colt Python in my hand, eh?'

'Thanks again, Toomey. For—'

'Get the hell off the line, Shannon,' he said. 'Before you have me crying in my Bourbon.'

I hung up with a lump in my throat. Turned my attention quickly towards the screen.

There were thirteen David Whitleys. But only one where 'The estate of' had been recently appended to the account name. I scrolled down to it and clicked the mouse. Up popped his account details.

Or were they?

The total wasn't anywhere near right.

Nor were the twelve payments coming into the account.

The dates matched those of the frauds, certainly. And the deposits were large, granted. But they weren't large enough.

I did a quick calculation in my head. Wasn't too difficult considering the bottom-line figure for each of the false policies was as near as damn it one hundred thousand pounds.

When a wrong figure divides by nine, it's a transposition error.

And when it divides by four?

It's a conspiracy.

CHAPTER THIRTY-TWO

I had a theory. A little late, maybe, but a theory nevertheless. But how to test it?

If Whitley's account contained only a quarter of the stolen money, perhaps I could find the missing three-quarters by trawling through the bank records of the other suspects.

It took an hour to check.

A fruitless hour. I looked at Tresor's account, Beaumont's, Stephanie's, even scraped the barrel in desperation by turning over the likes of Meg and Plimpson.

Nothing.

It didn't prove the theory. But it didn't disprove it, either: there was no law stating that employees and directors could only bank with City and County.

If at first you don't succeed, Shannon, keep digging away. These people weren't professionals — not at fraud, for that had been marred by a careless error, nor at murder. They were amateurs. And amateurs make mistakes: they don't have the experience to think of everything, the foresight to cover all the angles. Find one small slip, Shannon. That's all you need to do.

I emptied the drawers of all the audit files. Spread them across the top of the desk. Stared down at them, hoping

— praying — for inspiration. I picked up schedules at random. Examined them. Sighed. Put them back. Rearranged the mess of papers into an entirely different mess of papers. It didn't help.

I switched off the computer, reached down into the pockets of my jacket hanging over the back of the chair, fished out my valuables — cigarettes and lighter — plus wallet and car keys, and took a break. Fresh air, fresh thoughts perhaps.

Leaving the building, I walked over to the Lancia. Sat on the bonnet, lit a cigarette and gazed across at the entrance. Pictured Whitley on his last night on this earth. Ran the sequence of events through my mind. He's been working late. Steps through the front door. Dusk is gathering around him — blood-red sunset, clouds scudding across the sky, birds having their last tweet of the day, all that pulp-fiction stuff we know and love so well. He goes over to his car. But doesn't drive off! Instead, according to the security video, he unlocks the boot and takes something out. And then sets out on foot. Now, there are only two places within walking distance: the pub and St Jerome's. Maybe he needed a drink. But, if he's going to the pub, why does he need to retrieve something from his car? No, he's off to St Jerome's. But in order to get there he has to pass through the narrow corridor that cannot be scanned by either of the cameras mounted on the front of the building. He enters the blind spot. Where his murderer has been lurking. Whitley stares Death in the face.

But whose face is it? Toby Beaumont — Mr Gullible — is supposedly thundering up the M1 at the time; has receipts to prove it, too. Tresor — he of the phoney black hair — is tucked up in bed staining the pillows of nubile-lipped Stephanie. Unbreakable alibis all round.

A gaggle of young girls — or should that be a *giggle* of young girls — slipped out of the building for a late-afternoon smoke. Leaned casually up against the wall, puffing away furiously; a few months ago it would have been puffing away furtively — behind the bike sheds at school.

Forget the face for the moment, Shannon, I told myself. I closed my eyes to blot out the distracting sight of the sweet innocents in their short tight skirts and skimpy summer tops exposing bare midriffs. Whitley and Death meet face-to-face, right? And Whitley welcomes Death with open arms. That's the only explanation left for the absence of defensive marks.

A burst of laughter broke my concentration. The lady from behind the counter in the staff restaurant had joined the young girls. She was looking in my direction — they were all looking in my direction. And laughing merrily at some private joke at my expense, it seemed. Maybe they'd never seen a bloke sitting atop a car with his eyes closed before. Or maybe . . .

Mr Gullible? Mr Naıve, more like it.

I searched in my pocket for my car keys. Unlocked the passenger door. Took my road atlas from the glove compartment. Hurried back towards the building. Ran the gauntlet past the sniggering girls. Blushed a little. But what did it matter? The last laugh would be mine. I knew it all now. At long last everything made sense. I was going to find that small slip. Check and double-check, Shannon. That's the way alibis can be broken.

Back at my desk, I opened the top drawer and swept all the papers inside with one decisive careless movement. Cleared valuable working space to spread out the evidence. Then marched over to Meg.

'I need the expense claims for last month,' I said, trying to rein back my excitement.

'I thought you'd finished with those,' she said, her eyes dwelling on several new versions of the spreadsheets she'd printed out and collected from the inconveniently situated laser printer in Administration. 'They're all filed away now.'

I stood my ground, waited for her to look up, and then smiled.

She gazed past me at the clock on the wall and stifled a sigh.

'There's not much time left this afternoon, Nick. Can't it wait till the morning? Surely tomorrow's budget meeting is more important.'

'I'm sorry, Meg,' I said, shaking my head firmly. 'But now can't be soon enough.'

She didn't bother to stifle the sigh this time.

'I also need the invoices for the mobile phones,' I added.

She took one last lingering look at the spreadsheets and rose, not a little petulantly, from her desk. 'Go and sit down,' she said, her voice betraying weary resignation. 'I'll bring them over in a minute.'

It wasn't a minute. More like ten. Or maybe time was just playing tricks on me. I sat at the desk drumming my fingers on the almost bare top and watching her get side-tracked by a frustrating succession of queries from members of her staff.

'There you go,' she said, dumping two ring binders groaning with paperwork on the desk. 'Happy now?'

'Soon will be, I hope.'

I opened the binder containing the purchase invoices. Flicked rapidly through till I located the two relating to Tresor's and Beaumont's mobile phones. Thank the Lord for cost control and itemised billing.

Tresor's statement of calls ran to three pages. The day of the murder was on page two. There was Beaumont's number right at the bottom — call timed at 22.35. No joy there: Whitley's body had been found by the security guard at half past ten that evening, and reported to Tresor straight away.

Maybe the second binder would help. Extracting Beaumont's expense claim, I set it on the desk and turned to the page in the road atlas which showed the route of the M1. The receipt for petrol (a whole tankful, it appeared by the number of litres indicated) was from the service area at Toddington, thirty miles up from the start of the motorway, forty-five or thereabouts from Docklands. The cashier had written down Beaumont's car registration number (I verified it was actually his car by finding the last invoice for servicing): the electronic till-receipt showed the time of the transaction as 21.10. That meant he'd left the office late, too. It also meant that, theoretically, he could have turned round at the next junction (only one mile up the road) and made it back to Future Assurance by the time of the murder. But what about the coffee and the exorbitantly priced Danish he'd bought later?

Beaumont had stopped at Trowell Services. I added up the mileage. Eighty-three from his previous stop. Checked the time on the till-receipt from the cafeteria. 22.45. He'd stopped for a coffee and a Danish all right. But on his way back! After the phone call from Tresor to inform him of Whitley's death.

Was he the coolest customer in the annals of motorway service-area history?

Was he hell.

Was his blood sugar at such a dangerously low level that only a sticky-sweet Danish would produce the surge needed to get him home?

Was it hell.

This wasn't the action of a man who had just heard the distressing news that a fellow director, a colleague of long standing, an old friend supposedly, had been murdered. No, sirree, bub. This was the premeditated action of a rational man. A man establishing an alibi.

Meg interrupted my chain of thought.

'Will you run your eyes over these before tomorrow's meeting, Nick?' she asked, placing a neat pile of spreadsheets on the now cluttered desk. 'My head's swimming with figures. I'm calling it a day.'

I glanced reluctantly up from the desk. The boot was on the other foot now. Meg had her bag over her shoulder and briefcase in hand. I looked around the office. The place had emptied while I'd been engrossed in numbers, times and mileages.

'Sure,' I said, in the mood to agree to anything if it meant I could be left alone to return to my investigation. I was almost there. Instinct told me that.

'Have you finished with these?' she said, gesturing at the two binders. 'Would you like me to put them away for you?'

'Just a little longer. I'll leave them on your desk.'

'See you in the morning, then,' she said finally.

'Yes,' I said distractedly. 'See you in the morning.'

'By the way,' she said. Go, woman, go. 'Did you make your phone call? She sounded very upset. I hope it wasn't bad news.'

'What phone call?'

'The one that came while you were outside. Having a cigarette, I presume.' She clucked like a mother hen and shook her head reprovingly at me. 'I left the message on your desk. You must have seen it, even amongst all that mess.'

I groaned.

'Sorry,' she said. 'I should have mentioned it earlier, but . . .' She nodded apologetically at those damned irrelevant spreadsheets.

'It's not your fault,' I said, pulling open the drawer in which I'd cavalierly swept all the papers that had been littering the desktop.

I rummaged about and found the message. 'Urgent,' it said in big red letters. 'Ring Arlene.' The number I didn't recognise.

Meg shrugged her shoulders sheepishly at me. 'I'll be off, then,' she said.

'Good night, Meg,' I said, already with the phone in my hand — and a sinking feeling in the very pit of my stomach. Don't let it be the baby, I prayed.

'The Savoy,' a female voice trilled in my ear. 'How may I help you?'

'I'd like to speak to Mrs Arlene Tucker, please.'

'Just one moment, sir,' the voice said, before I could explain that Arlene wasn't actually staying there.

'Miss Tucker has checked out, sir.'

Well, what a surprise. Mary Jo had taken the quickest route back to the Savoy — researched in advance — and was probably sipping champagne in Club Class by now.

'If you would give me your name, sir, I'll check for messages.'

'Shannon. Nick Shannon.'

There was a long pause. I sat there anxiously, toying with the pages of Tresor's mobile-phone bill.

'I'm afraid,' the voice said, sounding genuinely sorry, 'that there are no messages, Mr Shannon.'

'Could you try Mr Timpkins's room?' I pleaded. 'Mrs Tucker may be there.'

Another long pause. More idle flicking of pages from me as I sought escape in displacement activity.

'There's no answer from Mr Timpkins's room, sir. And no messages, either.'

'Sorry,' I said, staring down at the bill. 'I wasn't concentrating. I didn't catch what you said.'

She repeated herself.

I paid more attention this time. But not much more, I admit.

I dropped the phone back into its cradle with trembling fingers. Didn't know whether to scream in frustration at being no nearer to finding out what was so urgent with Arlene or to punch the air in triumph and dance round the room in celebration.

I did neither. Just sat back and smiled. And stared again at the telephone number at the top of the third page of the invoice.

A telephone number that, once seen, was simply unforgettable.

Stephanie's special number.

And alongside it?

The time, of course.

And not just any old time, either.

A truly wonderful time.

22.36.

They don't write numbers like that anymore.

Got you, Tresor! Or may I call you 'murderer'?

I had the evidence at last. The theory was proven beyond reasonable doubt. *Quod erat bloody demonstrandum*, as we mathematicians say. Tresor hadn't been with Stephanie; he'd phoned her while speeding away from the scene of the crime.

It was all over.

What a day.

Prospekt stitched up. And Whitley's murder solved.

I stretched out a shaking hand towards the phone to call Collins.

CHAPTER THIRTY-THREE

It rang before I could touch it.

My nerves were so jangled I almost hit the false ceiling. 'Shannon,' I said with quivering voice. It was a bloody miracle I'd been able to speak at all.

The security guard on Reception — Soup of the Day must have gone home with the rest of the office staff — was stammering incoherently in my ear. In the background I could hear Arlene screaming incoherently in *his* ear. My eardrums got the better of the exchange. He broke off for a moment. 'Will you shut up, *please*?' I heard him shout. 'Get over here right away,' he said despairingly to me. 'This bloody woman is uncontrollable.'

I ran across the room, cursed the slowness of the turnstiles, picked up speed again as I sprinted through a deserted Administration. Could see Arlene as I neared the final hurdle outside Reception. Her face was red. Her eyes were shining wet, two dark effluvial lines of mascara streaking her cheeks. Her right foot was stamping in anger and frustration.

'It's all right,' I said, running the last few yards and throwing my arms round her.

'No, it's not,' she sobbed. 'It's Mary Jo. She's . . .'

I whisked Arlene outside, and out of earshot. Held her tight. 'Easy. Easy,' I said, as calmly as I could.

'You didn't ring me,' she cried, the words streaming from her mouth in tempo with the tears from her eyes. 'Why didn't you ring me? I was trying to warn you. I waited as long as I could. Then just had to come here. Mary Jo double-crossed you.' The stream became a flood. Arlene clung to me like there was no tomorrow. 'Oh, Nick, Nick, my Nick. You're going back to prison.'

'Calm down,' I said. 'It's OK. Everything's fine. I promise.'

'But you don't understand—'

'I do, Arlene. Believe me. Trust me. Like you always have done before. You mustn't get so excited. It's not good for you. Or the baby. Just take deep breaths. And listen to me.'

'But—'

'Just do as I say,' I said firmly. 'I don't want to have to slap you across the face.' She looked up at me in horror. 'Not good for my reputation,' I said with a smile. 'Or my delicate fingers. I might never play the violin again.'

'But,' she said again — a little calmer, though.

'I know,' I said, 'I can't play the violin now. But is this the time to get picky?'

Her shoulders shook a fraction. I took it as some sign of progress — probably as close to a shrug as she could manage under the circumstances.

'I hate to have to tell you this,' I said, embarrassed and ashamed — although God knows why. 'But I didn't trust Mary Jo. Her transformation was too rapid, too complete to ring true with me. I thought she might try to pull some stunt. So I checked her work after she'd left. Hacked into the City and County computer and put the money she had so altruistically placed in my account back where it belonged. There's no trace, Arlene. I'm in the clear.'

She smothered me with kisses. Hugged me so tight I thought my eyes would pop. Then drew away.

'If you were suspicious of Mary Jo,' she said angrily, wiping her eyes so as not to dilute the accusing look, 'then why the hell didn't you say something to me? And why give her the opportunity to stitch you up?' Her face softened as she thought more rationally. 'Or is that a stupid question, my fine English gentleman?'

'Stupid question, my adorable American lady. Let's just say that sometimes blackmail can be a more efficient persuader than trust.'

'OK, then. How about this question? How did you manage to hack into the computer? Did Mary Jo let her magic password slip out?'

'All she let slip was that the password had been used to gain entry to a computer at a military establishment. I simply got Toomey to phone around until he found which one, and what password was used.'

'Nick,' she said sweetly. 'Do you know something?'

'What, my darling?'

'You can be an insufferably smug sonofabitch at times.'

'How about you take a turn, then? How did you suspect what Mary Jo had done?'

'I'd like to say it was brilliant logical deduction — or even fall back on female intuition — but I'm afraid it was neither. Mary Jo left me a note at the Savoy. I wasn't supposed to get it until this evening when we were due to pick her up and take her to Toddy's. And by then it would have been too late.' She shuddered involuntarily. 'But I couldn't wait until this evening. I was so damn proud of her.' Arlene paused to shake her head in sadness and in shame. 'I bought a bottle of champagne and took it to the Savoy. Thought that mother and daughter could have a private celebration.'

'Save it for when the baby's born,' I said. 'What did her note say?'

'A load of diddlysquat about how I might not be able to forgive her now, but I would in the future when I was able to think straight. How you weren't the white knight of my dreams. Just a freeloader and a no-good gold-digger. So she'd fixed it for you to strike it rich — have all the money you could ever wish for.' Arlene gave me a sorrowful look. 'If you don't mind,' she said, 'I'll pass on the smug. Somehow it don't seem right. Not when you've given birth to the world's biggest—'

'Starts with a B,' I interrupted, so that she wouldn't actually have to use the word to describe her own daughter, 'and ends in an irritating itch.'

'Well, she's certainly done it, this time,' Arlene said threateningly.

'Or, thankfully, not done it. Come on,' I said, lightly kissing her lips. 'Let's go home.'

I gave her the car keys. 'Won't be a minute,' I said. 'Sit in the car and relax. I just have to fetch my jacket. And a couple of pieces of paper.'

But the couple of pieces of paper weren't there when I got back to the desk.

And, as if that wasn't bad enough, Arlene wasn't there when I got back to the car.

CHAPTER THIRTY-FOUR

Neither death, nor life, nor angels, nor principalities, nor things present, nor things to come,
Nor height, nor depth, nor any other creature, shall be able to separate us from the love of God.
Romans 8:38

Stephanie was wearing a dark red skirt, a plaid jacket in red and white, red high heels, and a wide smile on her painted red lips. She stood at the entrance to the Hive, the Queen Bee beckoning me towards her with a slow movement of her index finger. In different circumstances, coming from a different woman, I might have mistaken the gesture for a seductive come-on, but I'd watched enough Hammer Horror repeats in my youth to distinguish vampire from vamp.

I trudged away from the empty car on leaden feet and headed back to the building. My mind was in turmoil, a dozen different negative emotions using it as a killing field in their no-holds-barred battle for supremacy. Despair, dejection and desolation joined forces against anxiety and anguish: the cold sweat of fear crept over the hill preparing to ambush the victor. My heart fought a lone resistance movement, trying to persuade me that there was some perfectly innocent explanation for Arlene's disappearance — a pregnant woman's urgent need to visit the Ladies perhaps. My head scoffed. As scoffs go, it was one of the best. Came complete with an invisible row of exclamation marks just in case I'd missed the inflexion of absolute derision. 'Big trouble, Shannon,' Head said. 'Think it's time I pushed the button on the adrenalin. Again.'

'What have you done with Arlene?' I said, biting back the burning anger. It was directed against myself and, if I fanned the flames and let the fire take hold, would only serve to cloud my thinking. Breed carelessness. And hadn't I been careless enough for one day? When you're in a hole, stop digging. Use your brain, Shannon. Form a plan. Harness the adrenaline. Leap from the hole when the time is right.

'She's with Tresor,' Stephanie said, her tongue flicking over her lips. 'She's safe. At the moment.'

'I would have thought that was a contradiction in terms — safe, and with Tresor.'

She smiled humourlessly. 'I did add *at the moment.* If you want to see her again, Shannon — alive, that is — you'll do exactly as I say.'

'And what if I don't? What if I march up to the security guard and tell him to call the police?'

'Then, don't hold me responsible if she's dead by the time the police arrive. We've burned our boats, Shannon. There's nothing else to lose. What's one more death now?' She rocked on the heel of one shoe, looked at me with wide eyes and said: 'On the other hand, we think we may have come up with a way out of our problems. With your co-operation, that is. Why not come and listen to what we have to say?'

'What choice do I have?' I said. And, I thought, what good would it do? One more death, two more deaths — what's the difference?

'Absolutely none, Shannon,' she said, probably answering all my questions. 'Now, we're going to walk straight past the guard, eyes directly ahead — no stupid macho heroics, no meaningful looks or mimed cries for help. Is that clear?'

'Lead on, Macduff,' I said. How did the (mis)quotation continue, according to Meg? 'And damned be him that first cries, "Hold enough!"' How do you like your epitaph, Whitley?

I smiled at Stephanie, bent my back into an exaggerated bow, swept my arm invitationally through the air.

She gave me a long scornful look: it was the least of my concerns right now, and playing the fool wasn't going to do any harm. The deck was stacked against me. They held all the cards. Bar the Joker.

Prudently obeying her instructions, I entered the building and strode past the guard, watching him only from out of the corner of one eye. I could have looked him full in the face, jumped up and down, even done Basil Fawlty impersonations, for all the difference it would have made: the guard was too busy concentrating on the wasteful sway of Stephanie's pneumatic hips to notice me.

When through the turnstile, she hesitated slightly — that was enough to tell me where we were going — and then led me on the clockwise of the two alternative equidistant routes to the now expected destination of the Computer Department.

The room seemed very different from the red-alert bridge of the Starship Enterprise of my first visit. There was barely a movement, the two occupants unnaturally still like some tableau in a seaside waxworks. Barely a sound except for the low, verge-of-consciousness hum of the DEC machine in the background. Only one terminal was switched on, its screen flickering with a hundred planets fast approaching each other on a collision course.

Arlene, I was pleased to see, looked more foolish than frightened. She was tied to a chair near the middle of the room, a cable from one of the computers wound tightly round her arms and the elasticated waist of her soft pink trouser suit. Tresor stood watchfully behind her. In his right hand he held the heavy wooden handle of the machete slicer dismantled from the guillotine. He slapped the flat of the sharp blade impatiently into the palm of his left hand.

Arlene raised her eyebrows at me, gave a small sigh, brought both hands up to the available limit and flapped them impotently in the air like a bird whose wings had been clipped. 'Sorry, Nick,' she said. 'He said you'd been delayed. That I should come inside and wait.' She screwed up her face and sucked at her teeth. 'I've blown it, haven't I?'

'Well,' I said, 'let's just say it's not exactly how I planned for us to spend the evening.' I shrugged my shoulders. 'Don't blame yourself. How could you be expected to suspect these two? Up until a few hours ago we thought we had it all worked out. In our real-life game of Cluedo we'd already put our three cards into the envelope: Brother James, in the car park, with the chisel.'

She gave me a weak smile, simultaneously flicking her eyes briefly down and to the left.

I glanced in the direction she'd indicated. The safe door was open. A body was lying on the floor, legs splayed at odd angles. At the ends of the legs was a pair of scuffed brown Hush Puppies.

Plimpson.

As if I didn't have enough to worry about.

'What have you done to him?' I said.

Tresor mimed hitting Arlene over the head with the heavy handle of the machete. He gave a low guttural laugh. 'Sit,' he said.

'Woof, woof,' I replied with the heavy breath and wagging tongue of a dog in obedience classes. Come on, Tresor. Get angry. Get careless. Tip the odds a little in my favour.

'What are we waiting for?' I said, selecting a chair with my back to the safe. I sat down, crossed my legs casually. 'You haven't any proposition to put to me, Tresor. So why not get the show on the road? Skip the overture and first couple of acts. Move straight on to the grand finale, the inevitable climax: three more dead bodies to add to your list.'

'What's your hurry, Shannon?' he said. 'Don't you want to bargain?'

'I wouldn't give you the satisfaction, Tresor. I repeat the question: what are we waiting for?'

'Not what, but who,' Tresor said.

God, he was a such a bloody pedant. But the personality failing had served him well at our first meeting when he'd conned me by speaking about *calling* Beaumont and *telling* Stephanie. Very clever. A worthy, if highly detestable, opponent.

'I get it,' I said, nodding my head exaggeratedly. 'Beaumont's not here yet. Can't have the denouement without all the key players on stage, can we?'

Tresor raised his left arm high so that he could look at his watch without taking his eyes off me. 'You've got about fifteen minutes, Shannon. How shall we . . . kill the time?'

He chuckled, pleased with his pun.

I sneered pathetically. Lowest form of wit. Seemed fitting, coming as it did from the lowest form of life.

'Fifteen minutes?' I said. 'What do you reckon, Arlene?' I gave her a wink, hoping to reassure her by appearing relaxed and confident. 'We could boil five eggs consecutively, but unfortunately we don't have a stove. If Tresor untied you, we could give them both a treat and make love.'

'No,' she said, entering into the spirit of things by grinning at me and adding: 'He said fifteen minutes — I couldn't manage twice.'

I stared thoughtfully at the ceiling, then turned my attention quickly back to Tresor. 'Seems like we'll just have to talk, then,' I said with a sigh. 'Only fair, though. I mean, if Arlene's going to die, the least you owe her is that she should know why.'

Stephanie walked over to the desk next to Arlene, skirting me warily — or, rather, short-tight-skirting me warily. She perched on the edge, removed her jacket to reveal a black camisole top, wrapped one long leg over the other and looked up at Tresor. 'Shall I tie him up?' she asked.

'By all means,' I said helpfully, holding out my hands. 'I won't resist. Just as long as you untie Arlene. Otherwise,' I added, putting on my Violet Elizabeth voice, 'I'll scweam and scweam till I'm thick.'

'You wouldn't dare,' said Tresor.

'I would,' I said, grinning.

'He would,' said Arlene. 'When Nick's in one of these moods, well . . .'

Tresor sighed wearily. 'God, you're a pain, Shannon. It seems like you've been around for ever. No matter how uncomfortable I tried to make you feel, how much I insulted you, you wouldn't go away and leave me in peace.' He passed the machete to Stephanie. 'You take over here,' he said. 'I'll take care of Shannon.'

Stephanie moved behind Arlene as Tresor untied the cable. 'No tricks, Shannon,' she said, giving me a threatening look. She took a lock of Arlene's hair in her left hand. Twirled it distractedly. Brought the blade of the guillotine against it. Sliced through it quickly, and frighteningly easily. Then brought the blade to rest against Arlene's throat.

'Hands behind your back, Shannon,' Tresor said.

I complied — bald women don't turn me on. Neither do those with blood gushing from their jugular veins.

Tresor trussed me up like a turkey, winding the cable around my neck, waist and finally wrists. It might be worse, Shannon, I consoled myself — no signs yet of a packet of Paxo.

My confidence began to creep back. I couldn't see how they expected to kill all of us and get away with it. Your average policeman isn't exactly Sherlock Holmes, granted, but is still likely to smell a rat when confronted by three throat-slit bodies, one of whom is tied to a chair with a length of computer cable.

'I suppose a cigarette is out of the question?' I said hopefully.

'And how do you propose to smoke with your hands tied?' Tresor asked, quite reasonably.

'Arlene can feed it to me,' I replied. 'She could come and sit by my side.'

'Why not?' said Tresor, to my surprise. 'What a touching scene. And how could I deny you a last request?'

The man was all heart. Made up for the lack of brain, I suppose.

Stephanie led Arlene, blade still pressed against throat, across the room and pushed her roughly down into a chair next to me.

Arlene leaned over and searched awkwardly in my pocket. Found my lighter and cigarettes. Lit one. Pressed it to my lips. I inhaled deeply. Exhaled casually upward from my bottom lip, keeping my eyes off the long blue-grey plume as it drifted towards the ceiling. And the smoke alarm.

'Let's run over it from the top, eh, Tresor?' I said. 'Which of the four of you first had the idea for the fraud?'

'Hard to say,' he shrugged.

'It just seemed to come up in conversation,' Stephanie said. 'Toby, Robert and I were talking about David one day — a few weeks after the car accident, it must have been. David was in a such a state, we all wanted to do something. Someone — I can't remember who — suggested that money might help, and that we could pay him out of the company by creating a false policy.'

'And Whitley went along with it,' I said. 'Could hardly refuse, I suppose. Not when he was *in such a state*. And, of course, it wouldn't occur to him that this was just the start. Was that the plan all along, Tresor? Once Whitley was implicated in one fraud, he wouldn't be in a position to blow the whistle on a whole chain of them? It *was* you who suggested repeating the swindle, I take it?'

'And why not?' he asked, seeming affronted by the question. 'It was our money — by rights. Not our fault that the company wasn't making enough profit to trigger the earn-out clause. It was City and County's: they'd encouraged us to spend. "Invest for growth,"' Tresor whined. 'So we'd geared ourselves up for expansion. Bought the new computer.

Acquired the millstone of these bloody offices. No,' he said with all the decisive post-rationalisation of a petulant child caught with his hand in the cookie jar. 'We were only taking what was due to us.'

'My heart bleeds for you,' I said, my voice and eyes filled with contempt. 'Never crossed your crooked minds that you had signed a contract? Made a deal? Should honour it? For better or worse?'

It was his turn to look at me with contempt.

'Stupid question,' I said. 'Not the first time I've been guilty of naivety lately.'

Stephanie tossed her head back and laughed.

'I'll come back to that, if you don't mind.' I took another long drag on the cigarette.

'As you wish,' Stephanie said, pouting those lying lips at me.

'I should have worked out a lot earlier that it was too risky for Whitley to be operating the fraud on his own. He would have needed to hang around Administration for an opportunity to take blank proposal forms from the pile, and to collect the printouts of the letters about change of reference numbers. And the cheques required two signatures. No, the conspiracy theory was always much more likely. With all the directors involved, you could put up a united front to City and County about the claims record being initially pure bad luck, and later lay the blame at Plimpson's door.'

'You were careless, Shannon,' Tresor said, tutting dramatically. 'In thought and deed.' He shook his head mockingly. 'It would have been better for you to remove all the files of the fraudulent claims rather than trying to hide them in one pile in the safe. And, luckily for us, the only one you still have in your possession points the finger squarely at Whitley.'

'Hindsight is a wonderful gift,' I said. 'Neither of us seems to possess it, though.'

'There are some things you can't legislate for,' Tresor said philosophically.

'So,' I said, nodding my head in agreement, 'everything was going swimmingly. Until Whitley does the unpredictable. Or did you see it as the unthinkable? After all, no insurance policy ever provides cover for an act of God.'

I looked at Arlene to see how she was bearing up. A little pale perhaps, but that wasn't surprising considering that she had a sharp blade up against her throat.

'Do you know what Whitley did, Arlene? Why he had to be killed?'

'Tell me, Nick,' Arlene said, helping herself to a puff of the cigarette and adding her smoke to mine. What a girl. She must have worked out what I was up to. 'What did Whitley do?' she asked.

'He got religion,' I said, shaking my head sadly. 'He went and bloody got religion. And with religion comes a conscience. In Whitley's case, a guilty conscience — not only feeling to blame for his son's death, but also compounding the sin by accepting money. Now he'd broken two commandments. Had both "Thou shalt not kill" *and* "Thou shalt not steal" to cope with. He tried to atone through prayer and self-inflicted pain — flagellating himself with a scourge, even refusing to eat so that his ulcer hurt. But nothing really helped; the problem was too deeply rooted. His only way out was to confess. That's why Tresor had to kill him.'

'I never meant to kill him,' Tresor said. 'I just wanted to reason with him. The bloody fool was going to spoil everything. Tell City and County what we'd done.'

'So what happened?'

'When David told us all what he intended to do, we tried to talk him out of it. Sat in my office for hours that evening wasting our damn breath. The man was totally irrational. Just wouldn't see sense. Up he gets, cool as a bloody cucumber, says his mind is made up, and goes back to his desk to leave everything straight for whoever would eventually take over his job. So the three of us left him to it, hoping he'd have a change of heart overnight. Toby drives north, Stephanie goes home, and I decide to go to the pub.'

'But drowning your sorrows didn't help? You just got more stewed up, I reckon. And gained a little Dutch courage. So you left your car at the pub and walked back. One last try, was it? Do or die?'

Arlene stubbed out the cigarette on the carpet tile. Lit another. How many would it take to set off the damned alarm?

'David was off to St Jerome's,' Tresor said. 'I watched him take a bundle out of his car. It was his precious bloody tools.' Precious, yes, I thought, but not bloody — yet. 'Going to make some more of those crucifixes, I suppose. Leaving his car in the car park where it would be safe — as if that mattered in the circumstances.'

Tresor stared at the ceiling in utter disbelief. A bead of sweat rolled down my forehead.

'And you waited,' I said quickly, 'in the blind spot. You knew about that, of course. The security guard would have gone to the nearest director — that meant either you or Stephanie — for a signature on the purchase order form.'

'Must have had a premonition,' Tresor said, smiling proudly at me. 'I told the guard I was much too busy to sign forms. Sent him off to David. With a flea in his ear.'

'So what happened to poor Whitley?' I asked.

'He tried to push past me,' Tresor said, shrugging his broad shoulders as if what was about to occur was all Whitley's fault. 'I gave him a bit of a shove. He dropped the tools. I picked up the chisel. Held it to his chest. Told him I'd use it if he didn't change his mind.'

'But he wouldn't play ball?'

'He just smiled serenely at me. Spouted some biblical quotation about death like he was standing in the pulpit giving a sermon.' Tresor's face flushed with remembered anger. 'So I jabbed with the chisel to show him I wasn't joking. Before I knew it, he'd moved forward and the chisel was in his chest.'

Toby Beaumont entered the room. He was struggling with the weight of a large holdall. He set it on the floor and sighed with relief.

'Welcome,' I said to him. 'You've missed some of the fun; but there's plenty more to come, I imagine. Tresor's been telling us how Whitley more or less committed suicide. Oh, how we laughed.'

'It was an accident,' Beaumont said seriously.

'Whitley didn't fear death, I grant you. Probably welcomed it as the final act of absolution. That's why he didn't defend himself. But that chisel penetrated deep into his heart. It takes a thrust, not a jab, to do that.'

Tresor unzipped the holdall. Removed a gallon can of petrol.

Arlene gulped and hastily stubbed out the second cigarette on the floor. My heart sank. It didn't matter how many cigarettes we smoked, the alarm was never going to trigger. Tresor, as part of his plan, had disabled it.

* * *

'Is he going to take the money?' Beaumont said to Tresor.

'We haven't got round to that yet,' Tresor replied.

'How much do you want, Nick?' Beaumont asked. 'To keep quiet.'

'I see now,' I said. 'They've told you they're going to buy our silence, is that it? Wise up, Toby. They're not going to let us go. Can't take the risk. No guarantee that we wouldn't leave here and go straight to the police. Tell them the whole story. Or, maybe, try a touch of blackmail. Like Mickey.'

'Mickey?' he said.

'Didn't Tresor tell you? Tut, tut. How very forgetful. Mickey was one of the "undesirables" from St Jerome's that Security was supposed to keep away from the building. He was washed up on the shores of the river. Not a pretty sight, Toby. But death rarely is, I suppose.'

Beaumont stared undecidedly at Tresor.

'Shannon's just trying to stir things,' Tresor said. 'Don't listen to him.'

Stephanie nodded supportively.

'What was it, then, Tresor?' I said. 'Not another accident?'

'The kid had seen me throwing David's tools in the river. He wanted money to keep his mouth shut. I went to pay him, and he slipped in the river.'

'Not his lucky day, was it? Especially since you'd already clubbed him over the head and pumped him full of drugs. Oh,' I said, as if the flash of the inspiration had only just hit me, 'and we mustn't forget the other premeditated act of placing Whitley's credit cards in his pocket. So fortunate you'd kept them to make the murder look like a mugging that had got out of control.'

Toby looked at me uncertainly, then across at Tresor.

'You've been conned, I'm afraid, Toby,' I said. 'Nothing to be ashamed of. I imagine this pair can be very persuasive. But it can stop here. Still time for a happy ending. Untie me. Let the three of us go. Before there's another of Tresor's deliberate accidents. A fire this time, it seems. How very convenient. Disposes of two problems simultaneously: all the physical evidence — and us, of course.'

'It's up to you, Toby,' Tresor said, impatiently weighing the can of petrol in his hand. He walked across to Beaumont. Spoke softly and reasonably. 'We can lay the blame for the fire on a vengeful Plimpson like we agreed. Or we can take a chance and let them all go free. Whichever we choose, we have to stand together. Stephanie and I will abide by your decision.'

Like hell they would.

'Run, Toby,' I shouted urgently. 'Run, for crissake. Get out of here. Call the police.'

He turned to give me a reassuring smile. It froze on his face as the can of petrol hit him on the back of the head.

Toby stumbled forward from the force of the blow. His eyes assumed a momentary perplexed expression before glazing over. Then he crashed to the floor.

Tresor acted quickly now. I swivelled my neck and watched as he grasped Plimpson's ankles and pulled till the body was lying behind me. Took Beaumont by the scruff of the neck and dragged him inside the safe. Unscrewed the cap from the petrol can and liberally poured the contents over the files. Then he set about soaking the carpet tiles in the room.

'You next, I reckon,' I said to Stephanie.

'No chance,' she said. 'Robert and I alibi each other, don't forget.'

'And very convincingly you did it, too,' I said. 'The little charade in the pub, I mean.'

'*That's* where I've seen you before,' she said to Arlene.

'I'm flattered,' Arlene replied. 'I thought you only had eyes for Tresor.'

'Terrific performance,' I complimented Stephanie. 'The police could hardly miss it. What a pair you made. You, Stephanie, all legs, lashes and lips. And Tresor with the so noticeable jet-black hair. Brilliant ploy, Tresor. And there was I thinking it was pure vanity on your part.'

He paused in his spreading of the petrol and looked at me with hate in his eyes.

Oh, well. Seems like I was right the first time.

'Look at it from Tresor's point of view, Stephanie,' I said logically. 'After the fire here, there's only one potential threat left. Or, should I say, one weakness? Yours.'

'Shut your mouth, Shannon,' she said, moving away from Arlene so she could brandish the machete in my face.

'I reckon you're lucky to be alive as it is,' I said. 'I dread to think what might have happened if Mary Jo hadn't been on her best behaviour the day you laid your hands on her. Not only us men who get turned on by the St Trinian's look, it seems.'

Stephanie placed the tip of the machete against my shirt. Drew the blade down to slice off the buttons. Then, pressing harder, back up, leaving a thin red line on my chest. I felt the blood begin to trickle down to form a pool in my navel.

And a cold hand on my wrists.

Plimpson was back in the land of the living. And trying his best to undo the knot in the computer cable.

'It took a long time to realise,' I said, holding Stephanie's eyes. 'Can you believe, Arlene, that I could be so naive?'

'No problem,' she replied.

'When the lady in the staff restaurant said you were spoken for, Stephanie, I naturally assumed she was referring to Tresor. It was only when I became the butt of the office in-joke, decoded the giggles and sniggers, that the penny dropped.'

The cable felt looser now. Plimpson's Boy Scout badge for knotmanship was paying off.

'I blame the media personally,' I said, playing for time. 'All too easy to portray the average lesbian as a stereotypical Rosa Klebb lookalike, saving money on make-up and hairdos in order to have steel blades installed in the toes of a pair of custom-made shoes. Still, the day of the lipstick lesbian will come.'

'Surely you can think of better last words than that, Shannon,' Tresor said, coming close and bending down to pick up one of the cigarette butts from the floor. He threw it inside the safe. Next went my pack of cigarettes. Lastly my lighter.

I could imagine what was going through his mind. What he hoped would go through the minds of the Fire Service forensic team. Plimpson, disgruntled sacked employee, starts a fire in the computer room. Beaumont, Arlene and I take shelter in the supposedly fireproof safe, unaware that petrol has been splashed there, too. Shannon, seeking solace in his habit, lights a cigarette, real cool like. Whoosh.

My hands were free at last. I tapped Arlene lightly on the back of her arm to signal that all was not lost. Felt her give a little start.

'Get her into the safe,' Tresor ordered Stephanie.

'I'd watch your back if I were you, Stephanie,' I said, still employing the wooden spoon.

Stephanie lowered the point of the machete so it touched my crotch.

'And I'd watch your front if I were you, Shannon,' she said, the sick smile reappearing as she increased the pressure. 'You don't have to die in one piece, you know.'

Arlene let out a loud groan. Clutched her stomach. Began to writhe in the chair.

'Get up,' Tresor snapped at Arlene, roughly grabbing hold of her shoulders.

'Can't walk,' she gasped painfully, drawing their attention from me.

It was now or never.

Ignoring as best I could the threatening presence of the machete, I clenched my fists behind me. Then swung them in two arcs to smash on to Stephanie's ears.

She howled like a wounded animal. Collapsed in a heap, clutching her head. The machete, discarded now, bounced along the floor.

Tresor and I grabbed for it simultaneously.

I was faster.

But he was closer.

I jumped back and out of reach of the first jab. Ran to the desk. Snatched up Stephanie's jacket. Wrapped it, like the tea towel in Arthur's training session, around my left forearm. Advanced on Tresor.

'Fire escape,' I shouted to Arlene. 'Hit the alarm and get out.'

She started to rise unsteadily from the chair. Tresor elbowed her in the stomach, sending her slumping back. Then slashed at me with the machete.

I used my protected forearm to parry the blow and glance it aside. Sent a straight right into Tresor's chin.

He staggered back. Blinked at me with startled eyes, his face reddening with anger, veins pulsing on his forehead. He lifted the machete high in the air, took aim at my shoulder and chopped downwards.

I ducked under the blow, sweeping his arm up with the jacket. Hit him in the solar plexus this time. He doubled up in pain.

I glanced quickly at Arlene. She was crawling slowly across the floor, Stephanie's fingers desperately clawing at her ankle and impeding her progress.

Tresor recovered more quickly than I had expected. Swung the machete at my leg. I stepped quickly back. But felt the tip of the blade slice across my thigh. The old wound reopened. Blood gushed out to form a rapidly widening pool on my trouser leg.

The sight of blood — that bloody Shannon's blood — seemed to give Tresor new strength. He jabbed powerfully and repeatedly at me, forcing me to retreat back towards the safe. I concentrated all my attention on watching his hands and his feet, judging his balance so as to predict the angle of the next attack.

That's how I missed seeing the petrol can.

My foot turned on it. I lost my balance. Tumbled awkwardly to the floor.

Tresor leaned over me, the cold steel of the machete chopping down in a line aimed at the middle of my forehead. I reached out to my right. Grabbed the can. Used it to hit him hard on the wrist. Immediately reversed the direction of the swing to bring the can thumping against the side of his head, the last of the petrol spilling out over his shirt. He stood there swaying, looking down at me in a daze. I kicked upward, my foot connecting between his legs. Then rolled over and away, as he sank groaning to the floor.

I ran to Arlene. Plimpson was by her side, struggling to break the hold of Stephanie's talons on her ankle. I stepped on Stephanie's wrist — now wasn't the time for old-fashioned sexist niceties or 'Pretty please'. Took Arlene by the arm. Began to help her up from the floor. Froze as I heard the rasping sound of a match being struck.

The first flash of flame was a blinding yellow. It spread across the carpet, an eerie blue tinge at its edge, picking up speed as it licked thirstily at the petrol. Within seconds the whole of the room and the inside of the safe had been transformed into an inferno.

Tresor was on his knees, smacking at his burning clothes. The biter bit.

I propelled Plimpson and Arlene towards the fire exit. Turned my head from the nightmare vision of Tresor, his hair now a fireball. Sprinted back to the safe. Stretched my arms inside. Took hold of Beaumont's legs. And pulled with all my strength.

He was alight now.

I was alight now.

Everything and everyone in the room was bloody alight now.

Flames ran up my legs. Smoke billowed in my lungs and stabbed at my eyes. I glanced over my shoulder. Took aim at the door and dragged Beaumont backwards.

Stephanie, encased in a red aura, stumbled past me. Terminal screens to my left imploded in the rapidly building heat. The red hessian on the walls bubbled and turned to black. Tresor staggered around the room, blindly bumping into furniture, his hands ineffectually shielding his face. His screams echoed in my ears as I finally fell through the open door.

I rolled on the grass, smothering the flames on my clothes. Then gave Beaumont the same treatment. With a cough and a splutter he regained consciousness.

Exhausted, I sat there for a moment looking across at the burning building. Watched in fascination as the Plexiglas dome over the restaurant began to sag in the middle. The Hive was melting.

I left Beaumont. Made my way to where Arlene was sprawled. Collapsed at her side. Took her hand. Squeezed it tightly out of love, and in gratitude for diverting the attention of Tresor and Stephanie.

'Hold me,' she said, clutching at her stomach and writhing in pain. Tears filled her eyes. 'Hold me, Nick, like never before.'

CHAPTER THIRTY-FIVE

Sitting by the side of her hospital bed, I looked down at Arlene's white face. Had to turn away in shame from the sad eyes and the grimace of remembered pain that was revealed now the artificial veil of the anaesthetic had lifted. I took her cold hand in mine. Placed my head on her shoulder. And cried.

I was crying for Arlene. For the disappointment — no, the deep and tragic sense of loss, the emptiness she must be feeling in her stomach, heart and soul.

I was crying for the baby. For a life so unfairly snuffed out. Hadn't even made it that far — the candle had never even been given a chance to flicker.

I was crying for the baby girl I'd so selfishly wanted to balance the scales of life and death.

Last of all, self-pityingly, I was crying for me.

How could I tell her?

No happy endings this time, Arlene.

'You're better off without me,' I said into the coarse material of her gown. 'You didn't blow it, Arlene. I did. I'm so sorry.'

She put a hand on my head. Stroked my hair.

God, what a bloody mess! You're supposed to be comforting her, Shannon. Not the other way around. Step out from the pages of your *Boy's Own* adventures, for crissake. It's time to be a man.

'I've got something to tell you,' I said.

* * *

Half an hour later, nothing more to say, no apologies left unsaid, I limped into the waiting room. The stunned look on Arlene's face was etched on my brain. Her so justified words were ringing in my ears.

'Leave me alone, Nick. I can't take all this in right now. I need time to think. About the future. And whether we have one. Most of all, Nick, I need to think about you. Can you change, Nick? Is that possible? Can you stop acting on impulse and damn the consequences? I wish I knew, Nick. I wish I knew what to do.'

Arthur and Norman were standing in silence, staring morosely at the linoleum floor.

'Go to her, Norman,' I begged my friend. 'Stay by her side. It's not my place any more. I've done more than enough. It's all my fault. Her losing the baby. And her dreams for the future.'

'Don't be stupid,' he said sharply.

Arthur put his arm round me and led me to a chair.

'That's just what I have been,' I said. 'Bloody stupid.'

'You're still in shock, Nick,' Arthur said. 'It's only a matter of hours since you stepped out of that burning building. In that time you've seen Arlene go into the operating theatre, heard the bad news about the baby, and had nine stitches in that leg wound of yours. You don't know what you're saying. Or what you're doing.'

'But I know what I've said. And what I've done. Take me away from here, Arthur.'

'If that's what you want,' he shrugged. 'Maybe if you had some rest, got out of those clothes, took a shower, you might see sense. Come on, kid.' He wrapped an arm round my shoulder. 'I'll take you home.'

'No,' I said. 'Not home. St Jerome's.'

* * *

The policeman on guard outside St Jerome's wasn't very keen to let me in. I didn't blame him. My clothes were scorched, my trousers slit at the thigh from the machete. I smelled like hell, and must have looked pretty much the same. But I guess he saw something in my eyes. Sheer unbending determination, probably.

'I don't have any right to ask favours of you,' I said to Brother James, when we finally gained admission. Admission. Confession was going to be more apt. 'I misjudged you. Believed that you were capable of murder. Thought you were the one who had killed Whitley and Mickey. If you tell me to clear off, then I'll understand. But I need help, Brother James. The sort that only you can provide.'

'I think you have every right, Nick,' he said with a benevolent smile. 'After what you've done today. A man called Toomey called earlier to see Rhiannon. He told us everything. Ask, Nick, and you shall receive.'

He opened the door to the meditation room. Arthur and I followed him into the candlelit gloom. Sat ourselves down on the cushions. Arthur wriggled about uneasily and avoided looking directly at Brother James.

'Were you really expelled from the Order?' I asked, prevaricating as usual.

'Yes,' he said. 'I'm human, too, Nick. Succumb to temptations from time to time. Not the sins of the flesh, though. That was just the product of a hysterical nun's fertile mind. But I did weaken when confronted by the prospect of power. And money. All the better to pursue my crusade. Redeeming the young, showing them the path to God.'

He gazed into my eyes.

'When you first came here,' he said, 'I told you I knew your pain. I had a brother once. He was only fifteen when he died of a drugs overdose. That's why I entered the abbey. Made the decision as to how I should devote my life.'

'Maybe I should have done the same,' I said, thinking of how history might have been rewritten.

'You can't live by maybes, Nick. I could say that maybe things would be different now if I'd told you earlier all I knew about David. But such are the demands of professional confidence. And, I'm ashamed to admit, I coveted his legacy. Rationalised my silence with thoughts of all the good his money would do.' He shook his head sadly. 'I will just have to work harder in the future to make amends. Luckily, Nick, God forgives. No maybe about it. Or what hope would there be?'

'There's someone who is finding it hard to forgive me, Brother James. That's my first favour. Will you talk to her? Use all your powers of hypnotism to soothe the pain of the miscarriage, the baby she has just lost?'

'Why him?' Arthur interrupted, pointing his finger at Brother James. 'Why can't *you* do it? You were going to get married to Arlene, for crissake. Doesn't that make you the person closest to her? The best person for the job?'

'It's my fault Arlene lost the baby,' I said. 'Getting her involved in the plan against Prospekt. Leaving her alone in the car park at the crucial time. I'm trouble, Arthur. You said so yourself, remember? Arlene was damn near killed today because of me.'

'We all knew the risks, Nick,' Arthur said. 'You can't take all the blame on yourself.'

'There's something else, Arthur,' I said. 'The final straw that looks like breaking Arlene's back. I'm not emigrating to America.'

'But I thought it was all arranged,' he said, frowning with puzzlement. 'Toomey was getting you the visa. He promised. That was the deal, wasn't it?'

I nodded.

'Sort of,' I said. 'The deal was for one visa. And one visa was what Toomey delivered. But it wasn't for me, Arthur. It was for Rhiannon.'

'I don't understand,' he said, shaking his head.

'After the attempt on Rhiannon's life I realised the position I'd landed her in. If she stayed in this country, she'd be a sitting target. A murder waiting to happen. What could I do? Wasn't it me who'd persuaded her to buy the drugs? To give the evidence that now puts her life at risk? It seemed only just that I should put it all right. Sacrifice my chance of emigrating so that Rhiannon can live under an assumed name, safe from Prospekt.'

'Oh, no,' Arthur said.

'Oh, yes,' I said. 'Now you understand just how much I've let Arlene down. Hell, she deserves better than me, and more than I can ever give her.'

'I'll speak to her,' Brother James said. 'Do what I can. Perhaps if I take Rhiannon along with me?'

I shook my head. The sight of a pregnant Rhiannon would only rub salt in the wound.

'One last favour, Brother James,' I said. 'Before you go to Arlene.'

He looked at me with steady eyes. 'Whatever you want,' he said with a nod.

'Spare a prayer for a poor sinner from time to time.'

* * *

One last call to make before going home.

I sat in the van in the car park at Holborn police station while Arthur trooped off unhappily to fetch Collins. I was in no fit state — mentally, physically, sartorially even — to go inside. And what Collins and I had to discuss was better spoken out of earshot of Walker.

'Christ Almighty,' Collins said, on seeing me. 'Arthur said you were in a bad way, but . . . Here, drink some of this.'

He removed a quarter-bottle of Scotch from its hiding place within the folds of his jacket. Unscrewed the top. Passed it to me.

I took a long pull. It seemed to go down without touching the sides. I gave a hollow laugh from the bottom of the pit.

I tried to light a cigarette. My shaking hands couldn't manage it. Delayed shock? Excitement about what Collins might say? Or were they just making a protest? Unwilling to help me dig a bigger hole for myself?

Collins pressed a cigarette between my lips. 'You should be in bed,' he said. 'You need sleep.'

'But first I need help,' I said. 'Did Professor Davies discover what was missing from the file?'

'You don't want to know,' Collins said. 'Believe me.'

'If I didn't want to know, I wouldn't ask.'

Collins looked at Arthur. Arthur waved his hands helplessly.

'Davies found someone who had worked on the case,' Collins said. 'A secretary who typed the original report and remembered what was in the missing page. It contained a description of a boot impression found at the scene of the hit-and-run.'

'So why was it removed from the report?'

'The officer in charge of the case deemed it not to be material evidence, the secretary said.'

'But how can that be? Surely any evidence is material.'

'The pattern on the sole of the boot was very special. It could only have been made by a policeman. The rationale was that it was left by one of the local lads.'

Not another dead end, please. Let me have something to fill the void.

'There has to be more to it than that,' I said scornfully. 'Otherwise why would someone try to bury the file? Why couldn't you, a detective superintendent, officially get sight of it?'

'I agree entirely,' he said. 'That's why I did some checking through the personnel records. The print that was found couldn't have come from the policemen who attended the scene.'

'How can you tell?' I asked, my pulse beginning to race.

'Because they were ordinary run-of-the-mill coppers,' he said. 'And, like the vast majority of the police force, are given a boot allowance as part of their pay. They are free to spend that allowance in any shop, on whatever make of boot they choose — as long as it's black. But the boot that made this impression can't be bought in any shop.'

'So,' I asked, heart beating like a drum, 'how does one get hold of a pair of these boots?'

'By undergoing special training. Pass the course and your prize is a free pair of customised boots. Non-flammable, a mixture of leather and fabric, very lightweight, more like a trainer than a boot really.'

'What sort of special training are we talking about?'

'Public Order,' Collins said. 'Or, perhaps more to the point, my suspicious mind whispers in my ear, *firearms*.'

'Should narrow the field down a bit, then,' I said.

He nodded. 'Gives us somewhere to start, Nick.'

'So you'll help?' I said.

'Why not?' he replied. 'You know my feelings about rotten apples. And,' he gave me a conspiratorial wink, 'I reckon I owe someone for wrapping up Prospekt. We managed to trace the pipeline, by the way. Money was being channelled through a dozen different accounts, across the seas to Liechtenstein and then, for some strange reason, back to a newly opened account at City and County. The long arm of the law didn't have to stretch too far in the end. So, Nick, since no one seems keen to own up to being the catalyst behind cracking the case, I might as well push my gratitude in your direction.'

'Thanks,' I said.

'You always keep your promises, don't you, Nick?'

'I try to,' I said. 'But *sometimes* seems to be about my limit.'

CHAPTER THIRTY-SIX

August — I think.

All days tended to seem the same lately. Long and empty.

Jameson Browns had dispensed with my services, a pre-emptive move brought about by an unwillingness to pay the increased salary I would be due on completion of my two-year apprenticeship. And that had produced the knock-on effect of terminating my sponsored secondment to the Fraud Squad, there being no official machinery to allow me to be placed on the payroll. I'd applied for other jobs, and received depressingly short letters of rejection by return post: no one appeared to be in the mood to risk taking on an ex-con. So most of the days were spent moping about the flat, reading, listening to music, watching daytime television — and thinking. I'd even managed to remember the end of the quotation: 'Justice is such a fine thing that we cannot pay too dearly for it.'

All nights tended to be the same, too. But longer and emptier than the days.

Arlene's clothes had been spirited out of the bedroom by Norman on the day following the fire; her make-up cleared from the dressing table; even the peach-scented shampoo had been removed from the shower. Nothing remained of her but memories. And there were plenty of those. In the many sleepless night-time hours, I tossed and turned in the lonely bed, cursing Metcalfe and his damned fifty-four pounds — the fuse that had ignited the bomb to blow apart my life. Arlene's life. And the life that now would never be.

'Well,' said Norman, sitting himself down in the arm-chair opposite me and fixing me with the stern eyes of a surrogate father. 'I do believe it's time we had a little talk.'

'That will make a pleasant change,' I replied. 'I was beginning to think I was the victim of a conspiracy of silence. You've been avoiding me. Arthur hasn't been round. No word from Brother James. Or from Arlene — although that's not unexpected.'

'What has there been to say? The three of us all went as a group to see Arlene and speak up on your behalf. What more could we do?'

'I suppose my fate is in her hands now.'

'And your own, Nick.'

'I don't understand,' I said.

'And you won't,' he said, 'all the while you insist on wearing your cloak of self-pity.'

'How is Arlene?' I asked, jolted by the wounding dart.

'What do you care?' he taunted. 'I thought you'd given up. Settled for a nice clean break.'

'It wasn't like that,' I said defensively.

'Really?'

I looked searchingly into his eyes. Bit my lip, using the pain as a stupidly macho means of holding back the tears.

'Christ, I've been a fool,' I said, closing my eyes. 'It's about the only time in my life I've ever given up on anything. What am I going to do?'

'Progress at last,' Norman said. 'At least you're thinking about the future for a change.'

I shrugged. 'Not much point dwelling on the past, I suppose.'

'That depends, Nick. On whether, by doing so, you are able to learn from it.'

'I remember saying the same thing to Meg and Mary Jo that last day at Future Assurance. "The past is there for a reason. Learn from it. Try not to make the same mistakes again."'

'And can you take your own advice? Can you truly profit from those words? Or, like Future Assurance, is it just another case of false profits?'

'Give a guy a break, Norman.'

'You're good at dishing it out, Nick. But can you take it? You tested Mary Jo and found her wanting. How would you fare if tested?'

'OK, Norman,' I said with weary resignation. 'You're obviously not going to be content until I say it. I was wrong, I admit it. I see that now, after the weeks of sitting here alone contemplating my navel.'

'And . . . ?'

'I won't act impulsively again. I will always think ahead of the consequences. I have learned my lesson — the hard way. Satisfied?'

'What have we here?' he said, falling back in the chair with mock shock. 'Not just a small step on the path of progress, but a bloody quantum leap. Am I right in assuming this to be a new leaf in the Shannon textbook of life?'

'I'm a changed man, all right? Can we drop the subject, please?'

'Of course,' he said, a smug grin on his face. 'It's time to celebrate. There's a whole wide world outside beckoning its finger at those who have seen the light. Not to mention those who have this very day finally qualified.'

He dropped a letter, already opened, into my lap.

'No, dear pupil, don't thank me. Virtue is its own reward. *I* am going to ring Toddy. *You* are going to get changed. *We* are going on a picnic.'

* * *

'Where are we going?' I asked, as we stowed the heavy Toddy-stocked hamper in the boot of the minicab.

'Island Gardens,' Norman replied.

I groaned.

'Yes,' he said, reading my reaction perfectly. 'And we're taking the route that passes what is left of Assurance House. A spot of exorcism to banish for ever the ghosts of the past.'

'Maybe you're right, Norman,' I shrugged, forgetting Brother James's parting sermon.

'Where you are concerned, Nick, *maybe* doesn't come into it.'

The cab driver sped off in that time-honoured, time-is-money fashion that comes with the local-authority licence.

'I've been thinking,' Norman said, a little later, as we passed the all too familiar buildings of Docklands. 'Did Whitley do it on purpose? Or was it subconscious, perhaps?'

'Do what?' I asked.

'Use your brain, Nick,' he said, smiling. 'It's a little out of practice.'

The cab stopped at Norman's instruction outside the burnt-out shell of the Hive. I thought back to my first entrance through those doors. The carefree demob-happy sense of fun, the repressed grin at Pat's name badge, the jokes with Meg. And the search through the Sales Ledger.

'The fifty-four pounds,' I said. 'You mean Whitley made the transposition error deliberately, at a time when he couldn't yet bring himself to confess? Let it carry through from month to month in the hope that we — the auditors — would spot it and then go on to uncover the fraud? It's possible, I suppose.' I shrugged again, appreciating that it was becoming another bad habit to add to my list. 'Hell, we're never going to know, Norman. What's the point of bloody speculating?'

'In this life, Nick,' he said, 'you have to speculate to accumulate.'

I shook my head uncomprehendingly. Climbed out of the car, lit a cigarette and stared pensively at the building. A *For Sale* sign wobbled in the wind.

'What happened to everyone?' I asked Norman.

'Moved into the City and County headquarters. Future Assurance, my boy, is rising like a phoenix from the ashes. May even make a small profit, now that the false claims have been eliminated and the overheads have been trimmed back. Meg and Plimpson kept their jobs, by the way.'

'So they all lived happily ever after?'

'Ain't life a peach?' he said.

We stepped back inside the car and drove further up the road. The car park at the Cox and Eight had lost its Portakabins and the boost in trade from the investigating officers.

'Stop here,' Norman said to the driver as we neared St Jerome's. 'We'll walk the rest of the way.'

Everything had changed since my last visit. The weatherboarded warehouses had acquired new coats of paint. A rough square of sacking covered the door where once the nameplate of St Jerome's had been.

'Is Brother James still here?' I asked.

'Moved on too,' he said. 'This place is being developed.' He pointed to an impressive hoarding bearing the name *Unicorn Unity — Commercial Properties.* 'Brother James was paid to leave. Got himself and his disciples a nice modern place across the river. Electricity and everything. That's progress for you.'

Norman carried the hamper and set it down on the jetty. Began to unpack the contents.

'Let's forget Island Gardens,' he said. 'Have our picnic right here. Open a bottle of champagne and raise our glasses to Brother James. For all his good work.'

'Norman,' I said, my suspicions aroused, 'are you up to something?'

'Use your brain, Nick,' he said for the second time. 'And, while you're at it, get me that piece of sacking. I need something to sit on.'

The sacking was secured by four drawing pins. I prised them out of the door with my nail. There was a brass plaque underneath.

Shannon Investigations Ltd, it said in gothic script.

I looked at Norman. He had that cheesy grin I knew and loved so well on his face. And a glass of champagne in each hand.

'Congratulations,' he said. 'On becoming a qualified accountant. And on your new career.'

'But . . .' I stammered.

'Niche marketing,' he said matter-of-factly. 'You're specialising in fraud detection. Or forensic accounting. Use whichever term you prefer. There'll be lots of demand from banks and other financial institutions who need a top-quality, and very discreet, service. Cheers, Nick.'

I took the glass he was holding out to me. Clinked it against his. Raised it to my lips. And paused.

'This is *you*, isn't it?' I said, pointing accusingly at the developers' sign.

'The ad in the *Financial Times* produced another offer for the Windsor Club,' he said. 'Too good to turn down. I thought it was time I did my bit to help this fine country of ours out of recession. Shall we go inside and see your new offices and your new living accommodation?'

'Hang on,' I said, raising my hand. 'Unicorn Unity — Commercial Properties. You old rogue.'

'I'm sure I don't know what you mean,' he said with a deadpan face.

'Bloody coincidence, isn't it?' I said scornfully. 'That the initials of your new company spell out UUCP.'

'Just my little joke,' he said.

'You struck a deal with Mary Jo, didn't you? While you were cosseted with her in the lap of luxury at the Savoy. What percentage did you have to pay her?'

'Percentage of what?' he asked innocently.

'The escrow account,' I said. 'The one that Prospekt wouldn't be needing any more. Mary Jo changed the name for you, didn't she? While I was away getting her a cup of coffee she didn't ever drink. She made you the sole account holder.'

'All's well that ends well,' he said.

'Thanks, Norman,' I said, embarrassed. 'For giving me a fresh start.'

'This isn't charity, Nick,' he said, switching off the grin for a moment. 'As chief shareholder in Shannon Investigations Limited I expect to see a return on my capital. Not to mention the odd bit of lucrative consultancy coming my way. This is purely business. OK?'

'Sure,' I said, suppressing a giveaway smile. 'Purely business.'

'Right,' he said. 'Glad we got that straight. Time to view the premises. Bring the bottle.'

He opened the door. Waved me inside.

The smell of incense still lingered faintly in the air. But, in all other respects, the building had been transformed. Bright paint on the walls. Light flooding in through the windows of the room to my left, and running along the corridor from the glass-paned back door that overlooked the river.

'Living accommodation is upstairs,' Norman said. 'We'll look at that after you've met your staff.'

'I have staff, too?' I said with surprise.

'You certainly have,' replied Arthur, stepping through the door on my right. 'I told you I was getting too old for the bouncing lark. Not that watching over you is going to be a piece of cake. Still, the hours will be a bit more sociable, I suppose.'

'Good to have you on the team, Arthur,' I said, clapping him on the shoulder.

'One last member to meet,' Norman said. 'Office manager. And receptionist, too. I trained her myself. Word perfect, she is.'

He pushed me through the door to the main office.

'Good afternoon, sir,' Arlene trilled from behind the desk. 'Soup of the day is oxtail. And humble pie is finished.'

THE END

ACKNOWLEDGEMENTS

All the passwords (including the magical UUCP) cited in this book have been used in the past to enter computers illegally. My source was *The Cuckoo's Egg* by Clifford Stoll. Proof that truth can be stranger than fiction.

The story of Brinks-Mat (including the asset-sharing episode — yes, the money really was returned by the Metropolitan Police to the DEA/FBI) is told at riveting length, along with other case studies of money laundering, in *The Laundrymen* by Jeffrey Robinson. One of the accounts used for the washing of the money was in the name of G. Reedy!

In terms of forensic information, my source was *The Encyclopedia of Forensic Science* by Brian Lane — packed with detail and fascinating true-life (true-death?) cases.

I would like to thank: Gordon Harpin and Alan Gibson of Commercial Union for verifying at first-draft stage that the scam was feasible (what a relief!) and for providing the finishing touches of scanners and seals. Just in case anyone gets the wrong impression, Future Assurance PLC was *not* based on Commercial Union, nor any other insurance company for that matter. I would also like to thank Paula Fells for the inside story on boots, etc.; my agent, Sarah Molloy of A. M Heath, for unflagging support and encouragement; my editor, Hilary Hale of Little, Brown, for the benefit of her experience, and for knowing a good synopsis when she doesn't see one; and my wife, Melanie, for her patience during the many hours of (repeated) type checking and the many days when Shannon wouldn't leave us alone.

In all cases, any mistakes that have made it through to the finished product are mine alone.

* * *

This book is dedicated to John Hartgill of Harley Street who saved the life of our daughter, Victoria. Maybe if he had been there for Arlene . . .

ALSO BY PAUL BENNETT

JOHNNY SILVER THRILLERS
Book 1: MERCENARY
Book 2: KILLER IN BLACK
Book 3: ONE BULLET TOO MANY
Book 4: NO EASY WAY OUT

NICK SHANNON THRILLERS
Book 1: DUE DILIGENCE
Book 2: COLLATERAL DAMAGE
Book 3: FALSE PROFITS

STANDALONE NOVELS
CATALYST

Thank you for reading this book.

If you enjoyed it please leave feedback on Amazon or Goodreads, and if there is anything we missed or you have a question about, then please get in touch. We appreciate you choosing our book.

Founded in 2014 in Shoreditch, London, we at Joffe Books pride ourselves on our history of innovative publishing. We were thrilled to be shortlisted for Independent Publisher of the Year at the British Book Awards.

www.joffebooks.com

We're very grateful to eagle-eyed readers who take the time to contact us. Please send any errors you find to corrections@joffebooks.com. We'll get them fixed ASAP.

Printed in Great Britain
by Amazon

16935934R00201